RED HAND

RED HAND

RED HAND
AMERICAN BY BLOOD

Robert Ross

MACh/4 Press

Published by:
MACh/4 Press
1032 2nd Street, Suite 202
e-mail: bob@roberthross.com

Printed in the United States of America

Cover Concept: Robert Ross
Cover Design: John Espinoza

ISBN: 0-9669588-6-7
LCCN: 2010908290

Ross, Robert

      Red Hand/Robert Ross

      FIC014000 FICTION / Historical

      1. Native American adventure--Fiction.
      2. Friends relationships--Fiction. 3. Spiritual journey--Fiction.
      I. Title

to

Mom, Dad, Bill and Sheila

Other Book
by
Robert Ross

Journey Within:
A Tale of Astral Travel

*C*ontents —

The Buffalo

There was a time when the great herds
roamed the western plains cutting a massive swath
across the land. They would appear suddenly as if out
of nowhere to feed off the high grass, fill their bellies,
then vanish like smoke on the wind.

John Connor

The dampness of the dawn belied a day soon to be filled with an early summer's heat when the pony soldiers broke camp. Seven hundred strong had ridden west from Fort Lincoln to this wilderness on the Rosebud, and now it was time... time for the men and horses to break their feed, time for the bugler to blow his trumpet, time for boots and saddles.

Crook had been beaten, driven into an embarrassing retreat by Crazy Horse only one week before, not more than a mile from this very spot, pondered the general. The man sat resolute on a rock facing east gazing across the river, a few stray locks of hair blowing lazily in the wind, his coffee long cold. How could that have happened? Crazy Horse must pay, he demanded of himself. Of course, there had been broken promises with Red Cloud, Spotted Tail and the rest. But who were they? What have they and their people done to make this magnificence a better place to live?... roam its endless expanse breeding like rabbits, killing game only for food and necessities, and each other for the vainglorious adornment of a few eagle feathers? Well, my short red bastard friends, it is your time no longer. You have outlived your preeminance over the land. I, Long Hair, shall see to that. And presently, I imagine.

*

"Yi yi yi yi yi yi..." they came, thousands, firing rifles, wielding lances and battle hatchets as the men of the 7th scattered over the low hills south of the river. Moments before the smoke from many fires rising from the treetops a half-mile off had warned the bluecoats, but still they rode down Medicine Tail Coulee into this place where death greeted them, each man tall in the saddle like the general at the lead. Without hesitation the Indians kicked their ponies, racing to the fray. These were not old men, women and children huddling in fear as they had at the Washita. These were young men, braves, painted for battle. They met the soldiers head on, forcing them to abandon ranks and form small groups behind their fallen mounts. Sioux and Cheyenne and Arapaho rode through the forthright as well as the faint of heart, bloodying them with lances, shooting the dead and the dying, hacking them to pieces. Scalps were taken, later the bodies mutilated by squaws who delight-ed in their plunder until there was but one survivor, Comanche, the large bay who stood alone beside the remains of his master, Captain Keough, as the life poured from him glowing crimson in the sun.

Some claimed they had been the one who killed Long Hair, but no one knew for certain. The fight had been a frenzy, a gorging, a wild bloodletting that seemed much too swift to those who remembered the bluecoat tune called Garryowen, the killing song of the pony soldier trumpets. But now it was done. The 7th Cavalry was destroyed, and Long Hair, the boy general who had meted out his share of cruelty and death to the redman of the western plains, was dead.

As the warriors rode back across the river with trophies dripping from their lances, the wailing of Comanche for his fallen master rode with them, melting into the cries of new life coming from the Indian camp. It was a child crying for his mother's milk, crying instinctively for that which sustains life while the rich purple hue of the placenta still covered him. Rather than give him her breast, his mother held him high in the air to witness those returning victoriously from battle, to paint them into his mind so somewhere deep within his spirit he would always know his legacy. The child turned silent, focusing on the picture before him — men and hors-es crowding into one another with weapons raised, firing rifles, kicking up dust all around, becoming one together drunk with the moment. It was then the young Sioux princess chose to name her son. She would call him Red Hand, for the blood of the soldiers still on the hands of so many.

*

The days when the Sioux and Cheyenne lived as one with the earth, when their lodgepoles stretched across a thousand miles of plains and their only enemy was hunger... the better days, had long since passed when Red Hand rode into camp from an afternoon herding strays with the other boys. He was big for his age, eager since he first sat astride a pony to grow up and go with the men. It was not as before, however, nor would it ever be again. Not long after the Little Bighorn, the Indian Nations were broken by yet another army of bluecoats. Sitting Bull escaped to Canada while most of the other chiefs took their tribes to the white man's reservations. At least there they would not starve, or freeze to death as many had before hunting in the bitter cold of winter for game no longer plentiful enough to fill their bellies.

The boy entered the tipi, placing the buffalo hide back over the small entrance, and warmed his hands by the fire. He picked up some jerky before asking his mother yet again to repeat the story. It was one she recounted with difficulty, for it was the story of the only man she had ever loved... the man she still waited for, longed for.

"Please, mother?" He looked at her with his blue eyes, blue like the summer sky, like his father's eyes, and she relented as she would always.

"All right, my child. But only this last time, for you must know it by heart."

"This last time then, mother."

The fire warmed the distance between them, the flames licking at the hunk of venison on the spit, and Willow That Weeps began her tale. "It was a cool morning, the earth once again beginning to blossom when he rode into camp, a day I will keep in my heart long after I have left this earth..."

*

"Whadya think, John, wanna go on in? Looks quiet enough."

"It's all right with me. I could use some people aroun' me fer a change."

The two rode out of the treeline down a grassy slope into the valley below. Closer to the encampment they counted more than fifty tipis huddled along the river bank, enough to hold four times that number of men, women and children, but no matter. The Indians John Connor and his partner Ethan MacCall had encountered during three years of trapping were often sullen and suspicious, some dangerous, others unpredictable. The Pawnee, who would just as soon take your hair as look at you, they had learned to avoid. The Sioux, as these were, were generally friendly and accepted the white trappers, even traded with them, for they saw that these whites lived mostly as they did — wandering the great plains, taking only what was needed to sustain life, using the sky above as their blanket for a night's rest.

When Ethan and John were within sight of the camp, some of the young men rode out to greet them. One recognized the two from a year ago along the Shoshone taking beaver pelts down to Slatton's Post, and he raised a hand inviting them in.

Most everyone turned out to see the white men now. Although it was nothing new, whites visiting their lodges didn't happen everyday, and there was a curiosity about them still. These two seemed more like their own kind than the others who'd come. These were young men with keen eyes, well outfitted for hunting these hills. As they rode among the people with the labor of many months strapped to their mules, the scent of the skins filled the air causing the dogs to fuss.

"This way," their escort told them, and they continued towards one of the larger lodges in the middle of camp. A tall man, his hair adorned with eagle feathers, stepped from the entrance. They would learn later his name was Two Bears, that he was a chief among the people. Dismounting now, the eyes of the two trappers turned to Two Bears' family who followed him from the lodge. A boy of about sixteen, not yet as tall as his father, stood to his right, eyeing the two like game not often encountered. A woman, striking for one who lived the life of a squaw as all Indian women do, stood at his other side gazing at John and Ethan, her kind eyes giving her away. Then she appeared and joined her family. She of the raven black hair, and of still darker eyes that pierced the very soul of John Connor, bidding every muscle of his body to ache for her touch. For her part, she too was fixed upon him, her eyes smiling at his, this white stranger dressed in buckskins, with broad shoulders and sky blue eyes and as kind a face as she had ever seen... as kind, she would allow, as her own father's.

"What brings you here," Two Bears asked them.

"We been huntin' these hills fer many months," John answered, "away from the company o' others when we saw yer smoke. We missed the warm fires of our Sioux brothers since we las' stayed with Red Cloud an' his people on the Tongue. It was in our minds ta visit yer village, ta talk trade, an' sit once agin with those which we share this earth."

Two Bears stared at the two white trappers for some moments longer, looking beyond the surface of what was plain to all, looking instead inside, to where the truth of their words lie, and he welcomed them.

"It is good you have come." Gesturing to the beaver pelts on their pack mules, "you have hunted well. The Sioux have always been willing to share what the Great Spirit provides. Come, we will talk."

The men entered the lodge first — Two Bears, his son, Running Wolf, then John and Ethan, finally the wife of Two Bears, Star Rising, and she, she whose blue-black, velvet eyes again glanced to John, lingering forever before taking her place on the opposite side of the lodge with her mother and two other women. She, whose softness continued to reach out to John, a softness as soothing and gentle as the sound of her name, Willow.

The conversation among the men touched on the bounty of the land, the coming summer and, hopefully, the promise of good hunting before autumn came and winter set in in earnest. Running Wolf, who was nearing his seventeenth year and so was allowed to sit and talk with the men, asked the whites how many of their kind were on Sioux land. Two Bears admonished him some for being direct, but John and Ethan were not put off by the boy's eagerness.

"There's a smatterin' of us in these parts," Ethan said. "John an' me come up from Colorado Territory goin' on three years now, so we don't really know 'xactly how many white folks there might be. Not too many I reckon."

"Do you travel far?" Two Bears asked them.

"Down to the Powder on our way south," John replied as his eyes darted quickly towards the girl, and not for the first time. "Good fishin' on our way ta trade, an' a chance fer a few more skins to boot."

"Will you come this way again?"

"I reckon we like the country an' the trappin' well enough. What we need is a few days res' fer Ethan's horse. Seems he picked up a nettle an' we cain't git the dern thing out. He's been hobblin' real bad. We'd be obliged."

"You can make camp along the river. We will look at your horse in the morning."

*

The two men sat over a fire that evening warming their bones after they'd hobbled the horses and pack animals a ways downstream. John had scavenged some kindling while Ethan'd cut a few strips off a flank of elk they'd shot the week before. With the coffee and dried biscuits, they sat eating in silence staring at the lodges of their hosts. The moonlit night offered a backdrop of varying shades of blue, purple and orange while the smoke from many fires climbed skyward through the scene, the pony herd breaking the stillness now and again after catching the scent of a stray coyote.

"Ya think that chief'll be able ta do anythin' more fer old Soldier, John? That nettle's in deep."

"Don' know, but he looks like the kind that won't give up on somethin'. Strikin' son of a gun... he an' his whole family. An' no lack o' gray matter neither... his English is dern good." John wasn't ready to admit just yet being smitten by the chief's daughter. He was merely asking for Ethan to pick up his thought and engage further conversation about the girl, hoping to gain Ethan's opinion without having to ask it directly, but silence remained. No matter, he thought gazing back at the Indian camp, attempting to pick out the lodge of the chief, and of her, tomorrow will come soon enough. As he and Ethan hunkered down for the night in front of a still smoldering fire, he found he couldn't wait.

*

The ducks woke the two men early next morning with their squawking in the marsh at the river's edge. John, scratching himself awake, got up first and started a fire, giving Ethan a nudge with his boot.

"Gonna git the rest o' them biscuits out whil' I make the coffee, pard'?... or ya gonna lay there an' sleep like the King of Siam hisself 'til one o' yer harem props

6

ya up on a pilla an' serves ya roasted pig, with the dang apple an' all?"

"I hear ya, I hear ya," and Ethan slowly crawled from under his blankets in his longjohns and socks trying to sidestep the pricklers as he made his way towards a thick scrub of oak muttering something about first draining his pecker. John watched him hop along, only seeing the top of Ethan's head now from behind the oak as the man stood motionless for what seemed like an hour. Jeez, that boy could pee, thought John. He's like some damn camel er something, just saves it up fer days then lets 'er fly. As John smiled he also thought a man couldn't have a finer partner, one who knew the mountains and its peculiarities as well as any white man he ever knew, and one who wouldn't turn tail when trouble came calling.

"Any more biscuits?" John asked as the two sat sipping their coffee, hands cradling tin mugs.

"No biscuits, jes more o' the elk, an' not a whol' lot neither. We gonna have to scare up some meat b'for we ride down to Slatton's. With 'at Sharps yer carryin', pard', that shouldn't be no trouble."

John's thoughts wandered back to the girl with the raven hair and sweet, soft name as his eyes strained to catch a glimpse of her among the many in the Indian village now up and about. From this distance, the people were no more than the size of insects — women gathering up firewood and kids, men heading to a thicket to relieve their night's swelling — and John strained all the harder, attempting to find her until he noticed three figures in the distance growing steadily larger walking his way. Nearer, he saw they were Two Bears, Running Wolf and a third, older member of the tribe he and Ethan had not yet met.

Within twenty yards of John's and Ethan's makeshift camp, Two Bears raised his hand in greeting. The two hunters replied as the five men now faced each other, and Two Bears spoke first.

"This is Santin, an elder of our tribe, one who works with herbs and roots and the moss from the riverbeds. He has cured many of our horses from going lame. He will look at your horse, Ethan McCall, and take the sickness from him."

The old man moved easily to the horses. The others followed, watching him as he approached the animals. He placed a hand on Soldier's forehead who snuffled, shaking his head slightly. Santin waited some seconds, then placed his hand again on his forehead, all the while speaking to him, gentling him before lifting his left foreleg to inspect the soreness that had begun to fester. Santin moved away and muttered a few words to Two Bears before heading back towards the Indian camp.

"What is it?" Ethan asked.

"Santin will gather what is necessary and return soon," the chief told them. "There is little time."

Ethan was taken aback by Two Bears' remarks. He knew Soldier's limp was getting worse, but neither he nor John were doctor enough to have been aware just how perilous the situation was. Without asking the chief more, knowing he'd get little information, Ethan stayed close to Soldier holding him as the horse nuzzled his master.

The sun was near its apex and the old Santin had not returned. Two Bears and Running Wolf had remained, however, and after some time shuffling about with their two guests making small talk about the game in these parts and the presence of the buffalo, John invited them to sit by the fire, its flames still licking the air, throwing off heat. Ethan declined without any apparent offense to Two Bears, choosing to remain with Soldier, all the while keepin' a keen eye peeled for Santin. As John settled in with his guests across the charred cottonwood and lingering flames, he reflected... you're never certain with Indians, even peaceful tribes, if you might offend them by doing or saying the wrong thing simply out of ignorance of their ways. But then he thought, these Sioux have been nothing but friendly, and if he had his way right then and there, Two Bears might be a whole lot closer to him than a mere acquaintance. So he went on with his question.

"Two Bears, how long have you and yer people camped along the Bighorn?"

"For my father's and his father's lifetimes. We have survived the winters and the wrath of our enemies for as long as I can remember, but now the whites seem to be everywhere, swarming over the land like the tall grass in Spring. And the bluecoats follow, killing off those with whom they would make treaties. I do not think my son will live as my father did. Our way is changing."

"We can live together, you and I, we proved such these past three years... me and Ethan huntin' these parts, you and yer people invitin' us to share yer fire."

"This is true, but you are only two men who live as we do... off the land, taking only that which is needed, then moving on to allow the earth to replenish herself. It is not the way of the others who would grab up the land and fence it off for only their use. That is the way which will ruin us... first fencing off the Indian, then corraling us as the whites do their own animals, as they have done to the tribes across the great river to the east."

"I can't argue that. But it is the way of the world... people needin' to stretch their boundaries, to breathe easier. It's been the way since the beginning. I jes hope you and I can live together peaceably." Then John collected himself, sitting up straighter, wanting to look every bit the man he considered himself to be after surviving three years in the wild with only his rifle and his wits, and he added, "and I've got a reason for sayin' such."

It was not the Indian way to respond to a statement left unfinished. So Two Bears looked at John Connor, waiting, staring into the eyes of the white man he would soon call son.

"I...," John continued now, searching for the words, "I wish ta court yer daughter... that is, with yer permission... an' hers, Two Bears."

The chief looked deeper now into the blue eyes of John Connor and discovered to his surprise he did not see a white man before him, but simply a man, one who carried himself with the strength and bearing of his own people. However, Two Bears hesitated before answering, examining John closer, looking for the tiniest flaw of character, the smallest trace of weakness, but found only resolve.

"I will speak with her," the chief stated matter-of-factly, showing no emotion, the words hanging in the air until Ethan hailed them all with, "he's comin'!"

When Santin arrived they found the old medicine man had just two items with him — a pouch of hide with an odor so strong John and Ethan picked it up from ten paces, and a sliver of a stone knife sharpened to a fine edge. He walked straight on to Soldier, only nodding to Two Bears as he passed, and soothed the horse as he had earlier. Setting the poultice down, Santin picked up Soldier's foreleg in the same motion and began poking about with the knife until he found the spot he was looking for. To Ethan's astonishment, Soldier allowed Santin to whittle away, slicing at the oozing gob of puss and gore as it dribbled down onto the old man's shaggy leggings. Just a slight whinny and shaking of the head was all anyone heard or saw out of the animal until Santin let out a triumphant, "Heya!..." holding up a thorn as long as your small finger. Without letting go of Soldier's hoof, he stooped to pick up the godawful smelling poultice, untieing the top of the pouch. He placed Soldier's hoof inside, then retied the pouch to the animal's leg, but not so tight as to rankle him.

Santin joined the others now and, once again, spoke only with Two Bears before walking back to the Indian camp.

"Keep the pouch on the horse to draw the poison out," Two Bears relayed to Ethan and John. "Santin will come every day with fresh herbs. He will say when the horse is cured."

*

Two days passed, then three, with Santin coming every morning to change the dressing on Soldier's hoof with more of the herbs. Even though Ethan had kept the horse hobbled, he wasn't going anywhere. The animal seemed to understand the old Indian was doing him some good, and simply waited after sunup everyday for Santin to arrive, then comply with his wishes as a good patient might an attending physician.

After the fourth day, and still without word from the old man about the health of the horse, John told Ethan he'd better go shoot some meat quick, or else the two of them were going to be worse off than Soldier in a couple days. They'd run out of the elk, and the fresh biscuits Ethan had cooked up weren't far behind. Without waiting, John packed up his bedroll and enough ammunition to keep him occupied for the better part of a week, and rode west, disappearing with the setting sun over the hills in the distance. What he didn't see as he headed out was the silent gaze of Willow from a small stand of trees on the edge of camp, her face only a silhouette within the twilight, watching him for as long as she was able, then longer still in her own mind's eye, dwelling on what it would be like to feel his touch, the warmth of his breath, the sweetness of a caress.

—A few miles north as darkness fell he found a gully no more than ten feet wide stretching along a riverbank when he decided to bed down. The moon was bright, the stars dancing about, with some shooters from time to time to entertain him as he drifted off into his world of the Indian girl he'd only just met. But knowing the first light of dawn would bring the business of finding fresh meat, he put away his thoughts of Willow, nodding off for what remained of the night.

*

The following day the air was crisp with patches of white clouds hanging harmlessly overhead when he eased Stoney down a bank into a gully. Instantly he heard what he thought were birds or some kind of critter in a thicket off to his left. He kept moving at the same pace, only glancing in the direction of the thicket, making no sudden move, riding deliberately, waiting until he was farther into the gully before he would dismount and come back on foot to surprise whatever it happened to be. He kept riding, turning down a dry creekbed some hundred yards or more before reining in Stoney. There he dismounted, grabbed his Sharps along with a few extra rounds and headed back down the creekbed. When he reached the gully, he was crouched low to the ground, making his way carefully back to the brush where he first heard the sound. Thirty yards away, he stopped. No movement from him now, barely a breath... an intruder only slightly curious to the watchful eyes of the creatures who called this land their own.

It was another three minutes before he heard another sound from the brush just ahead, but this time there was no mistaking it. The cracking of branches told John it was bigger game, and he welcomed the thought of bringing down some meat this early on the trail. Don't rush, he thought... don't run it off, least ways not in the wrong direction. He looked at the ground around him. There were small twigs and branches about, and pieces of broken granite. This offered what he was looking for... a decent size 'throwin' rock.' He picked one out, cradled it in his palm for some seconds, then let it go. With it still in flight he set up on one knee, brought his rifle into position and cocked the hammer, staring intently at the brush before him. The missile crashed into the thicket ... then another split second... then a moment later, the buck was breaking from the heavy brush running straight at him. There was no time to think... no time, just react. He rode the sight of his Sharps and fired. The buck had moved so quickly the bullet struck him flank high, buckling his forelegs, bringing him down head over hooves. John exhaled, wiping the sweat from his brow as he watched the animal struggle to right his body without success, yet he struggled.

Some moments later with the life pouring from him, his breath shortening, barely moving, the buck's eyes followed the hunter as he circled around behind, slowly, carefully. He could see the hunter pulling something from his belt... what was it? But by then John had slit the animal's jugular, trussing him up and bleeding him before rigging a sling for the trek back.

*

As he rode back into the Indian camp with the buck strapped to a travois, some of the younger men came out to see. They watched approvingly as he made his way to his and Ethan's campsite. Bringing down an animal such as this wasn't easy, even with a rifle. So the young men raised their hands in salute, and talked of his feat around their fires.

"The white man named John hunts well, Father," Running Wolf stated to Two Bears at the first opportunity. "He brings back a large, male deer. It is good because Santin says the other's horse will take some time to heal. Maybe one moon."

"When did you speak with Santin?" asked his father.

"Today, fishing at the river."

"I will tell this to John Connor. And also I will tell him of Willow's reply."

The boy couldn't wait for his father to reveal Willow's thoughts about the white. Running Wolf had liked the two hunters from the beginning. If his sister felt as he did, the boy knew he would soon have a brother among them. But Running Wolf also knew the price would be steep for his sister... six, maybe eight horses. So he chanced one last question, hoping his father would share Willow's thoughts.

"And what is her reply, Father?"

He is old enough, Two Bears thought. He can keep such things to himself.

"She likes the idea." As he rose to go see John, the chief added, "so do I."

12

It was twilight when Two Bears was within sight of their campfire, and John was ready. As soon as he'd returned with the buck, he began dressing it out, skinning and cutting it into strips for the chief and his family. Naturally, he wanted to impress him with his skill at hunting... to be known and respected as a good provider. But there was a stronger motivation. John wanted to thank Two Bears for his hospitality, for he had a feeling he and Ethan would be in the Indian camp for some time, and he hoped the time could be put to good use... courting Willow.

"Hau, kola. I see you have done well on your hunt. It is a good kill." John nodded as the chief continued. "I bring news of MacCall's horse." As the words were spoken, Ethan came over to join them. "Santin says the horse will be well, but only with time... maybe one moon. He will bring more of the medicine when it is needed. He says to watch the horse closely so the wound is not reopened."

Two Bears began to rise when John caught his arm, asking him to wait. He pointed to the freshly cut strips and stated as formally as he was able, "this is fer you an' yer family, Two Bears... in gratitude fer allowin' us to share yer camp and the bounty that surrounds it. I hope you'll receive this gift in the manner it was meant, one of friendship."

The chief nodded, his eyes softening barely, but enough for John to see. Lingering for a few more seconds before rising to leave, he stated, "bring the meat to my lodge this night. We will eat and talk."

*

The Indian camp was abuzz with the news of the white stranger and Willow. Somehow word of their courtship had spread and now as John walked through the maze of lodges and tipis with the strips of meat hanging from a pole, the eyes and smiles of the people gathering followed. It was dusk when he arrived at Two Bears' lodge, but the sky to the west was still a flaming crimson and gold, rays bouncing off a stream of clouds slowly passing over the hills beyond. It was beautiful, a storybook reflection he remembered as a child, with one flaw... he was alone, with no one there to greet him.

Am I too early?... he asked himself. Did I misunderstand? No... no, he

13

thought. This is what he said. So the suitor stood there, holding the meat, shuffling about, feeling every bit the fish in the bowl he now found himself to be. He cleared his throat conspicuously as twenty or more of the Sioux continued to look on. Some giggled at his awkwardness while others were more sympathetic, but they watched, and waited... with him. What John didn't know was that other young men had attempted to court Willow, coming to call with a variety of extravagant gifts, but all were left standing for hours, waiting for an invitation that never came. Would it be the white's fate as well? The Sioux, like John, could only stand, and look, and wait. When Two Bears pushed back the skins covering the entrance to his lodge, their curiosity was answered. He stepped outside and looked briefly about at those who had gathered, waving them away before extending a warm welcome to John, inviting him in to the place he would soon call home.

*

"What happened?" Ethan asked excitedly as soon as John arrived back at their campsite. "Is she for it?... Is the chief?"

John had told Ethan of his plans earlier as he was gathering up the meat. He said he'd been struck by Willow from the very first, and couldn't take his mind off of her. It just felt right... her, this place. It was the right thing for him... the right life. Ethan had been surprised, completely. But John had not seen shock on his partner's face. In fact, Ethan's surprise had turned to genuine interest, then happiness for his friend. Now, though, John saw Ethan's excitement tainted with a modicum of apprehension. But he'd made up his mind. Ethan was just going to have to fend for himself for a time until he found somebody else to partner with.

"Yep, she's for it... an' Two Bears... an' her ma."

"Well, what happened then? And when will it happen?... the weddin' I mean."

"Not fer a spell."

"What's a spell?... and what happened tonight?"

John was pleased to find only excitement in Ethan's voice again, so he continued. "After shufflin' about some outside Two Bears' lodge, he finally come out and rescued me from the rest o' his people. Seems I was the village idiot fer a minute there."

Ethan pulled the log he was sitting on a little closer.

"When I got inside I saw only Runnin' Wolf at first. He was sittin' by the fire, and Two Bears indicated I should sit down and join 'em, which I did. Then I noticed off ta one corner, where the light wasn't s'good, there was two women — Willow's ma, Star Risin', and another. Their backs were to us, but they were movin' like they were attendin' ta somethin' er someone. Finally I realized it was her... Willow. Well, ma heart starts jumpin' an' poundin' an' b'for I c'n even offer the meat ta Two Bears, she rises from the corner and steps into the light by the fire... an' now my heart jus' plain stops. Two Bears an' her ma see this... even Runnin' Wolf... and they're all amused 'cause I cain't hardly talk at all. But Willow isn't amused. She's smilin' too, o' course, but her eyes're kind, lookin' directly inta mine fer what seems like ferev'r. When she knelt to sit across from me, her eyes nev'r left, and it took Two Bears' voice to break the moment, caus' I sure wasn't goin' ta."

"What then?"

" 'John Connor,' he said, 'this is my daughter, Willow, and her mother, Star Risin'. I have explained the reason fer yer comin', and both agree it is good. We accept the meat from yer hunt.' Then he took the strips an' handed them to Star Risin' who placed them on a spit ov'r the fire. Whil' the meat was cookin', Two Bears inquired as to what I intended to do... where we might live. I told him I expect we'd be livin' mostly like they did... off the land in these parts, not mor'n a few days ride. It seemed ta set well with him... an' Willow's ma. But mostly, I think, she liked the idea... to be close enough, but still far enough away to feel on her own... on our own. When the meat was cooked an' ever'one was enjoyin' it, the conversation got right friendly. Runnin' Wolf even threatened to spill some of his sister's secrets if she didn't make him that pair of moccasins she kept promisin' him... ta which Star Risin' raised a hand in jest, givin' all o' us a good chuckle. Well, it got later an' ever'one got full up with the buck, so not knowin' Indian manners real well, I decided to take ma leave. I didn't want to overstay ma welcome the first night. When I was gettin' up, I was havin' trouble takin' my eyes from hers. Our eyes were stuck together, glued like, an' I tell ya, Ethan, it was the hardest thing I ev'r done. But then I could hear Two

Bears sayin' somethin' 'bout Indian tradition... that it was right I should offer some gift fer Willow's hand. When I was fully standin' agin lookin' at him I asked what'd be proper to give. After some hesitation, he said he'd think on it."

"Well, pard, I hear tell that kinda tradition c'n get mighty expensive. Ya know it ain't unusual for a maiden like her to fetch half the beaver pelts west o' the Ohio... er a string o' fine ponies." Ethan was getting worked up now, worrying about what wasn't his concern in the first place. Though he had a point, John wasn't about to be put off by material items... not now, no matter how difficult they may be to come by.

"I don't give a hoot what Two Bears considers a proper gift fer his only daughter... I'm gonna git it."

Ethan saw a look in his partner's eyes he'd seen often enough. As soon as John knew the price he'd have to pay for Willow, there'd be no stopping him. May as well give the man a hand. "All righty then, pard, I'll help ya. I ain't got nothin' better to do fer a spell 'cept get you married off an' lose the best partner I ev'r had. Now that's brains fer ya. I'd do better ta tie ya down an' sit on ya, but I know that won't do no good. I'm goin' ta bed. Most likely we'll be gettin' started b'fore ya know it."

John smiled as he watched Ethan crawl into his bedroll, and he thought... yes, most likely we will be getting started tomorrow, so he offered, "night, pard. Get some sleep."

*

"Dang if I didn't know it'd be the ponies," Ethan was harping on Two Bears' firm request as the two rode south towards the open plains. "It could'na been pelts... any kinda pelts, piled high n' deep!... nah, it had ta be a string o' ten o' these here parts finest horses! Now tell me, how're we gonna accomplish 'at, partner? I ain't seen hide ner hair o' one good Injun pony since las' spring. How'r we gonna..."

"What about that mount yer ridin' right now? Mighty nice o' Two Bears ta let ya borrow him 'til ol' Soldier is sound... an' him watchin' ov'r 'im an' all whil' yer off with me."

"That was mighty nice, an' I 'preciate it. I told Two Bears as much on our

16

way out. But that ain't gonna find us ten others, now is it?"

"Well, I ain't so sure. Member that ol' timer when we put in to Wiley's Landin' the summer b'for last?... Riggins I think his name was... member?"

"Yeah, I believe."

"Well, if I'm not mistak'n, ol' man Riggins mentioned a wild herd runnin' b'tween the South Fork o' the Shoshone an' the Yellowstone this time o' year. Good grass there."

"What's that got ta do with this here Injun pony I'm ridin'?"

"Two Bears told me that pony was caught along with fifteen er twenty others beneath the great breasts... in the valley where the grass is thick."

"I don't foller ya."

"Look up... way off ov'r ta there. See that?... those two peaks? That's them."

"That's what?"

"The Grand Tetons, pard! That's what Two Bears and his people call 'em. Another three, four days ride and we'll be smack in the middle o' that rich grass-land... the same valley ol' Riggins was talkin' 'bout. Fact that's where he picked up his own string... an' that's where we gonna find ours."

For the next two days, they continued southwest bypassing scant herds of buffalo, finally stopping for rope and tack in Digg's Fort, then hugging the Shoshone until the evening of the third day when they saw the Rockies looming. So far, the travel had been without incident, but trappers and traders never knew what might surprise them on what was still the frontier. John and Ethan weren't raw by any stretch, and had experienced such travails, coming close to disaster when a small band of Pawnee jumped them near Granite Pass the year before, and on another occasion when a grizzly went territorial on them. In both cases, it took all their wits and some of their skin to survive, the net of it being to this day they travel easy, look-ing for sign, listening for any aberration within the more familiar sounds they had come to know.

"What's fer dinner?"

"Buck n' biscuits," John answered without hesitation.

"Agin?"

"Less ya wanna fry up some o' them beans with it."

"Buck n' biscuits n' beans! The three "Bs" over an' over. Seems like if we were ev'r ta scratch up somethin' besides buck n' biscuits n' beans it'd have ta be a "B"... fer beaver er butterflies er bats er somethin'." Ethan was goin' on like he did from time to time, but John didn't pay it any mind. Ethan was just bein' Ethan.

"Ya want them beans, pard? I'll fry 'em up if ya do."

"Na, don't go outa yer way... buck n' biscuits'll do me jus' fine. I'll get the coffee on," and Ethan went down to the river to fill up the pot while John cut off a few strips of venison.

They ate their fill around a low burning fire with the sound of the river rushing behind. Now and again a night owl would raise a hoot or a coyote would howl a greeting to whom or whatever, but they'd heard it all before around a thousand campfires, so they set at ease and talked some before turning in.

"Ya know I been thinkin' on this some... yer betrothal an' all... an' ya know I'd tell ya ma mind. I think yer doin' the right thing, pard. It's gonna cost me I know... ridin' together these past years like we done, but you an' WIllow are right together. I saw it when we were ridin' out the other day and she was watchin'."

"I nev'r expected to find someone like her out here. Life's funny, I guess." John hesitated before he went on, looking for the words, "Ethan, I ache all over from not seein' her... not like a bad ache, but a wantin' one... one I expect'll keep callin' me to her, so's she's nev'r mor'n a few days ride." He paused again before reaching for his blanket. "Get some sleep, partner... tomorrow could be interestin' if we find a herd."

*

The morning was clear as John and Ethan sipped at their coffee and had more of the biscuits. They'd awakened before dawn, but now that the sun was at their backs showing them the first light of day, the two gulped the last of the coffee and packed up. In a few more minutes they were heading west, straight at the Tetons, making decent time as the land opened up before them. The ridge in the distance looked to be fifteen or twenty miles off, but loping the horses at a good pace it didn't take long to cover the ground between. At midmorning, they'd reached its peak, and there sat aghast atop the ridgeline, jaws dropping. They turned to one another for a moment, then looked again. Below lay the richest land John and Ethan had ever laid eyes on... rivers and lakes intertwined with rolling hills and stands of pine and willow and cottonwood that stretched for miles until it half climbed to the summit of the Tetons themselves. The movement of game here and there in the valley had John grabbing for his spyglass, and upon further inspection he announced an abundance of elk, moose, buffalo, deer and, yep, that wild herd of ponies.

"Right ov'r there," handing the glass to Ethan, "near the smaller o' them two lakes. See 'em?"

"Yes... yes I do. Mus' be twenty-five er thirty in the bunch. This is yer party, John. How d'ya wanna handle it?"

"Let's watch 'em a spell... see what they're up to."

From the ridgeline they could see the herd was still on the move, and John figured they'd keep moving until high noon or so, then pick one of their favorite spots, fill their bellies and doze a while before moving again. If he and Ethan waited until they stopped to feed, they could count on them being in the same spot in the hour or so it would take to ride over there. So the two waited, watching as the herd moved easily across the valley below. As John trained the glass back on the ponies, he was startled once again. At the lead, standing tall and erect like some crowned prince, was a pure white stallion with black stockings on both forelegs.

"Look at that animal!... he's gotta be near sixteen, seventeen hands... he's a beaut! We get him and we got the whol' bunch."

John handed the glass to Ethan, "on the lead... the white."

"I see what ya mean, partner... he's a han'some one," adding, "look, they're slowin' down," and Ethan kept watching until the herd had stopped and were grazing, lazily, as the sun warmed their backs. "I think it's time."

They spurred their horses from the ridgeline into the valley of dreams, riding easily, loping over the land, splashing through streams and creeks only deep enough to wet the bottoms of their leggings. An hour later and still loping easily John pulled the spyglass out of its sheath and took another look. In a moment he raised two fingers. The herd was lolling after that midday feed only two miles ahead.

"Let's pull up ov'r to that grove o' trees," pointing to his left. Reining in the horses under the shade of a tall pine, they let them drink some. "We'll rest these two here fer a spell... they're gonna need all their juice when we go after that stallion."

Thirty minutes later, they were walking quietly on the blind side of their mounts as they approached the herd. The ponies were still lazing about, well satisfied with their foraging, and would be in no mood to take off on some 'yahoo.' But John and Ethan took no chances, using hand signals to communicate until the White pricked up his ears, looking in their direction. The two hunters only hesitated, continuing on, moving carefully, cautiously, closer to their prize. When the animal raised his head again to catch a scent, John and Ethan were already aboard their mounts, laying prone, walking them directly at the herd now only fifty yards off. They were hoping the White would mistake them for part of the herd, or strays, and they continued on, whispering.

"We go right at him. Whichever way he goes, get a rope on him... the rest'll follow." John had barely breathed out the words when the stallion reared, screaming a command to the bunch. The others snapped to, waiting for his next move, but by then John and Ethan were closing fast, lassos looped and raised, ready to throw. The stallion reared again and bolted to his left — Ethan's side — as the two were upon him. Ethan whooped and yelled out, "whahoooo!!"... letting his rope fly.

The loop caught the horse around the neck on the dead run, the animal kicking furiously as he felt the encumberance take hold, then bolting again. Ethan was barely hanging on, spurring his pony to keep up, all the while giving the stallion more slack until John could get another rope on him.

"Come on, Stoney... come on, boy," John urged, kneeing him over some as he looped his rope, swinging it overhead, closing fast. "Come on, boy, just a little closer now... that's it... yahooo!"... as his loop grabbed hold. John gave two quick jerks, slacked off, then two more. Ethan followed likewise, and the White slowed. But there was no stopping him, not yet, so they let him gallop easily, every now and again jerking their ropes on both sides, then slacking off. After another two miles, the animal was tiring. More than that, he sensed his predicament. He didn't like it, but he understood it, accepting capture when the two men, together, were able to rein him in, tie off their ropes, jump down and hobble him.

The White reared, screaming displeasure. John walked to him slowly, all the while talking, showing the palms of his hands to calm the animal, hushing him to neighing. When he attempted to stroke the stallion's forehead, the horse jumped back, but without striking out. John tried again, and again. After three more attempts the animal was still reluctant to allow John contact, but with each attempt the horse grew calmer, gentler.

"We got us a wild one here, Ethan, but he's no killer. I don't know if Two Bears is gonna be happy, though... when I give him to Willow."

"You're gonna give that rogue to Willow?! You'd best think on that one, pard."

"I have. Two Bears can have the rest."

*

They were within sight of the Indian camp now and John and Ethan had been right. Over the past five days, the rest of the ponies in the herd had stayed near the leader. Each morning the two men would lay a rope over the stallion, tieing him off to their saddles and climbing aboard before one of them leaned down to unhobble him. The first morning he took off, faster than dogs on the scent, and it was hell bent for more'n four miles until they got him straightened out and slowed to a cantor. Next day it got a might easier, and the next easier still, until they had the White full in hand with another twenty-seven paints and sorrels, roans and bays sticking close.

It was when they were riding the herd down the long, sloping bank towards the Indian lodges in the distance, like they'd come in that first day, that the people saw them. A great cry went up from the camp, and John and Ethan saw braves jumping on ponies, coming fast. Running Wolf arrived first with a half dozen others, and he was grinning from ear to ear as he greeted John, welcoming him back, saying with pride, "my father will be pleased... and also Willow." Then he turned to the others, exulting, "Yi, yi, yi, yi..." and they wheeled and drove the herd down to the river.

John and Ethan, still holding the stallion, didn't follow, but held their prize close, trotting him into the camp below. As they led him through the maze of tipis, the people gathered while a dog or two sparked to the unfamiliar scent, the White prancing all the way like some show horse understanding the importance of the moment, him being the center of it all. Everyone followed them to Two Bears' lodge where there was much excitement and scurrying about as each person maneuvered for what was to be the coming nuptials. As John climbed down from Stoney, Two Bears, Willow and her mother appeared from the lodge. It was enough for Two Bears to see the look between John and Willow. He had made up his mind, even if John had come back with something less than demanded. He wanted happiness for his daughter first, and he knew this white man would bring that to the marriage. So he looked at John approvingly, then to his daughter, and finally to the stallion. He approached the horse, quieting him, gently stroking his forehead. The White neighed warmly to his touch, and Two Bears looked at John, "this is a very fine horse, much better than I had hoped. But he is only one."

"It is true, Two Bears, he is a very fine animal, the best I've ev'r seen. 'At's why I intended him fer Willow. But he ain't the only one. Me and my partner here have brung ya twenty-six more, all as good as anything ya got in yer own herd. Now you only asked fer ten, so the rest are on me... my gift to you and yer people... an' still not near enough, in my mind, for yer daughter's hand."

He reached out to Willow, for he could no longer wait to feel the closeness of her. She came to him, as she would always, and his gesture was taken by Two Bears as it was intended, for he too remembered the impetuousness of youth, and his own longing for Star Rising when they had become betrothed so many winters ago.

"You have done well, my son," the words not lost on John or Ethan, or the rest who had gathered round. "Let us begin the marriage."

With that a great cry went up, the drums bellowing the call as Willow was led away by her mother and another of the women. She reappeared in her finest deerskins and moccasins, her hair braided meticulously with beads and feathers for the coming ceremony. Two Bears smiled, taking her hand, leading her to John who'd used the time with Ethan to hobble the White with the rest of the herd by the river's edge. John had splashed the dust off himself, slicking his hair back some which inspired Ethan to tell him he at least looked presentable.

"Thanks, pard, you'd bes' do the same. Yer ma bes' man, ya know."

Ethan slicked himself up some, too, then together they hiked back to where

Willow, Two Bears and the rest were waiting. Approaching his bride-to-be, John walked slowly, taking in the moment, savoring the feeling he held for the girl who stood before him.

Two Bears, in his eloquence, was every bit the proud father, not only of his daughter who was beautiful, but of his new son, who had grown in stature with his gift of many ponies. And the White, the magnificent stallion who John had given to his daughter was considered good luck for the couple as they started their life together, for he was bold and brave as all could see, yet with a good heart. When Two Bears finished speaking, he took the right hand of Willow and the left of John, clasped them together in his, holding them high above his head for all to see. Stating that these two are now one, and should be considered such, he said simply, "go into your new life together, bring only happiness to one another, and may your days be filled with hunting grounds that are plentiful, and the bounty of many children."

The people shouted in approval, their voices rising as the drums turned what had been just another day into a long afternoon and night of dancing, eating and revelry. The women changed into their finest deerskins, but not before slitting the throats and skinning three good sized dogs to add to the backstraps of buffalo and elk that had survived the previous hunt. John and Ethan still had some of the buck, and they added that to the pot. By dusk, the drums had become the elixir for all, the women dancing clockwise to the beat in one circle, the men in a larger circle dancing counter to them. Willow and John, with Two Bears and Star Rising next to them, sat watching, attentive to all who from time-to-time would come to congratulate them, or give them some small token, or offer them a piece of dog, considered a delicacy. One of John's particular delights was watching Ethan enjoying himself, dancing in the circle of men that would stop with the beat, each in front of a single maiden. Ethan, in his good nature, cared not if the girl happened to be particularly plain or heavy or toothy or, in one instance, sport what appeared to be a substantial amount of hair on her upper lip. He was whooping it up like the rest of them, catching on pretty well, John thought, as did Two Bears, to the rythmn of the drums. With a full moon rising to its apex and the light of many fires burning brightly, John and Willow turned to one another and the look they shared spoke only of a common desire. Let us leave the celebration, leave the dancing and the merriment to the others, and begin our life together, truly as one. Willow reached over and gently touched her mother, next her father, then held her hand out for John to take. She motioned to the wedding lodge that had been prepared earlier in the day. As they walked into the night from the rest of the tribe, another great cry of jubilation followed them, but they paid no mind, continuing slowly, hearing only the gentleness of their footsteps on the earth beneath them, and the soft breathing of one another.

*

The months passed quickly after their wedding night, a night John would recall often when he was off hunting with Ethan or some of the other tribesmen. It had been dark inside their wedding lodge, with only the light from a small fire offering he and Willow a glimpse of the other as they slowly sank to their knees in an embrace, discarding their deerskins, she revealing the sweet suppleness of her body. John remembered how they'd touched somewhat shyly, not knowing how to act or react to the moment they had longed for, prayed would one day come. But soon they discovered their way together was as natural as the sun rising each day, and the night lingered for them as would many after. They lay awake long and late, conversing with the few words each knew of the other's language, more deeply and passionately with their eyes, the soft touch of a hand, the warmth of a kiss, and the tender, endless lovemaking every part of their bodies ached for, would die for.

*

Willow That Weeps paused for some moments in her recounting of the story of Red Hand's father. The boy had noticed this before, that at this point his mother would stop and reflect before finishing.

"One morning, when the first snows were falling, your father rode out with Ethan MacCall to find meat for the coming winter. It was the last time I saw him, the last time any of the people saw either of them," Willow That Weeps stated softly, the memory of that time washing across her face, exposing, however briefly,

24

the hurt and sorrow that remained. Then, breathing deeply, her mood changed. "It has been many moons since that time, my boy. Why," she exclaimed, "you are nearly a man!"

Red Hand sat a little taller at his mother's comment, but he could see the pain, and he wanted to console her, to soften what for too long was plain for all to see. But he didn't know how. He didn't think he would ever know how.

"I'm sure mother, if he could have returned, he would have."

Willow That Weeps smiled, reaching out to hold her son's hand.

"Yes, my son, he would have."

It was a conviction she'd held for the past seventeen years, but like all of the women who'd lost loved ones without witness or explanation, she secretly held out hope. At times, she could convince herself that one day, one wildly happy day, John would ride into camp, announcing he'd been hurt, or captured and taken far away, far from the homeland of the Sioux. He would get off his horse and embrace her once again, announcing he was home, he was sorry, and that his heart soared at the sight of her... as it had and will always. But then, the reality of those years without her husband would take hold, and set in, and as he had before, Red Hand caught his mother gazing off into the mysteries of her own secret thoughts and dreams.

*

"Gonna throw another piece o' wood on the fire, pard?"

Ethan and John were bedding down for the night after three days ride. It was early November and there was near two feet of snow on the ground, but game was still in these parts, and John had figured they'd need some, paticularly with Willow in her condition. Only the week before she told him there was a baby on the way... that she was sure. And now as he sat by the fire of yet another camp out on the prairie, John thought of their coming child, and their life ahead. Then his mind would drift, consumed once again by the thought of Willow, and their first night together.

"Yeah, why not, I'll grab another log. This weather here's turnin', I c'n feel it. Let's bed down, pard, tomorrow'll be here right quick." Then he added after

25

pausing, "I feel lucky."

The morning brought with it a steel-gray sky that seemed to melt into the snow all around. Another three or four inches had fallen through the night, covering the tracks that might have been made the day before by any game that hadn't yet cleared out, so John and Ethan knew they were going to have to get lucky. One thing for sure, they weren't going anywhere without their coffee to thaw them out, so the two sat glugging down cup after cup, trying to figure which way to start out.

"I think we go south, John. Any beast with half the sense the Lord give 'im gotta be headin' south in this weather. We ain't goin' after jackass, ya know."

"Ya gotta point there. Let's pack up an' git goin' b'for we have ta track 'em clear ta Mexico. I'm still feelin' lucky, but that ain't gonna hold forev'r."

It was no more than two hours later when they picked up the tracks of the small herd. It looked like elk — a good-sized bull leading six or seven others moving southwest, taking their time. The two men tracked them over the gently sloping hills for another five miles, through cottonwoods and pine dripping with fresh snow, across streams and creekbeds beginning to ice up at their banks until John thought he caught a glimpse of the herd about a quarter mile ahead.

He said in a low voice to Ethan, "let's circle 'round an' come up on 'em."

The two lit out, putting another low rising hill between them and the herd until they pulled up and tied off their horses in a small meadow some two miles distant.

"I think this'll do," Ethan opined, "they should be comin' off that rise right ov'r there. Still some grass showin'. Let's jus' wait in these trees fer a spell."

A half hour later they saw the bull poke his head over the top of the rise. He was a good eight-hundred yards off, but when he breached the hill, one of the cows appeared with him. It wouldn't be long now before the rest followed, marching behind the bull, heading straight for them. Easy pickings, if they stayed lucky.

"Lookit 'em wapiti, pard!..." Ethan was excited, but quiet at the same time. " 'At bull in the front's gotta have eight points a side."

" 'At he does," John agreed. "Let's hunker down."

For the next hour the elk grazed some, but all the while moving steadily towards John and Ethan. They were less than two hundred yards off when John laid his Sharps across a branch directly in front of him, Ethan doing likewise.

"I'll take the bull, you got the cow jus' off ta his right. On three. One... two..."

The sound of the two rifles firing shook the serenity of the little meadow blanketed with winter's first decent snow, shattering whatever plans elk in the wild might be capable of devising. The bull went down like he'd been struck by the wrath of God, one shot through the heart. Ethan got the cow, his bullet piercing her brain. Frantic, the other cows twisted this way and that, finally bolting directly at the two hunters, their calves following as best they could.

"One more fer the trail, pard," John said, as he pulled off another round, dropping the lead cow. With that, the next in line veered into the trees with the calves right behind. In another instant they were out of sight within the dense brush, a mother and her babies, with one or two orphans tagging along.

"Whew!..." Ethan let out, "that was some catch. We got work ta do, here. I'll start on the bull."

"Soun's like a plan. I'll rig up the travois, then help ya with the res.'"

They were at it for more than an hour when Ethan heard the sound, like a branch breaking. He looked over to John, but he'd already rigged the travois and was hacking away at one of the cows, pulling off the backstraps. Ethan shook his head, saying to himself, 'nah,' and went back to work on the bull. When he heard it a second time, he looked at John again. Now, his partner was looking back, their eyes meeting, their minds reading the same sign... 'get yer rifle... now.'

John spoke first, "wanta knock off a spell?"

"Why not, I could use somethin' ta eat," and Ethan started walking towards John who was already on his way to the horses thirty yards off.

'Gotta get to that rifle...' John was thinking as he took his time, not wanting to show any hurry-up. 'This here hand gun'll do in a pinch, but that rifle'll do us a whol' lot better.'

It was then he felt the arrow plunge into his thigh, deep, to the bone, then the rush of braves that seemed to surround them. Ethan had caught a glimpse of them the instant before. They were Arapahoe and he was already firing his Colt, stopping two of them as he dashed for the horses. John was struggling, pulling his own hand gun, firing point blank at three more who were almost upon him. His leg was on fire. He fanned his Colt, knocking the onrushers down, but couldn't stop the third brave from falling on top of him. The bullet had spun the warrior around, but he was able to wield his hatchet in death, leaving a deep gash on John's temple. Ethan could sense disaster. He knew it wasn't going well for his partner as he got to his rifle. He pulled it from the scabbard, wheeling and firing as quick as he could cock and aim, chasing what remained of their attackers back into the woods. But they'd be back. Too big of a prize to leave behind... especially since more than a handful would not be returning from the hunt. He had to get John out of there, and right quick. He crouched low to the ground, sweeping the woods with his eyes as he made his way over to his partner. John was hurting, but Ethan was able to help him to some brush behind a fallen tree. Then he saw it. John was spitting blood from an arrow dug deep in his chest.

"I'm a goner, pard," John spoke weakly. "Ain't got mor'n a minute er two. You bes' get outa here... an' pronto."

"I ain't gonna leave ya."

"I said git. One o' us hasta git back an' tell Willow. Now, go on. I got my Colt here. I'll take one er two more with me when they come."

Ethan looked at his partner for some time, not finding the words to say what he wanted... that the man in front of him was like a brother, someone for whom he would have gladly given his own life. He put his hand on John's shoulder, then took his gun out for him, cocked it and placed it in his hand. Before he turned to leave he said, "I'll see ya in the long beyond," adding, "git a fire started."

The screams came at them again just as Ethan mounted his Indian pony. Four were charging from across a bog only some twenty, thirty yards off. Ethan pulled up his rifle and had barely enough time to knock down one of them before the arrow caught him in the right shoulder. His arm went limp and he nearly dropped the Sharps. All the while John was yelling at him to get going, "git outa here!... Ethan, git!!"

He was riding hard now, his pony jumping the brush, over fallen trees and stumps that lay in his path. He heard two more shots ring out in the distance. It was

John's Colt, he was sure. Musta taken two more of the bastards with him. Good boy. With the sound of the next shot he felt a sharp sting in his hip and he muttered aloud, "Good Lord, they're still chasin' me... how'n hell they git after me?" He kicked his pony harder, heading deeper into the woods rather than the open range he knew was just up the next rise. 'Gotta lose 'ese bastards,' Ethan kept saying to himself. 'Gotta find some shelter.' He pushed his pony for the next hour 'til the animal was stumbling beneath him. No good, no good. He quickly jumped off and grabbed the reins, walking the horse into the dense brush. Twilight was upon them. If he got lucky, the coming night would cover his tracks, and the Arapahoes would leave him be. It was a chance, Ethan thought, probably his only chance, except maybe for one other. 'Why not?...' he reckoned, 'I got nothin' to lose but ma life,' then tweeking his hip, wincing, he added wryly, 'I'm about half way there anyways.'

Ethan got what sleep he could after checking to see if the bullet had just grazed him or went in. He determined it was stuck somewhere inside because the wound was more of a puncture than a gash. He was going to need some help dislodging it, but first things first. He had to get out of these hills, and he was ready to take any risk, even if it meant walking out. So an hour before dawn, with he and his pony well rested, Ethan slipped his saddle and bridle from the horse, held Two Bears' blanket up to the animal to give him the scent, then spanked him hard, saying, "Go on now... go on home."

He waited until the sun was cresting the bluffs southeast of him before starting out, leaving his gear well hidden, not wanting the burden. If he got the chance he'd come back for it, but for now it was do or die, smirking at the thought, dragging his right leg from the pain in his side. 'Geez, the whol' right side o' me is all shot to hell,' he thought, packing the wound with snow to ease the bleeding, then sucking on a handful to take what little nourishment it offered. 'Some water'd do nice 'bout now. Don' know why I ain't seen a stream er ev'n heard the rushin' o' water in these woods yet... they're plenty green.' By midday Ethan was barely moving, the bullet causing him more pain and the wound bleeding again, leaving a dark trail down his leggings into his boot. He was near delerious when he heard the faint sound off to his right. The more he urged himself along, the louder the sound grew, until he was sure of it. It was the rushing sound of water... the sweetest, most alluring sound, he thought, he'd ever heard... more even than the soft whisperings of the only girl he'd ever dreamed of marrying as a boy back home. Ethan ran towards the sound, dragging his leg with him as if it was an extra appendage, an unwanted burden that now he wished he'd left behind with his saddle and his gear. He saw the falls in the distance breaking through a crevasse, then cascading fifty feet to a pool below before running off into a stream through a open glade. He stumbled towards it, falling once or twice, his last thought only of reaching the water, drinking it in, soothing the wounds he'd been given by the people of this wild land, the ones who had killed the only man he would ever call brother.

**

The Covered Wagon

Thousands of settlers packed up their belongings and
headed out from St. Louis — the Gateway to the West — all bent on
a new life etched in the timber of these prairie schooners,
"California or Bust." A good number ended up busted.

Ethan MacCall

"Pa!... Pa!!... come a runnin'!... we got a dead man here looks like."

The Latimer family had been on the trail west for going on three weeks now, except for the last two days. A wheel had cracked on their wagon, and the rest of the settlers in the train decided they couldn't wait.

"Pa!... come on!..." the boy was poking at Ethan with a branch, trying to determine if he was actually dead.

The remainder of the train, about ninety-some including animals, packed up their belongings and pulled out for Hamner to lay over 'til spring. The wagon-master, a man named Childers, wasn't about to let one busted prairie schooner stall the whole party, particularly if a storm was to come through. He gave George Latimer the choice of farming out his family to two or three of the others until they could get reoutfitted, or stay and fix what they got. The Latimers stayed.

"Jamie, hold on there," his Pa said, "lemme see 'bout this."

Jamie was the middle child, a boy of fourteen. Like his father, he was stout with dark, bushy hair and thick eyebrows to go with it. George slowly rolled Ethan over and inspected him for a minute. When he listened for a heartbeat, he grew excited and instructed Jamie to hurry and get his mother and older sister. This man was still alive.

The women arrived just as George was getting Ethan to sit up, and he quickly motioned for his wife and daughter to help get him to camp. Amy obliged her father almost as fast as he got the words out, noticing the wound in Ethan's side as she draped an arm over her shoulder.

"He's hurt bad, Pa. We gotta look after him."

*

33

"Stop all that bouncin', could ya Pa?" Amy was asking politely from the back of the wagon, keenly aware of her Ma's and Pa's notion of place as it related to parents and children. "He's mighty groggy, an' I can tell he's still hurtin' some."

"I understand yer concern, my dear, but if we don't make Hamner by the time this here storm hits, we're all gonna be hurtin'... an' mor'n some."

The day after they'd come upon Ethan, George and Jamie had gotten the wheel patched up with a few sturdy branches and spare wire they were carrying. George figured it'd hold for a spell, so they pulled out early the next morning, but not before Jamie had been given an earful for straying too far from camp looking for wood.

"I don't want ya outa ma sight agin, boy, 'les I know 'bout it first."

"You lis'en to yer pa," his mother added, with Jamie's younger sister Amanda punctuating the remark with a protruding tongue.

"Awright, Pa, ah won't anymore..." but he tacked on, "it's a good thing ah did er that man back there'd be dead."

The boy was right, his father thought, it was a good thing. But he might just as easily have been attacked by some critter or scalped out on this frontier, so George resolved to be more vigilant, particularly of his pups.

"I won't have that talk, Jamie," Amy broke in, "this here gentleman's gonna be fine, jus' fine, I'll see to that."

George and his wife Emma exchanged glances briefly at the remark just as Ethan began rambling some again... "come on... gotta git... John... come on, come on..."

"Whatever happened musta been awful, Pa. I wonder who this John fella mighta been?"

"I think that musta been a sidekick... a relation maybe."

She looked down at Ethan struggling some, shaking, and she scooted closer to the man she would one day wed, lifting his head onto her lap, steadying him, holding him gently. He slowly opened his eyes as the fog that had for some time shrouded his world lifted, and he stared up at the girl. He blinked to clear the distance between them, finally stating very clearly, "Martha?... Is that you, Martha?"

"No, it's Amy... it's me, Amy."

Before another word was spoken, Ethan fell back into the deep slumber that comes to shield the body from pain, pain of the flesh as well as the heart.

*

George and Amy had gotten the arrowhead out of Ethan's shoulder all right, just after they found him. When her father had jerked it out, she cleaned the wound as best she could and bandaged it with an extra pillow case, discovering she wasn't the least bit squeamish about the messy job.

"There," she'd stated directly, "now for that bullet."

"I think we better hold off on that, honey," George cautioned, "that looks deep. We better leave that up ta whatever doctor they might have up ahead."

"Well then, I'll just wrap him up good here in the back of the wagon an' tend to him."

"You do that, dear," Emma said.

*

It was their third day on the trail and Ethan was rambling again in his stupor, saying the craziest things it seemed, particularly to Jamie and Amanda who couldn't quite grasp the idea of hurt and delerium. However, Amy was as attentive as always, and when Ethan struggled, the sweat pouring from him, and he opened his eyes, he didn't remark on Martha as he had before. He looked up to Amy in what seemed a pleasantly lucid state, and asked, "who are you?"

Like before, she said simply, "it's me, Amy."

Ethan smiled, remarking he liked the name... "Amy." Then, while his strength held, he went on to inquire about where he was now... where they'd found him... was he alone... and so forth... just so's to fill in the blanks over, what?... four days now?

Amy took him through the story with her Pa and Jamie jumping in now and then, and the more she explained, the more his and John's encounter with the

Arapahoe came back. In his own mind now, the pieces had fallen together, from the time he rode off for his life, then walking through the woods hurt, and scared, looking for water... up until now, comforted in the arms of this young girl and her family.

"Well, Ethan MacCall," Amy said to him, "ya got a pretty bad bullet wound there in yer side. Soon as we git into Hamner, that'll have ta be looked after." She made the remark like the attending nurse she had become, but with so generous an amount of affection it was unmistakable to all, even little Amanda giggling at her sister's insistence.

"If you say so, Miss," Ethan replied to his orders, then adding more gently on Amy's behalf, "specially if you say so."

She looked down at him again, and as their eyes met, they lingered this time, neither of them seeing George and Emma exchange one more glance that only parents of children on the brink of life could share.

*

The Hamner settlement was teeming with every kind of two-legged creature found this far out on the frontier — families heading west, mountainmen and wagonmasters who guided and scouted for them, entrepreneurial types selling everything from maps showing newly cut trails through the Rockies to snake oil, store and saloonkeepers, blacksmiths, livery operators, hoteliers, those who let rooms, gamblers, cowhands and, of course, the ladies who'd gone astray... 'ceiling watchers'... found at every outpost where more than three men gathered west of St. Louis. However, what Ethan required most as the Latimer party arrived was the local doctor, something Amy would not put off for another minute.

"Pull up to that man over by the drygoods, will ya Pa? I'll ask."

George turned to her, trying not to let his daughter's initiative irritate him, though it did some, and he said, "you take care of Mr. MacCall, my dear, I'll locate the doc."

She understood and went back to soothing Ethan who'd been sleeping soundly the past few hours as George pulled up the team alongside the drygoods.

"Excuse me, sir, this settlement have a doctor in it? We got a man needs tendin' to."

The middle-aged, quite rotund gentleman with a ready smile beneath a broad mustache, answered directly, "yes, yes we do... down to the right, just past the livery."

"Thank you, sir," George replied, "we'll be gettin' along then."

"Hope he makes it," he yelled after them, causing Amy to wince. She never considered Ethan not making it, but hearing the remark it dawned on her there were no certainties in life... no guarantees, especially out here on the frontier. So she said a silent prayer that the man in her arms would make it, for even then, she wondered how she might ever be happy again if he did not.

*

"Roll him over... gently now," the doc was saying, "let me take a look here... doesn't seem too bad... bleedin's down... but we wanta get that bullet out right away... stop any infection that may be settin' in." He looked up at George and Jamie and Amy again and stated, "I'll need one of you."

George didn't hesitate. He and Jamie would get the wagon over to the livery so that wheel could get patched up and stable the animals at the same time, then go looking for a place to stay the night. After everyone was settled, he'd be back to see how things were going here.

"I'll be fine, Pa," Amy was saying to her father as he and Jamie were leaving.

"I know ya will, honey. You get Mr. MacCall back on his feet," and he winked at her, knowing she would do no less.

"All right, let's get these clothes off of him," Doc Mullins said to Amy, "we got some work to do."

Ethan had passed out again, his mind sparing his body the pain from the sticking and probing the doc had done to investigate the extent of his injury, so getting his clothes off was somewhat difficult, but the two of them managed. Amy pulled a clean, white bedsheet over him, carefully adjusting it to expose his wound, then swabbed away the excess blood with some of the cotton the doc had put out just for that purpose.

"Good," Doc Mullins complimented her, "now hang onto him, this may ruffle his feathers some."

Over the next twenty or so minutes, he dug into Ethan as gently as he could, employing his surgical tweezers, as Amy observed, with uncommon finesse, extracting the bullet on his third attempt. It was from a Winchester, he remarked. Amy had done her part, being firm with Ethan when he struggled from the pain so the doc could do his job, then soothing him when the round was dislodged and Doc Mullins was cleaning the wound, finishing up by installing a small tube before dressing it.

"What's that tube for, Doc? That looks mighty strange sticking outa Ethan like that."

"It may look strange, young lady, but it gives any infection a way out, stead o' seepin' in where it might do some real damage. Now let's turn him on his back where he'll be more comfortable. You keep him cool with that washrag over there."

Jamie came busting in a few minutes later saying how Pa had found them a place about a quarter mile out of town at a boarding house that was real nice, but before he could get most of it out Amy had hushed him with, "Jamie, can't you see we got a real sick man here. Now, quietly, what is it 'bout this here boardin' house?"

As he started up again in a more modest tone attempting to explain just where the family was bedding down for the night, Doc Mullins cut in, "that'd be Miz Scudder's place. Like the boy says, 'bout a quarter mile east o' here... not far. She's a good cook, too... best cobbler I ever et."

"Well I'm not leavin' Ethan. You just run an' tell Ma an' Pa I'm stayin' here the night. It is all right, ain't it Doc?"

" 'Course you can. I sleep in the back room. You c'n fix up a chair right here an' keep an eye on him between dozin' off. If he starts bleedin' heavily er grabs at that tube, you come tell me, ya hear?"

"I surely will, Doctor." Then looking at Jamie, "all right then, go on an' tell Ma an' Pa now. Tell 'em I'll see y'all in the mornin'."

—Two hours later there was another knock on the door of Doc Mullins' office, but Amy had already fallen sound asleep after checking on Ethan one last time. The doctor had given him some laudanum before heading off to bed himself, and it seemed to ease Ethan's discomfort. So now Amy was sleeping peacefully, and soundly, as the knocking continued. Finally, the door creaked open with Emma poking her head in before actually entering. She was not quite sure of what she might be walking into — Ethan all stretched out in the all-together or some such thing — so she eased herself inside before seeing both he and Amy were sleeping like babies. Emma had a plate for Amy Mrs. Scudder had fixed up with a large, red and green cloth napkin covering it to keep it warm. She placed the food on the bedside table, then shook her eldest gently 'til she awakened.

"How's Ethan doin', dear?"

"Oh... jus' fine, Ma," she responded, rubbing her eyes some. "I musta dozed a spell."

"No nevermind." Emma paused before continuing. She'd rehearsed some before coming, not wanting to say anything undue to her daughter as it might affect her feelings towards Ethan. "Musta been an effort helpin' the doc get that bullet out. That kinda thing can tire a person."

"I guess it musta, Ma. But I'm awake now. Is everyone else doin' fine?"

"Yes, dear. The boardin' house is comfortable, an' Miz Scudder's real nice... an' quite the cook, too. I brought ya some supper."

"I heard she was... from Doc Mullins. Thank you, I could eat something." Amy took the napkin and placed it in her lap to rest the plate on. The fried chicken was still warm and crisp, and there were greens and boiled potatoes. As she picked at her food, Emma continued.

"Did the doctor say how long Ethan might be laid up, dear?"

"No. I expect he'll know better tomorrow after Ethan has had a good night's rest."

"The man over to the livery told yer Pa it's gonna be two er three days before that broke wheel is put back together. He needs to fashion some new spokes fer it. We'll be here that long, anyhow."

Amy put her fork down and looked at her mother. "Ma, I'm stayin' with Ethan 'til I know he's all right."

"We don't know how long that'll be, honey."

"If it takes 'til I'm gray, then that's how long I'm gonna be sittin' here."

Emma expected as much, even though she was hoping Amy wouldn't be this determined. But she knew her daughter well enough to know she would not be budged.

"Let's just see how thing's are in the mornin', dear."

"That's fine," Amy stated just the slightest bit curtly. "I'll be right here." Then softer, "thanks agin fer the supper, Ma. I do appreciate yer bringin' it over."

*

It was three days later when George was told the wheel would be ready next morning. They'd learned the rest of the train was camped about two miles out of town, and both George and Emma decided it was time they rejoin the others. After all, they could've been scalped by Indians back in that glade where they found Ethan, and no one would've known the difference. The next day, however, instead of just hitching up and leaving, the Latimers would have a decision to make, which was all Amy's doing.

The day after Ethan had been relieved of the bullet he was carrying, Doc Mullins had inspected his work and determined the patient would not only live, but recover one hundred percent, that is if he stayed in bed for the next two weeks resting, and looked after. Doc said he could look after him some, but he had other patients as well, and babies to deliver... two he could name right off that were due any time now. That's when Amy had spoken right up and volunteered, saying it didn't make a bit of difference if the doc could look after Ethan or not. She was going to be the one doing the looking after.

"Honey, we got ta get goin' tomorrow mornin' now," her father said to her, "we gotta get back with the train."

Amy didn't answer her pa. She just got up and went back to the boarding house for supper and to gather up a few of her things. After the stew and dumplings, she'd finally gotten a piece of that cobbler and told Mrs. Scudder it was everything

Doc said it was, which pleased the woman no end. Then she faced her father.

"Pa, you an' Ma an' the kids go on. I'll stay here. I'll be all right 'til Ethan gets better. The doc said I'm just fine where I am."

George looked across the table at Emma who'd been resigned to this eventuality since her talk with Amy three nights earlier. However, she was also determined not to leave her daughter alone here in the Hamner settlement while the rest of them went off, even if it was just two miles away. She'd made this quite clear to George only an hour before Amy had arrived for supper.

"I suppose we could stay 'til Ethan is back on his feet," George replied after a short silence. "We'll be more comfortable here than huddled together in the wagon. I'll ride on out tomorrow and see Mr. Childers and the others... tell 'em were alive and kickin'."

"Oh thank you, Pa... thank you," and Amy ran over and hugged her father, squeezing him until he blushed.

"Why I haven't had this much attention in a month o' Sundays," George said, trying to hide his embarrassment. "Guess I better turn in early if I'm gonna get up tomorrow and geta goin'."

With Emma looking on, her eyes meeting her husband's, thanking him as well, Jamie and Amanda let out a whoop. They didn't want any part of cramming into the wagon any sooner than was necessary, so the news they'd have their own room and Mrs. Scudder's home cooking for the next two weeks was worth whooping about.

*

After three or four days Ethan was feeling a whole lot better, but orders were orders. The doc wouldn't allow his patient to get out of bed except to take care of the bodily necessities and, every once in a while, to shuffle around the tiny room a bit, maybe for just a few minutes. All the while, Amy was by Ethan's side, holding his arm, helping him as he struggled to regain his strength, and every afternoon and evening, tending to his meals. For entertainment, she would read to him from selections out of the doc's library... Dickens, Whitman, Hugo, de Maupassant, and that new fellow Ethan particularly liked, Mark Twain.

As the days passed, the two grew more comfortable with each other, often engaging in conversation about a particular passage from one of the stories Amy was reading. Inevitably she would set the book down and they would continue their conversation at length until neither could remember how in the world they got to talking so much about whatever they happened to be discussing next. It just seemed natural. The words flowed, which for Ethan was surprising since he'd never been what you might call a conversationalist, even with his best friend John Connor. Most times, people had to pull the words from him, except on those rare occasions like his old partner's wedding in the Indian camp when he kicked up a good fuss celebrating over the affair. With Amy, however, Ethan was different. He was relaxed, unfearful of what he'd always considered was a regrettable lack of refinement and education on his part. He found he could let his thoughts flow freely, without so much as wondering first if it was the right thing to say... at the proper time. It was more important to both of them he soon discovered that he simply say whatever it was he had on his mind. That was what lead Ethan to blurt out his now unmistakably truer, deeper feelings for her on the eleventh day of his recovery, just as she was about to serve him supper.

"Amy," he started, she noticing the change in his voice... she standing, waiting for him to continue, the tray still in her hands. "Amy, we spent a lot of time together this past week er two, an I thank ya for everything ya done fer me. I know ya didn't have to do any of it, but I..." She tried to interrupt, wanting to say she wouldn't have had it any other way, unless of course he hadn't been wounded in the first place, but he put up a hand to hush her and went on. "But I don't think I woulda done nearly as well as I done so far..." Ethan was choosing his words carefully now... "if it hadn't a been fer you. I don't jus mean yer nursin' me an all, although ya do a very fine job o' that. I mean ya bein here, by ma side, readin' to me, talkin' 'bout heaven knows what an all, keepin' me company when you an yer family coulda been off with the train. What I'm tryin to say, Amy, is 'at I couldn't a made it this good without ya, an I'm feared if we part I'm gonna have a real hard time gettin on if ya..."

She couldn't help herself now. She put the tray down on the table, and hushed Ethan as she sat up near him on the side of the bed. She took his hand in her's, then ever so gently so she wouldn't lean on his still weakened side, kissed him very slowly, very sweetly. As her eyes began to moisten with joy, she whispered, "I love you, Ethan. I will always love you... and I will always be with you. That is," and she smiled faintly, raising one of her eyebrows, "as long as you want me."

Ethan gazed up at the woman he would spend the rest of his days with, as content as he would ever be in this life, "I do want you, Amy... I want you fer always... an I'll love you as long."

*

They sat alone in the tipi, the two of them. Santin lit a pipe, taking his time, then studied Running Wolf with eyes of the hawk, looking well within the boy's spirit. The old medicine man knew the youth would understand what he was about to tell him, the boy was old enough, but first the old man inhaled deeply from the pipe, waiting until he saw the vision clearly once again before he spoke.

"Hear me, my son," Santin stated solemnly, "I have seen your brother and his friend. They are in some trouble. But they have been in this kind of trouble before," he recalled, his mind wandering back to the time of his forefathers...

—As the young boy crested the hill he saw the strange creatures in the distance... large, four-legged animals with man-like bodies atop their backs that could detach themselves from their lower half. It was strange to him, he had never seen creatures like this, and he hid in the brush to watch more closely. Now two of them were leaving the others and coming his way. He was not worried since he knew they could not see him, but they were close, maybe two stone's throw distant, and the boy could not be sure. Perhaps these foreign creatures had special powers, greater even than those the mystics of his village possessed. So Sansaqui dug in a little deeper within the blossoming mangroves, waiting for the creatures to pass before he felt it safe to follow.

It was late in the afternoon, the sun beginning its penultimate decent before Sansaqui again caught sight of the two creatures. They were relaxing by a river separated from their larger, bottom halves who wandered nearby, peacefully grazing, stout, powerful. The two by the river were talking, much like two of his own people discussing the changing weather, or the village's crops, or the result — good or bad — of a recent hunt. Sansaqui noted, the larger halves never spoke, only nuzzling one another from time to time. He took this to be a kind of communication on a level surpassing that of the smaller, talking halves, even of his own people. However, he saw the smaller halves were the ones in charge, coming and going as they pleased, forcing their larger halves to bear them on their backs, even making them run. To allow such humiliation, the larger halves must have attained great patience and inner peace, the boy concluded.

The drums of war, faint in the distance, broke the boy's ruminations, just as they did the conversation between the two disjointed creatures he'd been studying so intently. The smaller halves, who had been resting beneath a tree, rose quickly, adorning their gleaming bonnets, and in another instant jumped atop their larger halves heading south towards the sound of the drums. Sansaqui followed as fast as he could, but was not able to keep pace with the two creatures who disappeared over the rise of a hill as the drums grew louder in the distance.

The youth ran and ran towards the drums and the sounds of battle, of men shouting encouragement to their own kind and insults to an advancing enemy, of women wailing the misfortunes of husbands and children lost. He ran faster as he now heard the familiar sounds accompanied by strange popping noises. He had never heard such noises before, but still he ran on, hoping to find his family unharmed. He was frantic, desperate. As he approached the outskirts of the village, he winced as he saw friends and neighbors scurrying about, attempting to flee the carnage, to escape the great creatures silhouetted against a waning sun that bounced brilliantly off the gleaming bonnets of their top halves, while their sturdy, four legs pranced victoriously among the dead and the dying, their huge, angry heads all the while snorting defiance.

'There... there,' Sansaqui thought to himself, 'the lodge.' He dodged two of the creatures charging towards him, barely escaping the popping noise as he crawled under the back of the deerskin lodge, not knowing what he might discover within. He looked up, trying to focus within the darkness. In the corner his younger sister huddled, silent, but only she. His parents and two older brothers were gone. He went to her, hushing and consoling her, telling her they must remain quiet, then very carefully he looked out from under the skins. He saw most of the creatures had gathered what remained of his people at the far edge of the village, and he studied the group looking for the remainder of his family, but could not find them. 'This was good,' he considered, 'maybe they have escaped, and maybe, if the little one and me are lucky, we can make a run for it with the sun as our shield.' All they needed was some distraction, something that would keep the creatures from discovering them until the sun decided to set.

Sansaqui turned to reassure his sister when the first screams came. He turned back quickly, watching as the slaughter began, raging through the helpless, the great creatures wielding their long knives, slashing his people to pieces — severing limbs, heads, hacking massive chunks of flesh from the bone, devouring all. The bloodlust continued as the sun seemed to hang, still, unable to fall into the west when Sansaqui saw two more of the creatures coming fast with a handful of captives. They raced towards the melee, confronting what looked like the leader of the slaughter, a massive creature with a coal-black, lower body. One of the two was waving his long knife at the leader, shouting at him, but the great creature stood his ground, defiant, until turning away slowly. Seeing this, the villagers edged towards the brush as the two creatures who had stopped the killing watched for some moments longer before wheeling to leave. But in the next instant the great creature raised his long knife, bringing it down swiftly on the shoulder of one of the peacemakers. As he raised the great knife a second time towards the other, the wounded one turned, slashing out with his own weapon, burying it in the side of the leader's bonnet, causing a great gushing of crimson to flow forth as the creature's smaller half tumbled to the earth and lay writhing in the dust. The two interlopers, one hunched over and bleeding badly, leaning on his companion, fled to the north. The others started after them until another of the creatures raised a hand and they stopped, turning back to resume the slaughter, but not before many of the villagers had slipped into the brush, away from the long killing knives. It was then Sansaqui saw their chance and he whispered to his sister, grabbing his bow and quiver from the corner of the lodge, "now, Mezatil, now run... run towards the sun... run until your legs can carry you no longer."

They covered the first twenty meters in the open, then darted into the brush west of the village, hoping they'd not been seen by the creatures executing the few remaining who were unable to escape. The two did not look back amid the wails and cries, they ran, faster still, Sansaqui leading his sister by the hand further west for some time until he decided they were not being followed, then they turned north, into the twilight. He remembered what his father and some of the elders had said around the campfires... that there were others of their kind to the north. The elders did not know how far, but they thought it must be a great distance — two or three moons walking — for they had never seen their sign, only hearing of them.

Sansaqui found a suitable pace his sister could match, and they loped onward into the night, the stars lighting their way through a land known well by the youth who'd accompanied his father and brothers on many hunts. Mezatil was holding up for the time being, but he worried about the days of travel ahead, so they stopped to rest for what remained of the night, scraping together some dried leaves to serve as pallets, curling up side by side for warmth until the light of day broke through a canopy of palms above.

"I'm cold and hungry," Mezatil told her brother as soon as she'd awakened. She wasn't complaining, she was only being truthful, Sansaqui thought.

"We'll chance a fire," he told her, "you stay here and warm yourself. I will find us something to eat."

He left reassuring her, then made his way over the crest of the next hill, discovering to his delight a fertile valley with game in the distance. Loping down the other side, the boy checked the arrows in his quiver making sure the shafts were true, and with sharp heads. Then he heard the sound and stopped, frozen, listening. 'What was that?' It sounded like voices... off to his right. He waited, not moving. Now the sound came louder and he dove to the ground, prone, listening for more, waiting. It came again and this time it was familiar. He crawled towards the sound, bellying to the edge of a glade and it was clearer now and he remembered what it was... it was the two creatures he'd followed the day before, the two who had saved the last of his people... the kind ones.

The boy wasn't sure what to do. He saw the one was badly hurt. He'd shed his shining skin and, except for the hair covering his face, he looked similar to

46

Sansaqui's own kind. But the wound was deep. The boy knew of special plants and roots that offered healing remedies, but in this forest he wasn't sure where to find them, so he decided to hunt, for he had his sister to look after. Later, he would return.

He crept away, soon finding a flock of wild hens, taking one down with his first shot, reclaiming the arrow for further use. He made his way back to his sister not wanting her to think too much of the previous day's events without him being there to explain, though he knew he could not. To his surprise he found her in pleasant spirits, warming herself by a fire she'd started, drawing images lazily in the dust.

"Pluck this, little one," Mezatil's older brother told her, "then we will eat."

In a ravenous display, they devoured the hen without speaking before Sansaqui told her of the two creatures over the hill, resting, the hurt one salving his wounds. He said to her, "let us see if they are still there."

Two hours later they were at the top of the hill overlooking the glade. The two creatures were there still, under the large tree where the boy had left them. The one was worse. As the two spoke, the one would raise his voice at times then fall back against the tree, exhusted, then rant again... finally waving off the other as if to say it was time... there was no more to discuss... no more he could do.

It was then brother and sister rose up to show themselves, walking towards the two. The sturdy one stood, ready for whatever surprise they may have, but they continued on, arms up, palms forward, gesturing in peace as they came closer. Now within their camp, Mezatil knelt, reaching down to the wounded one, caressing his cheek with a hand in reverence, expounding softly, "Quetzalcoatl..."

The two creatures had heard the word before used by other natives to describe their great leader, Captain-General Cortés.

"This girl must think all of us Spanish are alike," Enrique laughed, until his amusement caused his wound to reopen.

"Take care," Julio cautioned, "you are bleeding."

Now Mezatil said something they could not understand, and motioned to her brother. She and Sansaqui hurried to the small stream running through the glade and tasted the water. It was good. They quickly broke a large leaf from a nearby palm, twisting it into a container, filling it with the cool water. Mezatil brought it to the dying Spaniard, applying it gently to the gaping wound. She let him drink some, not too much, for she knew it would do him more harm than good. They stood in silence for a while, watching with the other as the wounded one slipped into unconsciousness. Mezatil knelt beside him and whispered, "Quetzalcoatl, haz hecho bien...," and the young Spaniard, so far from home, drifted off to another place, away from the New World to which he had fled seeking adventure and glory. The two youths waited a moment longer, then rose, bowing their heads and taking their leave, Mezatil following her brother farther into the forest, heading north.

—"Was it your grandfather from long ago, Santin?... Did he pass the story down to you?" Running Wolf asked the old medicine man, wanting to hear more of it.

"No," Santin told the boy, hesitating some, "it was me."

Running Wolf was perplexed by this... how could it be?... the boy thought. Yet he was excited about learning more of the old man's adventures, particularly his knowledge of John's fate. Would he see his white brother again, in this life?

"And what of the two creatures?" he asked.

"They were the spirits of your white brother and his friend, good men who have lived many earthly lives, traveling at times the same path until, like today, one of the two dies young, in battle, saving the other."

"Which of the two has died, Santin? Was it my brother?"

After some silence, his mind's eye racing through the ages, he said only, "it is not clear. It may be one day, but now I am tired. I will think on it," and with that Running Wolf knew Santin wanted to rest, so the boy took his leave.

Walking back to the lodge of his family, Running Wolf considered telling his father and mother of Santin's story. Then he thought better of it, deciding to wait until the old one was sure of what he had seen.

*

"I should go, honey. I know we discussed it before a number o' times, but when I got the las' letter back I decided then I had to try to find Willow."

Amy was reluctant to say yes, although she knew Ethan was right. The kids were old enough and the three girls were all helping with the chores. There was the youngest, Bessie, now nine, and her two older sisters, Mathilda, thirteen, and Ellie, fourteen. Amy noticed the two older ones had stopped bossing their little sister around, and so determined the worst of the squabbling was over. Anyhow, she was the one who stopped all the bickering while Ethan simply doted on his girls. Then there was Hamner, the only boy and the eldest, named for the town where Ethan and Amy were betrothed. He was precocious for his seventeen years, proving on more than one occasion he could assume his father's duties when Ethan was away. He had Ethan's tall stature and strong back, along with his mother's considerable will which he'd put to good use during roundup the past two years when his daddy was up to San Jose with the buyers. That was an annual trip for the ranchers in these parts, and it took Ethan the better part of two weeks. On both occasions Ethan'd left Ham in charge, and upon his return found the beef at the stockyards weighed and ready to ship. By Ethan's account, he couldn't have done a better job of it himself, so he hadn't the least concern about making this trip east, back to the country north of the Yellowstone, back to those wilder times of his younger days... with John Connor.

Amy knew her husband was right about going... trying to find Willow so he could be certain she knew of John's fate.

"You better go, then, Ethan. But you be careful, I don' wanna have ta come get ya an' nurse ya back to health agin." She was trying to be strong, but he could see she was wavering, and he went to her. "I don' know what I'd do if anythin' happened to you, Ethan." He held her closely now. "I can't bear the thought o' losin' you."

"Nor I you, my dear... nor I you. That's why nothin' is gonna happen ta me," and he went on, "I've gotten a lot sneakier in ma old age. I'll be jus' fine." Ethan looked at his wife, still noticing her concern, so he changed his tone, carressing her cheek with his hand, "we're gonna be babysittin' the grandkids in our dotage, honey, you wait an' see." She smiled up at him, and they held each other tightly, their lips longing for the others, softly kissing, as they often did.

*

Three days later, each morning warmer than the one before with the coming of spring, Ethan was ready to ride. The night before, the whole family had eaten together as they always did, Ethan asking Amy if she wouldn't mind if Ty, their foreman, dined with them. He was going to be helping Ham out in case of any emergencies with the herd, and Ethan thought it would be nice. Ty had been with them almost twelve years and was like family anyhow. Of course it was all right, Amy'd told him, so they had all eaten together, filling up on stew and green beans, sourdough bread, and peach cobbler for dessert, washing it all down with buttermilk from the dairy. The girls giggled through most of the meal like always while the men talked some about the herd, but they'd covered most of that already. So when the banter turned to Ethan's trip and how long he might be and such, he could see the concern coming over Amy, if only slightly, and he changed the subject, going through Ham's chores again and what was expected of him, as if the boy didn't already know, or hadn't been doing them for three or four years now. Ty saw Ham roll his eyes and he smiled to himself. He remembered his own pa doing the same to him just before he took off for good, reminding him to be wary on the road, to watch his back, and pick his own friends. That was twenty-five years ago, and Ty Harris had been on the move ever since, that is until he found the MacCalls, a family much like his own had been. For no good reason, all those many years ago, Ty had felt the itch to leave home... felt he must leave, and to this day he could put no good reason to it, other than to call it good old-fashioned curiosity, to find out what was around the next bend. But after stumbling on Ethan's place some twelve years back, he'd come to think the MacCall's were as close as he'd ever get to seeing his own again.

"That was good, Mrs. MacCall, I enjoyed it, and as always, the company... mostly the company."

"Well, I hope the girls weren't too much fer ya, Ty... they can be too much fer a body sometimes."

*

"How long d'ya expect to be gone, Ethan?" Amy asked her husband later that night.

"I don't know, honey, a month er two... maybe more. It's been near twenty years... Willow an' her people could be almost anywhere. The army put the Injuns on reservations all over the west. I'm gonna have ta do some inquirin' aroun'... probably even get a little lucky."

"Well, I don' want ya comin' back here findin' me in a rockin' chair. You come home soon."

"I will, honey," he said leaning over, whispering to her, "you know I will," and Ethan reached out, snuffing out the lantern on the stand beside the bed, only the moon now lighting the room as they lay together, their bodies rediscovering an inescapable longing for one another, over and over again.

*

Ethan could feel the thaw in the Sierras as he climbed upwards toward the Tioga Pass through Yosemite, much of winter's snow already only a memory. It was beautiful country, he thought to himself, although the last time he'd seen it was with Amy and her folks in what seemed a lifetime ago. Ethan reflected on those times, and these now present. Amy's ma, Emma, had died only two years ago this summer from what the doctor in Monterey said was a blood clot on her brain. Life is unpredictable, he thought, riding higher and higher into the redwoods and pines. Emma'd been healthy for fifty-seven years, then one day she up and keels over and is dead the next. Her husband, George, hasn't been the same since, but luckily for the rest of the family he didn't go off into some dark corner of his mind like Ethan had seen others do. George had his down spell in the beginning, but now he was just quieter, keeping to himself on his vineyard near Los Gatos, his eyes and mind, whenever Ethan and Amy see him, off to distant places, distant times. However, when the grandkids visited, well, that was a different story... a different George, or Poppy, as the kids called him. He would light up and talk all the tomfoolery the girls could come up with, especially little Bessie. And he wasn't above getting down on the floor in the pantry of an evening with Ham, arm wrestling his grandson to find out who was still king of the roost. George had let the boy be king ever since he was ten, the

51

grin on Ham's face everytime he won always his grandfather's greatest delight.

Jamie came home after a year managing the warehouse in San Francisco. He was getting the itch to get back anyway when his mother died, so when he arrived for the funeral, he just stayed on, for which his father was truly grateful. Except for the year in the city, Jamie had been on the farm with the old man since he started up the vineyard fifteen years earlier. Before then, George and Emma had a small store in Monterey outfitting the ranchers and farmers in the area. After a Frenchman named Etienne Thee had been in a few times, he and George'd struck up a liking for one another. Thee had a winery near San Jose, but he preferred the ride down to Monterey come summer, to savor the ocean's coolness and pick through George Latimer's dry goods, which he found to be the best quality within a week's travel. It didn't take long after three or four such visits for the Frenchman to make George a proposal.

"How do you like your business here in town, my friend, does is suit you?... or are you a rancher or farmer at heart?" Thee asked one day.

"Hadn't thought about it much lately, Etienne," George replied, somewhat suspicious as to his friend's question. "Why do ya ask?"

"Were you ever a landowner?... do you like the land, I mean working it?" Thee went on.

"Back in Missouri, we had 'bout three hunnert acres... corn, beets, a mix o' things... best in the county I always thought. Always got top dollar."

"I would have thought no less... just as your store here, my friend, is in my opinion best in the county."

George appreciated the compliment, but he knew Etienne Thee to be a shrewd man. "You still haven't told me what yer drivin' at. I know you, Etienne, an' you got somethin' in yer craw."

"You are right, George. As you know I have been a winemaker for many years, both here and in France. And like all lovers of the art, I am always looking for the next great wine. That has always meant, to my mind, beginning with the very finest foundation. And what is the foundation of a great wine?... the fruit... the grape."

George was eyeing his friend carefully, noticing he was taking the long way around the barn.

"This is my thought, and I have not come upon it hastily. I need more grapes, not just in quantity, but quality... like the contents of your store here... like the crops you once raised back home... grapes of the highest quality."

George still wasn't quite sure of Etienne's meaning, but he was sure of one thing, "well, I don't stock 'em, if that's what yer askin', Etienne, but I know a fella down in the central valley who might be able to help ya out."

"No, no, thank you, George. My proposal is for you only. I am looking for someone I know, someone I can trust, to join with me in my search for greatness." Etienne could see his friend still did not fully understand just how he might be of some help, so the Frenchman continued. "I have discovered some land for sale in Los Gatos that I feel might be ideal for experimentation with a variety of cuttings I get annually from France... mostly clarets... hybrids. I would purchase the property, however, my proposal is that you, my friend, oversee the project. Over time, you could buy the land with the profits. If things go as I suspect, I calculate that would take no more than six or seven years."

"But why me?" George asked, "I don' know a dang thing 'bout grapes er wine er cuttin's an' whatnot."

"I can teach you that in a few short months. My problem is, I do not have the time to oversee the nuturing of the crop, or have another man in my employ whom I can trust to deliver what I know is possible. You, my friend... in you I see someone who takes pride in his work."

This whole thing had taken George by surprise, and he wasn't sure how to respond. "Ya know, Etienne, I don' know just what ta tell ya right off. Hadn't ev'n thought 'bout farmin' lately... jus' seemed like the store here was the thing ta do when we arrived a few years back. Farmin'... grapes..."

"Have you a desire to get back to the land, my friend?"

"To be honest, I do miss it... having our own place... some acreage around to stretch our legs in."

"Well here is your opportunity, then. I can tell you growing the kind of crop I am interested in will not be easy. It will take a lot of time and effort... and patience. It will be a challenge, my friend. However, if I did not think you up to it,

I would not have asked."

"A challenge is somethin' I've always looked forward to."

The particulars were worked out on Etienne Thee's next trip into town, after of course George getting the okay from Emma, who to his surprise was all for it. Turns out she'd been missing the country as much as he. So three months later, after finding a buyer for Latimer's Ranch & Farm Supply, George, Emma, Jaimie and Amanda were packed up and on their way north, making their way up the coast beside Monterey Bay.

"It'll be nice ta be closer ta Amy an' Ethan, George... an' little Ham," Emma was saying, "them bein' in Felton is only a stone's throw."

"Soon as we get settled, Em, we'll have 'em over fer a few days, I promise. I wanta see that little feller myself."

*

The years passed with the two families seeing a lot of each other, especially around the holidays and birthdays, one or more coming almost every month. Ethan remembered Amanda being the instigator in all of this... a stickler about getting everyone together on the correct day, as in her mind it wasn't right to put off celebrating something as special as a birthday. In fact, it was downright rude behavior. So Amanda kept them all on their toes, planning far enough in advance so there was no excuse. It was this concern for others that'd gotten George through the worst of it, Ethan thought, as he began his descent down the eastern slopes of the Sierras. When Amanda'd told her fiancee she had to spend time with her father — all of her time — it just about broke the boy's heart, but Amanda was strong, telling him if the two of them getting together was meant to be, it would be... one day. Right now, her daddy needed her. And that was that.

Now that two years has passed, and with Jamie back, it's been different. George is still quiet and reflective, but not like he once was... not withdrawn. So Amanda and her beau have taken up their courtship again, and from what Amy can get out of her sister, the wedding's been set for next spring. I guess things do work out, given time, Ethan considered. Now he hoped there was enough time left to find

Willow.

*

Riding through Jackson's Hole on Handsome, the big bay Ethan kept as his own for the past six years, he saw times past flash before his very soul... he and John running down the white stallion all those years ago. The two of them, whooping and hollering when they'd lassoed him, bringing him back with the rest of the herd to Two Bears... and Willow. Lord, that was long ago, Ethan recalled with melancholy in his heart, but what times those were... wouldn't have changed a thing, not one thing, 'cept for John o' course... and he urged Handsome on. It'd taken him the better part of two weeks to get to the Yellowstone country, turning north after leaving the Sierras, following the Humboldt River east across northern Nevada toward the Great Salt Lake. From there he'd again turned north, stopping in the tiny hamlet of Providence which lie at the foot of the Wasatch Range of the Rocky Mountains. There he enjoyed a bed, bath and hot meal... poached eggs, grits, with biscuits and gravy. By early morning he was on his way again headed towards Bear Lake, and just north of that, Montpelier, Idaho, before angling up the Salt River Range, then taking the Snake River cutoff up to the Yellowstone.

It was in Montpelier Ethan decided to stop and whet his whistle. He was passing the time with the barkeep at the saloon making his first attempt to drum up some information on the whereabouts of the Sioux when a sturdy looking gent came in, positioning himself at the end of the bar. Ethan noticed the man had a good view out the window to much of the town, which wasn't large to begin with. The fellow had a drink or two, always pleasant, smiling to the barkeep when he ordered. There was something about him though. He was no rancher or sodbuster, that was for certain... nor a drifter. And he had not, until now, made the acquaintance of the bartender, a friendly sort who took pride in knowing by name every man-jack in town. As he told Ethan, it's good for business.

Now for the Sioux, the barkeep hadn't kept up with their whereabouts. After the last massacre at Wounded Knee back in '90, the Army had rounded up the last of them and taken them to one of the reservations along the Nebraska border, or so the man thought. But he couldn't be sure. Best thing he could recommend was to ride back up into that country and head for the nearest Army outpost.

"They closed down Fort Laramie an' Lincoln, but I b'lieve there's a garrison 'bout a week's ride from the Yellowstone up near Crawford in the Dakotas. They should know where the Sioux been planted."

"Thank ya... I best be goin'," and Ethan walked through the swinging doors of the saloon, the sunlight making him wince some before he cinched up Handsome a might tighter, then climbed aboard heading north out of town. As he rode, and later as he bedded down for the night by a creek half way to Geneva, he couldn't help but keep the fella at the end of the bar back in Montpelier in his mind. Ethan thought, if I was a lawman, I'da been mighty suspicious 'bout that fella. But then the long day and days before caught up to him... his eyelids growing heavy as he leaned back against his saddle, his mind asking for slumber, his body answering the call.

*

Captain Rawlins at the Army garrison outside of Crawford didn't know his backside from a barn door, Ethan determined, after spending no more than five minutes with the man. He was unschooled as to the different tribes still surviving on the plains... their whereabouts... how many had been taken to reservations... which still had some recalcitrant braves running free... just about any question reasonable to ask. Apparently, the captain, because of rank only, had been left in charge while the colonel was east on Army business. Ethan presumed the colonel to have more sense than to leave his captain in charge of two-hundred men. He must have figured the frontier was peaceful enough these days, and not even his captain, buffoon that he was, would be able to bring Washington down around his ears in one month's time, particularly when he gave the man strict orders to sit tight in any eventuality... whatsoever!

After Ethan had left the captain's quarters and was preparing to mount up, the lieutenant who'd escorted him in came up to him.

"If you're on the trail o' the Sioux, I think I know a man can help ya."

"Who'd that be?"

"Name's Smoot. Did some scoutin' fer the colonel before that Wounded Knee debacle. You'll find him ov'r to the livery. Stays with his animals, mostly... an' a jug, but he knows his business. Kept all a us alive a time er two. You ask him."

"I'll do that. Thank ya."

*

The lieutenant'd been right. Smoot knew the Sioux Ethan was after to have been relocated to the Pine Ridge and Rosebud Indian reservations. That was many years ago, but it made no matter, according to Smoot. The Sioux'd been there ever since. In fact, the man'd been over that way just a year past, so if that's who Ethan was after, then there they'd be, if they were still alive.

"Ya want a pull on this jug, sonny?"

Ethan was about to say no, then reconsidered, "why, thank ya, I think I will. Been a while since I had a snort," and Ethan turned the jug over his shoulder, taking a good swig of the home brew. "Now that'll take the chill off yer bones," he said handing the jug back to Smoot, "thanks agin, I bes' be goin.'"

"You watch yer back, sonny, there's a few bucks out there still on the wild."

Ethan tipped his hat to the man, then mounted Handsome, turning him northeast to whatever he might find waiting, up ahead.

**

The Six Gun

To survive out west, many were asked to become
proficient with a weapon — the popular choice being a
sidearm — or turn tail when challenged by
a malcontent.

Red Hand

"Be careful, my son, the whites expect us to keep our place. Avert your eyes from trouble, and return as soon as you have gathered our supplies."

"I will, mother," Red Hand replied, "I will be back in three days," and he kissed Willow That Weeps before mounting the paint that was his favorite, then grabbed the lead to his pack horse and headed out of camp.

The boy would not be accompanied by his uncle Running Wolf on this trip. He was off hunting with some of the others, and anyway, Red Hand had been into town on several occasions and knew which stores were best suited for the supplies he and his mother required. It would be a simple matter to trade the blankets he was bringing in for however much seed and the necessary planting tools Mr. Bendt was willing to offer him, and if there was anything left over, he would get some of the whites chewing tobacco for his grandfather, who had developed a taste for it.

The ride into Mission seemed no different than it was the previous year in late spring. The thaw had come and gone, leaving the rivers and streams riding high, but nothing his mount and pack horse couldn't handle. When dusk settled on the land, the boy, nearer a man now as he'd grown considerably the past few months, found himself in familiar surroundings. He and Running Wolf had bedded down among these same cottonwoods only last year, so he turned the paint off to his left towards the rushing sounds of the Keya Paha, looking forward to a good night's rest and the short ride into town the next morning.

It was still brisk when Red Hand saw the town silhouetted on the horizon against the rising sun. As he crested a final hill, he headed straight for Bendt's General Store. He had seven blankets to trade, all newly woven; four by his mother, the other three by two others of the tribe whom she had done favors for this past winter. Red Hand was proud of the blankets, and thought he could get much for them.

With the town coming to life around him, the boy pulled up the paint and dismounted.

"Ah, Red Hand, haven't seen ya since last year. How are ya, lad?"

"I am good, Mr. Bendt. I bring blankets to trade... for seed and tools."

"I see... I see," the man said stepping down into the street next to the boy and his horses. "Why you've grown, my boy," Bendt continued, noticing the youth's stature next to his own, "you're as big as a man... good fer you. Now let's see what ya got here." Thumbing through the blankets, taking a good look at them for some time, then mumbling to himself before finally turning back to Red Hand, "seven of 'em, huh, all quality goods... mmmm... I'll give ya three dollars fer each... that's twenty-one dollars total. You c'n take it in cash er trade. That's a fair deal."

"Thirty-five," the youth countered. "Thirty-two in trade and three in money... then deal."

Alfred Bendt liked the boy, always had, ever since he'd first come into town years ago with Two Bears. He knew there was no other place Red Hand could sell his goods, but the man didn't mind. It was all part of dickering with the Indians. He'd make plenty on the blankets, and Red Hand knew it. So he said, "deal."

"Good," the youth replied.

"What ya gonna do with them three bucks, ma boy?"

"Tobacco... for Two Bears."

"Ahhh... say, how is the ol' bandit?"

"Good."

"Well, say hello fer me. Now let's get ya packed up."

Before long Red Hand had the seed and tools strapped tight to his pack horse and was waving goodbye to Alfred Bendt. He had one more stop down the street at the saloon to buy the tobacco his grandfather preferred. It was a particular type Mr. Bendt didn't stock... Cherokee brand, a thick chaw made by the Sioux's enterprising cousins to the east. Maybe that's why Two Bears preferred it, the boy thought, as he tied up the paint in front of The Divide. It was late morning now, and the early crowd was starting to drift in for a snort or two before dinner. Pushing through the swinging doors, Red Hand saw the bartender at the far end of the long mahogany counter. The bar was to the boy's right, polished to a sparkle with a large, inlaid laurel wreath in the center of the facade, and at the bottom a gold foot rail. He was making his way towards the proprietor when a voice came from the rear of the place to his left. He glanced over and saw three men sitting at a table in a small section raised two steps higher than the main room. They looked like rough men.

"Will ya look at that, Frank... I thought I smelled somethin'... either Injun er mule shit... one's same as t'other."

"I believe 'at's mule shit... on the hoof," his companion replied, all three laughing.

Red Hand continued on looking straight ahead, paying them no mind, remembering what his mother had told him. There was no profit in confronting the whites. There were no laws to protect him, no justice for his kind.

"Hey, mule shit," the first one taunted the boy, "get on outa from where we're drinkin'."

The boy kept walking towards the bartender, the others in the saloon now taking notice of the goings on. When he stopped and asked for the tobacco, the talker got up from his chair and stepped down to the main floor.

"You ain't buyin' that tobacca in here... not whil' me an' the boys are drinkin'."

The youth said nothing to the man, only waited on the barkeep to deliver his tobacco so he could leave.

"Boy, I said get yer mule smellin'' ass outa here... now," and he spun Red Hand around by the shoulder, throwing out a fist, knocking the youth down to one knee. Red hand was startled but unfazed by the punch. As he wiped the blood from his mouth, he thought for a moment about what his mother had told him, remembering her concern, but then he saw the cowboy raising his fist again. Before the man could deliver another blow, Red Hand leaped to his feet and shoved him with both hands, chest high, knocking him over a chair onto his back. The talker's two friends hooted, seeing their partner on his backside, laughing at his comeuppance. Their derision brought the man up off the floor throwing punches, wildlike, connecting with one, then a glancing blow until Red Hand was chased through the doors into the street. The cowboy continued flailing away, knocking the boy down now. It was then Red Hand began to sense the uneven nature of his punches, much like the men of his tribe swinging their sticks in a heated game of tewaraathon, a game the boy had loved playing since his childhood. He gathered himself, eyeing his opponent carefully, looking for an opening as the cowboy cocked his fist and waded in again. Red Hand waited, ducked, then stepped in, kneeing his attacker in the groin. When the cowboy bent down groaning, the boy whirled, driving an elbow into the side of his head, bringing him to the ground. Some of the townsfolk gathered as the Indian boy began getting the better of the man. He was a ruffian named Thompkins, one of a group that worked for Jedediah Strait, an ex-confederate who kept most of the smaller ranchers around Mission under his thumb, and it was good to see one of Strait's men taken down a peg. Thompkins dragged himself to his feet, but the youth was too quick. He stepped in, throwing three more swift elbows, then another knee, dropping the cowboy again. He stayed down this time until Red Hand turned to walk back inside the saloon for his tobacco. That's when he heard the sound... click, click, as Thompkins cocked his revolver.

"Turn aroun', Injun."

Red Hand turned as the cowboy rose to his feet. The boy waited. It was all he could do... wait for the gunshot, from the kind of man his mother so worried over. The youth looked skyward, beyond the cursing and ravings of Thompkins. He saw his mother... saw how much more pain this would cause her, how she would be left to fend for herself now that both her husband and son were gone. Then faintly at first, but with command, he heard a second voice, a stronger voice that split the moment, cutting short his vision.

"Drop it," the voice stated. Louder now, "I said drop the gun."

The cowboy glanced to his left, down a ways from the entrance to The Divide, and as he hesitated Red Hand saw the menace in Thompkins' eyes turn to doubt, then fear.

"Drop it or I'll take that arm off at the shoulder."

His head turned, and he looked at the intruder more closely. The man was tall, weathered. He had the look of one who'd seen his share of trouble, one who didn't make idle threats... and the cowboy did as he was told.

"Now walk away."

When Thompkins backed off, the stranger stepped from the shadows and picked up the gun. He pitched it into the horse trough before turning back to the cowboy and saying in a manner warranting no reply, "git on outa here."

Thompkins glared then looked back to the boy. "Ya bes' be carryin' a gun nex' time," and he mounted up with the other two and rode off, their horses kicking up dust.

*

" 'At was some doin', stranger. 'At man Thompkins is a bad'un. I seen 'im shoot a man fer no good reason mor'n once."

It was Alfred Bendt speaking. He'd been out front just after Red Hand came flying out the saloon. He saw the boy pick himself up and take it to the cowboy. At that point the storekeep thought he'd seen just about everything — an Injun kid kicking the tar out of a cowboy — but not until the stranger had gotten the drop on Thompkins did Bendt wipe his brow in disbelief, and mutter, "I swear..."

"My name's Bendt," putting out his hand to Ethan, "I own the General Store ov'r there."

"Ethan... Ethan MacCall. Nice to make yer acquaintance."

"Haven't seen ya in town b'for. Jus' ridin' through?"

"Well, I don' rightly know. I'm lookin' fer a group o' Sioux I hear settled near these parts... Yankton. Two Bears was a chief o' theirs' some years back, but I don' know if he might still be alive."

Alfred Bendt smiled at Ethan's good fortune. He liked the stranger, and was only too happy to announce to the man, "Two Bears ain't only alive, his camp's just two days ride, an' yer gonna be one lucky fella when he see's ya."

"How's that?"

"Ya jus' saved his grandson there, sonny. That boy's Red Hand, son of Willow That Weeps who's Two Bears' daughter. He dotes on her an' the boy. Seems her husband, a white man I hear, went off 'bout twenty years now an' nev'r come

63

back... musta got hisself kilt. Anyhow, the ol' chief'll sure make ya welcome, I c'n tell ya that."

What d'ya know, Ethan thought, feeling the wash of relief and anticipation race through his body, both at the same time. But now, seeing the boy walk back out of the saloon with the tobacco, he wasn't quite sure how to play it.

He decided it was best to go straight to him... no sense stalling now, so Ethan walked over and introduced himself, telling the boy right off who he was and why he'd come, then added in a gentler tone he wanted to relate the last days of his father's life to the boy's mother first. It was only proper.

That's when they heard another voice.

"What's all the ruckus?"

When they turned Ethan noticed the badge first, then the features of the kind of man who'd been lawin' much longer than he'd a mind to.

"Just a bad sort," Ethan answered, "mighta hurt somebody."

"The boy?"

" 'At's right."

"Was it the big one ridin' out with those other two?"

" 'At was him."

"You boys bes' come with me. It's jus' to fill out ma report, nothin' more."

The sheriff escorted Ethan and Red Hand to his office and after ten minutes asking them the whys and wherefores as to how all the trouble started, he smiled wryly, " 'at Thompkins is gonna git his... matter a time is all." When he was done he added, "now you two keep an eye out."

Ethan nodded and was turning to leave when he saw the poster on the wall. The face was familiar... man about twenty-eight, thirty years of age, intelligent eyes, square jaw. I know him, he thought... but where?... yes, yes...

"Say, sheriff, that thousand dollar reward for that fella in yer poster... what's it fer?"

"He an' his gang robbed the bank in Montpelier las' month."

Mighta known, Ethan thought to himself. "I seen 'im there myself... musta been jus' b'for."

"Well, we gonna get ol' Butch an' 'is bunch."

Ethan recalled the pleasant yet stoic nature of the man, his ambivalence, the way he removed himself from attention in the saloon that day. "I wish ya good luck with that."

Sheriff Lee Bell caught the facetious nature of the remark, but only tipped his hat as Ethan and the boy walked through the door.

—Riding back to the Indian camp Ethan and Red Hand talked mostly of life on the reservation... of Two Bears recounting their day of glory at the Little Bighorn... of the boy's mother and how she acquired the name Willow That Weeps. When the silence between them begged for more than civility, the conversation turned to John Connor, with Ethan attempting to explain as best he could the strength and fiber of the man who'd been only a ghost to Red Hand for these many years.

The next day as they approached the Rosebud, many from the village rode out to greet Red Hand, with much speculation and goingson about who it was riding with him. Hearing the commotion, Willow That Weeps ran from her tipi. She saw her son was home and well, but not alone. Grabbing her chest, her heart racing, pounding, she saw that... no, it was not John in the buckskin jacket riding alongside, but his closest friend and long ago companion, Ethan MacCall. She hesitated, then running once again she was nearly out of breath before reaching Red Hand, and greeting him warmly. Then, turning to Ethan who'd already dismounted, Willow That Weeps stepped closer to him, and clasped his hands in hers, knowing by the look in his eyes he would be relating the news she had feared would one day come.

"It is good to see you, Ethan MacCall. It has been too many years."

"It has been too long, Willow. I wished I coulda made it sooner, I truly do."

Despite the sadness, there was resolve on her face, and in her eyes, and she invited him to her tipi, telling Red Hand to invite the rest of the family as well.

*

They sat directly across the fire from one another, Ethan on one side,

Willow That Weeps and Red Hand on the other. Filling the space between them were Two Bears, Star Rising and Running Wolf. Santin was there as well, at Ethan's request. The old medicine man was ancient, but his mind was nimble, and for some reason it seemed appropriate to Ethan that he be there, and Willow That Weeps did not object.

Out of courtesy, she inquired as to Ethan's life and well-being over the years, which he related briefly, thanking her for asking.

He settled himself now, pondering just how he might tell the story of John's last days as gently as possible, sparing Willow the painful details. He stirred the fire in front of him with a piece of kindling, thinking back to those times and to that fateful day, the clarity of it all coming back, painful as it was, and he began the final chapter in the life of John Connor. As Ethan told his tale, he could not help, more than once, wiping a tear from his eye, or pausing for a stretch to regain his composure. And when he finished, he looked directly into Willow's eyes, asking her forgiveness for not coming sooner.

"I musta writ ya four er five times ov'r the years... first time the very next year when we arrived in California. But in those days, there was no tellin' if the mail'd get through... what with the hard winters an' lack o' any good roads... an' the troubles still kickin' up here n' there. Then our young'uns started arrivin', an' we was busier 'an bees makin' honey, but I promised myself one day I'd come to try ta find ya... to make sure ya knew about John... jus' how much he was achin' to get back to ya. When I saw my last letter nev'r made it, well, that's when I come a lookin.'"

"The soldiers moved us three times in those years," Two Bears stated. "Getting mail, or anything, was not easy."

Running Wolf was eyeing Santin, remembering his prophecy and concern about not seeing clearly enough through his mind's eye which of the two whites had died that day. Now as the old medicine man saw another clearer vision, Running Wolf watched when he smiled and turned to Willow That Weeps, telling her, "weep no more, for this is a day to rejoice. In the life to come, the man who was your husband will live long, with much happiness... and it will be possible only because of his brother, this man, Ethan MacCall." And the old Santin rested a hand on Ethan's shoulder in a gesture of friendship and admiration, then slowly got to his feet before leaving the tipi.

*

"Try it again... slower, more deliberate... then squeeze the trigger."

The boy was catching on, quicker than most. Red Hand had asked Ethan as soon as they were alone to teach him how to use the gun. He'd found it two years before out hunting, and he prized the weapon, carefully wrapping it in his blanket, hiding it in his corner of the lodge. Ethan saw right off the Colt pistol was in decent condition... holding the gun in his hand, checking the chamber, spinning it some. The balance was good, no missing or damaged parts, a good cleaning should make it as useful as any. When he told the boy the holster could use a good wiping, Red Hand returned with a hunk of grizzle and breechcloth. Ethan smiled and said that would do, then went to work on the pistol with what oil he had left in his saddle-bag, and in no time Red Hand was blazing away at the pine sapling Ethan'd picked out for him some thirty yards off.

"Good thing I brung extra ca'tridges. These here oughta do ya fer now... ya keep this box fer when I leave. We don' want ya runnin' into that feller without goin' heeled."

"When do you go," Red Hand asked.

"Couple three days, I reakon. Now let's try it again."

The two of them worked at the boy's new found skill over the next three days... Ethan making a sudden move towards his gun, Red Hand reacting, drawing his gun quickly, but easily, sliding it out of the holster, taking careful aim, then firing... pop!... at the sappling, smiling when another piece of bark flew from its trunk about waist high.

"Yer gettin' the hang of it, Red Hand, no doubt 'bout that. You keep that up fer another few weeks an' you'll be a hard one ta beat... that is, if you c'n stand up to a man. That's the tough part... keepin' yer nerves glued together when the time comes."

"How will I know? How does it feel?"

"Well," Ethan thought about that for a moment, "it feels kinda like yer all hollow inside, anxious like, jus' waitin' fer somethin' ta explode, not really knowin' what... maybe kinda like yer first hunt, when ya didn't know if that buck you was trackin' might come bustin' outa the brush smack at ya... an' if'n he did, what ya might do."

The boy nodded.

"The trick is... facin' another with a gun... well, it's pret'near gonna be his life er yours ever'time... ain't much in b'tween, son. When ya get that empty feelin' in yer gut right at the moment o' truth... it's jus' yer mind askin' yer nerves if they're ready. If they are, yer hand'll be steady, an' you'll know."

The boy considered Ethan's words, attempting to understand as much as he could of the white ways. After all, he was half white. He did remember the first time he had hunted alone. It wasn't a buck that surprised him, but a cat on the same trail of the prey he was stalking. He heard a branch crack directly above him. Looking up he saw the lion crouched, ready to pounce. He wheeled, falling to one knee as he reached for an arrow, letting it go while the cat was in the air. The arrow disappeared into the animal's mouth, piercing its skull as it slammed to the ground. The boy remembered being stunned by the suddeness of it, fearing death, how near it had been... but only after he'd killed the beast, and only for an instant. Afterwards, he lost what little breakfast he'd consumed, then slowly got to his feet and walked over to inspect his prize, feeling like he had grown much.

*

It was time. Many of the tribe had turned out to see Ethan off after they'd heard of his attempts to get word to Willow That Weeps about John over the years, but they were more taken by his efforts now... his tutoring Red Hand of the way of the white man's gun so the boy could protect himself when the time came, as it surely would.

"Take care, Willow. If I git the chance, I'll come visit agin."

"Keep safe on your journey home. I do not want both of you gone from this earth in my lifetime," and Willow, the name she would be called once again, held Ethan's hands warmly, and for a long while.

Ethan bid his best to the rest of the family... to Two Bears, Star Rising and Running Wolf before feeling the gaze of Santin upon him. He was standing in front of his lodge off to Ethan's left. Their eyes met and lingered some, then the old medicine man simply nodded before raising a hand in farewell, then turned to go inside... to sit and smoke and comfort his aching bones by the warmth of the fire.

Handsome was snuffling, anxious to get going, as Ethan stood before Red Hand. He held the youth's shoulders in his hands, and stated as he thought John might have, "practice like I told ya. You'll be as good as there is in a month, but you'll wanta stay razor sharp fer that fella Thompkins. He ain't gonna let ya walk past him nex' time. An' when that time comes, stay steady. You keep safe," and Ethan mounted up, his eyes scanning the faces before him... the Yankton people, Two Bears and Willow... most of all, Red Hand, son of John Connor, a boy who in a few short weeks time would leave the innocence of youth behind. He waved one more time, then turned Handsome toward what was left of the setting sun, spurring him to a cantor.

**

Viet Nam

It wasn't a war, it was a military action. Tell that to the
half million who came back wounded, and to the families of the
50+ thousand who never did come back, unless to be draped
in the stars and stripes while taps played.

Eddie McCabe

"Yowza... yowza," Eddie bellowed over the incoming, a couple of clicks into the jungle off the trail between Que Son and Binh Kieu, "I told you it was gonna rain."

The company had dug in just after Charlie'd hit them early that morning. They were on recon. "Just patrol the area," the Captain had told Lieutenant Gonzalves. "If you run across any gooks, take 'em out. But make sure they're the enemy. I don't want any fucking fiasco like that My Lai disaster. Got that!"

"Yessir," the Lieutenant had replied. But he already knew the routine. This was Gonzalves' third hitch, which meant the Lieutenant was not only good, he liked it. Of course everyone agreed it was better to take orders from an officer who was good, but not necessarily from one who liked it... meaning the action... the juice. He just might find you something for breakfast you didn't like so much... such as this mortor fire the company had been taking for the last ten minutes.

"Cramer," the Lieutenant barked over the sound of the shells, "take McCabe with you and find out where this shit's coming from... and take a radio. I'm gonna move the rest of the company due south a half click and try to get us outa this spot. Stay in touch."

"Yes sir." And with that Sergeant Joe Cramer grabbed some clips and slithered down the line, motioning to Eddie to follow him. Moments later, the Lieutenant saw their backsides disappear down an embankment into what was more the size of a creek than a river, and Gonzalves motioned, moving the rest of the company off.

The two were in dense jungle staying low but moving fast, adjacent to the trail where they'd first been hit, when Eddie said, "over there," and they turned slightly to the southwest, heading towards the sound as it grew louder with every

71

step. Suddenly a burst of rifle fire cut through the trees directly in front of them, grazing Joe's left leg.

"What the fuck..." he yelled, rolling to his right, taking cover. Eddie had gone the other way, burrowing into the underbrush where it was thickest, but not so far that he couldn't see Joe. They'd done this before. One of them was going to have to bait Charlie... stand up and fire a burst, raking the trees, trying to draw more fire so they could locate the fucker. It wasn't that Charlie didn't know the game, he just couldn't help himself, dreaming of sending one or two of the Yankee imperialists to an early afterlife before he'd be blown into the next grid himself. So Joe caught Eddie's attention, motioning to him to be ready, then began counting with his fingers. On three Joe burst from his position emptying a full magazine into the trees fifty yards ahead, about thirty feet high. When he stopped firing he remained standing for another heartbeat before diving to his left, scrambling ahead another ten yards. The second burst from the sniper came just as he moved, blowing the space he'd occupied the moment before all to shit. But the ploy worked, as it usually did. Eddie saw right where Charlie was... up ahead about fifty yards, just as Joe'd figured, but another twenty, thirty feet higher. The monkey could climb, Eddie thought to himself, now let's see how fast he can move with two clips up his ass.

Eddie got into a crouch, making sure he had a clear shot. After checking the clip in the magazine of his M-16, he gave Joe a thumbs up. Joe waited another second before jumping up again, firing a short burst, moving, firing another, moving again, finally drawing enough attention from Charlie to get a fix on his position. That was the monkey's last living act. First one clip, then a second from Eddie's rifle raked the crevice where two large tree limbs joined some sixty feet in the air, shredding Charlie, silencing the gun fire. Through the stillness that followed they heard the sound of something falling, bouncing off the leafy branches as it descended to the ground below.

A minute later Eddie remarked, "hey Joe, lookie here, an AK-47 direct from Moscow." He picked up the rifle, slinging it over his shoulder. "Beats the hell outa my M16."

"No mistaking that," Joe added. "Let's go find that mortar."

*

It was their sophomore year in high school when Joe and Eddie had first met, after Eddie's folks'd moved down to Columbus from Canton at the beginning of the school year. The two boys didn't like each other much at first. Joe'd staked out the middle linebacker position on the JV football team for himself that fall and hadn't counted on a kid like Eddie moving into the neighborhood. Coach Duggan saw right away Eddie was his man. He had Joe by twenty pounds, and if not as fast, just as quick. So after drills the very first day, coach hollered to Eddie, "McCabe, you take middle linebacker," then saw the look of disappointment on Joe's face. But coach was no dummy. His JVs had won the league title for the past three years, and he had plans. The coach of the varsity was retiring after the season, and Jerry Duggan saw his ticket to college with these fifteen year-olds right in front of him. All he needed was a little Butkus or Nagerski, a kid willing to run through a wall, and Jerry Duggan was certain he'd not only win again this year, he'd dominate. If he did, the president of the school indicated the head coaching job would be his. So after Eddie lined up in the middle of the field behind the nose guard, stalking and snorting like a stud bull waiting to head butt something, anything into the next county, coach smiled to himself, thinking of the weeks ahead... how much fun it would be. When his attention returned to Joe, still shuffling on the sideline, still confused and disappointed, the slightest smile crossed his face. Then Coach barked to the boy who was about to begin one of the most storied high school careers in Ohio football lore, "Cramer, you go to free safety... and you play it like you see it!"

It was beautiful to watch those first few weeks. While Eddie cleaned house on any back running between the tackles, Joe roamed the deep middle looking for play action or coming up in run support. When the offense optioned, or called a straight pitch, the two boys worked the quarterback and trailing back to precision, putting hits on the ball carrier that could be heard all the way to The Horseshoe. From time to time, more out of embarrassment than frustration, the opposing coach tried to go up top, which brought an even broader smile to Coach Duggan's face. If Eddie didn't get to the quarterback before he got the ball off, which was early and often, Joe was there roaming the secondary, waiting to pick off the throw. After five games, Joe had run six of his eleven interceptions back for scores, and Franklin's JVs had shutout three opponents, allowing only a combined total of nine points to the other two. Joe and Eddie were so good, the crowds were growing with every game. Even the varsity players were showing up, not just for the helluva it, but to watch two kids who could play the game and lay the wood to the opposition like no one had seen in a long, long time.

"Coach, your boys are looking good. That defense of yours is top notch, I must say." It was Gordon Parry, president of Franklin High speaking just as the team was heading for the showers after a Tuesday practice.

"I couldn't have asked for a better group, sir." Jerry Duggan called anyone he perceived in a superior position sir, whether that person deserved the deference or not. Jerry had been a Westpoint man, graduated in '51, and served in Korea. He understood the meaning of the word, in every sense. It was part of his own self-discipline, and the discipline he applied to his family, and team. Anyone who'd watched him for any length of time knew this, and knew also that Jerry Duggan was a fair man, never asking more than he himself was prepared to give in any life endeavor.

After being discharged from the Army a first lieutenant, he took his purple heart and bad knee back to Columbus from Fort Ord in Northern California, married his high school sweetheart, and went to work for his father in commercial real estate. What kept him there seven years was loyalty, and discipline. As the eldest son, he felt he should not only join the business, but be the one to, one day, take over the reins. But then two events changed everything: the untimely death of his father, and a lingering desire for something he had brought back with him from Korea. It was the rush, the excitement he'd felt before combat. He knew it was crazy. Someone... some unseen, unknown enemy a quarter mile off could have put a bullet through his brain at any moment, and he would've been worm meat. But still he had found he liked it... liked the rush to arms, the anticipation of battle, the ebb and flow of the conflict. So after his dad keeled over and died that Sunday afternoon from a massive heart attack and was buried five days later, he went to his little brother Danny and said, "it's yours, baby bro... the business, the whole kit and kaboodle."

"What?!"

"What do you mean, 'what?' You're twice the real estate man I'll ever be. Dad knew that. He just didn't want to hurt my feelings."

"How do you know that?"

"Believe me, I know."

"But I wanted to do this together... with you. Dad named the company Duggan and Sons, you know."

"Well... have some!"

"Very funny."

"Look, Danny, sooner or later, if he'd lived, Dad would've made sure the business was in the proper hands. I'm just doing it for him."

Danny smiled at his big brother, "you sure about this?"

"I'm so sure I've already got the attorneys drawing up the papers. I did give myself a small severance package, though. Nancy and the two squirts gotta eat until I find some work."

"You got any ideas, Jer?"

"Yup. It's back to the action for me, little bro... except not quite so intense as Korea. But it'll get the blood flowing again... give me that rush I've been missing. I'm gonna be a coach... a football coach!"

— "Got anything in your bag of tricks for the rest of the season we haven't seen, coach?"

"I think so, sir. Remember Doc Blanchard and Glen Davis? Mr. Inside and Mr. Outside? They were at Westpoint in the "40s."

"Why, I believe I do." While Gordon Parry wasn't a fanatic, he did like sports, particularly when one of the teams at this highly acclaimed academic institution which he presided over was, as the kids liked to say, kicking some serious ass.

"Well, sir, I believe it's time we got a little more punch on the offensive side of the ball. You know, I couldn't ask any more of Eddie and Joe defensively. They're two of the best I've ever seen. But with a week off before our final three games, we've got time to work on the offense. So I thought I'd take Eddie off the line, and Joe from his end position, and put them where they really belong — the team's new Mr. Inside, and Mr. Outside. I've been studying some old film of Blanchard and Davis a buddy of mine at The Point sent me. Great coach Red Blake was. Really nice stuff."

"You think those two can play as well on offense, coach?"

"I know they can."

"So, what should we expect the final three games?"

"As they say in Hollywood, sir," Coach Duggan winked, 'you ain't seen nothing yet.' "

*

'We gotta get outa this place... if it's the last thing we ever do...'

The song was spinning through Eddie's mind from the week before when a bunch of the guys were in the 'E-club' late one night drinking 'em down, as per usual. It was one of the anthems of the war, and when it came on, which was often, everyone boomed it out with the image of those closest to them dancing across their mind. So while Eddie hurried into the peril before him, thinking of home, and of Evie, he didn't see another flash of light from yet another tree as he and Joe continued their way towards the mortar fire growing louder in the distance.

"Eddie!... duck!..." was all Joe had time for as he dove into the jungle before him, scurrying off to his right, lodging himself behind the first good cover he could find. The rifle burst from high above had come an instant after he'd yelled to his partner, and Joe didn't know if Eddie'd had enough time to react. He hoped so. God he hoped so. He whistled to his partner, a call the two of them had practiced for just such occasions... a 'life and location' signal... something to tell the other guy, 'I'm over here, I'm okay.' Joe called to Eddie again, finally getting the response he wanted. Shit, he said to himself, okay, time to go to work again.

*

"Hut one, hut two..." Billy Smithers, the quarterback of the JVs was barking the signals at the opponent's 20-yard line. "Hut three..." he took the snap, pivoted to his right handing the ball to the fullback off tackle. Eddie hit what was only a small hole, burying his shoulder into the end trying to fill the gap, knocking him back three yards. As the linebacker came up, Eddie head faked, dancing left until the two safeties wrestled him to the ground nine yards downfield. It was a typical McCabe run, making nine yards out of one or two.

"Okay, your turn, Joey." Billy had them huddled up quickly. This school had knocked off the Franklin varsity by twenty points just two weeks before, and it was time for payback. With the clock winding down, and the score thirty-eight to three, the JVs vowed to double the insult. "Play action, pitch left, on two."

They lined up... "9, 8, 7..." the crowd roaring in time with the clock, Evie and Wendy together, pompoms flashing through the crisp air to the beat of the drums... "5, 4, 3..." deafening, adrenaline rushing through every vein of every player on Franklin's JVs... to score one last time, evening the score of the varsity's lone defeat.

"Hut one... hut two," Billy took the ball from center, this time turning left, faking the handoff to Eddie with his right hand as he hid the ball with the other on his hip for a split second. The defense bit. The middle and right side linebackers pinched inside just as Billy released a perfect pitch to Joe with one pulling guard out in front of him. Eddie could see their eyes as they crashed into him, the look of 'oh, shit' on their faces when they realized Joe — the second coming of Howard Cassidy — was turning the corner with a blocker. Joe hesitated allowing Wayne to pancake the cornerback, then had one man to beat. Wendy and Evie were leading the cheers... "go, go, go!..." just as Joe put a move on the free safety that no one, as far as anyone could remember, had ever seen. He set his man up, dipped inside at the five, and with the defender leaning left, stopped on a dime, made a complete 360° turn back to the outside, and walked in for six. For the slightest instant the crowd hesitated, awestruck by what they had just witnessed, then exploded as Joe was mobbed by his teammates. The noise was deafening. Both he and Eddie had each scored three touchdowns and were being carried off the field, arms raised, triumphant, as Wendy and Evie, hugging, jumping with the unbridled joy of youth, were suddenly stricken with the thought that, deep in their hearts, they'd met the boys, soon to be men, with whom they would want to spend the remainder of their lives.

*

'I wanna tell you how it's gonna be... you gonna give your love to me...'

Eddie was singing along to his favorite tune, Evie hanging on, draped all over him as she had been at every dance and school function since their sophomore year when he'd walked up to her after the fourth game and introduced himself, finally. He'd seen her at school the first week and was aching to say, 'hi'... just talk to her, anything... but the thought of it felt awkward to him. All he'd been able to do was harbor the thought, tuck it away until he hoped some bright, sunny day would come calling when he'd wake up with the nads to say to himself, 'fuck it,' walk up to her and, at the minimum, suggest maybe they could sometime, that is if she would like, meet at a dance or down at the Dairy Queen or out at the quarry with some of the kids.

Now it was two years later, they were seniors, and as close to one another as they could have possibly hoped to be.

"I love you, Eddie," she said, softly. The music had moved to a slower song, Ed Townsend, which she always made sure they danced to, and she meant every word she whispered to the melody... 'I would do anything... for your love...' Evie knew she loved Eddie from the first day she'd seen him. It was easy for her. She was an only child. Her parents had been high school sweethearts who were still holding hands after all these years, so she'd grown up with the idea that life, if nothing else, was magnified so much more by the true and everlasting love of another. And the sooner the better.

"I love you, too, Honey," Eddie told her, holding her tighter tonight, not really understanding why, just feeling the need.

"What is it?"

"I don't know," he said, "I just want to hold you forever. You know what I mean, Evie?"

She knew exactly what he meant, but she didn't answer him right away. She caressed the back of his head with her hand, her body close to his, feeling his warmth. "Just love me, baby."

They danced together well after the song had ended, Joe and Wendy smiling at them, thinking to themselves how wonderful it was to see their best friends so crazy about each other.

"How ya doing, Wen?"

"Fine... just fine." She could have been doing a whole lot better if Joe'd had the same intensity with her he displayed on the football field, but she appreciated his effort. She believed he wanted to be with her, it just wasn't easy for him to show. But when she saw the look in his eyes as he watched Eddie and Evie, she realized he had it in him... somewhere... deep inside.

"You ready for the game Friday, Joey?"

"You know it, Wen. It's gonna be tough, but we can handle 'em. Coach has it figured out. All we have to do is perform. Are your folks going to be there?"

She was mildly surprised. Joe hadn't asked if her parents were coming to a game since their junior year, his first varsity season. Now it was more than a year later. If they won this one, they'd go to state, and from there... who knows?

"Sure they're coming. Everybody in town's coming... everybody in the state I think is coming... just to see you and Eddie."

Joe smiled somewhat sheepishly. "Well, we're gonna whip 'em. You know I'm planning on going to college and get a degree. Maybe this game can help me do that... and then, well, maybe then I can get a good job so I can make you... make you happy, Wen."

Joe caught himself. He'd just blurted it out, rapid fire like. He had no intention of doing such, but it felt natural, the pure honesty and spontaneity of the moment, and it felt good.

Wendy looked at him, her eyes smiling then welling up, "Joey, you make me happy now... I'm happy now."

*

Six months later Eddie and Joe were heading for Turley's Flower & Gift Shop in Joe's '58 Chevy Impala. It was a two-tone, scarlett and gray, Buckeye colors... a red flag to most of the folks on the north side of Columbus who knew the boys from their newspaper clippings, but more recently from the car Joe'd gotten last Christmas after making first-team, All-State halfback. As they cruised down 2nd Avenue, they heard the familiar greeting, "Joey... Eddie... how ya doin'..." and the two of them waved back to one of whom Evie and Wendy continued to remind them was a growing number of their fans.

Now, however, they were on a mission. Each had one last errand to run before the senior prom on Friday night, only two days away. They'd been sent shopping for the corsages they were to give Evie and Wendy, and told in no uncertain terms they had to pick them out themselves. It would not do to have their mothers, or most definitely some store clerk or stranger, make the selections for them. They had to do it... personally.

Pulling up in front of Turley's they saw Coach Duggan walking out carrying a small plastic container. Inside was a white orchid.

"Hey guys, what's up?"

"Hi, Coach. Just a little shopping," Eddie told him, "for the girls."

"Let me guess," he said holding out the box, "something like this?"

"That's right, Coach," Joe replied, "they wouldn't let us get out of this one. We have to pick out their corsages ourselves."

"Well, I think that's a darn good idea. A corsage is very special to a woman. Look at me here. My wife wouldn't take one step out of the house with me if I didn't pick out hers."

"By the way, Coach, what is that?"

"This is a white orchid, which I discovered long ago, along with a little help from Nancy's mother, was her favorite. So I've been sticking to it ever since."

"Sounds good to me," the boys almost stated in unison when Coach Duggan cut them short.

"Now hold on a minute, guys. Not every woman is alike. You've spent enough time with those two girls to know a lot about what they like. So think about that before you decide. Then when you present them their corsages, explain why you picked out what you did. Even if you don't get it right the first time, they'll appreciate the thought. And in the future, they'll drop enough hints so you'll get it right from then on."

"How do you know all that, Coach?"

Jerry Duggan smiled before answering, then said with as much assurance as he'd had when he called that double reverse to put the game away against Fillmore for the state championship last fall, "survival, guys. Survival."

As Coach was walking away, Joe and Eddie looked at each other, thinking... 'survival?'

*

After a lifetime of lying perfectly still while the slime of the earth crawled over the feast they hoped would soon be theirs, Eddie heard the call from Joe one more time. Eddie'd been reluctant to brush the vermin off, not knowing whether the slightest motion might be enough for this second tree monkey to recognize and, in an instant, make the worms and the ants covering his lower body delerious with a warm meal. But now he heard Joe say very quietly and deliberately, "eleven o'clock, forty yards, about fifty feet." Eddie answered, "right," and scanned the area squinting through the rays of light that cast a haze angling across the giant kapoks and tualangs. He located the one he thought Joe was describing and concentrated, focusing on a large branch stretching obliquely from the trunk high above the ground, waiting, waiting as the ants began to sting and the worms continued their ascent above his torso to the juicy flesh about his neck, waiting while from time to time Evie smiled to him within a dream of home etched in his mind, waiting until, at last, he saw the movement in the tree, and he whispered back to Joe, "got him."

The rest they'd practiced and prepared for... just like the last monkey left to rot back down the trail. This time, however, Eddie was the bait. His turn... and not too soon, he thought, these fucking bugs are eating me alive. On the count of three, with the heat of a new day sapping the dawn, Eddie burst from his cover and, in the same motion, emptied a clip into the tree high above.

At first, he didn't feel the bullet pierce his lung. He thought the pain was from the stump he'd landed on when he dove headfirst into more cover. Then he saw the blood staining his shirt, and he felt a deeper sharpness in his chest as he heard Joe yell out, "Eddie... move!" Before he could react, he felt his abdomen implode from another round. "Shit," he looked down, and began crawling as fast as he was able, instinctively grabbing his rifle, taking it with him. Joe was on his feet screaming at Charlie, firing, reloading, firing again. When Eddie looked back, Joe was spinning sideways, falling from a bullet that caught his shoulder. The monkey was raking the area where Joe went down, and Eddie heard him cry out. He turned, emptying another clip into the tree until he saw two legs appear, dangling from a large limb, but still they took fire, first a quick burst back at Eddie, then another where Joe had fallen. Eddie thought, 'shit,' as he slammed his last clip into the magazine, taking careful aim at the sniper's legs. He began firing, slowly raking the barrel of his rifle from left to right across Charlie's thighs, back and forth until the right leg was completely severed, falling, disappearing into the brush below. A cry of agony rang out, then silence, but Eddie waited before giving away his position. He was bleeding, hurting, but he waited until his body begged him to move, to leave this place of death. He was making his way towards Joe when two final bursts from the sniper high above punctuated the moment. Then once again silence, total and complete.

*

'Love, love me do... you know I love you...'

It was grad night. Eddie and Evie were dancing to one of the Beatles' latest hits, with Joe and Wendy close by. The two boys were not the best dancers on the floor, but they needn't be. Their accomplishments were made on the football field and track, as well as in the classroom, and when the girls dragged them onto the dance floor, which was often, they did their best. In fact, most of their classmates admired them more for this act of fallibility than for all the records and accolades they'd accumulated the past two years at Franklin.

After the last dance ended and the lights went up, Gordon Parry thanked the class, each and every one of them for helping make Franklin the "best darn high school in the state," which was about as flamboyant as he could get and brought a rousing cheer from students and teachers alike that rocked the old gym to its foundation. Later, when everyone was saying their good-byes, Joe turned to Eddie and Evie, "what now, guys? You two want to go to the river with the rest of the gang?"

"Heck, yes," Eddie said without hesitation. "You want to, don't you, Evie?"

"Sure, baby." She knew Eddie wanted to be with the kids, all of them, this one last time, and so she added, "Sure, Eddie, I wouldn't miss it."

—"Hey, Eddie... Joey, come on over here."

It was Billy Smithers, their QB, standing by the bonfire with Charlie Polk, Dave Delmon, Alan Moore and a few of their other teammates passing a jug around.

"Don't you two get wasted over there," Evie scolded them coyly.

"We'll only be a minute, honey," Eddie said, kissing her. "We're only being sociable," and the two big men on campus strolled over to join the rest of the boys.

"Have a taste," Billy offered. "Best hard cider Uncle Ray ever made. Slipped me a jug when my mom wasn't lookin' before the dance."

Eddie took a swig, then handed the jug to Joe. "Whew! That's down home, Billy... the real McCoy!"

"You ain't kiddin', Fullback."

"Hey, what're you guys gonna do next year?" Dave had been an outside linebacker on the team... a good one, but he was also known for his willingness to take chances. And now, he was taking another, but only a slight one. He was well liked because of his honesty and candor, and he was asking what most everyone wanted to know, particularly the guys, as well as Evie and Wendy. Were Eddie and Joe going to accept the scholarships they got from Ohio State, or like some of the others graduating this year from Franklin, were they going to join up? Get their hitch in Nam over with. After all, it was only a matter of time before Uncle Sam would come calling. So Dave pressed the question. He'd drunk just enough of Uncle Ray's home brew to ask Joe and Eddie straight up where they stood on the matter. "You guys gonna join me in stoppin' the Communist oppression?..." he half stammered, "or are you goin' off to college?"

Joe hadn't made up his mind, but he was leaning towards college, ever since last fall when he'd blurted out his feelings to Wendy. He wanted to keep his promise to her and get educated, so he'd be able to take care of her in the years ahead. Eddie, on the other hand, felt more of a sense of duty to volunteer for any war, no matter how minor, in which America found herself. Over the past two years, he'd had long talks with Evie's father about his time in the Pacific during the Big One, and it seemed to Eddie since those discussions, that if Viet Nam should escalate, he would consider it a rite of passage to do his part.

So as the bonfire burned brightly on the best of Franklin High's graduating class, their silhouettes dancing across the river in the moonlight, Eddie decided. "Dave, I think I'll take you up on that."

With that, Joe looked over at his closest friend, catching his eye, thinking... what the heck have you gotten us into now, just as Dave howled, "praise the Lord and pass the ammunition!"

Then, Billy, Dave, Charlie and the rest of the guys on the Franklin Wildcats' State Football Championship Team huddled up, passing the jug around as they reveled in the thought of the battles to come, chanting, "Cats!... Cats!... Cats!... Cats!..."

*

It was the hardest phone call he would ever have to make, but he'd asked the captain for permission, and it was granted, this one time. He'd made up his mind two days before in the jungle he didn't want some stoic, starched officer walking up the front steps of her house, unannounced, with the news that would surely shatter her world. So despite a shoulder still throbbing with pain and a broken right leg, Joe volunteered for this last mission. During the eight minutes it took to connect the call, he was sweating, nerves giving way, hoping, praying he could find the words to stem the tide of emotion that would soon come to call. He heard the phone ringing now in the parlor of the little cottage on Beacon Street a million miles away, and in the next moment, a familiar voice bright with the new day, so sweet with the fullness of life answered, "Sims' residence."

"Hello... Evie?"

"This is she." There was a pause as much for the connection as there was for the suspicion in her voice. "Joe? Is that you?"

"Yes." He waited a second then said, "look, Evie, are your folks there?"

"My dad is." Why was Joe calling?... she thought, and why did he want to know if my parents were home?... what's up?... what's going on? The image of Eddie, of the two of them, in some foreign land in constant danger for what the politicians refer to only as a police action was racing through her mind, and now she was desperate. "Joe, what is it? Where's Eddie? Joe?!"

There was no good way to say it. No easy way. The only thing he felt might cause her some solace in the years to come was that he had told her.

"Evie, I'm afraid I don't have very good news. I'm sorry, but on our last patrol, just two days ago, Eddie didn't make it. We were on recon when this sniper jumped us. The guy got us both pretty good before we took him out. Eddie was just hit too bad." Joe waited a moment, then asked, "Evie, are you still there?"

"Yes." Her voice was hollow, weak, "yes, I'm still here, Joe."

"Evie, he saved my life. Eddie saved my life out there. When I finally got to him, he whispered, 'tell Evie I love her, tell her I love her more than anything.' Then he just... he just fell asleep in my arms, and that was it." Joe waited for a minute before adding, "he didn't suffer, Evie. I know he didn't..."

"Joe." There was another voice on the line. "Joe, this is Al Sims. What is it? Evie is in a state."

"Hello, sir. I'm sorry to have to tell you, but it's about Eddie..." And Joe recounted the story to Evie's father, this time in more detail, finally telling him about the ceremony the military is planning upon his return home, after he's able to travel, and about the silver star Eddie will receive posthumously.

"Joe," Al Sims asked him directly, "are you all right? I don't mean physically, I know the army'll take good care of you. Are you all right with Eddie being gone?"

It was only then that Joe's emotions got the better of him. "Well, I... I... he was like a brother..."

"Joe, son, there was nothing more you could have done, believe me. I lost two buddies, one on either side of me in the Canal in '42. It was just their time, like it was Eddie's. There's no other reason to it. Now you take care of yourself. You've got Wendy waiting for you. And Evie's going to need your shoulder from time to time... least for a while. Now you get healthy, Joe."

"I will, sir."

"You don't call me sir anymore, Joe. You've been to hell and back. You call me Al."

**

85

Crosstie Walker

Some men take to riding the rails for a time when money is low and they have a need to get here or there right now. Others live their lives as flatcar riders and crosstie walkers and few, if any, ask the why of it.

Red Hand

Red Hand was sitting with the old man, trying as he might to understand Santin's musings, for now, as all of the Yankton knew, the old medicine man did not have much longer in this life, and his remarks were whimsical and fleeting, like smoke on the wind.

But the boy was not detered. Ever since Running Wolf told him of Santin's ability to see beyond the earthly world, Red Hand had sought out the old one, wondering how he too might attain such powers. While Santin would never answer him directly, particularly about his comments to Willow the day Ethan MacCall returned, he did encourage a continuing dialogue and thirst for such knowledge, telling Red Hand, "if you continue the quest, in time you will understand."

It was with this thought Red Hand rode with Two Bears towards Mission to purchase some of his grandfather's favorite tobacco, along with a few month's staples from Bendt's store. Although Willow warned her son again to be watchful of the white named Thompkins, Red Hand had not seen him on his last two trips into town, and so had placed him in the back of his mind. He would not forget the danger, but neither would he let it rule his actions.

"Do you carry the white man's gun?"

"Yes, Grandfather. It is on the pack horse."

Two Bears waited some moments as he watched a hawk circle lazily against the billowing clouds, then finished his thought. "Let us hope you will have no use for it."

"Yes, Grandfather."

When they reached the town limits and Alfred Bendt saw them coming, he glanced over to The Divide and hurried out to meet them. They noticed the storekeeper's concern and reined in their horses.

"Good to see you Two Bears... you too Red Hand." He looked towards the saloon again, then continued, "but you've come at a bad time."

They waited for him to continue.

"Red Hand... you know that fella you beat the tar outa last spring? Well, him and some of his friends have been at it all night, an' if he catches sight o' you there's gonna be gun play sure 'nuf."

Two Bears looked at his grandson, remembering his wish... hoping there wouldn't be trouble, but as it has always been with the whites, ever since he was a youth himself, trouble seemed to be, in the end, unavoidable.

So the old man motioned to the holster and Colt pistol lashed to their pack horse, then nodded to Red Hand.

The boy jumped from the paint and grabbed the gun. He checked the chamber quickly, making sure it was loaded. He untied the holster and strapped it on, securing it to his hip, sliding the gun in and out once or twice to reacquaint himself with the feel. It had been a few days since he'd fired it, but nothing had changed. It was comfortable, his hand caressing the pistol like a favorite bow. But as Ethan had warned, when it comes time to face a man, he must also summon the nerve.

Red Hand looked at Two Bears, then asked Bendt to go tell the man he was outside.

The storekeeper hesitated, "I don' wanna see ya gittin' yerself kilt, son. 'At man Thompkins is..." but Red Hand stopped him. "I'm all right, Mr. Bendt. Go get him. Now is the time."

The Divide was due east from where they were standing, but now it was late morning so the sun was high; it wouldn't be a problem.

He was ready. As he stood watching Bendt, he felt no fear, no trepidation, only a slight dryness of the mouth. He looked down. His hands were steady. Now from the saloon he heard the whooping and hollering of the men inside just before Alfred Bendt came flying into the street from the entrance, with Thompkins and two others following behind.

"Where's the bastard?..." Thompkins bellowed. "Where is that red son of a bitch!?"

Red Hand remembered Ethan's words. 'Remain calm... always remain calm.' "I am here," he replied evenly. "I am right in front of you."

Thompkins was grinning as he fanned out the other two.

"Lookie here, fellas, the boy's gotta lil' ol' gun. Well, don't 'at beat all. Ya know how ta use 'at, boy?"

Red Hand didn't answer. His only thought was how to attack the three men. First, two quick shots to Thompkins, then one to the man on his right, anywhere to slow him down. Then the other, one or two shots, then back to the second.

"I say, boy, ya sure you know how ta use..." and Thompkins went for his gun.

What happened next, by all accounts from Alfred Bendt, Two Bears, and the citizenry of Mission, which at that time of the morning amounted to ten or twelve close enough to see, was a sight to behold, and to recount for years to come.

Before Thompkins had uncased his weapon, he was falling to his knees, already dead from two bullets chest high. The second man had barely gotten his pistol out when he was spun around by Red Hand's third bullet as it tore into his shoulder, leaving his arm hanging, his weapon falling to the ground. The third cowboy, seeing the youth turn towards him, dropped his gun and raised his hands. Red Hand motioned to him to step back just as the second man reached again for his pistol. The boy's fourth and last shot, aimed almost casually, shattered the gun's chamber, knocking it away.

There was silence, stillness, as the onlookers stared, some shaking their heads, others in awe. Three or four of the townsfolk inched forward to inspect Thompkins, realizing only after they'd turned over the body the sheriff and his deputy had arrived on the scene. Lee Bell had cut his teeth helping to tame cowtowns like Salina and Ellsworth in his youth. But some time ago, as others of his ilk had done, he'd chosen the easier path when Jedediah Strait convinced him it was in his best interest not to buck the tiger, the odds were stacked against him.

"After all, Lee," Strait had told him, "you ain't gettin' any younger. An' that wife and daughter o' yours', well... you catch my meanin.'"

Lee Bell had considered standing up to Strait. He'd abided by the law his entire career, never accepting money offered him to look the other way, not in thirty years of wearing a badge. But when Strait saw the first beads of sweat begin to appear on the man's forehead, he sneered, " 'at's better, Lee. Yer workin' fer me now." Then Strait had added before he turned to walk out of Bell's office, "There's plenty here fer the takin'... I'm gonna make you a rich man."

As the sheriff was leaning over Thompkins' body, inspecting the corpse, he knew what he had to do. He remembered Thompkins run in with the Indian boy, and he knew Strait's top hand deserved whatever he had coming to him. But all that didn't matter. Strait would want the boy taken to task... to show the people around Mission who was in charge.

The sheriff walked up to Red Hand and asked him what happened. When the boy told him, he said, "come with me, I'm gonna have to hold ya 'til the court hears from all the eye witnesses." Sheriff Bell then told him, "gimme the gun, son," and held out his hand.

Red Hand glanced over to Two Bears before obliging the sheriff. The boy's grandfather nodded slightly, feeling secure enough people had seen what happened, and would come forward. So Two Bears packed up their supplies at Bendt's Store alone that day, then mounted up and rode west out of town towards home.

Later that night camped under a full moon the old chief wondered if his grandson might be treated differently than others of their tribe. After all, didn't the blood of the whites run through his veins? Surely this would be considered. But the more Two Bears deliberated on the matter, the more he became unconvinced the actions of Red Hand would go unpunished, for deep in his heart he knew the boy would have to pay some price. He just hoped it would not be the ultimate.

*

Judge Elias Carver had only just called his court to order when the Sioux made their entrance. First Two Bears, then Running Wolf appeared in the doorway of the small courtroom, causing the judge to look for wall space where the two might find some standing room. The court had been packed since early morning, the entire town waiting for an outcome rumored to have already been engineered. But the judge was a fair man, and as he studied the two Yankton chiefs he saw the resolve in their eyes that the accused should be treated justly, as any man. He nodded motioning them to a far corner just as they stepped aside allowing Willow room to enter the courthouse. Silence fell. All eyes turned towards her as Elias Carver leaned forward in his chair, staring shamelessly. He'd seen Indians before, close up and plenty of them as they had from time to time been in front of him for a variety of offenses, most often the result of too much whiskey. On occasion, their squaws had even come to plead leniency from the court so the men could continue providing for them. But the Indian woman standing before him now was no ordinary squaw. Willow had retained the beauty and bearing that had so captured John Connor, and the judge could only gawk until he had the presence of mind to take a drink from his water glass, clear his throat and state, "you..." pointing to the front row opposite Jedediah Strait and Lee Bell, "you men there... you three... give way for the family of the defendant."

Willow acknowledged the judge's deference to her, and with Two Bears and Running Wolf by her side strode to the front of the courtroom and sat down. Red Hand turned and smiled to her over the grumblings of a few who questioned his decision, however the banging from his gavel soon silenced the courtroom and the proceedings began.

As the third witness to the shooting was testifying, a farmer named Haller, it became clear Strait's men had been convincing during the prior week. They'd called upon each man who'd been in the street that day, puting the barrel of a gun in his mouth and explaining in great detail what they would do, first, to his wife and family, then to the man himself. Even Alfred Bendt, the last witness called, stammered, "I... I don't rightly recall if... ah, the boy pulled his pistol, ah... after the deceased or, ah... it was awful fas' action, yer honor..."

Even Two Bears' matter-of-fact statement that... "the whites went for guns first... all three..." could not sway a jury that, when all was said and done, had to coexist with Jedediah Strait. They didn't know exactly what he'd said or done to the witnesses, but to a man the jury knew they wanted no part of it. After deliberating barely an hour they charged Red Hand to be guilty of the killing, self-defense being unproved beyond a reasonable doubt, and left his sentencing to the court. When Judge Carver heard the verdict he admonished each for his spineless behavior considering what he'd learned of the matter before taking the bench. But he was left with no recourse. Under the law the minimum sentence was five years hard labor, and in Red Hand's case, because he was an Indian, that was in a hellhole fifteen hundred miles east buried in the swamps of Florida known as The Stockyard.

Willow watched as her only son was shackled and taken away, and she felt what remained of her strength leaving her. Her breath shortened, and she reached out for support from her brother and father. During the commotion, Red Hand had barely enough time to turn and make eye contact with her. But in that moment she saw a likeness to his father she'd not seen before, a strength of will and purpose, and she drew from that, steadying herself, as she would in the years to come.

*

The stench was what he noticed first. After the 3-day ride from Mission to Omaha in a makeshift cage mounted on the back of a wagon, then locked inside a cattle car with three Northern Cheyenne traveling by rail to Topeka, on through Shreveport to the town of Bartow in central Florida, then back in the cage for the final seventy miles to his new home just north of Lake Okeechobee, the stench rising from every crevice of The Stockyard filled the air. Red Hand winced from the odor of sweat, blood, human waste and rotting flesh. The mixture was like some recipe from hell, and as he looked up, hell was where he believed he'd arrived. Without warning, a guard pushed him from the wagon. He landed on his back in the muck, unable to break his fall because of the shackles. He struggled to his feet, glancing at the man who stated, "don't you eyeball me, boy," and jabbed Red Hand with the butt of his rifle, knocking him back into the muck, blood now flowing from a gash on his cheekbone. "Don't you ever eyeball me."

Just the four of them were checked into the prison that day. At times, twenty or more would arrive at this outpost on the Okeechobee, and it took some time to strip them down, wash them down, outfit them in convict stripes, shackle them and have each say his name and make his mark. But on this day there was just the four... Red Hand and the three Cheyenne, two bucks named Talks Little and Pony, and an older warrior with years of the white man's brutality etched into his face. Red Hand saw at once the man had a bearing about him. He was surely a leader of his people the boy was thinking as the guard asked him his name.

"How're ya called?..." the guard snapped.

The old one's English wasn't good. He didn't understand the question, and he hesitated. The guard stood, raising the butt of his rifle, but Pony quickly translated. The old man nodded to Pony, then stated clearly, "Walks Over Them."

The guard began writing the old man's name in his log book then stopped, first smirking, then chuckling before yelling to another across the yard, "hey, Teddy, here's a real moniker for ya. This one's called Walks Over Them. How'd ya like to carry that aroun'?"

"Jus' one o' them damn Injun names, Jasper. Now let's put this bunch to bed."

"In a minute... in a minute." Turning back to the old man again, he asked, "Walks Over Them, huh. What the hell is Them?... just who the hell is Them, old man?"

Pony saw his old comrade was again befuddled, so he quickly translated. Walks Over Them listened to Pony, making sure he understood before answering in his native tongue, taking his time, his remarks punctuated with a firmness and finality the other two Cheyenne had not heard before. When he finished, the guard asked Pony, "what'd he say?"

Pony shuffled his feet before replying, unsure if he should relate the old one's words. But he decided he would. What was there to lose? Only life in this world, a world that was becoming more white with each passing day. So he looked the guard in the eye, attempting to add a forcefulness to his own words as Walks Over Them had. "Them," he stated, "Them were the bluecoats of the great warrior chief Long Hair... wiped out at the Little Big Horn many winters ago. It was Them," and Pony's voice rose with finality, "the old one Walked Over."

*

Jasper Peadle was suited to his work. He'd grown up orphaned after his mother died of consumption when he was three, and just two years later his father left this earth by way of disagreement with a longshoreman in Panama City. Seems old dad accused the man of cheating at cards one night after a few too many whiskies. The longshoreman had been on a hot streak for about an hour, and Ike Peadle was betting into every hand the man held, whether it showed good or not. Ike could get stubborn that way, and this night he was paying for it with five dollar gold pieces, lots of them.

" 'At's the third time t'night ya beat ma flush, pardner. I ain't nev'r seen 'at b'fore."

The longshoreman had been in and out of this particular saloon over the course of the last year, and he was known to be a rough sort. Those who frequented The Masthead had seen him carve up more than one man and take the ears for trophies.

"Well then, I guess ya seen it all now, haven't ya?"... he stated, looking right through Ike, raking in the coin.

It was Ike's move, and he'd had just enough whiskey to give him the starch to make the one that'd be his last.

"Roll up yer sleeves, you cheatin' som' bitch... roll up them sleeves!"... Ike yelled, leaping over the table, reaching for the man's arm.

The longshoreman, Dawson was his name, sprung to his feet. He grabbed the scruff of Ike's neck, dragging him across the table onto the floor. As Ike tumbled over, he drew a small pistol from his coat, aimed and fired. Dawson's boot arrived just as the pistol discharged, sending the gun flying, the bullet splitting the shinbone of another man at the next table as Ike scrambled for the weapon, but too late. Dawson was on him, delivering one, then a second thrust to the hilt into Ike's belly with what bystanders described later as a Bowie knife, or something awful close. After the second, Dawson ripped the weapon up to Ike's heart, blood flowing like a river in spring. Then he took the ears.

"Well, that's it," the sheriff said. He'd seen Dawson's work before, and he was growing weary of cleaning up his leavings. But after he'd heard everyones' story, he knew he couldn't hold the man.

"Dawson, if I was you, I'd be smart an' move on. Cause next time, I won't care 'bout the circumstances. I won't ask."

Dawson studied Bill Allen for a moment, then uttered, "yer bluffin.'"

"Try me?"

Later, one of the men came up to the sheriff and said, "I hear tell he had a kid... a youngun."

"If he did," Bill Allen answered, "the court'll handle it."

*

Little Jasper was five when the State of Florida took him in. As a child with no surviving kin he became a ward of the state and sent off to an orphanage near Tallahassee. There he quickly learned the lessons that were to serve him well years later when he joined the government as a prison guard. The secret, he remembered, was to find a person's weakness, then exploit it, attack it at every opportunity until the person was so desperate for you to stop they would do anything, anything to make the pain and humiliation go away. Little Jasper Peadle had learned the lesson as the bigger boys, one in particular named Jelly for his fondness for preserves, got to calling him Peed-a-little instead of Peadle. This so upset Jasper one night he in fact did pee the bed, something he hadn't done for more than a year. When the older boys discovered his sheets, they were relentless. Peed-a-little became Peed-a-lot. After supper they would surround him in the dormitory before lights out, making faces and laughing hysterically, chanting the ditty Jelly had penned... Peed-a-little like as not, peed a little peed a lot. Before the dean got wind of the goings-on, little Jasper was near institutional.

"You realize the older boys are just having fun with you, don't you Jasper?"

Mr. Folks was doing his best to put the whole mess into perspective for the lad, but to no immediate avail. Jasper just sat in the overstuffed, leather armchair in the dean's office opposite the great mahogany desk he could barely see over, both hands firmly holding his pecker as if to avert any further peeing. Folks looked down at him with more concern for an orderly dormitory than fear of any emotional damage the boy might endure. What to do?... he considered. What to do?

Over the next few weeks after repeated tauntings by Jelly and the rest of the boys, Mr. Folks made his decision. He called a colleague of his in Orlando and had little Jasper transferred to an orphanage of equal size, but one where the boys were of predominately younger age. Jasper would fit right in, Folks imagined, and his Tallahassee Home for Youths could get back to normal, if there was such a thing.

*

It was eight years later when Harold Folks ran into his old colleague Tremaine Lewiston at a conference in Chicago. After exchanging pleasantries over a glass of sherry one evening, Folks remembered little Jasper Peadle and how Lewiston had helped him out, and he asked after the boy.

"Oh, yes, yes, I do remember Jasper. He did come out of his shell. Actually, by the time he graduated he ran the dormitory with an iron fist. Scared the beejeesus out of every little tyke who came through. Damn tyrant, he was."

*

He'd made a habit of visiting the old man every night about this time, just after the residents of The Stockyard heard the familiar call for lights out. Walks Over Them understood this and waited, huddling in the corner of his cell bathed in darkness, his only companions the crawling insects and stinging mosquitoes. He listened for the heavy footsteps, waiting as the faint sound of Jasper's distinctive shuffle grew closer until it would stop, for only a moment, before another sound... more ominous and deadly. No matter how often the old Indian prayed to the Great Spirit to make it stop, make it go away, the sound of the key sliding into the lock of his cell always came, and with it a gruff voice he could not understand, "this is for the boys in the 7th." Then the heavy blows would follow, first to the abdomen, then the rib cage, never to the head or face where their affect might be seen. Lately, the old man could take only so many of the blows before rolling to one side and covering up. But he knew the attack was not finished, not yet. Walks Over Them had become accustomed to the routine, and so he waited once more, waited for the toe from the avenger's boot to plunge into the small of his back, again and again, then more of the angry words, "who's walkin' over who now, you red fuck?" One last kick would punctuate the moment before the cell door closed and the sound of keys jingling amidst more hurried footsteps slowly faded into the night.

*

They'd broken for lunch after digging a latrine for a new bunch of bucks set to arrive soon. Pony and Red Hand were leaning against a tall palm, fingering mush from tin bowls between gulps of water tainted a murky brown when they saw Walks Over Them stumble. The two rushed to him, catching him just before he struck the jagged stones lining the pathway. As Red Hand cradled his head, they felt his shortness of breath and Pony went for water. Red Hand tore open the old man's shirt to allow his body what breeze there was when he saw them. The bruises were everywhere, covering Walks Over Them's torso and continuing around to his back. His rib cage was badly swollen, and Red Hand could feel the rough edges of bone beneath the surface of his skin. Pony was back with the water wetting Walks Over Them's mouth when the voice rang out.

"Get the hell away from him," Jasper Peadle barked, "I'll take care o' him," and he pushed Red Hand aside with enough force to cause the boy to lose his balance.

Red Hand stared at the guard as he stood, taking care to avert eye contact. He knew what Jasper could do. He'd just seen the evidence, and he was already plotting retribution.

Since arriving at The Stockyard, he and Pony and Talks Little had spent many hours with the old man, learning much about the happier days of the Cheyenne and Sioux and the other tribes that once roamed the western plains. Walks Over Them's stories filled the young men with pride, pride that turned to bitterness as they reflected upon the fate of their brothers at the hand of the whites, then to regret that they had not been born in an earlier time so they, too, could have ridden against the Long Hair, wiping him out, taking scalps to adorn their lodge-poles. Red Hand had told Walks Over Them of his birth that day in the Indian camp along the Little Big Horn, and the old man had looked at him with a tear welling up, saying it was a great and terrible day, the red man's finest hour, and the beginning of their long journey to hopelessness and despair. Red Hand understood the old man's meaning, and as the words echoed within his mind he saw Jasper Peadle turn and shout to another one of the guards, "Jimmy, git on ov'r here and git this carcass to the infirmary... it's trashin up the yard."

*

Red hand had been allowed to visit Walks Over Them on one occasion while the old man was recovering, and during the few minutes they were together a plan was devised. Walks Over Them told Red Hand that because of his birth on the day of the Little Bighorn victory, he was special. He carried the greatness of that day within him, and its power was doing him and his people no good in this place. He must escape and find his way in the white man's world, and use the power to help his people... all people. He told Red Hand to get him a weapon, a knife of some sort. He would use this against the guard, and gain Red Hand his freedom.

*

"All right, out the way." Jasper Peadle was leading Walks Over Them through the other prisoners towards the row of cells in Building II. While the old man was much better, he wasn't up to manual labor and the doctor recommended he be given, at the minimum, two more days rest. Jasper didn't like the idea, but it was not his call. At least, not yet he thought, smiling.

The past three days Red Hand had heeded the old man's request. He'd spent every available moment fashioning one of the metal bowls used for meals into a crude knife. Using two rocks, he'd smashed the bowl flat, then late at night sparked a small fire in his cell, heating the metal to where he could fold it into a thin, cone-like shape, flatten it once again, then sharpen the edges. After wrapping a piece of cloth around one end and tying it off it was ready. The weapon would be no match for Jasper with his rifle handy, but in close quarters, unsuspecting, it could be lethal. He just hoped Walks Over Them had the strength to use it.

"Move away," Jasper was telling the men when Walks Over Them saw Red Hand approaching. When he was close enough the old man feigned another stumble, and as Red Hand held out his hand for support, Jasper failed to see the object pass from one to the other.

"Get in there," he snarled, pushing his prisoner into the tiny cell. "I'll be seein ya later."

*

Lights out came as usual, nine o'clock, however the old one was without trepidation this night. He felt young again, like the days when the bluecoats first appeared on the great plains, and the warriors, painted for battle, anticipating the fight to come, rode out to meet them. This night, it was the same. Walks Over Them was renewed with the feelings of his youth, and so rather than dreading the familiar sound of the jingling of keys and the lock to his cell sliding open, he waited with one final purpose: this night he would die in battle, and deliver Red Hand if he could.

The footsteps came clearer as Jasper approached, close now. Then the jingling of keys, and the lock. It was time. He felt the rush of adrenaline, and he crouched, ready to spring at his enemy as he did in his youth. The knife Red Hand had given him was in his left hand, blade pointing up, so he could strike upward toward his enemy.

"Had a week off, did ya?... ya red bastard. Not no more."

Jasper Peadle had leaned his rifle against the far wall as always before commencing his punishment. This night, however, he removed his jacket so he might take freer swings with his arms as he delivered his blows of redemption. He moved slowly across the cell. The old man sensed his nearness, the footsteps edging closer. Jasper was upon him now, fists clenched, feral, but the old man was ready.

"Now come git some," the guard growled, swinging a right fist when he felt the pinch in his abdomen. He wasn't sure what it was. It was sharp enough to have deflated the blow, causing his fist to stop short of its target. He looked down, then felt the warmth of his own blood flowing freely from the wound. He didn't understand, couldn't grasp what had caused the injury, or how it happened. The old one? It couldn't be. Then he felt another blow, a sharper pain from a blade thrust directly into his midsection, and now he understood. He was incredulous, frantic with the knowledge the old Indian was fighting back, stabbing him, killing him.

He lunged at Walks Over Them, his weight taking them both to the ground, the violence of the fall knocking the wind from the Indian. Jasper was scrambling to find the knife now, knowing he had to kill the old one quickly and find the Doc. He searched desperately for the weapon, brushing his hand back and forth on the dirt floor of the cell... here, over here. His breathing came quicker, the beads of sweat profuse, covering him. He felt something. His palm struck an object. It was sharp. He found the handle in the darkness and thought, now you red sonofabitch...

As Jasper raised the weapon, he didn't hear Talks Little. The young warrior had been busy the past few days himself manufacturing a crude key. After he picked the lock of his cell, he slithered down the dark corridor towards the sounds of the scuffling.

Now Talks Little stepped in behind the guard, grabbing his wrist. In one move the boy wrested the knife away and slit Jasper's throat quietly, then scalped him. Talks Little had moved so swiftly he was stunned by his own actions. He stood motionless for an instant, then a fire he'd not known ran through him, consuming him. He rose up, wanting to hold his prize high for all to see, but caught himself, remembering this night was about business. As he began to drag away the body he heard the old one groaning from the corner of the cell.

Walks Over Them reached out, barely whispering, "Red Hand... Red Hand..."

"Yes, old one, what about Red Hand?"

"Release him... release Red Hand. He is the one."

Talks Little did not understand, but he nodded he would do it. There wasn't time for understanding, except knowing he must dispose of the body before daybreak. He grabbed the guard's rifle and keys and headed to a far cell.

"What happened?..." Red Hand whispered.

"Walks Over Them is near death. I killed the guard and must try to bury him."

"Good, do that. They will think I killed him, and come after me. Hide the body well."

Talks Little unlocked the cell door, and Red Hand stood next to him for a moment, placing a hand on his shoulder. "I will come with you, Red Hand."

"No, you can stay alive here, serving your time. Chances are I will soon be dead."

"Take this then, it is Peadle's rifle. You will need it."

Red Hand took the Winchester, cradling it in his hand, then lingered for a moment before he turned to leave. "Tell Pony I will not forget my brothers."

*

Ascending the wall of The Stockyard had been the easy part. The perimeter of the prison wasn't well guarded, because it needn't be. With the swamp surrounding them and the inmates locked down tight at night, there were only a handful of men working the walls after lights out. He slipped over the top at the east end of the fortress, making the leap from the roof of the livery. He had eight hours before daybreak, so he felt comfortable putting some distance between him and those sure to follow, that is, if he could avoid the miles of swamp water that would grab hold and devour even the hardiest who invaded its reaches.

He was heading north, following the trail of an Arapaho the warden kneecapped after trying to escape some years back. The man had related to Red Hand how he made it through the worst of the swamp before the dogs ran him down, so the boy was ever grateful as he followed the trail at an easy lope figuring the warden wouldn't notice his absence until first call. More perplexing would be Peadle's disappearance. They'd look high and low, raking the area until they found something that explained what'd happened to the man. No telling how long that might take, but Red Hand knew Talks Little would do a good job of hiding the body, so he gave himself an extra three to four hours. That would put the time at just about noon before they'd get serious about coming after him.

When dawn showed its light, Red Hand could see the sun's rays slicing through the trees, bouncing off the glass of Lake Kissimmee to the west. The boy was tired after running for eight hours, but he wasn't spent. This was no time to stop and sleep he thought, that would have to wait. Another hour went before he watched the lake disappear from view behind, and the land changed. There was an order to the terrain taking shape as he continued to lope easily, rifle in hand, and he could sense the human element creeping into the day. He noticed the groomed, fenced off pastures with animals grazing, set side-by-side with rows of crops, vegetables, citrus, all attended to by the white man, displaying at once his affection for and dominance over the land. The boy felt some amount of pride which he thought must come from the seed of his father, although he'd been told many times the man lived like the Sioux. No matter, I am half white, and this is the way of their world.

The mid-morning sun greeted him as he emerged on the far side of a glade loping at the same steady pace when he saw in the distance to his left a small lake. This was the shortest route to Haines City he remembered the Arapaho saying, and to the iron horse. Once there, he could steal aboard one of the great boxed carts and travel north to Gainesville, then on to the great water that is near Savannah, Charleston and beyond. They would be looking for him to head west, so go north, the Arapaho said, and stay to the byways and gullies, get a change of clothes, and always travel at night. So with weariness setting in and the heat of the day disappating, he found a cool bog among a gathering of palms, and sleep came.

*

The squawking of parrots high above awakened him, birds he'd observed with great interest during his time in the Yard. He recalled the stories told by some of the inmates of the ability of these birds to talk, and he had marvelled at this, hoping one day to engage one of them in conversation, if for no other purpose than to exchange pleasantries. But that is for another day, and his mind jumped to the task at hand. It was twilight. Good, he thought, I didn't lose any time. He rubbed the sleep from his eyes, focusing on the lake to his left. Hatchineha, he remembered the lifers calling it, and he picked up the rifle and began to lope once again, heading into the white world that lay just up ahead.

*

It wasn't the voices that caused him alarm, nor the fact he was inching around the far side of a barn next to a small farmhouse with a candle still burning in the window. It was the anger in the man's voice, and the screams from the woman that followed. His skin crawled at the sound, remembering how some of the men of his tribe, mostly when drinking the white man's whiskey, would abuse their women. He made his way to the window and could see the woman cowering, the man taking off his belt as he approached her. The boy tried the latch of the door, gently. It was open. He made no sound as he entered. In the ebbing light, the man had enough time for one blow, catching the woman across her shoulder and back with the belt as she turned away. When he raised it a second time, Red Hand swung the butt of his rifle catching him on the side of the head. The man's knees buckled and he fell to the floor in pieces — calves, knees, torso — as the woman screamed louder still. Red Hand put the rifle down, holding out his hands, palms up, in reassurance, but she was wary, and waited. Then placing a finger to his mouth to quiet her, he reached out. After another moment she took his hand and regained her feet. He brought her a chair and took another opposite.

"Who are you?..." she asked, adding before he could answer, "I know yer an escapee by yer clothes, but who are you? Why you helpin' me?"

He felt he could trust the woman... must trust the woman. "My name is not important, but you are right. I have escaped from The Stockyard. I have been there three moons, and was lucky to get out."

She studied the youth. "Yer not full-blooded, are ya?"

"No, my father was white."

"Was white?"

"He died before I was born. I never knew him." Then Red Hand wanted to satisfy his curiosity. "Why does he beat you?"

The woman's eyes began to well up as her voice quieted to a whisper. "We had a son, but he died too... of the fever. He was only eight. When my man's drinkin', he blames me."

Red Hand didn't know why, but he reached out and touched the woman's hand, barely. She smiled.

"Do you need anything?"... she asked.

103

"Food... clothes."

She went to the stove and served him up a plate of stew still warm, a slice of sourdough, glass of cider. While he was stuffing himself she went and found him a shirt and pair of pants saying, "try these in the other room."

When he came out still wearing his moccasins, she said, "those won't do. They'll give ya'way sure," and went and fetched him a pair of boots. "These were ma brother's. He an his misses used ta come here ever' year. He left 'em a while back."

He put them on. "They feel good," the boy said. "Thank you."

She looked at him for some time before saying, "it's me who owes the thankin'. I won't ferget what ya did. Now scoot, an' you take care."

Red Hand took her hands in his. "Get rid of the whiskey. And when he awakes, talk of the good times... always the good times."

*

As the sun was beginning its slow tumble off the western edge of the world, Red Hand was nearing Haines City. He'd passed Lake Hatchineha earlier that afternoon, stopping to scavange a few fruits and vegetables from the farms in the area, making sure to stay well clear of the inhabitants. He'd heard voices once, but they were far off to the east and he was heading northwest.

With the darkness of night looming, he found a kind sky... stars smiling, a full moon lighting his way as he kept on, the even pace acceptable to the weariness he felt throughout. Farther north he thought, it must be farther still until I see the glow in the distance from the lights like the old ones told me. He kept on, his boots pounding the earth, relentless, fearing what might be behind gaining ground.

An hour later, his legs now heavy, his spirit waning... that was when he first heard the sound. It was barely audible, yet unmistakable. It was the sound of the huffing and puffing of the great iron horse, growing nearer in the distance. Then he saw it, silhouetted against the moon rounding a bend no more than half a mile off with clouds of white smoke billowing from the engine, and he heard its call... Come, follow me, follow my tracks to Haines City, and to freedom.

*

The train yard was a deep, ink blue, darker than the night sky making it all the more difficult to decifer which direction to take. He needed to reach Gainesville, another one-hundred twenty miles up the line. Once there, he figured anyone chasing him would think he'd headed west to Tallahassee and beyond, not turned east to Jacksonville and the coast. But there were too many tracks crisscrossing in all directions like so many trails, each one identical to the next, and he could find no sign to it. So he left the yard and continued north on foot looking for only one trail of the iron horse.

He was loping again, hurrying, his mind telling him he must. No more than a mile out of town, with only the moon lighting his way, he rounded a bend and saw the track up ahead. It had been off to his right on the far side of a stand of trees, parallel to the path he'd taken. The boy felt a rush of anticipation. He didn't know how long it might be until the next train, but he relished the idea that once aboard he would soon be puting more distance between himself and his pursuers.

He saw there was a gully up ahead running alongside the tracks just as they became visible beyond the trees. He headed for it, slowing his pace some. The gully was narrow at first, then widened to ten meters, with maybe a three meter drop to the bottom that was barely visible. That would be a good place to wait, good shelter he thought, and he neared the edge.

He didn't know what it was at first, perhaps a voice like a harbinger, and it whispered, go slowly... be watchful. He saw the embankment sloped gently to the bottom, and he could see there were rocks and clumps of brush below big enough to hide a man, so he crept along the edge listening, not yet ready to slide down into the darkness.

The two sounds came almost simultaneously... the scuffing of his boots on the gravelled bank of the gully as he began his slide into the abyss, and the sound of a man moaning, needing help. He had no choice now as he continued down the side of the embankment, his own weight carrying him faster, the sound of his boots against the gravel blurring any other he might have detected.

When he felt solid ground beneath him again he crouched, rifle ready, but the two were upon him. He had enough time to duck out of the grasp of the one at his back, swinging his rifle like a club as he rose to his full height. He felt the butt strike flesh and bone. He wheeled, his eyes focusing better now on the dark figure standing before him. It was enough to simply cock the weapon, slamming one of the shells into the chamber, and the man turned tail. He looked down. The other was on the ground, dazed but moving. The boy placed the barrel of the rifle under his chin, raising his head. The man pleaded, "no, don't... please don't." Red Hand said nothing, just stood staring. "Oh God, don't pull it." The boy waited some time longer before raising the rifle still higher, forcing him to his feet. He pushed the barrel against the man's throat, "you have three seconds." The man froze. He didn't understand. Three seconds?... he thought... three seconds to live? "Oh my God, no... no!" Motioning the barrel of the rifle towards the gully, again Red Hand said, "three seconds," this time beginning to count, "one... two..." The man's eyes bulged as he turned, scrambling away, falling, crawling until he was out of sight and into the darkness beyond.

*

The groan he had heard before came again, only this time he could tell it was to his left. The boy again shrunk to a crouch before heading further into the gully. He heard the sound again. It was close. He stopped and focused, squinting his eyes, looking for shapes that didn't belong with the underbrush and rocks and stumps strewn about. The sound came again, then movement no more than fifteen feet ahead. He continued on. Whoever it was must have had worse luck with his two attackers.

Red Hand crouched beside the man now, waiting for some movement before rolling him onto his back. He was about middle age and was clutching a small cloth bag tied tight with a piece of leather. The boy patted him down, finding no gun or knife.

"Are you all right?" The boy's hand was on his shoulder, shaking him slightly. "Can you hear me?"

The man moved, attempting to reach his head with his left hand.

106

Red Hand asked again, "are you all right?"

"Wha... what do you say?..."

"Are you not hurt? Can you sit up?"

"What... what!... who's that?!..." The man was delerious, still half conscious when he began to crawl away, "no, no, don't! Don't hit me!... don't... hit..."

"I won't hit you. Stop, I won't hit you. I want to help you," Red Hand offered calmly, settling the man some. He asked a third time, "can you sit up?"

"Yes... yes, I suppose," half-struggling as the youth held one arm. Studying this Good Samaritan more closely now he asked, "who are you?... an how did you stumble across me in this godforsaken ditch?"

"I had come into this wash when I heard you. You sounded hurt. I am heading north on the great iron... on the train. I was lucky to find you."

"That is an understatement, sir," the man replied as he attempted to right himself, "although I would suggest I am the lucky one. Two rascals accosted me as I lay sleeping, waiting for the 11:33 to Sanford, however I feel I am not too worse for wear."

"Good," said the boy, "let's find the water. We can drink and you can wash."

"What water would that be?"

"Ahead... there," pointing. "I can smell it."

The two made their way to a small stream fifty meters farther up the gully. The water was clear, cool, and the man bathed his face and arms before drinking his fill. Red Hand drank enough to satisfy his thirst, then sat for a while, contemplating his companion. He thought he must be a man of the road... of the iron horse, so he should know the track that leads to Gainesville. But can I trust him?

"I thank you for coming to my aid, kind sir. However, there is one thing... how did you miss those two who attacked me? It couldn't have been more than a minute or two before you came along."

"I didn't miss them. I ran them off."

"I see, that makes sense... your arriving on the scene so soon afterwards." He looked at the youth differently. There was more respect in the man's eyes which Red Hand saw to be those of someone down on his luck, except for tonight that is. And he thought, even if he is not yet one to be trusted, he is beholding.

"My name is Woodleigh," the man stated more formally, holding out his hand as he continued to gather himself, "Ransom Woodleigh III of Pembroke, Georgia... formerly, that is. Nowadays I am, how should I put it... a man of the world, and of the road. And I might add, happy to be... quite happy to be."

The boy looked closer at Ransom Woodleigh without speaking. He wanted to trust him... felt he could trust him. He'd mentioned a place called Sanford and Red Hand wondered if it was near Gainesville. He considered the question before deciding to take the risk. Afterall, he had the rifle.

"Sanford. Is this a town?"

"Yes. Why do you ask?"

"Near Gainesville?"

"No, Gainesville is north from here. Sanford is northeast, and not quite as far. Do you know people in Gainesville?"

"No, I am just heading in that direction... north."

Ransom Woodleigh's interest was peaked.

"Listen, my boy. If you are asking these questions with respect to needing directions, I would be most happy to assist you. However, to do that properly would require my knowing something of your plans. Now, you say you are heading north. Is that north to Gainesville?... or north beyond Gainesville?"

Red Hand had already decided to be truthful with Mr. Woodleigh. There was no one else.

"Beyond... to the Canadas."

"To Canada! My good fellow, you do have plans!"

"I am being followed... guards from The Stockyard."

"I see..." Woodleigh contemplated this for a minute. An escapee. But dangerous?... hardly. The lad had rescued me. "Then we do need to get you moving as soon as possible, don't we? You said Canada. Any particular place in Canada?"

"No. Just out of this country, where they can no longer hunt for me."

"Well, my boy, I would advise you to travel with me tonight then. The 11:33 to Sanford is going to get you out of here a lot quicker than the 3:10 to Gainesville. And from Sanford you can switch trains and travel non-stop to Jacksonville, then Savannah. As you may or may not know, most trains going north travel through the central part of Georgia... to Atlanta. Staying along the coast should throw off anyone who might be following, at least for the time being."

The boy paused before answering, searching for a sign he could trust. It came from the man's eyes.

"We must hurry, lad. By my grandfather's watch, we have only eight minutes to reach the point where the track turns. That's the only place these old bones will allow me to jump on."

Red Hand was sure. "Let us go."

*

Ransom Woodleigh III had been right, Red Hand thought after the two had successfully jumped the 11:33 out of Haines City to Sanford, the boy grabbing the older man by his collar, half dragging him aboard a boxcar before they rode the remaining two and a half hours up the line comfortably and without disturbance. The train yard in Sanford looked much like the one in Haines City, but it didn't surprise the boy, thinking all of the white's train yards must look the same, just like all of their towns, all of their wooden houses.

"We had better get moving, my boy. The 2:12 to Jacksonville is half way across the yard, and it would be better if we caught it outside of town. However, that is looking chancy. I'm not as spry as I once was."

"Which way," said the youth.

"That way," replied Woodleigh as Red Hand prepared to jump, "wait, wait, look before you leap. There are bulls in these yards. If they catch you, you'll wish they hadn't."

The boy looked, then leaped, with Woodleigh right behind pointing the way to the far side of the yard and the embarkation point of the next train taking them farther up the line. They danced through the heavy iron, Red Hand marvelling at the immensity of the cars silhouetted against the night sky, each one like the next, silent, waiting. But soon, he told himself, one of them would be transporting him at speeds no horse could travel, taking him to the far reaches of the north... to the Canadas, and to freedom.

"Hold on, son," Woodleigh whispered, grabbing Red Hand's arm, "there's a bull in the yard."

The two slid beneath the flat car in front of them, waiting while one of the guards sauntered between the line of cars swinging his night stick back and forth, back and forth, his other hand hanging loosely by his side next to his revolver. He was heading their way, and he was in no hurry.

"We've got to get going," Woodleigh whispered, "we have only four minutes before the 2:12 pulls out. I'm afraid we'll have to catch it in the yard."

"Wait here," the boy told him.

Red Hand slid away, crawling under the cars farther down the line towards the guard. It was less than a minute when Woodleigh heard only the faintest scuffle, and only for an instant, then saw the boy reappear.

"Let us go."

The older man shook his head slightly as they heard the huff and puff of the engine, wheels skidding and grabbing track followed by the clank of iron against iron, one car coupling after the next like elephants in a circus locking together trunk to tail before they saw the Jacksonville Flyer inching away.

"Make a run for it, lad," and with that Ransom Woodleigh III bolted toward the next to last car. For a moment, Red Hand was taken aback by the man's temerity, then smiling he took off after him and once again grabbed the back of his collar before the both of them leaped into the car crashing to the floor laughing like school boys.

*

Over the next six hours as they sped north through towns like Bunnell and St. Augustine they spoke of one thing or another — the lay of the land, the towns ahead, what to expect farther on — mostly questions Red Hand was interested in, with Woodleigh doing his best to accommodate him. The boy appreciated his companion's knowledge of the comings and goings of the great iron horse, and now felt comfortable with the task that lay before him once Woodleigh reached his own destination up the line, wherever that may be.

They felt the train slowing about 8:00 o'clock when Woodleigh promptly announced he was famished and asked Red Hand if he would like to join him for the morning repast, since they had a good two hours to wait for the 10:08 to Savannah. When the boy hesitated, Woodleigh reassured him, "it's one of the finer hobo jungles... a group of hardy vagabonds like myself, harmless, save for their bluntness when inviting a newcomer to their midst. Dare I say, you will pass judgment lad." With that he slid back the door of the boxcar, perched himself on the edge and motioned, "shall we?"

Red Hand grabbed his rifle and scooted over by the open door, jumping just after Woodleigh, landing on his feet in a slow jog. His partner didn't quite make the jump, tearing his trousers and skinning a knee as he landed on all fours.

"Thank you young man," Woodleigh stated after Red Hand helped him to his feet. "Now, follow me, it's just over here."

About thirty meters off they approached grassy dunes, much like those found along the coastline only a few miles distant. However these had nettled scrub growing through them which could grab an arm or leg or piece of your cheek or lip, scratch you to bleeding and leave you stinging for some time after. Woodleigh warned Red Hand about it as soon as they started through a narrow path cut through to the other side. About halfway along Woodleigh smiled, "mmm, smell that? I believe breakfast is served."

*

Shortstuff was the first to spot them. He was sitting on a log across from the fire directly facing the path that led to the camp. Shortstuff liked that particular log, liked to see who was coming and going before they saw him, if he could manage it. Up and down the line the practice had saved his backside more than once, and he was under no illusions there'd be more times ahead. But on this fine morning a smile crossed his face revealing a sparse gathering of teeth stained from tobacco.

"Say, fellas, look who's a comin' ta breakfas'. I swar to Jesus his timin' is as good as the 2:10 to Lake City. Howdy, Socrates. Hungry?"

"Top of the morning to you, Shortstuff, and to the rest of you crosstie walkers. Yes I am, famished actually, but first let me introduce you to a friend who of late dispatched himself, single-handedly I might add, from The Stockyard down on the Okeechobee, then saved my bacon back in Haines City for good measure."

Only now did the other three men turn to look at Red Hand. They'd all heard of the prison, but not of any who'd escaped, and they were impressed even if it didn't show. As they eyeballed the youth more closely, Woodleigh made the introductions.

"Gentlemen, this is Red Hand, residing of late with family and friends of the Sioux Indian nation in South Dakota until his unfortunate circumstance brought him here to us."

Then indicating to Red Hand the men who either stood or sat before him around the campfire, "lad, meet Shortstuff, or The Watchman as we sometimes call him for his keen sense of survival; Billy Banjo, he may strike up a tune for us later if he's so inclined; Porkchop, who never met a pig he wouldn't make a meal of; and last but certainly not least, Bouncer, for obvious reasons of which even the bulls take note."

Red Hand wasn't sure of the proper protocol within such a circle of men, whether to shake hands all around, say hello or howdy in the manner of the whites, or just what. So he nodded slightly, adding in much the same way Woodleigh might have, "nice to make your acquaintence."

The men hesitated for only a moment before chuckling loud enough to embarrass the boy, with Billy adding, "he's been hangin' roun' you too much, Socrates, that's a plain fact."

"Maybe so... maybe so. Here you go, Pork," tossing Porkchop a large, red bell pepper, "throw that in with the mully."

The men chuckled again as Porkchop, who was shoving a concoction of wild leeks and onions, white potatoes, sour dock and red beans around an iron skillet quickly cut up the pepper and added it to the pot. Then he motioned to Red Hand, "come on over here, young fella, an' pull up a stump. This here's one of a 'bo's hardiest meals... mulligan stew. An' it's pret' ne'r ready."

Over the next hour the men ate while comparing stories of new faces, old friends... alive and dead, jobs available here and there, towns friendly, towns not, one thing or another that had Red Hand fascinated with the seeming pointlessness of it all. Between stories, he was trying to figure out the 'why of it...' why these men choose to remain in their present state of life. How they got here, the boy figured, would probably make for some very interesting listening, but the 'why of it' had him baffled.

Bouncer, who hadn't said a word, looked over at the boy after Shortstuff had made another wisecrack which was his wont and said, "jes' where the hell you headed, boy?" Bouncer didn't dislike Red Hand, he just needed to know where the lad stood, not from any keen sense of interest, more for his own comfort. After all, a stranger's just that, no matter how highly recommended.

After looking at Bouncer more closely, Red Hand judged him to be a direct man, no ill intent to his question which the boy liked, so he answered, "I am going to the Canadas. A man was killed when I escaped, so others will be coming."

The big man grunted. It was explanation enough.

"What about you?"

The question took Bouncer off guard, as well as the rest of the men.

"What about me what?" Bouncer retorted.

"Where are you headed?"

The big man looked at the boy again and saw only a search for an answer to a larger question in his mind, something the boy had not been able to answer for himself, so he chose his words carefully.

"I'm headed here an' there. We're all headed here an' there. But I got a feelin' 'at ain't what yer askin', is it son?. Yer askin' the 'why of it.' "

"I am."

"Well 'at there's another story, one I s'pose we all have diff'rnt reasons fer, an' I got mine, 'ats fer sure. So I'll tell ye, lad. Haven't ev'r tol' nobody, but I'll tell ye... tell all o' ye.

"Twas'nt 'at long ago, maybe ten, twelve years, I had what ye might call a conventional life... wife, two kids... boys, ev'n a dog aroun' the place. Then one day comin' home from the mines I seen a bunch o' neighbors roun' the house an' I don' know what's goin' on. I git a mite closer I see the sheriff, some o' the women holdin' each other, some cryin' an' such, so I come a runnin'. Well, the short of it is," and here Bouncer takes a deep breath, "one o' the other men, an odd sort who couldn't hold down a job... he'd come ov'r ta the house half drunk an' started botherin' the misses. Well, she ain't goin' t'ave none o' that, an' she goes after 'im with a kitchen knife near as anyone c'n figure. The boys musta jumped in too, though they were only sev'n an' nine at the time, an' he panics and pulls a gun an'..." Bouncer pauses again, looking down now to avoid eye contact, then simply states, "he got 'em all... jus' started shootin'."

Red Hand was transfixed... and stunned, as were the rest of the men. They'd not heard Bouncer's story before. It was common enough for men to share stories of their lives before they took to the rails. But if someone didn't offer, you didn't ask. It was enough to know they all had one, and leave it there.

"What happened to him?" the boy wanted to know. They all wanted to know, but the boy asked.

"Shot hisself."

Bouncer just stared now at nothing in particular, stared straigth ahead, eyes glazed, thinking back, remembering. "But 'at don't 'xactly answer yer question, do it son? The why of it is... 'at time did it fer me. Buryin' ma family... drinkin' a year off ma life... finally jes walkin' away from 'at town and jumpin' the first freight I seen. Know one thing. Don' want any mo' relations... any mo' family. No strings. Couldn't do it agin. I'd shoot m'self like he done. Almos' did."

Bouncer looked at Red Hand directly now. "Been on the move since, ridin' the rails... walkin' these backroads an' byways. I'll do that 'til ma time's up." Then the big man looked away again, stating barely in a whisper, "maybe then I'll git ta see..." and his voice trailed off leaving a silence that lingered while the men and the boy gathered in his story, and thought of their own.

*

Woodleigh and Red Hand were heading north again, sitting within the shelter of their own boxcar complete with a half dozen bales of hay to make the ride about as comfortable as it comes. They'd said little since breaking camp an hour earlier with the others, careful to wash out the plates and pans in a nearby stream and stash them away before they left. This was a popular spot to camp, and it was appreciated by all who passed by to have something which to eat off.

Rolling through the village of Kingsland, Red Hand asked his companion, "what did you think of the story?" The boy was curious, but more than that he found he was becoming much more direct when his curiosity got the better of him. It wasn't his nature to be direct. It wasn't the Indian way. In fact, in most instances it was considered downright impolite. But it seemed to the boy such frankness was acceptable in the white world. Certainly it was a much more efficient way to satisfy one's curiosity. So Red Hand asked.

"You had not heard the story?"

"No, I hadn't. Bouncer had not spoken of such things as far as I was aware. But then, it really doesn't matter, does it? It's enough to know we've all had some unfortunate circumstance, like yourself, that has since led us to where we are and what we are today."

"Bouncer is lonely."

"We're all lonely... or alone."

"Why are you called Socrates?" The boy was gathering his nerve, wanting to learn as much as possible about the man who'd taken him under wing, guiding him north.

"Well, my boy, in another time many centuries ago a man named Socrates was a great philosopher, and much of what he observed is still widely admired today. So, I suppose the boys call me that because I, too, am a philosopher... of sorts."

"A philosopher?"

"Yes, a... thinker of things. I enjoy observing certain earthly phenomena, such as how a sparrow feeds her young, or a caterpillar metamor... changes into a butterfly, or the movement of the clouds upon a gentle breeze. I believe in each of these there is a lesson to be learned... that is, if one pays close attention."

"You are like an old one of our tribe, a great thinker, and a healer. He is called Santin."

"A medicine man?"

"Like a medicine man... a shaman, with great powers to see into worlds we know not."

"I'm afraid I can't look into the beyond, Red Hand, but I do enjoy the small pleasures of this life. I could watch them all day long, and I do. It keeps my sanity intact."

"Sanity?"

"It keeps me from going crazy."

"I see." The boy now understood. Woodleigh, like Bouncer, had a story of his own, one which had driven him to the brink of insanity, then finally to the hobo life: pick up and go, don't look back, don't really look forward... just far enough ahead to satisfy the needs of the flesh... hour to hour, day to day.

The thing was, Red Hand considered, every hobo every once in a while, either too drunk to help himself or too sad to care, had to look back to whatever it was made him give up on society, choosing to live only on its edges. A man like Woodleigh, a philosopher, he surely must have looked back... probably more than once. So he continued with his questions.

"What is your story, Socrates? Why do you run?"

*

The train was pulling into Princeton Station, another six hundred or so miles up the line from where Red Hand and Ransom Woodleigh had parted company just outside of Savannah. Socrates had told the boy to take the trains heading for the major cities directly north — Columbia and Raleigh in the Carolinas, on up through Richmond, Virginia, Washington D.C., Baltimore, Philadelphia, then on to Newark.

"When you pull into that train yard, just find the first train heading due north for Canada, most likely to Montreal, locate that track and you're a free man," then he'd devised a plan for the boy to reach his goal successfully, a plan he'd used on several occasions before he became familiar with the comings and goings of every freight from the Florida Keys to Bangor, Maine.

First, Woodleigh had secured a map of the Eastern U.S., with all the major cities duely noted. After pointing out the route he advised the boy to take, he circled the cities on the map with a quill and made Red Hand memorize the names. Next, he jotted down adjacent to each the time of day or night when another train would be leaving for the next city he'd circled up the line. This was only for stops where the boy would have to change trains. To find the right one leaving the yard, Red Hand would have to enter the station, watch the board until he saw his train listed, then before it left, find another leaving sooner on the same track, jump it, then jump off before the switch and wait for his.

"Be careful when you're in the station. Make every attempt not to look suspicious. By that I mean, dust yourself off and slick back your hair, tuck in your shirt, and if you can, pick up a newspaper and pretend to be reading it while you're waiting for your track listing. The police are everywhere, and if they catch you hoboing, even just think it, they'll haul you in and ask questions later."

"Are you going to Pembroke, Socrates?"

Woodleigh had a look in his eye Red Hand saw, for the first time, had a glimmer of hope. "Yes... yes, I think I will. I'll be catching the 12:40 to Pembroke just after you leave for Columbia." Then he took the boy's hand firmly in his own. "Good luck to you, lad. Travel safely. Farewell."

"And you, Ransom Woodleigh."

*

"Princeton Station!..." The voice of the line conductor announcing the train's arrival pierced the morning air, and Red Hand was content in the knowledge gained from other stops at the smaller towns and villages they would be here for no more than twenty minutes. So the boy leaned back in a dank corner of the car, and thought about Ransom Woodleigh, how he'd been on the move since the great war between the states, how for thirty years he'd been living in his own words a life without reward, a life less than a man's...

— There was smoke billowing skyward everywhere it seemed, all throughout Georgia in the latter part of '64. Sherman had burned Atlanta in early fall, and ever since had been pushing southeast virtually unobstructed towards Savannah...

burning, looting, ravaging the land and much of the populace along the way. Of the three remaining Confederate forces in the vicinity of the city, General Wheeler had taken his men and worked his way down from Macon to set up a defensive near Statesboro, skirmishing with the Union's cavalry when he got the chance.

"This is where I joined the fray, my boy. My father and I had a small farm outside Pembroke, only twenty miles south of Statesboro, and in a direct path to Savannah. Most of the local chaps had joined Wheeler's men, so I did as well, although I admit I felt I had not the stomach for it. We'd all heard and seen some of the war's horrors by that time... tales of the thousands killed in single engagements, limbless men like the walking dead, certainly nothing I had any desire to entertain. However, the impetuosity of youth and the pressure of one's peers can make a young man do what he might otherwise not do."

"Did your father join you as well?"

"I dare say he would have. He was a fighter, but he had passed on two years earlier. The doctors said it was the whiskey and cigars, however I've always felt he missed my mother more than he knew.

"After that, I took over the farm and was actually making a go of it... mostly Sea Island cotton, some sugar and corn. We'd been supplying the troops since the war began like most of the farms, so I had not been summoned to duty. Although the days were long and at times hard, they were not so hard as to mitigate time for leisure activities. Mine lay over the hill on the adjacent farm. Her name was Emma. She was tall and slender, hazel eyes, light hair... almost blond, and with a way about her that captured my very soul. We had been stealing away and holding hands ever since I can remember, but when the war came calling everything changed... along with one's sense of duty. One evening walking the ridgeline between our two farms I told her I was joining up... that Sherman was advancing towards the valley. She was beside herself, but I was determined. I had to go, I told her, however foreign it felt to me, I must."

"Where is she now?"

"The last I heard... the last I saw, still there."

"You have seen this woman?"

"Yes, about three years ago. I was heading up to Macon for no particular reason than I hadn't seen it in some time. Passing through the old neighborhood, something just came over me. I grabbed my knapsack and jumped out of the car about five miles from the old place. I almost killed myself as well... that engineer must have been traveling close to twenty miles-an-hour going around the turn."

"When did you see the woman?"

"First, I went by our old farm and to my surprise it was still there, partially anyway... most of the main house and part of one barn. Standing there again, on that ground I had not seen for nearly thirty years, well my boy, I was so shaken I nearly fell over. I had to catch myself on the limb of a tree, then just crumpled to the ground for what seemed like hours, drifting back to those times.

"It wasn't until I was leaving I got the notion to see the Monroe place. That was where Emma had lived with her folks. It was only a short distance from ours, about two miles over the next hill, so I headed off in that direction expecting much the same. After cresting the hill that looked down into the little valley where their farm had stood, I was nearly knocked off my feet once again.

"It was twilight, the end of the day, and the men were just coming in from the fields. The place was well manicured, just as Emma's father had always kept it, and there were three or four fine saddle horses in the south corral. Then... then she came out of the house and stood on the front porch speaking with what looked like the foreman. They stood talking for quite a while... and I... I just sank to my knees... and watched. It was all I could do to keep from bawling like a child." After a while Woodleigh added, "finally I just got up and walked away, like I had thirty years before."

"You had done this before?"

"Yes, just after my first and last encounter as a soldier in the Confederate army. As I mentioned, I had joined General Wheeler's troops. In early December, we were camped near Waynesboro, not far from the Ogeechee River. We had gotten word of the Union advance and so rallied to a place called Rocky Point to engage them. In the following day and night, all my fears were realized. The battle was bloody and relentless. I saw things I can barely relate today, but worst of all, I... I did nothing. At each encounter, I was frozen with fear. I couldn't escape it... I buried my head beneath my hands, or tucked tail and ran, at every opportunity. The final encounter, when we were driven back to Waynesboro, I turned and ran again, and this time didn't stop until I reached home, nearly that is. A quarter of a mile away, I saw a company of Union soldiers setting up camp around the place, officers parading in and out of the house as if they owned it, and for all that mattered at the time, they did. Well, I just kept running... all the way to Emma's folks place. When I arrived at the top of the hill looking down, it seemed peaceful, like I had seen it on so many occasions. But considering events as they were, I felt I should investigate. As I started down the road it struck me, and I realized I couldn't do it... couldn't face her. What would I tell her?... what could I say?... I ran from the gunfire while so many around me were fighting and dying?... I ducked my head and wimpered like a child?... no, all I could think to do was walk away. But before I turned to go, she came out of the house with her father, onto the front porch. After they had talked for a few moments and her father had gone back inside, she suddenly looked in my direction. I had barely enough time to duck behind some shrubs. I watched as she continued to look up the road, as if waiting for someone to arrive. Only when the sun had completely set did she turn to go inside."

The youth pondered Woodleigh's story for some time before he said, "I have heard many stories of battle, from great warriors who fought the bluecoats. Many of them said the first time they rode against the Long Hair, they feared his sword. Then later, they killed him, on the day of my birth."

The statement startled Woodleigh. He looked at the boy more closely now. Yes, he thought, the lad would be about twenty years of age, just about the time Custer was killed.

"Do you mean General Custer, of the 7th Cavalry?... at the Little Big Horn River?"

"Yes, I am Red Hand, given this name by my mother, Willow, who bore me on the morning of the great battle. Many braves who feared the Long Hair before that day feared him no longer. They knew in their hearts what they must do."

"Yes, I know what you mean, my boy. I understand that... now. I have thought of those times more than I would care to, and more than once I wished I had another opportunity to prove, if only to myself, I could stand up like any man. But those days are gone, and I'm afraid I've been running for so long I don't know any other way."

"Maybe you have another chance. Maybe it's the woman."

"What do you mean?"

"Your war is over. But your fear is not. Face her. Let whatever happens between you and the woman bring peace to your spirit."

*

"Check ev'ry car... ya nev'r know where he might be a hidin'." It was Jimmy Tarver.

After the warden had discovered Jasper's body in a shallow grave under one of the barracks, he'd given in and allowed Jimmy to take three men and go off after Red Hand. The warden didn't like Jimmy much, just as he'd not been fond of Jasper, but a state employee had been killed and he had to make every effort to apprehend the culprit. So after a day of constant badgering by Jimmy and another guard named Springer, the warden had ok'd the chase.

"Damn, warden, ev'r minute we set here yammerin' he's makin' time!"

"All right, all right, Jimmy... you two take Butts and Critter an' the four of you have at it. But if the trail don't warm after a week er so, you git yer behinds back here, understan'?"

"Yessir, we sure will."

The warden knew they'd probably not find hide nor hair of the boy. He'd noticed the lad from the beginning, and watched him closely over the next few weeks. He was smart... helping those he could, particularly the old man, without drawing too much attention to it. He ate what he was given and did his work without objection. There was one other thing the warden remembered... the boy seemed to be constantly surveying his surroundings. The warden's assumption the boy was preoccupied with escape was correct, and when it happened it didn't surprise him. And now, frankly, he didn't particularly care if Red Hand wasn't caught and hauled back. The fact was, the warden had less than two years to go before his retirement and subsequent move back to his native Arkansas... and three of his favorite fishing holes.

*

"Ev'ry car, Nat. I want you an' Critter ta start back at tha far end agin. Me an' Butts'll take tha oth'rn. Now let's git to it."

The four guards had gotten a line on the kid from an itinerant named Smokey unfortunate enough to get himself waylayed just outside of Darien. He'd spent the previous night jawing with Shortstuff and Billy Banjo at another hobo camp, and they'd told him about Red Hand, a nice enough kid it seemed who'd been traveling with Socrates, making his way up to Canada after escaping from The Stockyard. Jimmy Tarver and his men were lucky enough to call on the authorities at Darien Station where Smokey was spending the night. On a hunch, the guards figured the boy was heading pretty much due north, and Darien was one of the hook ups on the quickest line in that direction.

"We got us a poor bastard locked up fer the night," the head bull had told Jimmy, "maybe you boys wanna talk with 'im."

It wasn't long before Jimmy had beaten enough tar out of old Smokey that he'd related his encounter with Shortstuff and Billy, what he knew about the boy, and that he would've advised him like Socrates had done. That was good enough for Jimmy and he and his boys caught the next train north to Columbia, checking in with the depot agents at every stop, making sure they were on the best line north, with the fastest hook ups. On a short layover in Alexandria just across the river from D.C., the station manager said they ought to catch him and pass him somewhere in Jersey.

"My guess is either Trenton er Princeton, take yer pick. But if ya wanna be sure 'bout it, go on up ta Princeton."

*

Red Hand heard Jimmy the first time. He grabbed the rifle, slipped from his hiding place and took refuge under the car just ahead. The station was bustling with people clambering aboard the first few cars as the four guards were making their way down the line. They were nearly upon him when he heard Jimmy again.

"Look un'erneath 'em cars, too."

He wedged his rifle in the draw bars pulling himself up as close as he could to the bottom of the car. Just then the train jerked forward, then a second and third time as it took up slack making its way out of the station. That's when he heard Jimmy again.

"Jump on, boys, we'll take this'n here ta the nex' stop."

He reaslized now he had no more time. The train was picking up speed. He had to take his chances and let go. When he hit, he hoped he'd hit flat and stay flat. His final thought was of Walks Over Them telling him he was the one on the day of his escape. He tried to loosen the rifle, but couldn't. Leave it, he thought... train's going faster... better let go... now.... now...

**

Tool of the Trade

Most of the early sportswriters weren't whizzes on the
gridiron, nor on the typewriter. They were hunt-and-peck
guys. The good ones, however, were whizzes with a
storyline and a 'way with words.'

Joe Cramer

The townspeople couldn't remember a funeral as large or as full with the outpouring of grief and condolences from family, friends, neighbors and complete strangers as that held for Eddie McCabe upon his return from the Far East. The mass took place at Old St. Mary's on a Friday morning beneath a blue cloudless sky, the sun shining brilliantly casting its light through large stained glass that lined the church walls marking the Way of the Cross. The mourners inside numbered five-hundred, with nearly as many spilling over the front steps out onto the sidewalk where two large speakers had been set up so all could hear the proceedings.

When the hour approached, Father Houk emerged from the sacristy and made his way to the altar. As he surveyed those seated before him, his eyes settled first on Eddie's casket with the Stars and Stripes draped over. Evie was in the front pew steadied on one side by her father and mother, Joe and Wendy on the other. The remainder of the McCabe and Sims families filled the next five pews... mothers, fathers, brothers and sisters, grandmas and grandpas, cousins, aunts and uncles. Directly behind them were Eddie's company commander, Lieutenant Gonsalves, along with two other high ranking Army officers with ribbons and medals covering their chests. Sitting shoulder to shoulder in the next two rows, the good father studied the somber faces of the 1967 Franklin High football squad... less six members of the defense positioned across the aisle as pall bearers, and Dave Delmon who was still in Viet Nam somewhere along the Mekong Delta. Then, raising his arms in praise to the Lord, robes flowing to the floor, Father Houk commenced the service.

After high mass lasting an hour and fifteen minutes followed by the Franklin High choir's inspired rendition of On Eagles Wings, silence filled the church. A child's voice asking for her bottle and the faint shuffling of feet broke the stillness as Gordon Parry stood and walked slowly to the lectern. It did not go unnoticed that after adjusting the microphone, he paused, composing himself. He spoke briefly, eloquently, reminding those in attendance of the fragility of life, particularly for those of us who at times seem indestructible. Death is near, he said, it is a simple fact to be remembered daily. Besides life itself, it is the one thing we all share. And because we do, we can rejoice in the knowledge we will see Eddie again, on the road ahead.

Coach Jerry Duggan was next to speak. True to character, he had come prepared with pages of notes he'd drafted and redrafted over the past three nights that had his wife, Nancy, worried about her husband for the very first time. She'd never seen him as vexed or precise about his preparation, including the state championship a year ago. But this morning she thought she noticed a little spring in his step again, and she knew then that however painful it was going to be for him, he'd get through it.

Taking the lectern, Coach genuflected making the sign of the cross, then turned and looked at the crowd. He spoke to Eddie's family members directly, paying particular attention to Evie without the remainder of those gathered feeling less a part of his eulogy. After recounting his association with Eddie from the very first day of JV Football practice three years ago, Coach settled on what, to him, set Eddie apart from the rest of the team members, although to a man, he admitted, each holds a special place in his heart.

"Eddie," he said, "was the quintessential warrior. I saw it the very first day when he stepped on the field as my middle linebacker. But like all warriors do, they put themselves at risk... put themselves in harm's way... take the hard hit." Coach paused for a moment, then went on, "that's what Eddie did... over in that jungle. But under the circumstances, I have a feeling he wouldn't have had it any other way."

He was doing fine Nancy thought, 'hang in there, honey.' But that's when she saw him waver.

Coach was choking up, not sure if he could get his final words out. He cleared his throat, raised up and stated, "Eddie... nobody can fill your spot... can't be done. Your number has been retired, and your jersey will be encased and hang in the Athletic Department... permanently." He paused one last time before adding, "I love you, Eddie... you fought the good fight... rest well."

Joe walked up the three steps to the front of the altar with a noticeable limp, his left arm in a sling, and he stood silently. Not until the voice inside of him, Eddie's voice he believed which said, 'okay, it's okay'... not until then did he begin.

"Eddie was my classmate and my best friend... and I miss him. But when I think of him, I'm going to think of the good times, because I know that's what he would want. Eddie wouldn't allow me to get all somber and depressed... he wouldn't have it... and the last thing I want is to have him come back here and straighten me out like we've all seen him do to every running back in the state of Ohio who ever tried to go off tackle." That produced a smile from everyone, even Evie, which Joe was relieved to see.

"These past three years were special... for all of us, because that's when Eddie entered our lives. And me?... I was the lucky one. When Evie didn't have him all to herself, I did. Eddie and I went to class together, played ball together, and... well... we became..." Joe's voice cracked, "brothers. Life was good. But as Dr. Parry said, it can also be fleeting. Eddie must have known that, because he didn't waste one minute of it.

"The last day we were together, it was... it was..." Joe couldn't contain himself. When he grabbed the side of the lectern for support, silently sobbing, Wendy rushed to his side, whispering, "it's okay, honey, it's okay." He looked at her and understood, for the first time really, he didn't want to live without her... couldn't live without her, and he smiled and took her hand, and felt her strength.

"The last day we were together was terrible and wonderful... at the same time. I'd never felt as close to Eddie. We were working as a team... left side, right side... but together as one." Joe paused briefly again.

"I don't know why we're eulogizing Eddie today and not me... I really don't. But I do know one thing... it's not for me to question. I did at first, but not anymore, not now... thanks to Al Sims. What happened out there to Eddie was... just life. And if for one minute you think Eddie didn't have a chance to live his life to the fullest, just ask me or Evie. He did. During the last three years Eddie lived a lifetime... his lifetime. And I thank God everyday I was lucky enough to have shared it."

Before taking his seat again, Joe put his arm around Wendy, feeling her closeness, and stated, "I love you, brother. I'll see you again."

*

"Atta boy, Joey, way to hit that hole," then turning to Joe, Dave said, "he may look like you, but he runs like Eddie."

Joe smiled at the comment as he saw his son and the rest of the Northside Bulldogs break practice when Coach Delmon blew his whistle and yelled, "all right, everybody in!

"Okay, listen up, guys, we've got a big game this week against the Southside, so tonight get your homework done early and get some sleep, all right!?"

The team answered, "yes, Coach!"

"I can't hear you!"

"YES, COACH!!"

"All right, tomorrow we'll work on technique, then Saturday..." and here Dave paused, like always, "then Saturday, we're gonna GO GET 'EM!"

The team answered again, growling, "AAARRRR!"

"We're gonna run up one side of the field and down the other!"

"AAARRR!"

"We're gonna rock 'em... we're gonna sock 'em!"

"AAARRR!"

"Then we're gonna knock the socks right off 'em!"

"AAARRR!... RUFF!... RUFF!..."

Above the barking Dave yelled, "all right, men, one lap and then that's it for today!"

"RUFF!... RUFF!... AAARRR!..." as the team circled the field still growling like bulldogs, Dave turned to Joe, "man, was that fun. Remember that, Joe?... when we were that age?... I never had so much fun."

"You're one-hundred percent right on that one, Coach," adding, "say, you and Evie are coming over after the game for a barbecue, right?"

Dave nodded, "right, I was told this morning."

"Good. See you Saturday."

*

The first six months after Eddie's funeral were the dark days. Al and Betty Sims watched Evie closely as Doctor Hayes recommended, and when they were unable, Wendy and Joe took over. At first she seemed to be doing well. After two weeks off she went back to work at the bank, but a week later called in sick. The next week she called in sick again. When she returned she walked in to her boss's office and said, "I'm afraid I'm going to have to take some time off."

She drove home, climbed the stairs and went to her room, staying there, rarely eating. When she did eat it was just enough to satisfy the minimum her body craved. She'd lost all sense of direction... all sense of herself. Her color turned a waxen hue, her hair unkempt. The circles under her eyes made her look beyond her years, as did the tattered cotton robe she was never without. She was lost, and neither her parents nor Wendy or Joe could reach her.

During the sixth month of her self-confinement Dave Delmon returned home from the war. Joe had called and told him about Eddie almost immediately, but Dave was in the thick of it and unable to get leave to attend the funeral. He'd always regretted that, swearing to himself the first thing he'd do after getting back home was visit Evie and Eddie's folks. What was waiting for him as he pressed the front doorbell of the Sims' residence with a box of chocolates under his arm he could not have imagined.

"Hello, Mrs. Sims."

"Why, David... you look wonderful. We're all so glad to have you home. Come in, come in."

"Thank you, ma'am. Here's a little something for Evie... and you and Mr. Sims."

Why, thank you, David."

"Dave!" It was Al Sims, "great to see you! Pull up a chair. Would you like something to drink?... coca cola?... beer?..."

"I'll take a beer."

"Fine, be right back."

"Thank you, sir."

129

Al Sims hesitated. "Now Dave, I told this to Joe when he first called and I'll tell you too... no need to call me sir. I understand where you boys have been these past months. Al will do just fine. Okay?"

"Okay then."

"I'll go get us a couple of beers. Honey, you want anything?"

"No thanks."

As Al Sims turned towards the kitchen, Dave asked, "how's Evie?"

Betty Sims expression changed. He could see the concern. "She's been better."

"Do you think she's up to visiting for a while?"

"I'll go on up and see."

Al was back. "Here you go, Dave."

"Now you two go on out to the parlor and chat," Betty suggested, knowing full well that's what the men wanted. "I'll be down in a bit."

As Joe had done after his return from Viet Nam six months earlier, Dave recounted his experiences to Al Sims. He'd lost a couple of buddies near My Tho, and although it took him some time to deal with the loss, he knew it was nothing like what had happened with Eddie and Joe. Nor, he said quietly, almost reverently, could he imagine the pain Evie was going through.

"I just hope she's doing all right. If there's anything I can ever..."

Dave thought he heard Betty coming back and stopped in mid-sentence. When he turned he was shaken by the girl standing before him. He rose to his feet. "Evie?..."

"Hi, Dave."

"Evie, hello. It's... it's terrific to see you."

Her father noticed his wife had gotten her to brush her hair and put on some lipstick, and although Dave didn't know exactly what to expect, he hadn't expected this.

"It's good to see you, too, Dave."

The short silence that followed was interrupted by Betty Sims. "Honey, why don't you take Dave and go sit on the front porch. You must have so much catching up to do."

The conversation was awkward at first... small talk about school mostly... their two families being part of the few who'd been on the north side of Columbus long enough for the two of them to have gone through school together since kindergarten. Evie smiled at that, as did Dave, not knowing it was the first time she'd smiled in eight months. As the conversation continued he guessed she hadn't opened up to anyone... expressed her feelings about what had happened to Eddie... broken down completely so the healing process could begin. Late at night, lying alone in the darkness, her mind racing with thoughts of Eddie and the secrets they had shared, she'd thought about it... thought about telling someone...

"You know, Evie, I don't think I ever told you this, but I had a major crush on you since... since all the way back in third grade." She smiled again. "I did!... major crush!... but you know, all of us guys... we thought we were too tough to say anything. Fact was, we were too scared. Then sophomore year at Franklin, when I finally had the guts, well here comes Eddie and..." Dave caught himself. "Evie, I'm sorry, I didn't mean to..."

"I know, Dave." She sat quietly for a moment before the tears came. She hadn't cried in quite some time, but now, finally, she couldn't hold back... couldn't stop the pain.

Placing her hands over her face, she turned away from Dave, but he said, "that's not going to help, Evie, believe me I know. You've got to let it out... at some point, you've got to let go."

She didn't know why really, but she felt comforted by his words. He'd only reaffirmed what her folks and Wendy and Joe had been trying to tell her for months, but from Dave it felt like it was time... time to start the healing... that is, if she could be healed. She turned to him, resting her head on his shoulder. He put his arm around her, as her father might, holding her as she continued to sob, stroking her hair.

"Dave, I miss him so much..."

"I know, Evie, I know. Now you go ahead, I'm right here with you."

*

The wedding took place a year later, with many in attendance who had been at Eddie's funeral, in particular the Franklin High football squad. Joe was best man, and Wendy was Evie's matron of honor. As Dave, Joe and the rest of the ushers waited by the altar in the front of the church for the bride to enter, Wendy walked down the aisle. Joe caught her eye, and just as she had done six months earlier on their wedding day, she took his breath away. He was hopelessly in love with her, and lately had surprised even himself by telling her so... more than once.

Now, Evie entered the church, she and her father making their way towards Dave who was waiting, shifting from one foot to the other, sweating more than slightly. Joe smiled and put a hand on his shoulder, whispering, "calm down my man, she's beautiful, and she's all yours." And she was. Evie had long since reconciled her feelings for Eddie, holding forever his memory in a special place in her heart. She'd openly discussed this with Dave after the second time he'd asked her to marry him. When Dave had looked distraught by her remarks, she added, "Dave, come here... come here. I can never forget Eddie... I hope you understand that. But with all the strength I have left... I want you to know that I love you. I'm happy, Dave. I couldn't be happier." Then she kissed him softly and said, "Yes... I do, honey. I do want to marry you."

*

The Northside Columbus Bulldogs nine and ten year-old division had a perfect season that year, Coach Delmon being the first to accomplish that feat, and Joey Cramer was his best player, on both sides of the ball. The fact was, even as a nine year-old, Joey had the other coaches verifying his age to make sure he was legitimate. But there was another boy the coach couldn't wait to suit up the following year when he would turn nine. He thought he had a good chance to turn some heads like Joey, particularly since they'd been friends and playmates from the day they crawled out of the crib. His name was Eddie... Eddie Delmon.

"You boys cooking out there or just guzzling up the beer? Everything's ready in here." It was Evie.

"We're cookin', honey... and guzzlin.'"

"I hope you're not burning our dinner."

"Not a chance, steaks'll be ready in three minutes." Then Dave turned to Joe stating matter-of-factly, "you know, Joey really tore it up this year... head and shoulders best kid in the league."

"I know... he surprised me. I thought he'd be good, but I didn't expect this. And you're right, Dave, he runs like Eddie did... north and south."

"Yeah, but he's got your speed."

Joe just smiled at the thought, then added, "wait'll Eddie joins him next year. That's going to be something."

"We'll see," Dave said, "I don't want to be accused of..."

"No, no, wait a second. The coach shouldn't hold a player back worrying about what other people think. You've watched those two play together as much as me, and you think Joey's not going to have to split time with the ball?"

When he felt Wendy's arms from behind reach around his neck, he smiled again. "C'mon Dave, let's eat. We can't keep these two lovely ladies waiting forever."

*

"Was the old man there again?"

"Yes, he was, Joe. He just likes to watch practice, Dave said, that's all."

"Well, I may have to stop by one day this week, Wen, just to check him out."

"He's harmless, hon."

"I'm sure you're right, but I haven't seen the team in a week or so. I think I'll swing by tomorrow."

*

Dave didn't see Joe arrive right away. It was now only three weeks until the season opener, and he was watching his running backs work with the first team. Joey was set to start, but Eddie was pushing him just like Joe had told him. As Joe walked up, Eddie took a pitch from the quarterback on a sweep. When he saw he was bottled up, he cut back, danced away from two defenders, and sprinted upfield

133

about thirty yards before the offensive coach blew his whistle.

"What'd I tell you, Davey boy."

"Joe. How are you, man?"

"Good... good. Well?..." Joe reiterated, gesturing to Eddie.

"Okay, he looks good... real good, in fact."

Joe just smiled. "You're right, coach. Now all you gotta do is coach 'em."

Then he looked beyond Dave and the kids to the small set of stands on the far side of the practice area. In the top row he saw the old man, hands folded in his lap watching the goings on. He'd become a curiosity for both the coaches and boys, but like Wendy had told him, the old guy was harmless.

At times, the boys would wave to him or one of the coaches would say hello, and he'd reply in kind, either smiling or waving back. During practice, after a particularly good effort by one of the kids, he would stand and applaud briefly, then sit back down. After this happened a few times the coaches noticed it wasn't always when Joey or Eddie would break a long run, or catch a pass and take it the distance. It might be a cornerback tipping a pass incomplete, or a lineman throwing a timely block, or any one of the kids not giving up on a play. The old man definitely knew his football.

"Dave, how long's he been coming around?"

"Who?"

"Him," Joe said pointing to the stands.

"Oh, you've heard about him."

"Yeah, both Joey and Wendy have mentioned it."

"Since practice began... I guess about three weeks ago."

"Has anyone ever spoken to him?"

"Not as I remember, Joe... just an old guy probably reliving his youth."

"Well, anyway, I think I'll go on over..." and as he looked up toward the stands again, the old man was gone. Joe was baffled. The field was enormous, with the stands and practice area out in the middle away from any shelter or trees... nothing. How could the old guy have vanished so quickly? And he stared into the distance, surveying the farthest point of the field and parking lot beyond, but saw no trace, no sign of him, only the sun beginning to set as the Northside Bulldogs circled the field growling, running their final lap of the day.

*

Just before their wedding, Joe and Wendy had discussed her dad's offer to have Joe join him in the car business. But it didn't feel right. Joe couldn't see himself pushing cars and trucks even though Avril Miller's Ford dealership was respected throughout the Columbus area for their honesty and fair play.

"No offense to you or your father, Wen, but I'm not a salesman. That summer after our senior year convinced me of that. I can't glad-hand people everyday. It's not my nature."

"Then what, hon?"

"Remember all those letters we sent each other when I was in Nam?"

"How could I forget?"

Joe liked that. "Well, I found I enjoyed writing them, I mean the actual composition as well as what I was trying to say. I think I'd like to pursue that... writing, I mean."

"That sounds good, honey."

"My plan is to go on down to the paper and see if I can catch on, maybe as a cub reporter or writing the want ads or something while I go to State and study journalism. If I work hard, I can still graduate in four years."

"What about playing ball?"

"That ended back in the jungle."

"I thought the doc said..."

"I know, the doc said there's a chance my leg will be a hundred percent, but I'm not counting on it. It hasn't felt any better the last three months."

"Are you okay with that?" She was hoping he would be. They'd gone to a few college games since his return, and she didn't want Joe taking the pounding those boys did.

"I am, Wen, I am. I had a good run in high school. It was just one of those things... where that bullet hit me. Could have happened to..." and Joe caught himself, as he did more than once in recent months.

"Honey," she pulled him close to her, "like Evie's dad said, it was just Eddie's time, that's all. No one's to blame."

"I know, it's just sometimes I feel like he's right here, right next to me... close enough so I might still be able to..."

"Honey, don't. Like you said at the funeral... remember the good times. That's what Eddie would want."

*

"So you want to be a newspaperman?"

Joe was sitting across the desk from Spencer Billings, editor of the Columbus Dispatch. Wendy's dad had gotten him the interview since his car dealership placed two-thousand dollars in advertising every month with the paper. But as Spencer Billings had explained to his best advertiser, 'I'll see the boy, Av, but I won't guarantee he gets a job... that wouldn't be right.'

"Yes, sir. I'll be going to the U. in the fall studying journalism. I'm getting married next month, too, so I'm serious about it. I'll have a family to take care of."

"I see." Then Spencer Billings raised his eyebrows some as he was scanning the second page of Joe's resume. "Ah, you were in Viet Nam?... and decorated."

"Yes, sir." Joe didn't offer more.

"Very impressive, Mr. Cramer." Joe Cramer, Spencer Billings was thinking now... Viet Nam... then he remembered... the funeral almost a year ago about the two local boys... one was killed over there, one survived. "Are you the Joe Cramer?..."

"Yes, sir."

"And what was the other lad's name?... Eddie..."

"Eddie McCabe."

"Yes, Eddie McCabe. I remember the story, now. You know, I wasn't much of a sports fan then, but two years ago when you and Eddie were playing at Franklin... well, the buzz was so great about your exploits I had to go see for myself. It was the state championship game, and you two won me over on the spot. I haven't missed a Franklin game since."

"That's good to hear, sir."

"Very sad about Eddie. From what I heard, he was a fine young man."

"The best."

Spencer Billings saw this was becoming difficult for Joe, so he changed the subject. "Will you do something for me, just so I can feel comfortable about hiring you, because that's what I fully intend to do."

Joe straightened up in his seat, "why, yes sir."

"Jimmy Dilford writes the high school column for us. He's a capable young man, but I do believe he could use some assistance. At times his take on a game doesn't have that little something extra, that spark that would make it original... make it its own. You know what I mean, Joe?"

"Yes, I do, sir."

"Well, then, I'm going to have Jimmy give you your first assignment... kind of a test, which I will strongly suggest to be covering the Wildcat's pre-season football practices. You know, which starters are back... who the team leaders are... how the competition looks... that sort of thing. Think you can handle that?"

"Definitely, sir." Joe's excitement filled the editor's office. "When do I start?"

"Expect to hear from Jimmy tomorrow."

"I will. Thank you, sir. I can't wait."

After Joe had left and Mrs. Milligan had come in to see if her boss needed anything before lunch, he said, "did you notice the young man who just left, Doris?"

"Yes, I did."

"I have a feeling we're going to be seeing a lot of him around here."

*

Joe's career with the paper took off with his first article on Franklin's upcoming season. In fact, it was the first of four articles, each in succession going more in depth than the one before... player by player, position by position. This was the idea he'd presented to Jimmy Dilford two days after his interview with Spencer Billings. Jimmy said, okay, but first he'd have to run it by the boss. Joe figured that wouldn't be a problem. Since he graduated only two years earlier, he knew half the players already, and the one's he didn't... well, Spencer Billings figured they'd like nothing better than to meet the best player ever to come out of Franklin. When Joe heard the same thing that first day from some of the sophomores, he corrected them, saying, one of the two best... so far.

School started for him in the fall at State and Joe kept right on working at the paper like he'd told Wendy. These were the tough years, only because they didn't have all the time together they would've liked. While Joe was in class or at the paper or studying, Wendy was working a full day at the bank, then tending to the chores around the house... their house right now being a two-bedroom apartment near campus. Wendy was excited about one thing... Evie was coming back to work at the bank. Over lunch at Pete's Pub with Wendy, Evie said she'd called Mr. Ossening asking if her old job was still waiting for her.

"What did he say?"

"He harumphed like he does... you know, Wen, then he said, 'your job, young lady, has been waiting for you since the day you left, and will still be waiting for you until the day I'm fired.' Then he added... 'and as you may know, Ms. Sims, I can't be fired because it's my bank.' "

Wendy smiled, knowing that beyond his sometimes gruff exterior, Mr. Ossening was like everyone's favorite uncle. "Evie, that's great. When do you start?"

"Monday."

"Come over for dinner Saturday, can you? Afterwards, we'll talk about stuff at the bank. I've gotta fill you in on all the gossip. Joe's usually studying then anyway."

"I don't know, Wen... I..."

"What is it?"

"I kind of have a date... sort of."

"What!... who?!"

"Dave."

"Dave?... Dave Delmon?!"

"Yes, Dave and I've been spending time together. He came to see me when he got back. You remember, Wen, that was my really down period. But since that very first day I've always felt so comfortable with him... like he understood... the way I felt, and feel now..." and Evie explained how she and Dave's relationship had evolved, almost unnoticed, from being just good friends to someone she looked forward to seeing more and more. This coming Saturday?... well, she was counting the days, doing anything she could think of... cook, clean, wash the clothes, do the ironing. Her parents were so delighted with her renewed sparkle they actually went to dinner one evening, sneaking out to their favorite hideaway, and coming home later than usual... cooing like lovebirds.

"What are you two going to do Saturday?"

"We haven't decided yet."

"Then come over. We'll barbecue, the boys can talk, we can talk... Joe hasn't seen Dave in eons... they'll love it. Evie, it'll do you good... it'll do us all some good."

Evie hesitated only slightly before agreeing, "all right, I'll call Dave and ask him."

That Saturday was the beginning of many barbecues the Cramers and soon-to-be Delmons were to have over the years. While at first Dave seemed slightly uncomfortable among the four of them, over time Eddie's memory became more palpable. Small anecdotes about him would surface in conversation, which was healthy for them all. In fact, the first to remark so was Evie.

One evening, when a full Ohio moon filled the sky above the trellis of Joe's and Wendy's back porch, and the four of them were reminiscing, she remembered how Eddie had forgotten to pick up her Dad at the mechanics after he'd dropped his car off for service one day. Eddie would pass right by there on his way over, so he'd said, sure, it wouldn't be a problem to give her Dad a ride home. Well, he forgot, and by the time he got to the house, Evie's father had been waiting for over a half an hour, twiddling his thumbs outside of Barney's Auto Repair.

"As Eddie walked in the door, you should have seen the look on his face when Mom asked him where Dad was," Evie said, chuckling. "He looked like the cat that swallowed the canary, with the feathers still flying."

They were all dying, remembering some of the gaffs Eddie was famous for. But when the laughing subsided, and Evie looked at Dave and smiled, then reached for his hand... that was the time they'd all waited for, the time they prayed would come. Evie was now officially back among the living... and Dave was as real to her as

Eddie had ever been.

*

Joe had just finished his first year of school and he and Wendy were excited. Along with the raise he'd gotten at the paper, and Wendy's promotion at the bank, they could begin saving for a house.

"Let's celebrate," she said. "Let's go out to dinner, hon, it's been a month... at least." Then she looked at him with those eyes of hers, sliding up close on the devan, kissing him slowly, softly, before whispering, "I'll buy."

"Oh, you will... with what?" he asked.

"I just stole some money."

"You did, huh."

"From the cookie jar... and it's burnin' a hole in my pocket."

He kissed her back. "Then let's go."

*

"We're jammed," the hostess said, "it's going to be an hour or more." They were at T.J.'s, one of the Northside's more popular eateries famous for their steaks, salads, and big ol' baked potatoes. But tonight it was not to be. T.J.'s was packed.

"Let's go to Pete's, honey. We can get in there."

"It's Friday, Wen, it's going to be full of college kids."

"I know, but they'll be in the pub. We're going to eat."

He smiled.

—"Joe... Wendy... how are you two?" It was Pete.

"Great. You got a table for us, Pete. We're celebrating, and Wendy's buying. How's that for a great wife?"

Giving Wendy a peck on the cheek, Pete winked, "If I was twenty years younger, Joe, you'd be in trouble. Come on kids, follow me."

They had the usual... Wendy, the fettuccini with baby clams in a rich cream sauce, and Joe the Pub's special meatloaf with mashed potatoes and gravy. They split a house salad, which was big, but Joe ate most of it like always. Over ice cream after, they were back on the subject of a house. Joe figured they'd be able to save a hundred dollars a month, starting next month. By the time he graduated, adding in one more raise, they'd have enough for a downpayment, particularly if their folks kicked in like they promised.

"All we've got to do is keep working hard, Wen, and stay focused."

"You sound like Dave, coaching the kids."

"I guess I do... but it's true. Hey, I'm stuffed, let's go," then he grabbed her around the waist after they'd gotten up, pulling her close and whispering, "but I'm not tired."

Joe guided Wendy through the pub on their way towards the back door to the parking lot. Over the din of students letting off a week's steam, he heard a voice. "Hey, check her out?"

Joe glanced to his left and saw four guys standing at the bar. The smallest was about his height, but thicker. Joe recognized him as State's second string tailback. He and part of the offensive line were out for the evening... carousing.

"Fine looking woman. Tell me, hotshot, just how fine is she?"

Joe considered his next move. Should they keep walking? Should he ignore the insult? He thought not, letting go of Wendy's arm.

"Don't worry, Wen, I'll be all right."

The crowd around moved back a step now as Joe faced the tailback.

"I recognize you. You're Kyle Tork, right? I remember playing against you in high school for the state championship. You had a bad attitude then, too. That cheap shot you took in the fourth quarter cost your team six, but that wasn't what lost you the game. Remember? Eddie stuffed you all night long. What was it?... five tackles behind the line of scrimmage?..."

The tailback didn't like Joe. He'd been reminded too many times that if Joe, or Eddie, had gone to State right out of high school, he'd be riding the pine permanently. He slowly clenched his fist and was about to raise it when he felt a hand grab his wrist. Joe's grip was strong, much stronger than he'd anticipated. The tailback tried to raise his arm, but it wouldn't budge. He was sweating now.

"Now apologize to my wife."

The tailback looked behind him. His three linemen just stared at him like they do most times after he'd carried the ball. The dumb bastard juked wrong again.

He looked at Joe. There was silence in the bar as the sweat poured from his brow, and he muttered, "sorry."

"Not me. My wife."

Louder, he stated, "sorry, miss... ma'am, I apologize."

It was only then Joe loosened his grip and backed away. He waited some seconds, then took Wendy's arm again. "One more thing," he said to the tailback as he turned to walk out, "you could be starting, if you ever learned how to play."

*

Three months later, with two-hundred dollars in their "house account" Wendy had opened at the bank, they got their second piece of good news. Joe'd gotten a promotion. Spencer Billings had come into his office one morning and said matter-of-factly, "Joe, get your things together, we need this office for our new high school writer."

Joe was taken aback. "Pa... pardon me, sir?"

"No 'pardon, me, sir' necessary. You've been promoted to the college desk. You're going to college, aren't you?... may as well start writing about it."

"You mean, I've got the college beat... covering State and the rest of the Big Ten?"

"That's right. Now get your things because you've also got a bigger office... with a window."

It didn't take Joe long to gather up his personal belongings... files, pens and pencils, notepads, his typewriter, a picture of him and Wendy on their honeymoon at Niagara Falls. His new office was on the third floor of the Dispatch Building overlooking the park. It was twice the size of his old office, with enough room for two stuffed chairs and a table and lamp in the corner opposite the desk. The window was behind him, to cast the day's light on whatever he happened to be working on. When he wanted to survey the comings and goings of those outside in the park or strolling the boulevard, all he need do was swivel in his chair and look out the window, which is what he was doing now, with his feet crossed on the sill.

"Honey, guess where I am?"

"I don't know... at work?"

"I am... calling you from my new office."

"New office?!"

"Right. The best thing is, it comes with a window... *and* a promotion and a raise."

"Joe!" Wendy exclaimed, causing two of her workmates to turn their heads. "Honey," she added quietly, "that's terrific."

"And guess what else?... no, on second thought, I'll tell you later."

"Honey, tell me now... what is it?"

"No, I've made reservations at T.J.'s for six-thirty. I'll tell you then."

It was a Wednesday evening. At Wendy's request, they were seated in one of the wall booths near the back of the restaurant facing the main dining area. She liked these tables because the two of them could sit side-by-side, holding hands.

After the waitress described the specials and left to fill their water glasses, she said, "well?..."

"Well," Joe replied, "let's order a glass of wine. You know it's becoming quite the sophisticated thing to do."

When the wine arrived, he raised his glass towards the light, inspected the contents, then announced, "here's to the new college beat writer at the Columbus Dispatch."

Wendy smiled at her husband. "Honey, I'm so proud of you."

"Yep, the old man walked into my office this morning and said, 'Joe, since you're going to college, may as well write about it.' Isn't that great, Wen?"

"It's great, Joe. It's great news!" In fact, it couldn't be better, she thought, as she was trying to find a way to tell him her own news, which she had verified only two hours ago. When Joe had called earlier, she'd forgotten about her four o'clock appointment. But now, she considered, since we're sharing news, big news, why not share all of it.

As he sipped his wine, she moved a little closer.

"Mmm, interesting," he stated, smelling the aroma. "I think I could acquire a taste for... what is it?" he said reaching for the bottle, "zinfandel," he remarked putting the accent on the second syllable.

Wendy moved still closer. "I have some news, too, Joe."

"Oh."

She hesitated, "get ready..."

There was a noticeable curiosity in his voice now. "What?"

"You're going to be a father."

"I'm going to be... Wendy, are you sure?!"

"Sure I'm sure."

"Wen, that's fantastic!... unbelievable!..." and he stood up and whooped, turning every head in the place, nearly causing one of the busboys to drop his chicken ala king. "We're going to have a baby!" he announced to one and all, capping the statement with another, "whaahooo!"

Everyone was chuckling now as Joe sat down again to a round of applause while Wendy, still blushing, said, "I wasn't sure how you were going to take it... having school to finish and saving for a house and all."

"How I was going to... honey, I couldn't be happier. I love you. Wen, nothing you could ever do will change that."

Later that night, tangled into one, they understood just how much closer they'd grown. And they revelled in the feeling.

*

"Hut hut," the quarterback barked out the signals just before the first team offense and defense slammed into one another. The QB turned to his left, faked a handoff to the fullback and pitched the ball to the tailback. Tork took the pitch and headed around the left side, outrunning the guard who'd pulled to lead interference. Near the sideline, the outside linebacker and cornerback hit him hard, dragging him to the turf after no gain.

"Tork!..." the offensive coach yelled, "wait for your blocking next time!" Then turning to one of the other coaches, "shit, is he ever going to get it?"

Joe had gotten his press pass from the athletic department earlier that day, and was in the process of getting to know the coaches and some of the players. To his surprise, most were coming up introducing themselves to him. This was after the 'Old Man' spotted him and exclaimed, "see that boy walking this way? I would've given my right nut to get him out of high school. Best runner since Cassidy. Hey, Joe!..." and the coach of the Buckeyes walked over to say hello.

"Tell me, Coach," Joe was asking the offensive coordinator now after Tork got blasted on the last play, "with Snell and Matte gone, how're your running backs looking this year?"

"All right, do it again!..." Coach Albright yelled to the offense before turning to Joe. "We've got a good bunch, Joe, I really believe that. Ya see Tork out there, he could be the best of the lot. He's got speed and power, but here," pointing to his head, "I don't know. He's not stupid, he just doesn't stop to think as the play is developing... doesn't make the right decision."

"I noticed. But I agree with you, he's got the goods."

"Well, if you've got any words of wisdom for him, be my guest. He sure could use 'em."

Joe just smiled remembering his run in with Tork.

"Say, Joe," Coach Albright said before turning to yell at Tork one more time, "I'm sorry about everything that happened over in Viet Nam... about Eddie and all. We sure coulda used you boys."

After practice Joe lingered on the field, considering the vagaries of life. If not for a kneejerk decision made at his high school graduation and a bullet from a VC sniper, he might have been the tailback running with the first team today. Might have been?... would have been, he thought, amused at his self assurance. But then he considered, hey, I've got nothing to complain about. In fact, I'm loving life right now, and he got up and turned to leave when he heard the voice.

"Excuse me... excuse me! Joe... ah, Mr. Cramer." It was Kyle Tork. He was jogging towards Joe before he slowed to a walk. "Mr. Cramer, sorry to bother you but... well, I've been thinking about what happened a few weeks back, you know, down at the Pub, and ah...

"Kyle, call me Joe. You're making me feel old here."

As Kyle Tork smiled, Joe could see the relief all over his face. "I just wanted to apologize."

"You already did."

"No, I wanted it to be my idea. I was out of line." He stood silent some moments before extending his hand, adding, "when I'm not playing like I think I should, well, I take it out on other people. I guess I still have some growing up to do."

Joe saw that he meant it and took his hand, "apology accepted... again. No hard feelings," and he turned once again to leave.

"Say, Joe, what did you think of practice?"

"Not bad... team's looking good, on both sides of the ball."

"C'mon, what did you really think?"

Okay, Joe thought, I am going to take Coach Albright up on his offer, because Kyle does have the goods, and maybe I can help.

"Kyle, you can play, I mean you can be all-conference, I really believe that. You've got size, speed, and when you get squared up you can take on any linebacker on the team. But like I said at Pete's, you're not playing up to your abilities."

"What do you mean?"

"I mean... well, take today. Remember those pitches Coach Albright was running?"

"Yeah."

"On half of them, you didn't wait for your blocking, and on at least two others that I saw, you had a cutback lane you could've driven a truck through. You gotta see the field. You know the play doesn't always unfold like it was drawn up."

"I know that."

"It's not just knowing it, it's seeing it, and later on when your instincts take over, feeling it... feeling the defense, feeling the pressure... and reacting."

Kyle'd never heard this before... a more visceral, instinctual description of what it was like carrying the ball. He'd always been told by his coaches to grip the ball... hit the hole... run hard... and he always had. It was just his speed and size that'd gotten him by.

"What can I do?... I mean, will you help?"

"Kyle, I'm not a coach. You've got good coaching. What can't be coached is seeing the play as it develops, and reacting. If it's a pitch, don't just take off and try to get to the corner... wait for your blocking... and react off the block. If the defense overruns the play, cut back. If it's a straight handoff off-tackle, bounce it to the outside if there's no hole... or take the tough two, three yards if that's all the defense is giving you. Hey, three yards and a cloud of dust... you know what the Old Man wants."

Joe could see the light starting to come on as he was delivering his lecture on carrying the pigskin. But he knew it would take Kyle time, some weeks anyway, to break old habits.

"I think I see what you mean."

"See it, feel it, do it. I use to say that to myself everytime my number was called. After a while, I just did it."

Kyle memorized those words that day, burning them into his brain so deep he would take them to the grave. "See you at practice tomorrow?"

"I'll be around. This is my beat, I'm the new sports writer for the Dispatch covering your games."

"Great. Then I'll see you around."

As Kyle was jogging away, Joe yelled after him, "hey, tailback, give me something to write about!"

**

The Old Pigskin

Teddy Roosevelt almost outlawed the game of
American football on account of its rough nature,
particularly referencing formations like the 'flying wedge' as
it was employed by teams that dominated the sport at the
turn of the 20th Century, such as the Princeton Tigers.

Red Hand

He was crouched behind some prickly pear near a livery that was adjacent to the train yard, his mind racing as fast as his heart as he contemplated what might have been. Just moments before, when he'd dropped from the bottom of the moving train, he in fact did bounce, causing the draw bars beneath to leave a good size gash across his forehead and left shoulder. Good thing he didn't panic, he thought, or the bulls would've been picking up the pieces by now trying to figure out if what they found was man or critter.

Slowly the boy looked from behind the dense shrubbery and saw no one. The livery was quiet, and over its roof through the gaping branches of a large willow he could see the sun making its penultimate descent before slipping away to other worlds. Better to stay until dark, he decided, then look for a place to hole up... until the trouble passes.

It was twilight now, but not so dark Red Hand couldn't make out the stone and brick houses as they grew in numbers the closer he approached the town's lights. They looked sturdier than the farm houses he'd passed traveling north, but they lacked the open land about them. Their proximity to one another was much like the tipis in an Indian camp, so the boy determined the people of this village must be of one tribe.

Some distance farther, when the faint sounds of music and laughter broke through the dampness of the evening, he came to a crossroads. One of the streets was named Prospect, which he'd remembered from school on the reservation when he and the other children learned about the early trappers and prospectors who were the first white men among his people, one of them his own father. He recalled the stories his mother told about the man who'd killed a buck and shared the meat when he came to court... who'd brought Two Bears twice the number of ponies he'd asked in return for his daughter's hand... who'd loved her, and she him, as much as two could share every part of themselves, so he followed the street called Prospect to see where it would lead.

The night shone from the lamplights lining his way as the stone and brick houses, some rising four and five times the height of a man, now stood shoulder to shoulder. Walkways lined the front of them like he remembered back in the little town of Mission on the Keya Paha, but most of these were stone, like the buildings themselves. He walked on into what seemed like a growing number of young men, much his same age, rushing here and there towards the great front doors just as a church bell rang out the six o'clock hour. He thought this strange, only in the sense it was more of the white man's ways of which he knew little. He smiled as he watched one of the young men barely make it inside the building called Tiger Inn before the large, carved oak door slammed shut. When he turned to continue on his way he was struck with a pervading quiet where, a moment before, there was noise and laughter about. He thought this strange as well, and this time hesitated before continuing on. It was then his curiosity got the better of him. He looked right and left and saw no one, and so slipped around the back of the Tiger Inn, and into a whole new world.

*

"Ya here 'bout the job?..." a voice call out. The man had come up behind him from the alley, startling Red Hand just as he'd peered through the back door that led to the kitchen.

"I... I..." the boy began to answer, searching for an innocuous reply, but the man paid no attention and continued.

"Well, the pay's five dollars a week plus room n' board." The man was now looking directly at him, his arms holding a large box filled with the afternoon's leftovers, waiting for a yes or no.

Red Hand was about to say no when the aroma of freshly cooked meat filled his entire senses, and his stomach answered for him. "Yes."

"Good, then, that's settled. You c'n go on ov'r there an' start by gittin' them meals out on the tables in the dinin' room. We got twenty-five hungry lads waitin' for their supper." Then before turning around to take another load of trash out the back, the man put his hand out and said, "I'm Chester McGinley, owner, manager and cook of the Tiger Inn. How'll I be calling you?"

The boy thought for a brief moment before extending his own hand. "John... John Connor."

*

The first week at the Tiger Inn went well for Red Hand. His duties included dishwasher, meal server, and occasionally, when one of the 'lads,' as Chester McGinley referred to his charges, got overly exhuberant and tossed a spoonful of mashed potatoes or yams at another, janitor. In spite of it all, the boy liked the atmosphere. While the food was spicier than he cared for, it was plentiful; and the small room he occupied with a cot and chest of drawers on the third floor?... why, it was an extravagance, particularly with a water closet at the end of the hall. However, what the boy found he indulged in most was the mealtime conversation. Everything from scholastics to politics, from the local news to the fairer sex was discussed openly and with great enthusiasm. After only six days at the Tiger Inn, he felt he'd spent a year in reservation school learning the white's ways... what leads them to the decisions they make... how those his own age approach life... indeed, how they think.

"Howd'ya like yer first week, John?" Chester asked.

"Good."

"Well," Chester hesitated at the abruptness of the boy's reply, "good, then. Here's yer five dollars. Ya git tomorra off, so we'll see ya Monday mornin', six-thirty sharp."

"Thank you," and Red Hand took the money, money which he'd already made plans for, for it was during his first week at the Tiger Inn he decided to stay in this village for some time. The cover was good. He had food and shelter in a building he rarely needed to leave, and if he dressed the same as these whites, he could disappear within the mob... become invisible, as the wise Santin used to tell him... when the time came.

So the first thing he did the following Monday between his shifts at dinner and supper was purchase a pair of tweed trousers and matching tan suspenders. He put them away in his chest of drawers, then continued his education during regular working hours as he alternately served and cleaned up after his twenty-five profes-sors who, between meals, attended what was now called Princeton College, not The College of New Jersey as it had been until this very year.

The following Monday, he made his second purchase... two white cotton shirts, sans collars, and a pair of dark brown, lace-up boots, or shoes as they were referred to.

By the end of the second week, his education was progressing nicely as the boy stored away common phrases and mannerisms which he felt could only enhance his ultimate escape to the Canadas. In the not too distant future, he, in his new clothes, would not only look like white, he would be able to speak and act the part. At least, that was his plan.

*

"You... there. I say, boy..." It was Neilson Poe, or Net as the lads called him.

"I believe the young man's name is John," said Robert Garrett, sitting to Net's right.

When Red Hand reappeared from the kitchen, Net Poe stated once again over the din of conversation, "I say, you there, John, come here."

Red Hand looked at him, not quite certain yet if it was he who was being addressed.

"Yes, you there... come here."

He walked across the room, negotiating several tables before reaching Net and comrades who were sitting in the far corner of the dining room next to the fire.

"Do you see what's on this plate, boy?"

Red Hand was somewhat confused by the question. He could see exactly what was on the plate, as he presumed anyone could, so he answered honestly, "yes."

"Yes. Excellent! The boy's a genius, Robert, for he must have the powers of the Allmighty to be able to see anything quite resembling food to be upon this humble platter set before me."

Red Hand wasn't sure if he was supposed to respond, or wait for another direct question or request of some sort, so while Net Poe was displaying the amount of food on his plate for all to see, Red Hand turned and began walking back to the kitchen to retrieve more meals.

"So, you see, boy... why where did he?... ah, there he goes... I must stop him at once," and with that Net picked up a small pork chop, stood up and flung it at Red Hand, hitting him squarely in the back of the head. "Bullseye!"

The lads roared their approval as Red Hand stopped, looking down at the pork chop resting by his feet. When he stooped to pick it up, they roared again.

Red Hand turned and eyed Net. He said nothing. He had nothing to say. He'd never seen men throw food. On the reservation, food was often scarce. It was not wasted.

"Boy," Net was smiling, mischeviously. "Come here."

Red Hand walked over to the table.

"Now, as I requested politely only a few moments ago, what do you see?"

All right, Red Hand decided, I will play his game. "Food."

"Aha!... I told you he was a genius. Yes, food... but so little I can only surmise that, one, there is a shortage of hogs hereabouts, or two, I had not paid McGinley my bill for the month, both of which I know are patently untrue. So take my plate back in there, boy, and tell the old geezer to pile it on."

Net was still smiling when Red Hand turned away, "and like this fine mug of ale here poured to spilling, put a head on it!... I've got a game Saturday!"

"Net, be kind," Robert Garrett said to his friend, "the lad is only trying to do his job."

When Red Hand was making his way back towards the table with a new plate, the starting halfback for the undefeated Princeton football team looked up and said, "ah, now that looks more like it."

When a moment later the plate holding five fat pork chops half-covered with an avalanche of mashed potatoes and countless peas was overturned on his head, he was not smiling, rather he was howling, jumping up, livid, "what the hell," then lunging.

Red Hand jumped back, avoiding Net, as Robert and two others now held him off.

Net was red with rage, potatoes and gravy dripping onto his collar, one pork chop resting atop his head, peas sprinkled about. At first the rest of the lads were as stunned as Net, but the longer they gazed upon the sight, the more they couldn't contain themselves.

"I thought you said, 'fill it up, and put it on your head,'" Red Hand added at precisely the right moment. Like before, the lads roared with laughter.

Brushing the food from his hair, Net looked at Red Hand more closely. He could see the person before him was no boy. There was a worldliness about him, a look telling Net this lad had been places, seen things he had not. As the muscles in his arms relaxed, Robert and the others relaxed their grip as well.

Red Hand saw the respect in Net's eyes and extended his hand. "My name is not boy. It is John... John Connor."

Net smiled at the irony of it all, as he would years later when the two friends would meet. "Neilson Poe... Net to my friends." And the lads cheered in approval.

*

The Monday of the third week found Red Hand making the final purchases that would fill out his white wardrobe... a three-button, tweed jacket with medium lapels almost identical to the trousers he'd bought; a stiff, white collar to match his shirts; and a brown cravat with small, angular stripes that were alternately cardinal and gold.

Walking back to the Tiger Inn with his packages in hand, the boy felt good, he felt ready about the transformation he would make when the time came, as he knew it surely would. Now, however, he would continue working at the Inn and save his money, for he didn't know how long the work would last, or how much of these American dollars he might need when it came time to leave.

Continuing up Prospect Street, he saw a food and grog shop he'd noticed on his previous shopping excursions, and so decided to stop for something cool to drink. I will save all of my money beginning tomorrow, he thought. Right now, I will find out if I've learned anything from the lads.

He walked through the double doors beneath a sign announcing The Blue Boar Tavern, squinting his eyes as they adjusted to the dark surroundings. He took a seat at a small table in one corner and in a moment a girl his own age meandered over. Taking the pencil from behind her ear she asked, 'what'll it be, then?"

Red Hand looked up as she waited for him to answer. He wasn't sure what he wanted. He'd just picked up the menu and found he could decifer only about half the items listed. Maybe he'd made a mistake thinking he could pass himself off as white. He was about to grab up his packages and leave when he reconsidered. He breathed deeply, and leaned back in his chair as he thought Net might. Then looking up he stated with an accent affected to match those of the lads, "yes, what shall it be?"

The tone of his remark caused the girl to roll her eyes, but he went on. "Actually, I'm not quite sure what I'm in the mood for. What do you recommend, my dear?"

She rolled her eyes again, shifting her weight to one side, which Red Hand found made her more attractive somehow, and she spoke evenly, "ale, cider, soda or lemonade. If all you want is water, there's a bucket n' cups at the end o' the bar."

He thought for a moment, "which do you prefer?"

"Ale when I'm out of an evenin', cider when I wake, an' lemonade when I've got a real thirst. Now, the soda we have is fairly new, up from Atlanta way... called coca cola. Ya may want to try that. Kinda sweet an' tart an' fizzy all at once."

The youth smiled and stated, "bring me a soda, then."

The girl was back in a minute with his drink. She placed it smartly on the table, this time smiling back. "One soda. That'll be a dime."

As he sipped the bubbly drink, Red Hand reached in his pocket for the few coins that remained from his shopping trip. Pulling them out he slid a dime neatly between his thumb and forefinger, placing it on the table in front of the girl.

"One dime."

She thanked him as she picked it up, however before she could turn to leave, he was holding out a nickel, smiling, waiting for her hand. She looked at him for a moment before extending it, blushing slightly.

"And one nickel, for an excellent recommendation."

Their eyes met before she stated, "thank ye, kind sir." She turned and walked away, leaving the lad to his soda and a view of her backside that swung in time to a tune the bartender was busy whistling.

In bed that night Red Hand found he could not stop thinking of the girl, how she seemed to warm to a little encouragement and kindness on his part. He thought he would visit the inn again the following Sunday, on his day off. Until then, he would pursue his book learning.

*

Over the next week by lamplight, John studied the words in the books he'd borrowed from Mr. McGinley. There were two by a man named Mark Twain which he very much liked, and a third filled with what Chester McGinley referred to as poetry. He'd also mentioned the author of this book, although long since having passed on, was a cousin once or twiced removed to one of the lads here at the Inn, Neilson Poe.

Neilson... Net, John thought, Net was family to this man? This piece of information caused the boy to pay greater attention to the book of poems, reading over and over again the words about the strange black bird, The Raven.

He remembered Santin had told him about those who could speak with the animals... medicine men and shamans. But never had the boy heard that of a white man. This Edgar Allan must have been a great man, and if Net is family, maybe he has the power also.

After the evening meal on Friday, John approached Net as he was leaving the inn. He had a game the next day against Lafayette, and was on his way back to his room to do some reading, then 'hit the sack' early as he put it.

"Mr. Poe," John started.

Net turned, placing a hand on the youth's left shoulder. "John, call me Net. I thought we'd agreed to that."

"Yes... Net. I have been reading a book of poems by one of your family, Edgar Allan. Mr. McGinley told me."

"Ah, the great Edgar Allan. Not my older brother of the same name mind you who was a footballer here back in '89 and '90... but my father's cousin, my second cousin, a man of literary renown I must say. I would have wished to have known him actually, but he died young, only forty years of age."

Forty years, the boy thought. It is a good age to die.

"And what are you reading?"

"The poem of the black bird."

"Of course, I should have guessed, 'Once upon a midnight dreary, while I pondered, weak and weary'... a classic, I dare say," Net smiled, "from Cousin Edgar."

"You know of it?"

"I know them all. The Raven, Lenore, The Valley of Unrest, A Dream, A Dream Within A Dream... all of us Poe brothers grew up on them. That and Princeton football. Now, my good man, I really do have to hit the old sack. We have a game tomorrow."

John felt a closer attachment to Net as he watched him walk from the room. Like his friend's excitement for the game called football, John recalled his passion for tewaarathon on the reservation... taking the balled up hide with his stick and racing to a goal sometimes half a mile distant, exulting in victory when he reached there first. It is something he would still be doing if the trouble with Strait and his men had not developed. But then he admonished himself for dwelling on day's long past. Where he was today is his reality. He knew he must concentrate on his condition as it is today.

*

The following Sunday John heard the revelers before he entered The Blue Boar. The noise carried half way down Prospect Street. As he walked through the double doors, the cacophony raised by so many students after so many pints yelling above one another to be heard, cheering those footballers in attendance, and from time to time belting out various school anthems, ribald and otherwise, was deafening. He was about to leave when he saw the girl carrying six mugs of ale in each hand to a nearby table poured to spilling. Then he saw Net sitting at the table. What caught John's eye was the sweater Net and some of the others were wearing. The letter "P" was emblazoned on the front above the heart in heavy gold, block type. He was deciding if he indeed belonged when Net glanced his way and motioned him over.

"John, my friend, what are you doing in this den of drink and debauchery? Have you come to celebrate our victory?"

The boy was unsure how to respond, but felt that was as good a reason for his presence as any. "Yes."

"Well, we were only victorious in that we did not lose... we tied... two goose eggs. Can you beat that? Have a seat and a drink. Lenore!..." Net yelled to the girl, "bring one more for my good man here."

John had been watching her, the way she moved easily from table to table serving the lads their drink, disarming those who attempted anything beyond social acceptability with charm, and a good sense of humor. When she arrived back at the table with his grog, she looked at John for a moment, and recognized him.

"Hello, then. How are you? No more packages, I see."

Before he could answer, Net piped up, "have you two met?"

"Last week. The lad stopped by with a few purchases and had a soda to quench a godawful thirst."

"A soda! Not a bad choice considering the rumors going around about the special kick it provides," he winked. "John, let me introduce Lenore, the prettiest maid in Princeton Town, and I dare say miles beyond."

John stood, and Lenore, to her surprise, blushed. She wasn't use to such gentlemanly behavior from any of the lads in The Blue Boar. She extended her hand and John took it, smiling.

"My name is John... Connor. I'm pleased to meet you."

Net was watching as John remained standing, holding Lenore's hand for some seconds longer than required.

"And I as well," she eventually responded.

"I believe you two are kindred spirits," Net interjected, "or so it appears, not to mention a quite handsome couple."

Net's last remark caused Lenore to blush once again. She released her grasp from John scurrying back to wait the other tables. But, as she went, both John and Net saw her glance back over a shoulder.

"The girl is taken with you, my friend. And lucky you are. I along with everyone else who frequents this fine establishment haven't been able to get to first base."

John wasn't sure what Net meant, he just continued to watch Lenore as she went about her business.

"Her name is like the girl in the poem," he said to Net finally, sipping at his grog.

"Lenore? Yes, in The Raven, and also more eloquently in Cousin Edgar's poem by the same name."

"I see why," John said, "with her yellow hair..."

"And angelic beauty," Net added.

After a while, John asked, "I wonder if she knows of the poems?"

"My guess is no," Net was raising his voice again as the lads broke into another Tiger anthem. "Lenore doesn't have the schooling we are privleged to have, but she has intelligence. I've observed that on more than one occasion right here, dissuading an unwanted suitor who'd had a bit too much grog to pursue his ambitions, and without embarrassing the chap."

John was beginning to feel the effects of a bit too much grog himself, and so said, "I think I understand what you mean. Congratulations on your victory," and he stood to leave.

"Thank you, my friend. I'll see you at breakfast tomorrow morning then."

"Yes, I will see you then."

Walking towards the front door to take his leave, John caught the eye of Lenore one last time. As they looked at one another, their souls embraced, and Lenore believed Net's words... that she and John were somehow kindred spirits. John thought only of the poem by the famous Edgar Allan, the poem by her same name, and he said a prayer she would not die young.

*

" 'At red nigra musta dodged us back down the line." It was Jimmy Tarver telling Springer to go round up Butts and Critter after the four of them had scoured the train yard in Newark, and before that Elizabeth and Perth Amboy. At each stop they'd spent close to a week checking the hundreds of boxcars that passed through these towns heading north, as well as sticking their nose in a variety of well known hobo camps the bulls were more than happy to point out. Even after Jimmy and Butts had kicked the shit out of one poor bastard sleeping in the shade of a large black maple outside of Elizabeth, the old boy could tell them nothing. There was simply no sign of Red Hand anywhere.

"Let's git on back to Princeton."

*

The train pulled in Tuesday morning on schedule at 10:09, and the men wasted no time. They looked up the depot agent and asked if he'd rounded up any 'good-fer-nothins' in the past three weeks. The man couldn't say for certain, telling them to check with the bulls in the yard, which Jimmy did. One told him they'd bagged three, but none fit Red Hand's description. After hearing the boy's age, however, he had a thought.

"If'n he's only 'bout twenty years er so an' was wantin' to hide out fer a spell, well I'd head straight fer the school, er some o' them lodgin' houses they got up there. I wouldn't be no needle in a haystack neither," the man went on, "I'd be one more piece o' hay."

He's right, Jimmy thought. Shit, howdy.

Thirty minutes later the four guards were walking up Prospect Street amongst a hundred or more students crisscrossing one way or another heading for their midday meal. Jimmy Tarver observed the scene, figuring if they were ever going to find the boy, some dumb luck would be required. So he thought, fuck it, divided up his troops, and haved at it.

"Spinger, take Critter with ya an' go on up 'at side o' the street an' find out if some o' these boys has seen any red nigras roun' here lately. Butts an' me'll go on up t'other."

It wasn't until Jimmy had persuaded the third lad he'd near accosted that the dumb luck kicked in.

He'd grabbed the youngster, George Firth, by the nape of the neck after the second student he'd approached bolted upon seeing his scruffy appearance from more than a month on the road.

"Seen any new boys in the neighborhood, sonny?... 'bout yer height, black hair... kinda long, dark o' skin?"

George thought of The Tiger Inn's newly hired employee, which Jimmy could see in his eyes, but he hesitated. He knew this man was up to ill doing, and that John would bear the brunt of his anger, so he attempted to avoid answering.

"I... I'm not sure..."

"Goddam it kid I'll wring yer fuckin' neck right here lessen ya tell me what ya know," and Jimmy pulled George close so the lad could smell the foul of his breath and witness the hate in his eyes.

"There... th-there is someone like that w-working at The Tiger up the s-s-street I think," George stammered.

"Yer sure 'bout that, sonny?"

"I th-think so."

Jimmy pushed him away telling Butts, "go git Springer an' Critter, I'll wait here... then we'll see."

A minute later George busted through the back door of The Tiger Inn and found John and Chester getting dinner on.

"John, John," he was shaking, "there're some men asking about you outside. I don't like the looks of them."

"Where?"

"Down the street, but they're headed here. I... I'm sorry, I had to tell them."

Chester came over, "are you in some kinda trouble, lad?"

"Some."

"They'll be here any minute," George was still shaking, "I'm sorry, John."

Chester now took control. "We can discuss 'at trouble later. You and

George git on up to yer room now an' stay put. No one goes up there, so ya should be fine. But if ya do hear footsteps on the stairs, git out the winda to the roof, an' lay low. Now go on with ya... an' George, send me Net on yer way."

When Jimmy and his goons came in through the front door the lads were sitting down to dinner. All heads turned as the guards walked into the room looking slowly from table to table. After some moments, Jimmy stated evenly, "any you boys know a breed 'at works this place?"

Jimmy's question, more a demand, was met with silence, and he was displeased.

"I'm askin' you college pukes polite," his voice rising, "now any you..."

"Jes who the hell er you!?..." Chester cut him off coming out of the kitchen, walking towards Jimmy. His remark was so unexpected, so direct, Jimmy was taken aback, but only for a moment. As Chester continued walking towards the guards, the lads tensed up.

Jimmy was getting back his nerve when Chester faced him and the two were standing toe-to-toe, but the proprietor of The TIger Inn was relentless, "I said who the hell er you, hayseed, er can't ya hear me with all 'at dirt in yer ears?"

Jimmy hadn't been challenged like this for years, and he was back on his heels again. "We're here on official business o' the state o' Florida..." he attempted to go on.

"I don't give a good morning shit what business yer on, hayseed. You take these peckerheads yer with an' git outa ma place. That plain enough?"

Jimmy tried one last time. "We were told you have a boy workin' fer ya..."

And on cue Net came out of the kitchen, his hair blackened from the coal bin out back, walking towards the far table carrying a tray of meals.

"We got anymore chicken, Mr. McGinley?"

Without turning Chester answered, "in the second oven, John."

"Yessir."

The lads were catching on now, and at the same time getting ired with these four bumpkins who'd invaded their domain. Robert Garrett stood up as did Junk Tanner, a lineman who played on the team with Net, along with two or three other of the lads. They walked over, standing slightly behind Chester.

162

"Everything all right, Mr. McGinley?" Robert asked.

Jimmy eyed Net going back towards the kitchen. That wasn't his man, he knew it, but doubt lingered.

"We'll be goin'," Jimmy stated.

"Damn right, 'an if I catch ya in here ag'in, you'll wish I hadn't," Chester added as he and the lads watched the guards turn and walk from the inn.

—Later on over chicken and dumplings, there was much chatter among the lads about their proprietor.

"Could you believe it?!"... Robert Garrett marvelled, still amazed, "our own Mr. McGinley walking up to that bruiser, a head taller than he, and saying, 'just who the hell are you?' He had that bumpkin on his heels. My god, I love the man!"

"I will not be pissing around with Mr. McGinley anytime soon," Willie Blake chimed in.

"Or a day late with your dues," Junk added, "or he'll turn you over and plant one of these chicken legs up your arse."

The lads laughed at that one, however, the feeling they shared tonight was more a renewed sense of pride at belonging to one of the university's most prestigious eating clubs. And this, all agreed, could not have been accomplished if not for the zeal and temerity of their own Mr. McGinley, whose verbal spanking of the four bumpkins was recounted over and over again until dessert arrived, which tonight was bread pudding with a caramel sauce, served by Net.

*

As a precaution the following week, John remained out of sight. Chester didn't want the goons snooping around, spotting the boy serving meals to the rest of the lads, so he kept him in the kitchen and asked Net if he would continue his table duties for the time being. Net, of course, complied and as the day-to-day events at the inn regained a more familiar look, John made plans.

Lying by lamplight late Friday up in his room, he decided he must leave. He couldn't allow Jimmy and his boys to beat up on George again, or any of the lads, in an attempt to flush him out. Once he was gone and his trail went cold, the guards would leave, most likely heading north again, but that would be out of Princeton. So early the following morning, after putting on his new store bought clothes and gathering up the rest of his belongings, wrapping them in a blanket, he started downstairs. What John didn't plan on was seeing Chester McGinley in the hallway at that hour.

"Going somewhere, John?"

The boy hesitated, then spoke. "I was going to leave you this," pulling a note from his pocket. "It explains why I must go. You will understand."

"Tell me instead."

Putting the note away he began, relating everything from the beginning of his trouble with Thompkins back in Mission to killing the man the following spring, his incarceration in Florida and eventual escape and travels all the way up here to Princeton.

"That is some story, John. But I don't hold nothin' ag'in ya. Ya killed 'at man in self defense."

"The court said no."

"Well, son, I guess ya got a point there."

"And now I am running."

"Yer right, being a fugitive is no life." Chester lingered in thought before continuing. "Seems ta me somehow ya gotta clear yer name... git some o' those folks back in 'at town... what was it called?..."

"Mission."

"Mission. Yup, git some o' them to come forward with the truth. Ya cain't have a thing like this a hangin' ov'r yer head ferever."

"That will take some time, which right now I do not have." He looked at Chester McGinley as he might have looked at a blood relation who'd taken him in and eased his journey to freedom, if such a place existed. "You understand why I must go. If I remain, it is too dangerous for the rest of you."

"I know, I know, yer right, so go if ya must, but know this... there'll always be a place rat here if ya need one. Don't ever ferget that."

"I will remember." John extended his hand, "thank you."

164

"You take care, lad."

*

He was crouched behind the livery next to the train yard once again, as he had been... what?... three, four weeks earlier? He wasn't sure anymore. The thoughts of his short stay in the college town now consumed him, thoughts tumbling in his mind... thoughts of Net and the lads, but also a sweet, clear vision of Lenore. He remembered wanting her, wanting to be close to her... somehow... but the shrill howl in the distance of the 8:12 to Newark broke the spell, and Red Hand cleared his head, readying himself for the jump. He waited, and listened, shaking away some of the morning's dew as the sun began to shed its warmth in earnest. Then he saw it, the great smoking engine, wheels pumping, pulling what seemed like an impossible amount of weight as the line of box cars sweated behind. He marvelled at the sight, as he always had, then smiled with the knowledge the iron horse would soon be pulling him as well, taking him to a place where he might be able to sleep soundly once again... taking him to the Canadas.

He was running through the scrub that flanked his side of the track towards the last set of cars when he saw them. There were about thirty cars total, half a dozen flat cars carrying mostly lumber, but there they were, two of the men standing on the back stoop of a passenger car about mid-way in line, the other two on the platform outside the caboose.

Red Hand dove into the scrub, hoping he'd been quick enough. But then he heard them.

"Did'ya see that?" It was Jimmy"s voice. The boy could tell even over the rumbling of the cars as they picked up speed.

"Damn, I knowed 'at sombitch was still..." then the voice trailed off and the boy knew they'd caught a glimpse of him. He figured he had about a minute. It'd take Jimmy that much time to get to the other two and tell them they were getting off... jumping. He thought for a few seconds more, then decided.

He was running now, sprinting back towards Prospect Street and The Tiger Inn, back to... no, he thought, no, and veered left towards campus. Not the inn, that would be the first place they'd look. I must go elsewhere. In the distance now he saw the throngs gathering... students, as well as what looked like half the town — men, women, children — all gathering and mulling about as if at some festive occasion. This is good, he considered as he slowed to a walk, looking quickly over his shoulder. No one. He continued on, wading deeper into the crowd, relaxing some. Then he heard a second voice.

"John!" It was abrupt, near, stopping him in his tracks. In the next instant he caught himself, recognizing its familiar ring. It was Net. "I heard you had left. What are you doing here all dressed up looking like a proper student? My god, you're pale."

Net didn't realize he'd just taken three years off of Red Hand's life. But the boy gathered himself, stating, "they saw me in the train yard and are close behind. I have to disappear."

Net wasted no time. "Come with me."

"Where are we going?"

"You'll see. We have a game today... Havard. And you're suiting up!"

The two of them turned and headed towards the field house at the far end of campus as Red Hand mumbled, "suiting up?..." barely hearing the students, alumni, family and friends around them with a drink in one hand and a pennant or some such school paraphanalia in the other, chanting, "Net... Net... Net..."

*

"Who the hell is that, Poe?" It was Briggs, one of the two team managers who'd just spotted Red Hand putting on some gear Net had given him.

"One of the lads, sir."

"Never seen him."

"Ah... he's been working out with me and Junk and some of the others only recently," and Net looked down to lace up his cleats, not wanting to give away the lie. He added, "damn good runner."

"What's your name, son?"

"John... John Connor."

"Connor, huh. Well, hurry up then,"... and Whitey Briggs walked away harumphing to no one in particular.

The team was walking out of the locker room now, bunched up, shuffling along like some giant centipede with several independently moving parts waiting to explode.

"John," it was Net, "have you ever seen football?"

"No."

"Well, just stay by me when we run out on the field. I'll put you at the end of the bench. You can just sit down and relax... enjoy the game."

John nodded. It sounded good to him... all of them in the same clothing, uniforms they called them. He would be hard to spot. Then a voice from in front shouted, "let's go boys!... let's go get 'em!..."

They charged from beneath the stands, each man filled with adrenaline for the battle at hand as the crowd roared their approval before segueying into a cheer that started slowly, then built in speed as the crowd repeated it over and over again...

Ray 'ray 'ray

Tiger, tiger, tiger

Sis, sis, sis

Boom, boom, boom, ah!

Princeton! Princeton! Princeton!

John noticed, it took on a strange resemblence to the sound of the great iron horse as it roars ever faster leaving the station.

The noise from the cheering crowd was intoxicating, and the players jumped about as John had remembered doing before a game of tewaraathon on the reservation.

"Have you ever seen anything like this, John!?..." Net asked, yelling over the crowd.

"Yes, back home."

"I mean the excitement before an athletic contest... like this?"

"Yes, when we would play the little brother of war... a game called tewaraathon."

"Te... what?"

"Tewaraathon. The young men would take sides, sometimes against other tribes, many on each side."

"What was the object?"

"To get the ball to the other's goal."

"Carrying it in your arms?"

"No. With a basket on a stick."

"More like our lacrosse, I would think."

"Yes, I think so."

"I see." Net thought for a moment, then asked, "were you a good player?"

"I was good."

"Did you ever score a goal?"

"Yes, many times."

Net smiled to himself, his mind racing ahead to another victory, hopefully, for the Tigers and their faithful, and the celebration that would surely follow at The Blue Boar.

As the whistle blew to begin the contest, Net turned to John before running out on the field, "now take a seat, but watch closely. I want you to see how the game is played."

The coach huddled up the team on the sidelines barking, "okay, we're receiving. Starting unit... v-formation wedge. Net, you're deep back." Then, with his starters around him, Coach gathered his voice in earnest. "Boys, let's show 'em what Tiger football is all about... run this kickoff DOWN THEIR THROATS!"

The team ran on the field to a deafening roar and formed what Red Hand noticed looked like an arrowhead directly in front of Net. When the ball was kicked, Net caught it out of the air, charging straight ahead behind the other players. As the two teams met, bodies exploded off one another, the men of the Tiger "V" knocking a half dozen of the opposition out of Net's way. One of the Havard players leaped high in the air, diving over the top of the Tiger blockers, grabbing a piece of Net's shoulder pad, spinning him around. The crowd roared as Net regained his balance, ducked and veered right towards the sideline, running through one tackler until being dragged down by two others somewhere near mid-field.

The referee's whistle stopped the action only until the Tigers reformed behind the ball. Red Hand saw what looked like six or seven players in a line near the ball, with the remaining, including Net, behind them. One of the back players then yelled out a signal, the ball was pitched to him by one of the line players, and the running started again.

This time, the player who received the ball ran until he was about to be tackled, then he pitched the ball to Net who continued on until he was downed again.

As Net told him, Red Hand studied the game, observing the ebb and flow as the two teams battled in similar fashion attempting to carry the ball to the other team's goal. Neither had been able to accomplish this when the sound of the whistle stopped play, this time for good.

Watching the two teams running off the field now, Red Hand wasn't sure what to do. Then Net yelled to him as he passed, "follow me... it's halftime."

"It is what?..." Red Hand asked back in the locker room.

"Halftime. The game is half over. We rest for a while then play again... one more half."

"And no one has a goal."

"No, those boys are tough, but we'll handle them." Then he asked, "tell me, John, what do you think of the game?"

"It is like our game of tewaraathon, but with less players, and smaller field."

"I see. But you understand what we're trying to do?"

"Yes, make a goal."

Net smiled, saying mostly to himself, "that does simplify the object, I dare say," then adding with a grin and some gusto, "and we will make a goal! I feel like scoring!"

Net was right. Three minutes into the second half, after Princeton had gotten the ball back, he took a pitchout and raced forty yards for the game's first score with Junk throwing a crushing block at the twenty yard line. He'd taken out two of the Harvard players as the crowd groaned, "ooooohhh," when he hit them simultaneously on the blindside. Even Red Hand appreciated the collision. Junk reminded him of Buffalo In Camp, a boy he had grown up with who was also big, and who loved the contact of tewaraathon. Red Hand had always made it a point to have Buffalo In Camp on his side.

Back on the bench sipping a cup of water, Net looked at John. "What'd I tell you," he winked, seeking in some small way, the boy thought, his approval.

"Good goal," John replied. "And good for Junk."

"Did he pulverize those two chaps or what?!" Net grinned. "I love the Junkman."

After the extra point it was 6-0 Princeton, but the Harvard boys were not through for the day. They took the kickoff and ran the ball perilously close to Princeton's goal after only five plays, but were stopped by a saving tackle at the one. As the runner limped from the field the crowd applauded generously. That's when Red Hand spotted them.

Jimmy and his men were walking through the stands, slowly, carefully. They wound their way up and down the aisles impervious to the game, every fifteen yards back at the bottom row, five steps from the field. They would turn, look up to the crowd, and begin again. John could see Jimmy in the lead, the scowl on his face, eyes fixed, working his way towards his end of the bench. Three more aisles and he would be right behind him, fifteen feet away. He grabbed Net by the arm before he could go back into the game.

"They are here," he said, motioning to his right, "coming this way."

Net saw them and understood. "Wait here... be right back." Seconds later, "John, this is Billy Tully. He's the third option in the backfield. Good man that he is, he's agreed to sit the rest of this one out. You're in. Let's go." And with that, the boy from the reservation of the Sioux Nation, who at no choosing of his own had travelled so far to this place, lined up at halfback for the Princeton Tigers as the game wound down against Harvard.

The up-back barked, "one-two, one-two," the ball coming to him as Net, then the second back, then John ran left following him. He pitched the ball to Net who cut up the middle of the field, bouncing off two, three tacklers before being stopped after a twelve-yard gain. The crowd approved as the offense lined up again. This time Net was the up-back taking the snap from center. On three, he got the ball, faked another run up the middle, then pitched to the second option, Mike

Povic, who headed for the sidelines before turning upfield for sixteen yards until cut down.

Princeton kept up the attack, first right, then left, Net and Mike alternately carrying the ball as John, once he saw where the play was going, sprinted ahead, taking out the closest defender.

"Look at Tully," Coach yelled to Briggs, "never seen him block like that."

Briggs just looked over and gave Coach the "okay," knowing full well it was not Tully who was in there. He'd seen Net and the new boy race onto the field together and figured Net knew what he was doing. Afterall, Net was the Tiger offense. But that's when disaster, or what at first looked like it, struck.

"One-two, one-," the ball was snapped, this time past the up-back directly to Net who, in one step, feinted up the middle, then cut left towards the sideline, sprinting beyond the frozen defenders with Povic swinging behind trailing. It was working to perfection. With one Harvard backer to beat, Net pitched the ball to Mike who... fumbled. Without a man near him, with his eyes on a clear path to the goal, he lost control of the ball. The crowd was stunned, then watched in horror as the Harvard defender recovered, scooped up the ball and was sprinting towards the Tiger goal. He had sixty yards to go with no one in his path. Only the sparse Harvard fans sprinkling the stands could now be heard as he crossed mid-field gaining speed. Then, as it would be retold countless times later that day, that season, for years, Billy Tully came out of nowhere running like the wind, flying like Mercury himself, catching the Harvard man at the Tiger fifteen yardline. But rather than tackle him, Billy tomahawked the ball out of his hands, picking it out of the air cleanly after one bounce. He turned back up field with, as eyewitnesses would argue, either eighty-seven or eighty-eight yards to cover. The first man to him was bounced two feet... "no, three feet if it was an inch," wrote a local scribe... off the ground by a forearm that rocked him like the Great John L. himself. Billy cut back to his left, sidestepping three more would-be tacklers before veering right again and into the clear. The last two defenders were flailing in slow motion at his backside as he left them in his wake before crossing the goal.

The entire Tiger team raced to the end zone to engulf Billy. Net reached him first saying, "John, that was the most spectacular display I have ever witnessed,

171

will ever witness... only, bad timing, my man. Those four over there are bound to see you now."

Red Hand nodded in agreement looking for a way out... anything.

Net's eyes widened. "Billy," he yelled amidst the team, still hooting and howling, "Billy!..."

Billy Tully scrambled through the other players, and Net explained... "You've got to do it, Billy... fellas... we've all got to do this. Now let's go!..." And with that Billy tore off his helmet as Net and Junk lifted him off the ground, onto their shoulders, the crowd chanting his name, "Tully... Tully... Tully..." carrying him off the field among hundreds... thousands, into Tiger lore.

*

Lenore saw him enter with Net and some of the other lads. She turned, catching herself looking into the mirror above the bar, breathing a bit quicker, straightening her hair.

What am I doing, she said to herself. But she knew, and she delighted in it.

"Lenore!" It was Net yelling from across the room which was already filling, motioning for her to come over. She walked up as Net, John, Billy, Junk and two more of the Tiger linemen, Morry Sanders and Chop Tingle, were settling in for a victory party they expected to last well into the night.

"My dear, we would like six of the House's finest lager, large, along with your close personal attention as we most surely will require six more quite soon after."

"Yes, Mr. Poe," she answered, smiling coyly. "Comin' right up."

Before she could turn to leave, John added, "thank you." And the look they shared for no more than a second or two was caught by everyone at the table.

"John, you rascal. How long have you been smitten?" It was Junk.

John looked perplexed. "Smitten?"

"Yes, captured by the charms of Miss Sinclair..." Net explained as the others smiled, not because Lenore was held in any disrepute. They were smiling in approval, and more than likely with a bit of envy.

John hesitated before answering. "I do feel something for Lenore I have not experienced with others... like a pain. But a good pain," he said quickly, which caused a chuckle around the table. The boy was embarrassed now, but Net set him at ease.

"That's good, John. That's how you should feel." No sooner had Net added, "now where is that lager?..." Lenore arrived with three tall mugs spilling over in each hand.

"Gentlemen, your refreshment."

"Thank you, Lenore." As Net raised his mug, the others followed. "Here's to victory," he started, "and to love. Because as they say, and I do believe what they say... to capture the heart of the lovliest girls, you must first become a football hero." Then winking at John, Net rose and stated for all the Tiger faithful packed inside The Blue Boar to hear, "Princeton, I give you BILLY TULLY!"

Billy rose on cue to "TULLY!... TULLY!... TULLY!..." and it would not be, either that night or for some weeks to come, the last time.

As all there chanted Billy's name again and again, Net caught a glimpse of Jimmy and his boys through a front window heading for the entrance to the inn.

"John, the guards. No, wait. Lenore, quickly, get him out of here... out of town... now."

At first she saw a look of panic in Net, only for an instant, then control. Whatever it was, she must act. She grabbed John's hand.

"Come with me. Hurry."

He picked up his belongings and they raced through the kitchen door as Henry Pierce, the proprietor, was supervising the night's fare when he saw them.

"Lass, what is it?"

"Mr. Pierce, I've got to get John out of here... out of town, quickly. Bad men after him... here... now."

Henry Pierce had made a decent living for himself serving the students who'd come through Princeton the past twenty-some-odd years, and like Chester McGinley, he'd taken them under his wing. With no wife and children of his own, he considered them his extended family, and not more than one or two bad apples over the years had made him regret it. More often than not, passing through town after graduating and getting on with their lives, most would stop by to chat, chew the fat as he liked to call it, reminiscing about the good old days. For those who worked for him, particularly Lenore, all of his fatherly affection went double. So it was without hesitation and to no one's surprise Henry Pierce offered them his own personal transportation.

"Take Pip and Tuck. They're both out back, fed and rested, and they need the exercise."

"Mr. Pierce, are you sure?" He looked at her, like she remembered her father had, the warmth and contentment palpable.

"You're lovely," and she kissed him on the cheek before taking John"s hand again and rushing out the back door just as Jimmy and his boys were coming in through the front.

Net had thought this part through as well, and had conveyed as much to Junk and Chop and the others.

"Just back me up, boys."

"Lead on, Net," Junk told him, "we're right behind you."

Jimmy was first through the door, then Critter, Butts and Springer trailing after. Jimmy surveyed the pub, moving ahead slowly. At the second table left of the door, he leaned down, eyeing a small group of freshmen. After barely getting out, "any you pissants see..." Net was right up in his face.

"See? Did you say, see? We can all see, hayseed, and we've certainly seen enough of the likes of you... haven't we, lads?"

"I would agree." It was Junk.

"As I," Billy added.

Jimmy hesitated. It was all too familiar... like the other night. He chanced another question but was cut off.

"You were not invited to speak, hayseed. However, I will tell you this. We will accommodate you in one respect, since we can all see so well. How about all of us seeing all of you out the door. What do you say lads?!"

The immediate roar of approval was accompanied by the entire Princeton starting eleven led by Net and Junk swarming over the four guards, lifting them overhead, heaving them like so much trash through the front door of The Blue Boar

Inn into the muck of a now drizzly afternoon as the rest of the lads within roared, "GO!... GO!... GO!... GO!..."

It was the last sound John and Lenore heard before kicking their horses to a gallop.

*

Pip and Tuck were at the bit headed north before the two riders slowed to a cantor just outside of Rocky Hill. They could see the town in the distance, its lights beginning to flicker here and there as the sun dropped from the sky, trumpeting a blanket of stars to guide their way. They bypassed the town, staying in the countryside, red oaks and dogwoods all around, until they found a shallow bank on the Stony River, and crossed. Night had fallen, but the stars cast a sheen. John could still make out the girl riding beside him, and his mind raced with the thought of her there, the two of them heading towards... he knew not. It was only later when they stopped outside of New Brunswick that Lenore told him her plan. If the guards did anything, they would continue looking up the line all the way to Canada, she reckoned, particularly in the small towns. Why not hide in the one place where the two of them could disappear within a sea of humanity as desperate as themselves?... a place she knew well... every block and corner, every nook and crany.

"I'm takin' ya to the Kitchen, Johnny," she half yelled over to him as they approached the Raritan River. "We c'n stay at me mums for as long as we like."

After stopping to rest for a while on the far bank, he asked, "the Kitchen?"

They sat under a tall oak munching off a loaf of sourdough Lenore had grabbed on their way out of The Blue Boar along with a few of her own particulars.

"Yes, Hell's Kitchen. It's a name been given to the neighborhood where I was raised. A policeman named Dutch Fred the Cop and his partner came up wid it when I was jus' a wee lass. Funny thing is, they was talkin' 'bout the tenements where we lived... at 39th an' 10th Avenue. Still do."

Red Hand listened, but could only guess at most of what she was saying. The boy had no notion of what a tenement was, much less the number of them along with the saloons, slaughterhouses, factories, warehouses and such that were

175

packed into the westside of midtown Manhattan in New York City. The very next day, however, he was about to find out.

After bypassing Metuchen, they stopped for the remainder of the night outside of Rahway, finding shelter in a thicket of blueberry. They tied off the horses and scraped together a pallet of leaves using their saddles as pillows.

"It's cold," she said, burrowing in.

"Come," he motioned, "it will warm you," and she moved closer, shivering some within his embrace until she could feel his warmth seeping into her body. It came slowly, and she snuggled tighter, wrapping one leg over his. He'd never felt like this. The ache he remembered back at the inn was only a ripple on a stream compared to what had now become a river overflowing with her touch, carrying him faster and faster along. His heart pounded, his mind racing with his own youthful desires which he'd experienced but once before with a girl of his tribe, and that only from a distance. There was no distance between he and Lenore now. They were tangled up like two bear cubs in winter waiting for their mother.

"Are you warm?"

"Mmmm," she answered, moving her arm onto his chest. She felt his heart, her hand riding its beat, and she looked into his eyes. They knew it was right... the two of them... the night. Their lips met gently, and they lingered, softly, indulging themselves, kissing over and over again, exploring every perfect part of the other's mouth, the smoothness of the skin, the tip of the nose, the curving of the ear, until at last a whipperwill announced the first light of day.

They hadn't wanted the night to stop, but with the second calling of the whipperwill, the boy said, "daybreak," waiting before adding, "we must go."

"I don't want to," she replied, causing him to smile. He was catching on to the white ways.

"Lenore..." when he spoke her name he was taken with how easy it was for him, how familiar.

"That was nice."

He didn't say anything more. He rose, reaching for her hand, which she gave him.

*

It was mid-autumn when they trotted Pip and Tuck into the city after ferrying across the Hudson, the chill in the air more noticeable than it had been the day before. Each day it would grow colder still, he thought, until the first snow which was soon to come... good for covering tracks. But now as they turned their horses north on 10th Avenue approaching the southside of Hell's Kitchen, John put the weather from his mind. He was awestruck by what stood before him. It looked as if all of the whites were gathered in this one place, thousands of them, neverending, like the buffalo on the great plains his forefathers had hunted. But the whites, unlike the buffalo, would not be wiped out. There were camps like this one, cities they called them, still farther east, and extending west through his own homeland to the great sea beyond. At that moment, the boy knew he could not return to the reservation. He would not be able to reconcile a life there, removed, isolated, after seeing all of this. After all, had not his father come from such a place? Am I not my father's son? Yet, as he marvelled at the sight, he had difficulty seeing these people as his own, until he looked at Lenore.

"John, this way. We'll stable the horses a coupla blocks over and walk the rest o' the way."

They pulled the horses up in front of Kilkenney's Livery just as the old man was coming around the far corner after putting away a team of bays.

"Well, if it ain't my favorite girl and, who's this?... have you given yer heart to another, lass?"

"I'm afraid so, Mr. Kilkenney. This here's John... John Connor."

Alan Kilkenney reached out and shook John's hand. The old man's grip and the look in his eye exposed at once his honesty and good nature, both of which he'd brought with him from the old country thirty years earlier.

"Then, I suppose, me an' the misses will remain united in holy matrimony for at least another day."

"I suppose," Lenore replied, smiling.

"Now let me take Misters Pip and Tuck from ye. They look like they could use a rubbin' down an' a bucket o' oats. Tell me, how long will ye two be stayin'?"

"A few days I'm thinkin'. Can I keep ya posted, Mr. Kilkenney?"

"Ye may, lass."

Before John untied his and Lenore's belongings from the horses' saddles, he extended a hand to the man stating, as he had practiced in his mind, "it was very nice meeting you, sir."

Alan Kilkenney was impressed, indeed.

"You've got a keeper there, Lenore," he waved to them as they walked back towards 10th Avenue. Both John and Lenore waved back.

"Now, I've someone else fer ya to meet." She took his hand once again, holding it tightly, and his heart raced.

*

The odor inside the tavern was a combination of strong drink, beef and tobacco, not unlike The Blue Boar they'd hurried from only the day earlier. Yet as John was squinting, his eyes adjusting to the light, he noticed a fourth odor, a fragrance, and was curious until he saw the small vases of flowers centering each table, and the one large one at the far end of the bar.

"Roses," he said to Lenore. "I like roses."

"There for me ma. It's her touch to the place after me pa passed on. Her name is Rose, ya see."

"Ah, I see."

And with that they heard her.

"Lenore... darlin'..." she was excited and crying at the same time as she ran from the kitchen to greet her daughter. "I wasn't expectin' ye. Why didn't ye send word an'... ah it's so good to see ya, girl."

Rose was half hugging her to death before she noticed John standing next to her.

"An' who might this be?"

"This, mother, is John Connor. I met him at The Blue Boar. He'd never been to the city, so we decided to come. Hope it's no bother, ma."

"None a'tall, dearie." Rose wasn't sure about things yet, but she decided to wait before inquiring. She knew her daughter was no fool, no one to be taken in by some flim flammer with a good story and a wink in his eye.

"It's very nice to meet you, Mrs. Sinclair."

"And you, Mister Connor."

"Please call me John. I would feel better."

She liked him at once.

"So, how long will ye be stayin' lass?... ah, the two o' yous, I mean?"

Lenore smiled at her mother's slight discomfort, and she told herself she would explain everything in due time.

"A few days, maybe the week. I thought John could use me own room, an' I could bunk in with ye... if that's all right ma?"

Considering the alternative Rose was quick to agree, "that'll be jus' fine, dear."

*

The next morning Rose was up early as usual, careful not to awaken her daughter as she threw on a robe, slipping out the bedroom door to make tea and scones and to see what fruit might be ripe. Entering the kitchen she was surprised to find John standing by the window staring into the street which was already filling with people.

"Why, John, lad, I didn't think ye'd be up this early."

"Good morning, Mrs. Sinclair."

"Call me Rose, John. I don't need ta be feelin' any older than I already am. I'm reminded o' that daily down at the pub by some o' the regulars."

"They tell you you are old?"... he inquired somewhat incredulously.

"All in fun, lad, all in good fun." She hesitated, then said, "but, ya know, sometimes..." and her voice trailed off into her own thoughts until she regained her focus and asked, "tell me, John, how'd ya meet my Lenore?"

"At The Blue Boar."

Rose waited some before adding, "and?..."

John was not quite sure what she was asking now. He was unaware of the whites natural desire for detail in conversation, particularly white women. Of course, she, not knowing his heritage, didn't understand he thought he'd answered her fully and completely.

She began again. "Exactly what were the circumstances, lad?"

He looked puzzled.

"I mean... fer instance, did ya boldly walk up and introduce yerself sayin', 'I'm very pleased to make yer acquaintance, miss?...' or did she accidentally bump inta ya and spill grog all ov'r yer coat?... or dump a plate o' beans in yer lap jus' so's ya'd look at her?... the circumstances, lad, the circumstances."

He understood... the circumstances. He would have to learn to share his thoughts.

"One day I walked into The Blue Boar and Lenore served me. She told me of a new drink they had that was sweet, and with bubbles. I liked it. But I remembered her more than the drink."

Rose laughed, "I should hope so, lad, even if I'm a wee bit prejudiced. Then what?"

John was catching on to the white ways again and answered, "I thought of her often each day. When I went back with the team, with Net, he introduced us."

"Net Poe?"

"Yes."

"Lenore's spoken of him. Nice lad I hear."

"Yes, we are friends. The last time we were at the inn, two days ago, some men came who have been looking for me..." and John told Rose about the events of his life over the past few months — his showdown with Thompkins, time in The Stockyard, his escape and travels north — and also of his life before, with his family on the reservation.

Rose had just remarked, "that is quite a story, me boy," when Lenore entered the kitchen.

Rubbing the sleep from her eyes she inquired, half yawning, "what story?"

Rose got up from the table, excusing herself. "I'll be gettin' down to the tavern now... got some orders to take care of... see yous later this evenin'."

John waited a moment for Lenore to settle herself then told his story once again, starting slowly, beginning with his days on the reservaton as they drank their tea at the table in the small parlor, telling her of the time his father's friend, Ethan MacCall, came to visit... explaining how his fight with Thompkins became unavoidable as they now walked up 5th Avenue, buildings rising on either side, John in awe of their size... finally relating the details of his trial and incarceration, and ultimate escape as the two of them relaxed on a bench in the Sheep Meadow in Central Park. Lenore was captivated, digesting every phrase, every word, burning them into her memory. She didn't ask a single question until he ended with, "then I met you."

"My lord, John, how'd ye get through it, I mean the past few months, without losin' yer mind?"

"It was hard in the prison, but I always thought, always knew, I would escape. I attached my spirit to this counsel, and it did not fail me. Many times, though, I wondered if it would."

"I'll bet. But now," she hesitated, "now, John, what're ye goin' to do?"

"Men are still after me. I must keep moving until my trail grows cold, so they will give up the chase. You and your mother are in danger, so I will soon leave... one or two days from now."

The words hung heavy in front of her, unwanted, yet inescapeable.

"That's the last thing I wished to hear," she whispered.

"I as well, but it is too dangerous for me to stay."

"I'll go with ye then." The excitement showed in her voice.

"I have had those thoughts, but no, not this time. We must wait until the danger passes."

Taking his hand in both of her's, easing her head onto his shoulder, she knew he was right, so she returned to her own thoughts of the two of them together, sometime...

*

The following day Rose came home before the evening rush at the pub with the news. Johnny Riley, one of the regulars, had heard earlier in the day four southern fellas with badges were roughing up some of the boys at The Black n' Tan down on Anthony Street near the Five Points. They were looking for a fugitive, a half breed, who they suspected had come this way.

"John, I'm afraid for ya, lad. They're here."

"John, we've got ta get ye outa here," Lenore said, almost demanded.

He didn't answer her, not yet. His mind was on the stories she'd been telling him about the neighborhood, how over the years, with all the political and cultural unrest, immigrants coming in from Ireland and Germany, then Italy, old prejudices flared, things happened, people disappeared. Hell's Kitchen simply ate them up.

"Here," he answered, "maybe it is here that I should face them. This is a hard place to be... to survive," and the look he gave Lenore and Rose showed he learns quickly.

"Where is this Johnny Riley?... can I meet him?"

Rose showed some signs of confusion but said, "o' course, he'd be at the pub tonight, I'm sure."

"Good."

*

John and Lenore arrived at The Raven's Nest at a quarter past nine o'clock. She entered first while he stood in the shadows of the butcher shop across Orange Street, watching both the men milling on the sidewalks and the entrance to the pub. Moments later Lenore poked her head out, signaling him to come on, Johnny's here, no troublemakers about.

In a back booth, Rose made the introductions.

"Johnny, I think ye met me daughter, Lenore, a while back..."

"I did, and I must say, darlin', yer as pretty as yer mum."

"Why thank you, sir."

"An' this here is John Connor, a good friend of Lenore's an'," hesitating only slightly, "mine as well."

"Very good to meet you," John stated.

"Likewise," said Johnny. "Well, then, what can I do fer yous?"

182

Rose briefly restated what Johnny had told her earlier that day, adding it was John they were looking for. As Johnny raised an eyebrow some, John gave him the short version of the 'whys and wherefores,' Lenore and Rose chiming in from time to time, damning the men who were after him. Johnny kept nodding his head in agreement until John had finished.

"I see... I believe ya, lad," Johnny started, "but as I said, what can I do fer ya?"

"I have seen these men. They do not frighten me, not any of the four. But for me to fight them alone, I would have to kill them. I have thought about that, and it is not what I wish."

Johnny was beginning to see his point.

"Lenore has told me of this place, the gangs, the violence. Are there any men today who might wish only to count coup with me, and drive these men chasing me back to their own land, for good."

"I see, laddie," Johnny smiled, "yes I do see the beauty of what yer askin'."

The three of them were staring at Johnny as he continued to smile, silent, his eyes all a glaze as if he was miles away in another place, another time... which he was.

"Johnny?..." Rose finally broke in.

Returning to the task at hand, Johnny stated matter-of-factly, "Ye must see Tipper. He can help ya."

"Tipper?"

"Yes, name he goes by... a warrior from the ol' days when the Irish gangs ruled The Points. Real names's Sean Spillane, from Tipperary originally. Got off the boat in sixty-four wit his folks who were murdered by some o' The American Guards fer their poke, which amounted to ten dollars an' a gold watch. The crushers took young Sean to Cow Bay an' dumped 'im. He was only eight years at the time. Fended fer 'imself since as a bootblack, then a runner... finally a full-fledged lay in order to eat an' help fill the growler back at the Bay. He was only twelve when he joined The Forty Thieves, but soon earned his keep. Turned out one of the best fighters in The Points, an' a tough act still. He's kept a small group o' the Irish immigrants together fer jus' this sort o' thing I'm guessin'... call theirselves The

Islanders, cause it's a mixin' o' The Forty Thieves, Kerryonians, Dead Rabbits, Plug Uglies an' a few o' the others who as wee boys had got off the boat wit their folks, an' now 'ave banded together out o' necessity... to survive."

"May I meet with him?..." John asked.

As chance would have it, he would, and sooner than later.

"You may, laddie. How's 'bout now?..." and Johnny nodded towards the door, smiling.

All turned at the same time seeing the two men entering The Raven's Nest. They came in easily, eyes darting this way and that. The bigger of the two had a full head of black hair, slightly graying at the temples, and a dark mustache. He was an inch or two over six feet, his muscled body apparent under a red flannel shirt and topcoat. He wore black trousers with dark brown work boots laced up. What appeared to be a hatchet hung from his belt. The other man was nearly as tall, but with short-cropped reddish brown hair trailing into three days growth of beard. His silk vest, slightly worn, covered a collarless, white cotton shirt save for the three-quarter sleeves. This was nicely tucked into forest green, flared trousers which were, in turn, tucked into tan, calfskin boots. A knife, holstered to the side of his belt, was barely visible. As they moved towards the bar, both of the mens' eyes never stopped scanning the room until the larger of the two saw Johnny Riley in the back. Their eyes locked for a moment before Johnny motioned for them to join he and the others. Tipper elbowed his companion, and they walked towards the table.

"Tipper, me lad, been a while... how are ye?"

"A bit jaded, Johnny... been on the piss since early."

"An' you, Cam, haven't seen ye since me sis got 'er knobs."

"Jus' foosterin' about. Who're yer friends, Johnny?"

"This is Rose Sinclair, she owns the place, an' her daughter, Lenore."

"An' this boyo?"

"This'd be John Connor."

"Bit of a bob," Cam answered, "aye, Tipper?"

Tipper didn't reply, just asked of Johnny, "what's doin'?"

"Have a seat, lads. John here has a story wants to tell yous."

—"Feckin' culchie crushers need a good puck in the gob... 'at's what I says," Cam was adamant.

John looked at Johnny for translation.

"Cam here thinks these country coppers require a good arse whippin'."

"Arse whippin'?"

"Ass kickin'... beaten up."

John nodded. "Yes, I agree... and then sent back to The Stockyard. I do not want to kill them... that would be easy. I just want to convince them their duty is done."

Tipper had been studying John as he told his story for the third time that day. The leader of The Islanders was indifferent at first, but as he listened, he began to understand the plight of the young Sioux, and the social significance that paralleled his own kind. If only a microcosym of the American Indians' greater struggle, the Irish, over the past forty years, had experienced similar hostilities in The Five Points, and by now had effectively lost control of that portion of Hell's Kitchen to the Italians and the Jews, an area which they once ruled and roamed at will. Tipper also liked the lad's savvy. He could kill these men, had killed in the past, but he was no killer. Tipper saw himself the same way.

"John... laddie," Tipper cut in, "fair play to ya, I say... we'll help ye. I know The Black n' Tan. Me an' Cam'll go ov'r an' 'ave us a chinwag wit Paddy Dunn. Sounds like the head crusher's thick as a ditch. They'll be back. Then we'll reef these boyos beyond all help... have us a ri-ra."

Although not understanding exactly what he'd heard, John liked the sound of it. "I'm going with you."

"Good fer ya," said Tipper.

"Yes, good fer ya," added Cam.

"John, are ya sure ya need ta..." It was Lenore whom he cut off at once with a gentle grasp of her hand.

"Yes, I can't let these men do all of my fighting. And I want the leader myself... for Walks Over Them."

He waited another moment until he saw resignation in her eyes, then got up and said to his new companions, "shall we go?"

As the three headed out the door Tipper said to Cam, "let's pick up the Dazzler. He should be ov'r to The Den." Then turning to John, "stargazer of a mot ya got there, Johnny. I could take a reddener fer her meself."

When they arrived at The Ferret's Den, Tipper was right. The Dazzler, one Richard Lonigan, was standing at the bar three shorts empty in front of him and a pint in his hand.

"Aye, Dickey, what's for?"

"Tipper, me good man, a might fluthered, but the night's young. Aye, Cam, how's that juicy sis o' yers?"

"All scrawbed by some sleeven bean flicker who reefed 'er good at The Maidenhead. Earned it fer actin' the maggot."

"An' who's this boyo?"

"This boyo's a lad, Dick, name o' John Connor."

John reached his hand out. "Very nice to meet you."

The Dazzler was surprised at the formality displayed by the young man in polite gent's garb standing in front of him. However, he was not lax in extending his own hand, for he knew anyone introduced to him by Tipper had surely been scrutinized.

"Pleased to make yer acquaintance, John."

As John shook the Dazzler's hand he examined more closely his attire. Cardinal and gray houndstooth suit accented with a scarlet cravat and pearl stick pin. Black calfskin gloves and hightop boots to match. Over one wrist, what looked like a walking stick, and above it all, atop a greased-down mane of hair, trimmed moustache and piercing, blue eyes, a gray felt tophat cocked to one side. He looked like, well... the Dickey Dazzler he was.

" 'Ave ye heard o' these culchies rabbitin' on aroun' The Points 'bout a runaway the las' coupla nights then, Dick?"

"I 'ave indeed... down to The Swindler's Inn, an' The Black n' Tan I'm thinkin'."

"Well, ya see, it'd be John here they're after, an' fer no good reason. So wees all are gonna reef these amadains 'til they gick their y-fronts then send 'em back home... all trussed up like in the ol' days."

186

The Dazzler was smiling at the thought. It had been a while.

"Do ya wanta join us then... fer ol' times sake. We'll 'ave us a hooley after."

"Not wit dos wagons whose jammy baz yous been aussie kissin' in the jacks," Dick smiled. Tipper and Cam chuckled at their friend's unique brand of humor as Dick added, "sure I'll join yous. 'Aven't 'ad a good dust up in donkeys years."

They headed first to The Swindler's Inn on Cross Street. Dick had heard from one of the fellas at The Den the guards had been there earlier in the day. After roughing up one of the regulars, they threatened to be back if they didn't get their man.

Stepping now out of the bright sunlight into the dank odor of smoke and whiskey, they hesitated, their eyes adjusting to the dimness about. The few locals drinking at a far table were talking amongst themselves, quiet like, so they walked towards the bar. Ian the Elder, as he was known for the daytime bartender was also named Ian and a younger man, had just returned from the kitchen.

"Ian," says Tipper, "how are ya?" Then he saw that old Ian was banged up a bit. "What's that on yer gob, Ian?"

"Them four culchies was jus' here. One o' 'em loafed me good when I couldn't tell 'em anythin'... fekkin' gobshites. If I was a younger man I'd..."

"We'll take care o' that fer ya, Ian. Which way'd they go?"

"Ov'r to The Black n' Tan, I'm thinkin'."

*

They were four abreast now, walking smartly down Cross Street until they came to an intersection where the road converged with Anthony and Orange Streets. This was the infamous Five Points, and it wasn't difficult to observe why. From these crossroads, in three directions, the streets were lined with groggeries, gambling houses, saloons and brothels, above which, take your pick, were tenements known to be the filthiest in the five boroughs. This night was like most... locals everywhere, a good portion half drunk ready for their poke to be taken, ladies of the night on the pimp, gang members milling about watchful not to get isolated, and the police, the crushers, grabbing a handful off the top where they could.

The lads turned the corner at Anthony Street, the crowd parting, cutting them a wide swath when they saw Tipper, then Cam and The Dazzler with a jump in their step and the look of business in their eyes. But who was this fourth lad?

John could see the sign in the distance now, The Black 'n Tan, just up the street on the left. As they neared the entrance, Tipper said, "They's here, I c'n smell 'em."

Just inside now, the place was full of a hundred or so of The Point's finest... drinking, gambling, carrying on, but not in the free wheeling, rollicking manner that was common, even expected. There was an edge to the revelry this night. Something was amiss. And as soon as the lads were fully inside with a view of the booth regularly occupied by Paddy Dunn, the reason was apparent.

"John," asked Tipper without taking his eyes off the guards, "which one o' these fekkin' eejit's Jimmy?"

"The tall one."

"Good. He'd be yours then. We'll take the others as they line up... right lads?"

Cam and Dick nodded.

"Now let's give 'em what for."

Jimmy had Paddy Dunn by the shirt collar, about to backhand him when the sudden stillness inside the saloon caused him and the other guards to turn around. Their surprise was evident as they saw before them the boy they'd been trailing for some weeks, and alongside him three others they'd just as soon not deal with.

"Let him go," John started.

Jimmy did so, adding veiled threats, "we cornered ya, boy. We takin' yer red ass back ta prison, an' you gonna be in 'at hole 'til ya rot. Now you boys," Jimmy half ordered pointing to the others, "y'all leave it be."

The crowd backed off slowly as the eight men faced each other. They knew what was coming from Tipper, and it wouldn't be long.

"No," John said evenly, "only you are leaving, and I would suggest now, and quickly."

Jimmy's faced reddened, his show of quiet force turning to ire as he raged, "we gonna drag yer red nigra carcass back if'n we got ta..."

Those were the last words Jimmy or any of the other guards would utter for some days.

Tipper raised his battle hatchet high above his head, cutting Jimmy off with the cry, "Islanders takes care o' their own!... specially when fekkin' culchies come actin' the maggot, loafin' the hard workin' people o' The Five Points! Now lads, let's send these mollies back to da rurals!"

The fight was over before it was on. Tipper lunged at Nat Springer, feinted right, then jumped left bringing the butt end of his hatchet down on the side of Nat's scalp just hard enough to stun him, then delivered a swift kick to his privates, and the man fell like a tree. Cam had already severed Butt's right thumb from the rest of his hand when he tried for his pistol. While he was still screaming, Cam snipped the buttons off his shirt and carved his signature "C" on his chest. Dick, a fan of the Great John L. and proficient in the art, was snapping back Critter's head with stiff jabs, then a right to the kidneys, then another left, putting the big guard on his knees. John hadn't a weapon, but he leaped at Jimmy just in time to grab his gun hand, twisting and jumping behind him, ripping the arm upwards, splintering it at the elbow. It was done. The guards were helpless, groaning, groping... the Irish lads and their adopted brother putting them to sleep for what remained of the night to the cheers from the patrons that filled The Black 'n Tan, that is until Paddy Dunn himself yelled over them all, "drinks fer the lads!... drinks fer YOUS ALL!"

*

Two hours later, Tipper and Cam walked around the corner from The Black 'n Tan to a warehouse they used for just such occasions as these.

"Theys lookin' like the gobdaws they be, aye, Tipper?"

It was Frankie The Rabbit, called such for talking all the time, or 'rabbiting on' as it was. Whether you liked his gab or not, Frankie was reliable at cleaning up the mess after the Islanders finished their handiwork around The Points from time to time. And this time, Tipper made it clear he wanted these four trussed up proper before they were taken to the trainyard for a fond farewell back to the swamps of the Okeechobee.

As Tipper and Cam looked over the guards, they found them stripped naked in the fetal position, wrists and ankles tied together, each with one of their socks they'd been wearing for six weeks stuffed in their mouth gagging them near to choking.

"Do yous like the spuds, lads?"

The two looked closer, seeing now each man had a potato shoved up his arse.

"Bit of a gickin' problem," Cam remarked.

"Aye, an' an Irish message to these boyos fekkin' culchie friends back home... 'stay out da Kitchen.'" After a pause for effect, Frankie added, "they'll be catchin' the 2:10 to the Liberty Bell."

"Good. Come to The Den after fer the hooley, Frankie. Mary's been askin' fer ye."

"Mary?... Mary Tansey?!... that sleeven header. I'd jus' as soon play with me knob."

"Aye, she's a bit of a chancer, but think of those grand jabs o' hers," Cam reminded him, smiling.

As Sean Spillane and Cameron Coyle walked into the shadows, heading to The Ferret's Den to join the revelry, Frankie gave thanks once again to the Lord above for their very existence on this earth, and most of all, that they walked the streets of The Five Points. For if that was not the case, the rest of the Irish lads and their kinfolk would have been banjaxed beyond all help long ago.

**

Entrance to Saint Patrick's Cathedral

Formally opened on May 25, 1879, the newspapers hailed
the new Cathedral as "the noblest temple ever raised in any land
to the memory of St. Patrick." Since that time it has hosted
royalty and heads of state for ceremonies of all kind and manner,
not to mention the sacred vow of matrimony
for a portion of the local gentry.

Lenore Sinclair

It was two days later when John attempted to explain to Lenore his anxiety, a feeling of unfinished business that presented itself so clearly. It wasn't what once had been the constant thought of escape to the Canadas, rather it was the state of those he loved back home — his mother and family — and in the back of his mind, the level of lawlessness Strait and his men were continuing to dispense.

"I couldn't stay here without seeing my people again, Lenore. You must understand that."

"I'll go with ye," she said excitedly.

"Riding the rails?... living off the land?... no. I must go back to my family once again and see to their wellbeing, then I will return. I do not know when, but I will return."

She clung to him, he brushing a tear from her cheek, looking into her eyes one last time, a memory he would carry with him always.

"Tell your mother farewell. I will think of you often." And he turned and walked down 8th Avenue towards the Hudson, and home.

*

Rose took the next two nights off consoling her daughter, almost to the point of exhaustion. She hadn't seen Lenore's spirit broken to such extremes in years, not since she was a babe, Rose recalled, and her cat went missing. But this was no passing flirtation with the young lad from the far west. And Rose feared Lenore would not recover.

The days passed with the girl shutting herself in the small tenement away from the world outside. Her mother would bring her tea and something to eat from time to time, which Lenore nibbled at, replying "thank ye," but nothing more.

It'd been nearly two weeks, the worry on Rose still plain, when one evening Lenore walked into the parlor and looked at her mother and stated firmly, as if more practiced than believed, "he will return." Then broke into tears.

"He will, darlin', I can assure ye o' that. He's not a man given ta idle chatter, I could see that straight away. Now," and she looked her daughter in the eyes, "ye've got ta grab hold o' yerself and face the days 'til then. Ye know that now, don't ya?"

Lenore shook her head yes, slowly, but yes nonetheless.

"All right then. Now I could use some help down at the pub. Let's get some sleep tonight, darlin', an' be chipper in the mornin'. Okay then?"

"I will, ma," then looking up, the pain welling in her eyes, "but I miss him so."

*

After surprising her mother early the next morning with the smell of freshly baked scones, Lenore went down to the stables and asked Mister Kilkenney if he would be so kind as to have his son drive Nip and Tuck back to The Blue Boar. She was sure Mister Pierce would be missing them by now, wanting to take them out himself as he often did. Mister Kilkenney stated that would be no inconvenience; his boy, Charlie, could use a few days away from the stables, and the city. She thanked him and walked across town to the flower market to pick up the day's ration of roses, then headed for The Raven's Nest.

"What's 'at in yer basket, lassie?..." one of the two men asked, picking up a rose, savoring its scent.

"Potatas," she answered, the scorn visible as she waited for him to put the rose back.

She wasn't sure which gang they belonged to, but she was certain they were not Islanders, for the Irish remnants of times past were not given to pestering those in the Kitchen.

"Potatas, eh... well then, let me help ye peel them, lassie," he grinned as he begun to pick the petals from the dark red rose, dropping them slowly as his companion smirked, knowing what was coming.

"Whadya think yer doin', ya feckin' mollies?... them's me mum's roses..." Lenore was adamant now, "hump off!"

They only grinned wider as the bold one moved closer, stretching out a hand, grasping at her breast. She retreated, holding the basket of roses in front of her, shielding herself, but he threw it to the ground, lunging, tearing her collar.

It was when she was stumbling backward that the large, meaty hand grabbed the bully's neck, nearly lifting him off the ground. Cam quickly had the point of his blade up under the chin of the other while Tipper continued to squeeze the breath from the bully he recognized as a member of the Whyos, an Irish gang who would attack any and all, even their own.

"He's a right gobdaw, idn't he Cam, actin' the maggot towards this stargazer," Tipper remarked as he continued squeezing, the bully's eyes bulging, his face nearly as red as the roses strewn about his feet. "Yer makin' some holy show, throwin' shapes fer this feckin' amadain wid ya."

The bully couldn't answer. He was clutching at Tipper's hand trying to pry it from his throat, now with both hands, choking, gagging.

"Shall we get to millin' wid deez two goms, Cammy, er jus' loof 'em good an' send 'em back to dat kip in da Bowery?"

Cam liked the second idea so well, in one swift move he sheathed his knife, grabbed the fella's shirt collar, headbutting him until his knees buckled. When he let go, the boyo stumbled away like he was on a three-day bender.

All Tipper had to do was let go his hold on the bully to effect the same result. He and Cam smiled, as did Lenore, watching the two weave hither and yon down the crowded avenue, heading as instructed towards that dive of a pub in The Bowery called The Morgue, named such because the proprietor, one Paddy O'Reilly, recommended his refreshments for embalming as well as drinking.

When the boys were helping Lenore gather up her roses, she thanked them. "Much obliged Misters Spillane and Coyle. I'm indebted to yas."

"Not at all, Miss Sinclair, not at all," Tipper stated, "bit of a ri-ra is all. Can wees escort ye to The Nest then?... just to fend off the headers in our fair city, o'course."

"Ye may, sirs," and she added, "an' ye may call me Lenore. I ain't given to such proprieties, ye know. I'm just a..." and the word lingered on her lips for a moment, "... a lass... from The Kitchen."

"All right then, dat's settled," Tipper said. "Now even though wees be a might older than ye, we ain't yer Gran'pas either. So I'd be Tipper..."

"An' I'd be Cam," Cam chimed in. "Shall wees," Cam bowing at the waist before the three headed off towards The Raven's Nest with the roses.

They chatted easily as they strolled the remaining six blocks to the pub. At various points, Tipper or Cam would remark on a particular establishment, giving Lenore a brief history of the place, most often the place being a pub, recounting an event or two to which they'd been a party. While Lenore had lived in Hell's Kitchen all of her life save for the past two years she'd spent in Princeton, she'd never heard such stories. As the boys explained, such stories weren't for the likes, or ears, of young lasses, particularly beauties like herself, and she blushed some.

"Aye, Cam, is the stargazer taken a reddener fer me or the remark?"

"I can't be sure, Tipper," then Cam turned to Lenore, "but I'm scarlet fer ye, darlin'. Tipper's a bold one, only slaggin'."

Lenore smiled, then slipped in between her two guardian angels, taking the arm of each after handing her roses to Cam. She didn't say anything, just held the two men tightly. At once they felt the bond between them seal, and both knew from that moment they would do anything for Lenore... anything.

*

"What kept ye, darlin'," Rose said the moment she saw Lenore enter the pub. "Were you not able to get..." then cut short her question when Tipper and Cam followed in behind.

Lenore saw the look of trepidation cross her mother's face. What were these two doing with her daughter? Their reputations were as notorious as any who had walked the streets of Hell's Kitchen in the past thirty years.

"Ma, look at ye," her daughter laughed, "you remember Tipper and Cam... the night Johnny Riley introduced us when John was here... right here in the back booth."

"Ah, yes... yes I do now," she replied remembering full well. "Good day to yous, boys."

"An' to ye, ma'am," both responded.

Rose's brow was still knitted when Lenore chuckled again, then explained why she'd been a might tardy returning with the roses... how Tipper and Cam had come along "in the nick," as she put it, rescuing her, sending the two bully's packing. When she'd finished her story, Rose's expression, already having changed from concern to gratitude for the boys' actions, was now filled with a mother's affection for her daughter's two protectors.

"Boys," Rose stated once again, " 'tis a very good day indeed. An' if ye would, do this one favor fer a grateful mum; make The Raven's Nest home as often as ye like... grog an' supper courtesy of the establishment. Yer money's no good here. Do I make meself clear?..." she stated, smiling broadly, giving each a tremendous hug. "Now sit yerselves down, I'll have Michael bring yous some stew an' a coupla jars," and she turned to her bartender, "Michael, could ye bring these two fine gentlemen some dinner?... an' two pints of our finest lager? An' Michael, take no money from these boys. At The Raven's Nest, they eat an' drink as they please." Then turning to her daughter, "Lenore, help me wit the roses."

It was later when Lenore was back at the table that Tipper asked her about John. She hesitated, looking away, brushing a strand of hair from her cheek before responding, knowing that keeping it locked up inside was doing her no good.

"He had to leave... to see his folks an' family back home... out west." There was quiet again for some moments.

"It's all right, Lenore, if ye'd prefer not to discuss it. We can chinwag 'bout da weather, or da way Willie O'Hairn has a gatch like a fluthered duck..."

Lenore was smiling again.

"Or," Cam went on, "how the Dazzler was throwin' shapes after Annie Donofan at a hooley las' Friday 'til she got pissed an' confessed to bein' a bean flicker..."

"Stop the lights!..." Lenore reacted like her old self, "Annie Donofan!?..."

"The very same," Cam replied, "she left Dick at The Hound's Tooth langered 'til he weren't da full shillin'. Juicy bird dat Annie is... a waste, aye Tipper?"

"Aye, dat it is. Well, my dear," Tipper changed the subject, "seein' dat yer happy out once again, Cammy an' me better be findin' the Dazzler. He's still a mite narky ov'r Annie."

Cam punctuated their leaving. "We better bring along a queer bit o' skirt he c'n wear da head off to brighten da boyo's evenin'."

Lenore blushed as the two men made their way towards the front entrance to the pub. There, they turned and bowed.

"Good day then, sweet Lenore."

*

It'd been six months with no word or sign from John. Although the memories of their time together, and the longing for more, was never far from her thoughts, Lenore was healing. She was enjoying helping her mother at the pub, seeing old faces she'd not seen for three years or more. To a man, all remarked how she'd flowered into a beauty, which of course embarrassed her no end, but she was thankful, replying how good it was to see them as well.

Tipper and Cam stopped in regularly for a pint or two, never more, for they didn't want to abuse Rose's gratitude. On occasion, they had no choice but to allow her to serve them a plate of the specialty of the day, which most often was stew. The boys would beg off at first, however they admitted to Lenore more than once they always looked forward to the feast. As chance would have it, one morning the two strolled in with a third lad. When Lenore saw them, she was taken aback some by the second look she gave the newcomer. It surprised her, startled her in fact, catching herself looking at another with the same interest she'd once had for John that first day she'd served him coca cola at The Blue Boar.

"Sweet Lenore, how are ye this fine day?" It was Tipper.

"Jus' fine, Tipper. Hello, Cam."

"Good day, Lenore. Allow me ta introduce dis young lad to ye, it bein' his birtday an' all. Wees takin' 'im on a piss up an' a bit o' malarky. Mister Daniel Coyle," Cam gestured to his brother, "Miss Lenore Sinclair. An' is she not the stargazer

Tipper an' me've been tellin' ye?"

As she attempted to scold Cam, Danny extended his hand, "a pleasure to make yer acquaintence, Miss Sinclair. As always, Tipper an' me brother are right as rain."

"Very nice ta meet ye as well," she replied. His hand felt good, warm. "This bein' yer birthday an' all, let me get yous all a round o' shorts an' some fry to lay a base. I'm thinkin' ye'll be needin' it."

"Pint o' plain fer me, miss," Danny said.

"All right, then."

As Lenore walked towards the bar Danny turned to Cam and Tipper, "yer not gettin' me all langers t'day. This evenin' we're comin' here fer afters." When Danny's eyes focused on Lenore once again, following her as she disappeared into the kitchen to order their breakfast, Tipper and Cam shared a knowing glance. Danny's interest was evident. Lenore's?... the two agreed, just as much.

*

It was later that night, after eleven, that the three arrived back at The Nest. Lenore'd been watching the clock since seven, losing hope about ten thirty she might see Danny again this day. As she was putting to bed some tables in the back, wiping them down, turning over chairs, she heard Cam first.

"Wees back," Cam stated loudly, throwing his arms out wide as he stood in the middle of the place, reeling a bit from nine hours of fluthering about Hell's Kitchen and The Bowery. "Danny was determined to come fer afters. If wees hadn't a, he'd a been narky 'til payday."

Danny didn't blush or lose eye contact with Lenore. He simply said, "Cam's right," waiting some before he added, "so, what have ye got left sweet ta eat?"

"Bread puddin' with caramel!?"

"My favorite," Danny answered smiling. Then turning to Tipper and Cam, "didn't I tell yous that very thing walkin' over."

Lenore just smiled and went for the dessert.

*

It was only one week more the two were walking in Central Park after Danny had stopped by to ask if she might get an afternoon off. Rose had overheard the excitement in her daughter's voice and immediately told her it was okay.

"Why haven't I seen ye before, Danny Coyle? Ye still lives ov'r ta 29th Street an' 10th Av do ye not?... with yer brother Cam and yer ma?"

"Yes an' no. I been in school fer the past two years up in the Bronx, at Fordham, studyin' the law. I've been boardin' up there mostly."

"While I been at Princeton... waitin' tables."

"Nothin' wrong waitin' tables, Lenore."

"Won't get me too far in this world, I'm thinkin'."

"It got ye here, didn't it," and he stopped and smiled at her, reaching out for her hand after another moment, which she gave him.

They spent the remainder of the day sitting under a tree in Central Park after buying sodas and sammies off a cart. It was a day Lenore thought, only weeks before, she would never experience with another man again. The peacefulness, laughter, sheer joy of being alive. The longing.

"The lads told me something of John," Danny said. She was leaning her head on his shoulder, his arm around her, just as dusk fell. "Not a whole lot, mind... they're not knowin' a whole lot... jus' that you and he were together... some time back."

"That'd be true."

"But he returned west."

"Yes, he did."

After some minutes Danny continued, "Lenore, I don't want to get in the middle o' somethin' that might upset ye. I'd take it as my fault, an' I wouldn't like meself much fer the doin'."

She'd thought about this day... about a time someone might come along who would erase her thoughts of John... escort her back among the living causing the blood to rush, swelling her breasts, her heart nearly bursting with desire... something Danny had done this day.

"Danny," she turned and said to him, "it'd upset me somethin' terrible if ye didn't stay."

As the sun melted into the Manhattan skyline bringing with it the last shadows of the day, their lips met softly, lingering, their desire never waning as they slipped lower to the ground, tangled together under the cover of night.

"I'm already in love with ye, Lenore," Danny whispered. "Is that strange? I've known ye a week, but 'tis how I feel."

She smiled up at him, putting her memory of John in a special place in her heart, but a place apart, " 'tis not strange, Danny, nor foolish, nor anythin' else o' the kind, for I feel the same as ye."

*

The wedding took place two months later at St. Patrick's Cathedral on Fifth Avenue, its graystone facade and flanking twin Gothic spires stationed like sentinels head and shoulders above the neighboring stores and shops.

As the eighty-odd guests filed inside, a mix of forms — Georgian classical, Romanesque, Byzantine — greeted them, bidding them sit either right for Danny, left for Lenore. In a far bay a choir sang the Ave Maria until all were seated. When Moira Feherty entered the rear of the church the music segueyed into a single organ as she strode slowly, deliberately down the aisle carrying a bouquet of roses. Once positioned just left of the altar, Danny and Cam appeared from a side gallery in traditional morning suits, and took their places just opposite. The organist stopped momentarily, then proceeded once again proclaiming the coming of the bride with the first four distinctive notes of The Wedding March.

All rose from their seats when they saw Lenore on Tipper's arm enter from another side gallery and begin walking towards the main aisle that would take them to the altar. At the head of the aisle the two hesitated, taking in the smiling faces. As little girls do, sitting alone painting a picture of their wedding day in their mind, it was as she always dreamed it would be... family, friends all around, and the man who consumed her entire being waiting by the altar.

With Lenore on his arm, Tipper felt like a god. He hadn't entertained the thought of family since his earliest days off the boat when the only one he'd known was taken from him. Tipper suffered from that tragedy more than he'd admit. To this day, at night in bed, his still youthful, loving parents would sing him to sleep, smiling down at him, and he would drift off vowing never to allow himself to be hurt that badly again. But now as he walked Lenore to the man of her dreams, Tipper felt a wash of affection sweep over him, and he was struck with the feeling. His eyes welled up letting Lenore go to Danny, but as all there observed... the toughest man in The Kitchen shed tears of parting and of joy like any proud father. And from that day forward, Tipper had a larger family than he would know.

*

The reception after was held at The Raven's Nest which Rose and Danny's mother, Emilie, had planned together. Lenore knew the two were getting on when one evening, just three days before the wedding, they surprised her in her room, popping their heads in the door, singing...

"Boxty on the griddle,
Boxty in the pan,
If you don't eat the Boxty
You'll never get a man..."

This was ancient Irish folklore, she knew, but was nonetheless flattered that both of her mothers would remember to make the boxty bread. As they proceeded into her room with the potato and flour concoction, hot out of the oven, she pulled off a large piece with her two mums joining her, and all three sat munching into the night, giggling like schoolgirls and talking of love.

The guests were filing into the pub now, family and close friends of course, as well as mere acquaintences and those one might see only now and again in the neighborhood. But this too was traditionally Irish... to have one and all partake in celebrating a young couple beginning a new life together.

The revelry, like the whisky and the ale, continued non-stop, the merry-makers dancing to a squeezbox, fiddles, fluted horns and percussion with all sort and manner of couples joining in... young ones like Lenore and Danny, fathers and daughters, grannies and grand kids, neighbors and friends.

When The Dazzler took center stage with top hat and cane, all gathered round anticipating the jig to come, for he possessed a reputation as a dancing man Eddie Foy himself could envy. The place grew still as a single flute began with Dick tapping his toe. As the band quickened the tempo, he transformed himself from the natty Dazzler he was to The Kitchen's version of a whirling dervish, everyone clapping in tune, urging him on until to the final beat of the drum he leaped high in the air, landing in splits form, throwing his arms out and head back. The place erupted... all alike cheering, hooting, whistling... and in the months to come, Dick would be rewarded with many a pint, as well as a warm bed by a lass or two, for the effort.

The Dazzler was still accepting congratulations for his grand performance when Moira Feherty's voice rose above the merriment, the sound angelic, the song a thousand years old...

Here they stand hand in hand,
They've exchanged wedding bands
Today is the day of their dreams and their plans,
And all we who love them want to say
May God bless this couple married today...

"Here, here," some of the men punctuated the ending as Moira held the last note until the clinking of the glasses, and the quiet that followed.

First to speak was Tipper, who'd been enjoying himself immensely. Not only had he been honored with the bride's first dance, he now had what he felt was family... of a kind. So with a smile as proud as any father's, he began, "Lenore and Danny... may ye be poor in misfortune, an' rich in blessin's... slow to make enemies, an' quick ta make friends... but rich er poor, quick er slow, may ye know only happiness from this day forward." The warmth Tipper displayed warranted a generous round of applause, after which he bowed and added, "an' should ye come upon any enemies, yous see me an' Cam... we'll give them feckin' mollies a good puck in the gob," and he winked as the laughter began in earnest once again.

Another clink, clink as Cam claimed the floor. He raised his glass, announcing after a hush came over all, "to me brother Danny, an' to his new bride, the beautiful Lenore," then with a reverential tone in his voice not many had heard, Cam recited the ancient toast, "may the road rise to meet you, may the wind be always at your back... may the sun shine warm upon your face, the rain fall soft upon your fields... and until we meet again, may God hold you in the hollow of his hand."

The hush that continued after Cam had spoken was as much for the manner in which he delivered his toast as the words. After some moments, Danny broke the silence, thanking his brother first, as well as all in attendance, calling Cam not only his big brother, but his best brother, adding, "after all, he's me only brother," to everyones' enjoyment.

Before he could continue, Tommy Coates, already well in his cups, blurted out from the bar, "may there be a generation of children on the children of yer children."

Danny boomed back, "Lenore an' I thank ye, Tommy," then he raised his own glass in a toast to all before him, turning a phrase or two along the way to these well worn words, "here's to you an' yours and to mine and ours," hugging Lenore, "an' if you an' yours ever come across mine an' ours, I hope mine an' ours will do as much for you an' yours as you an' yours have done for mine and ours... on this our wedding day. God bless all."

The roar of the guests and the music that followed carried the celebration far into the night, with Lenore and Danny responding to every request to dance, no matter if it was little Karri O'Connor standing atop Danny's shoes, or Ian the Elder waltzing with Lenore.

At the stroke of twelve, with the merriment at fever pitch, and the tables refilled once again with grand platters of sweet pork and marmalade, roasted potatoes and tomato salad, and deep dishes of apple caramel and whipped creme with berries, the Strawboys came.

"Look, ma?!"... Taddy Ryan cried out, tugging at his mother's dress.

Slowly they came, one-by-one from the back of the pub, dipping their shoulders and bobbing their heads to a silent tune, with high caps on their heads, pointed like, made of straw, and masks, and straw capes round their shoulders. There were eight of them, their peaked caps towering above all as they moved from guest to guest... dancing with the lasses, but never speaking.

"If they speak, they break the spell," Danny whispered to Lenore.

"Is it ta bring luck?" she asked.

"Tis," he said.

A long, intimate look passed between bride and groom as Tipper thought of the old country's ancient fertility rites, which never before seemed so near or real as they did this night.

"Do ya know where they come from?" Lenore asked.

"Somewhere... back in the hills," Danny said.

"Tis true," Tipper said, "but it's years since the Strawboys been in The Kitchen. Times past, back in the homeland, there'd be a great cheer when they'd be seen comin' high up cross the crags. Whoever sent 'em tonight blessed this marriage."

Later, after they'd left just as quietly as they'd first appeared, no one admitted to arranging their attendance, because no one there had. And it would be years before the mystery of the Strawboys was to unfold.

**

The American Bald Eagle

The eagle and the sun are linked in many cultures.
One tribe told of how the eagle and the jaguar fought over
who would have the honor of bringing warmth to our mother
the earth. The eagle settled the matter by flinging himself
into a fire, and becoming the sun.

Red Hand

"Darlin, I'm home. Where's that little ragamuffin son o' ours?... are you givin' him a good scrubbin'?

"I am me love," Lenore yelled back through the wall. "Come in an' take him off me hands, I feel I'm 'bout to pop."

Later that night after Danny had dropped young Terence off at his mother's, Lenore did give birth to their second child, Maeve Elizabeth.

"How do ya feel, darlin'?" Danny asked. "The Doc said everything went as he expected, except for a time there he thought she was a he... she's enormous," he exclaimed with a proud smile.

Lenore smiled back before whispering, "I'm fine... jus' a bit tired."

"Well, yer Ma's comin' later to stay the week, then my Ma next week... so ye can get back on yer feet."

Lenore nodded before drifting off once again, not to awake until Maeve's first feeding three hours later.

*

Spring came early the following year. With the weather already warming to shirtsleeves in early May and the sky a crisp, bright blue, Danny and Lenore decided to invite Rose and Emilie, and Tipper and Cam for dinner on the following Sunday.

When the day arrived, Danny spent the morning setting up the large, oak roundtable on a small patch of lawn in the back yard, then gathering up the four chairs and two benches they had which he judged would be adequate for all to have a place. Terence could sit between he and his Ma, or his Grandmas if he chose, and Maeve would have her highchair.

At precisely eleven o'clock the Grandmas arrived to help with the cooking, as they'd insisted. Since Tipper and Cam were due at half past noon, this gave the ladies ample time to get the large rump roast basted and garnished with rosemary and garlic before putting it in the oven, and starting the sauce for Tipper's favorite, potatoes au gratin. Cam would get his peach cobbler with an immense scoop of vanilla cream for dessert, but not before Danny had plied them both with as much rye and guiness as they pleased.

It was time. The juices from the roast were gurgling and snapping, spilling over into the pan, the hearty smell of the meat and spices filling the small kitchen. The potatoes were covered in two wide, glass dishes hot atop the stove, their brown crusts a perfect glow. The cornbread was thick and warm and moist.

Half past noon came and went. Then one o'clock. Then half past one. It was only then everyone began to worry some. To set the women at ease, Danny announced he would get over to Tipper's to see if they were still there, and if not check one or two of the pubs. As he was about to leave, there came the familiar knock, and it seemed all inside exhaled at once.

It was not until the door opened that the blood rushed from Lenore's and Rose's sweet faces when Cam stated, "brother an' sister, do yous have room fer one more? John's come home ta visit, an' we t'ought it only proper ta invite 'im."

John had changed. As Lenore and Rose studied him for some moments before introducing him to Danny and Emilie, they saw a man who looked years older, not physically, only from what his presense displayed and the gaze from his eyes. It had been three years and some months since he'd departed, but to Lenore it felt like half a lifetime.

After clearing her throat, she walked up to him, "John, 'tis... wonderful ta see ye," and Lenore hugged him as one might greet an aunt or uncle. "I hadn't expected as much... please, come in." And the three men stepped all the way into the pantry from the front stoop of the small apartment.

"John, ye remember me ma?"

"Of course I do. Good day Mrs. Sinclair... Rose," and they hugged much the same as had he and Lenore.

"An' this is me mother-in-law, Emilie Coyle."

"How do you do."

Hesitating, Lenore continued, "an' this is Danny, me husband."

John looked Danny in the eye, and at once the man who hadn't quite shaken the thought of John's return and the effect it might have on his wife felt a bond, a trust that would remain between them.

"I've been looking forward to meeting you, Danny. You're all that I expected from the man who would marry Lenore."

"It's my pleasure," Danny replied. And the two men held their grip until Danny said, "let me introduce ya to the rest o' the family, John. This here's Terence," putting his arm around his son, jostling his red head of hair some, "an' this, with her mashed potatas all over her face, is little Maeve... well, not so little as ye can see."

John smiled, shaking Terence's hand like he was all grown up. "Very nice meeting you, Terence." Then turning his attention to Maeve, he leaned over and picked up her tiny hand. Before another word, however, little Maeve delivered a mouthful of potatoes right between his eyes, much to the delight of all save Lenore and Danny.

With Tipper and Cam almost doubled up, John didn't miss a beat, stating, "Danny, was that your idea?..." increasing the level of laughter in the room twofold.

"I've learned me lesson," Tipper chimed in, "ye keep yer distance when dat one's eatin'."

Still bent down facing the little culprit, John wiped the goop from his eyes and continued, "and very nice meeting you, Maeve."

They were outside now around the table finishing up dinner, Rose and Emilie gathering up the dishes, making room for the dessert that was about to come, with coffee made up the Irish way. The crack had been good during the meal, but there'd been nothing much stated nor asked about John's activities over the past few years. That was until Cam, ever the bold one, could hold out no longer after he'd gotten his cobbler and cream placed before him, and a grand cup of the Irish.

"John, me lad, ye've been a bit tight in da gob about yer travels since wees las' seen ye. Now, I'm not wantin' ta be pryin', but tell us if ye would... how's life been treatin' ye?"

John hesitated some before speaking, shifting a bit in his chair. He first looked at Cam, then the others before continuing. "Life..." he stated, pausing, contemplating the word. "I've come to learn that, no matter how unpleasant at times it may be, life is good, and I look forward to each day. But let me tell you something about my life... so far..."

*

The day John left Lenore he headed for the only certainty he'd come to understand about traveling a great distance across this vast land in a short period of time... the railroad. When he found it, he made his way through the crowd inside the station and checked the great board to find the next train heading west, anywhere west... which was a town called Cincinnati. After inquiring if there was an earlier train going to Cincinnati than the one scheduled, he was told no, the train going to Cincinnati'll be the first one out today because of the freighter going to Newark leaving in twenty minutes. Why is that, he asked. The freighter, that right there, the man pointed, is on the same track as the train going to Cincinnati, which normally would be leaving at the same time the freighter'll be pulling out. I see, John replied. Then what time will... Thirty minutes after the freighter, the man said. Thank you, sir.

That should give me just enough time, he thought, as he made his way out to the yard, staking himself on the west end, waiting for the freighter. Once he saw the track it was on, and how fast it made the turn, he'd find a good place to settle in for the next twenty minutes, then get ready for the jump.

*

He felt free again, the wind blowing into the boxcar through the cracks in the slats, hard and crisp, as the great iron horse chugged west through open land, gobbling up miles of green, rolling hills and stands of willow and pine, taking him home.

He missed Lenore, he truly did, but he knew this was right. He'd been away too long, over a year, and no matter that he'd been sentenced to five years for killing

Thompkins, he was not sure what a man like Strait would do to regain his grip on the people of Mission... to show them what would happen to anyone with the brass to confront him or his men.

It was two weeks later when Red Hand crested the hill above his village on the roan he'd purhased only the day before in Clearfield from a farmer named Blythe. He wanted to ride the last forty miles to his home arriving on a good horse rather than straggle in on foot, so he'd spent the last ten days bending his back — baling hay, mucking stalls, mending fences, foaling calves — doing whatever needed done for Eli Blythe.

Riding down towards the village as the roan highstepped at a trot, his mind wandered to other days, earlier times, when he was a boy hunting small animals in the woods just across the valley with only a bow and arrows... and swimming the Keya Paha in the warm summer months, then afterwards sleeping beneath a blanket of stars, consumed by the mysteries of the world around him. He remembered he'd felt a great longing for knowledge... of not only his world, but also the white way. And he knew one day he would pursue such a quest.

As he neared his village, a small town in the middle of Ohio where the train had taken on water interrupted his thoughts, stealing his attention as it had before in the past two days. It was called Worthington, set just outside a larger village called Columbus. Although the train had stopped there for only a few minutes, he was not sure why this village was never far from his thoughts. There was a sense of peace there... a feeling of warmth and comfort that came not from the town, but from within himself. It was as if part of his own flesh was reaching out to this place, this white village, extending a hand, realizing he had been wayward, and was returning home at last. That must be what it is, he determined, because it was this same feeling he was experiencing now as one or two of the young men recognized him, racing to greet him, and soon after a great cry rose from the encampment... everyone rushing to him, whooping and hollering, welcoming him back to a reality that would tear out his very soul.

*

"No one knows for certain, Red Hand." It was Running Wolf speaking. "We found them two days after they were to return from town, in a small gully east of the Keya Paha. They had not been shot. It looked as if they had been clubbed to death."

"What did Sheriff Bell do?

"He came with some men and looked, but he could do nothing. Some of the others were Strait's men. They were watching."

"Did he say he would do anything?"

"Only that he would ask around, then come and tell us what he found."

"And he hasn't been back."

"No."

Two Bears and Willow had been placed together, side-by-side, next to the pyre that held Star Rising who had died six months earlier from the white man's cough. They were dressed in their finest deer skins, adorned with hawk and eagle feathers, and staked high above the ground. The funeral ceremony that followed lasted for four days. During this time many of the tribe recounted Two Bears' exploits on the battle field, and as a great leader to his people; and they spoke of Willow's strength and courage, enduring the loss of a husband, and a son.

"The white buffalo skin still hangs in Two Bears' lodge, Red Hand. You should take it now. It has been long enough."

"He was your father, Uncle. You should have it."

"No, it is yours. I fear you have lost much more than I."

There was silence between them as the smoke from the great pipe rose slowly, filling their nostrils. It was a long, reflective, deep quiet... one that overcame the everyday sounds from the camp outside, wrapping them up like a warm blanket in winter until they were taken somewhere above the earthly world, captured by the spirits of their lost loved ones dancing across their minds. While Running Wolf struggled with the vision — faint images of his father and sister speaking to him from a distance, the thickness of their words unintelligble — Red Hand saw them and heard them clearly. Theirs was a message of peace, not hatred, of kindness, not retribution. Red Hand drifted on the wind with their words, soaking them in, unaware he'd stumbled into another world, a higher state of consciousness where he could seek knowledge, find the way. As his whole body and soul drank in the feeling he began to wail, softly, waking Running Wolf, surprising him. Running Wolf had not seen anyone in such a state... their body levitating, their face contorting with anguish, then lighting up with wonder, then anguish, then wonder. Running Wolf was scared yet powerless to stop what he was witnessing. He shook Red Hand violently but with no effect. The boy continued his wailing, now supine some six inches off the ground as Running Wolf watched with awe until Red Hand's eyes suddenly opened and he crashed to the ground in a daze, his head pounding from the experience.

"Nephew," Running Wolf exclaimed, "where were you? Your body was here in my lodge, but your spirit was somewhere different. And you were making strange sounds like I have not heard. Where were you?"

Shaking the cobwebs from his mind, Red Hand said simply, "I was in a place of healing." Pausing again he stated, "I will go to the mountains, into the higher world. There I will see Santin again... and begin my journey."

At daybreak, with Running Wolf watching from the front of his lodge, Red Hand rode out from the Sioux camp on the roan he now called Truth. He had with him the white buffalo skin, and in his bedroll the sixshooter Running Wolf had kept for him since the day he was shipped east those many months ago.

*

The next day broke like it had the day before and the day before that when Red Hand had ridden from the village, the air crisp, the sky a robin's egg blue as Running Wolf sat outside his tipi perplexed. He was pondering Red Hand's statement about Santin. It had been many moons since the old one had gone to meet the Great Spirit, and he wondered what his nephew had meant about seeing him again. His confusion continued well into the day as Red Hand, now miles away, was urging on Truth, climbing higher and higher into the Black Hills, carving a trail amongst the green ash and pines rising all around.

At dusk, reaching the pinnacle of what once had been precious sanctuary for the Sioux and Northern Cheyenne, he studied the great plains below, imagining a sea of buffalo where now there was none... and he wept.

After some time, he knew not how long, his tears turned from sorrow for those who had gone on to hope for the future of those remaining. He lay his head back in silent prayer, breathing in the tranquility of this higher place, his mind open to imaginings of a more peaceful world to come. The picture in his mind seemed to stay forever, etched indelibly until, with a mournful cry that shook the very ground beneath him scattering the birds of the forest, he stretched out his arms, reaching up as high as his spirit would allow, and touched the heavens.

*

It was not until he was walking toward Sheriff Bell's office in Mission at daybreak three days later that Red Hand understood the moment of his transformation. Although his pain over the loss of his mother and grandfather would remain deep and lasting, his silent mentor, Santin, who had come in the dream, told him killing the men who took their lives was not the answer. The answer lies with those who are still living, with the townspeople of Mission and the man who has pledged to serve and protect them. Months earlier, when he'd been jailed and tried for killing Thompkins, Red Hand had judged the sheriff to be a fair man, only lacking in duty out of fear for his family's wellbeing, as had others. However, when he knocked on the door of Lee Bell's office, smelling the fresh coffee cooking inside, it was time for the men of the town to stand and be counted.

The door opened slowly as Deputy Lon Turley squinted into the rising sun before recognizing the young Sioux half-breed. His voice broke when he turned and said, "Sheriff, it's... it's the boy... Red Hand."

Rising from the chair behind his desk, Lee Bell set his coffee down saying, "let 'im in."

"Thank you, Deputy," Red Hand said as he entered the small office. The two men noticed a marked difference in the young half-breed who was tried for murder no more than a year ago. They saw a man standing before them, and wondered what might have happened in twelve months time to cause such a change.

"Good morning, sheriff. As you can see, I am home... and I am here to inquire about the deaths of my mother, Willow, and my grandfather, Two Bears. My uncle Running Wolf has told me you have been looking into the matter." And he paused, waiting for a response.

The sheriff studied Red Hand before answering. He liked the boy... man, now. He remembered thinking... Thompkins only got what was comin' to him, comin' fer sometime. But as Judge Carver ruled at Red Hand's trial, the law had to be observed, even when it served no good purpose.

"I could hold ya, son, then wire 'at jail down in Florida ta find out why yer out." He paused for the effect. "Not goin' to, though. Whyn't ya tell me yerself?"

Red Hand spoke right up. "I escaped, with the help of two others. One remains there, the other was murdered... for no reason. Just hate."

"Musta been pretty bad."

"It was. I will not return." It was not a challenge, only the truth. That is all that matters... as Santin counseled.

The sheriff eyed him.... the lad's resolve clear beneath the leather vest buttoned over a long-sleeve, white cotton shirt that was tucked into heavy jeans. When his eyes rested on the colt revolver tied down to Red Hand's right hip, he remembered the youth's swiftness with the gun. No matter, though. He wasn't going to send Red Hand back to that hellhole in Florida.

"I did look inta tha matter, son... much as I could. There weren't no trace... nothin' ta link anyone to it, although I suspec' Strait an' his boys. But, ya know, son, fer those o' us who lives here, well... you know the hard side o' that."

"I understand. But what if you had proof... something to put Strait there."

"That'd go a long way. But it'd 'ave ta be good, cuz if'n he got off, we'd all better run fer cover."

Reaching inside his vest, Red Hand produced a small piece of cloth, torn at one end, which he handed to the sheriff. "Is this good?"

The sheriff glanced at it before saying, "whadya mean. It's jes a piece o' cloth."

"Look closer."

The sheriff held the cloth up now, studying it, noticing the red and brown interwoven stripes which looked familiar. Then unfolding the one end which was

215

curled over as a result of the elements these past weeks, he saw them... the letters "JS"... Jedediah Strait's initials. Yes, the sheriff thought, I seen that bandanna on 'im... jus' yesterday in fact. Damn.

Handing it to his deputy, Sheriff Bell said, "take a look at this, Lon. Ya ever see sumpin' like it?... like a feller's bandanna?"

"Cain't says I have, Sheriff," giving it a cursory look, then more closely, "on secon' thought now, don't Strait..."

"Where'd ya git this, son?"

"In the gully... where they were murdered. It was under some brush."

"Mighta got snagged on a branch, or torn off jus' about anytime..."

"That was not a trail," Red Hand cut him off, "it was off the trail, in a hidden place. I believe it was torn off. My mother and grandfather would not be slaughtered, they would fight."

After another moment Lee Bell agreed. "I believe ya, son. I believe yer right. But what can Lon an' me do? Strait's got half a dozen men with 'im wherever he goes, an' twice 'at back at 'is ranch. We're outmatched."

"Get more men. Get Alfred Bendt and the other shopkeepers, and the farmer, Haller... all who are paying Strait only for the privilege of living."

" 'At's a nice idea, son, but when yer lookin' at a passle o' gunslingers... killers, well the fight goes plum' outa those who sell flour an' beans fer a livin'."

"They are men. If they want their town back... if you want your town back, sheriff, and you, Lon, it has to come to a fight. Today is a good day."

Lon straightened up now, a feeling of pride rushing through his veins by being included in Red Hand's remarks. He'd taken the job as deputy only three months earlier, more by default than anything. No one else was crazy enough. But as the weeks progressed, the sheriff took notice of his meticulousness, not only of his dress... always dark coat and tie with a vest, but his approach to the task... the detail of keeping precise notes of each arrest, major or minor, encounters with the drunken and disorderly, yahooers, stray cattle, even shinneying up Old Miss Longley's sycamore from time to time to rescue Dusty, her cat.

Now, with this renewed upswell of pride, Lon opened his heart to the feeling, and to an overwhelming sense of self and duty.

"I'll go git Bendt an' the others, Sheriff," and he was half out the door before turning and adding, " 'at is, if'n ya want."

It was then Lee Bell felt the power as well, his days in Abilene as a young lawman flashing across his memory, and with muscles taut and brow furrowed he said, "go git 'em."

—One hour later Alfred Bendt and Chet and Hanley Vespers, all of whom owned shops in town, were gathered in Sheriff Bell's office along with three of the local farmers... Tobias Haller, Vance Wrightwood, and Henry Busby. Counting Red Hand, that made nine of them, match enough for Strait and the six or seven men he would be riding into town with about noon. According to habit, he would stop at the bank first to take care of some business, then head on over to the saloon. His boys would be with him, flanking him the whole way. Red Hand liked that. If he could take out Strait, his men would be divided, making them much easier for the rest of the group to handle.

"Red Hand, hello," Alfred Bendt said warmly extending his hand, "it's good ta see ya, lad. Ya look fit... an' older."

"I am older, Mr. Bendt."

"I's sorry ta hear 'bout yer family... terrible thang 'at was."

The rest chimed in behind Bendt's remark, extending their condolences to Red Hand, shaking his hand.

"I am truly sorry," it was Tobias Haller now, "in paticular cuz fer these pas' months I felt I mighta prevented it back at yer trial. I seen what happened in tha street 'at day when ya took Thompkins out... 'at no account sumbitch, but Strait an' his men... well, they come out to tha farm an' scared tha misses half ta death. 'At bastard ought ta've paid."

"Here is your chance," and Red Hand showed them the piece of Strait's bandanna he'd found in the gully. "This was under some brush where my mother and grandfather were murdered. The sheriff recognized it as Strait's."

There were some seconds of silence before Henry Busby chimed in, saying what all of them were thinking, "can we take 'em?"

It was Lee Bell now. "Henry, an' fer 'at matter tha rest o' ya, how long 'ave

217

ya lived here?"

They all chimed in, Henry the longest now going on over twenty years.

"An' Strait's been rulin' tha roost fer the past three er more. Now jus' how long er we gonna let 'at continue?"

"Well, sheriff, you been pretty lax on Strait yerself, an' tha res' o'..."

"I know, Chet, I know, I'm as much ta blame as anyone, maybe more... but with this," and Sheriff Bell held up his evidence, "we got 'im. Now all we gotta do is be men enough ta take 'im."

The challenge was layed bare. Were they men enough, or would they cower, walk to the other side of the street as they had been doing, back down. And the silence returned, the air heavy with its presense, until it was broken by a voice from the back.

"Boys," the words came slowly, precisely, "you bett'r reach down 'tween yer legs an' check fer balls. If'n ya'll still got any, then you go on home an' git yer rifles. An' don't ferget ta kiss yer womenfolk. You tell 'em we're gonna take our town back today," Lon's voice was rising now, not in anger, but with empowerment for the men of Mission, "an' ain't nobody gonna take it from us again... ev'r."

Sheriff Bell and Red Hand stood almost as much in awe of Lon's words as the others. The men looked at Lon, then at one another. Chet and Hanley Vespers stood in the middle of the group. As brothers, they'd grown up fighting everyday, not really knowing why, not remembering why. But now here was a fight right in front of them that meant something... meant everything, and they nodded to each other, and left to get their guns. The rest followed, with Alfred Bendt saying on the way out, "damn, Lon, 'at was somethin'."

Another hour passed before they were back, outfitted for the fight to come. Henry, Tobias and Vance all had Winchester repeaters. All could get off six aimed shots in ten seconds or less. The problem was, none had ever shot a man, even shot at a man. Today would try their nerves, if not their very souls. Alfred Bendt and the Vespers brothers brought their Colts, as they were the preference of shopkeepers for their easy handling in close quarters. As it was, each of them had taken a pot shot at a thief or two over the years, but this would be different. Men would die today.

The silence in the office returned, draping the nine of them like a canvas, dark and complete. There was no angst, no trepidation, only anticipation of the fight to come. And they waited.

As expected, the clock above Lee Bell's desk showed five minutes past noon when they heard the clatter of horses on the red-brown clay outside packed down by the morning mist. Lon cracked the door and poked his nose out just far enough to see Strait and his men pulling up in front of the bank, then turned back to the others.

"They's here. What's yer plan, sheriff?"

Lee Bell didn't hesitate. His mind's eye took him back to the days when he'd made his reputation by knowing how to handle men like Strait. He stated matter-of-factly, "we'll go straight at 'em. Red Hand, Lon an' me'll take the middle, three o' you fellers on either side. I'm gonna give Strait a chance ta come peaceable, but I wouldn't be countin' on it if I was ya'll. Soon's he makes 'is play, I'm gonna stick one in 'is belly. Ya'll do tha same to who's ev'r directly in front o' ya. If'n they don' pull on ya, you cov'r 'em. We ain't gonna murder 'em, we jus' gonna shoot 'em... if we have ta. Got it?"

They nodded, checking their weapons, more than one or two swallowing hard before the sheriff added, "breathe easy boys. We need ya steady."

"What about 'at Libby fella?"... Lon asked. "He's tha gunhan' o' tha bunch, an' a sure 'nough killer."

"I saw his poster," Red Hand offered, "Merritt Libby. It said he's killed more than twenty men... and women and children. Is that true?"

"I'm sure 'tis, son. He jus' ain't done nothin' here I c'n prove. If'n I attempted ta take 'im an' hold 'im fer transport outa ma territory, well, we'd be in the same kind o' fight we're fixin' fer rat now."

"Which one is he?"

"He'll be next to Strait... 'bout yer height, slender, black hat with a silver band, two gun rig crossed ov'r."

"I'll take him."

Lee Bell looked at the men in front of him, studying them. He'd known them all for years to be hard working, most of them with families. But this was no barroom brawl they were getting into. This would be a watershed moment for the town, as it had been and will continue to be for other fledgling towns across the west where men like Strait attempt to grab more than their fair share. The sheriff only prayed they'd all come out of it alive.

As each of the nine men took a final minute to collect his thoughts... of family, or kin, or some seemingly insignificant event in their life that was now inescapably present, Lee Bell glanced out the window and saw Strait leaving the bank. He checked his gun one more time before barking out the words, "let's go."

*

The day the people of Mission got their town back would be told and retold for generations by those whose fathers and grandfathers had stood tall in the street that day. The story went something like...

"Well, ya see, Strait an' 'is men jus' come out tha bank when Sheriff Bell an' his deputy, Lon Turley, an' a... Alfred Bendt, the Vespers boys, the young Injun, Red Hand er John Connor, whichev'r ya please, an' a... Old Man Busby, Tobias Haller an' Vance Wrightwood... well, they confronted 'em rat in tha middle o' Main Street, jus' like in tha ol' days. It was some sight, I'll tell ya.

"Now Strait, upon seein' 'is many men... well, he was stunned sure fer a secon' er two, but 'at's all. After 'at, he jus' cracked 'at grin o' his he makes when he's on tha prod, an' he tells 'is men ta fan out. Now ever'body on tha street knows ther'll be gunplay an' runs fer cov'r, 'ceptin' o' course the sheriff an' Strait an' their men.

"Right then, Sheriff says, 'howdy Strait, how's business?'

"Strait answers rat back, 'good's always, Lee.'

" 'Good... good,' says the Sheriff, 'I got a little business with ya ma self.'

" 'Ya do?' says Strait.

" 'Yes, I do. It's got ta do with 'at bandanna yer wearin'.'

" 'Ya don' say?'

" 'I do say, Strait, 'at one rat there.'

" 'An'?...'

" 'I want ya ta take it off an' hand it ta me... real slow. I foun' somethin' tha oth'r day an' jus' want ta put ma mind ta rest.'

" 'What might 'at be, Lee?'

" 'Oh, jus' this here lil' ol' piece o' cloth,' an' tha Sheriff pulls the piece out o' 'is coat. 'Looks a lot like 'at bandanna o' yours. Jus' want ta check it, Strait... do ma job, 'at's all.'

"Well, 'at ol' grin on Strait's face gets ev'n wider now an' he says, 'hell, Lee, Billy Bones got one jus' lak it, see,' an' he points to one o' his boys off ta his lef' side.

" 'I see that,' Sheriff says, 'but 'is wouldn't 'ave tha initials "JS" on it... would it?'

"Rat then is when the color lef' Strait's face... an' he's white as a ghos' on Hollerween. 'What ya sayin', Lee?' he asks.

" 'I'm sayin' this one does. An' it was foun' in 'at gully where Willa an' Two Bears was killed.'

"Strait's han' was twitchin' all ov'r like now. 'Yer bluffin', Lee.'

" 'Try me...' an' with 'at both sides drew they irons an' changed tha course o' history aroun' these here parts. Red Han' was off firs' an' he put one 'tween tha eyes o' that gunslinger quiker 'an you could spit. The sheriff an' Lon, God love 'im, were nex' jus' a split secon' afore tha res'... then all hell broke loose. The sheriff put Strait down but he got poor ol' Lon afore Red Hand kep' 'im down fer good. Billy Bones winged Alfred and Chet Vespers b'fore Tobias put two in 'im chest high, pop pop, jus' lak 'at. Tha res' o' Strait's men, only four o' 'em now, kep' tryin' ta make a fight, ah'll give 'em 'at, wingin' Vance perty good. Ol' Henry took a bead on one whil' tha sheriff an' Tobias were busy bloodyin' tha oth'r three 'til they throw'd their guns down an' give up. Then, as suddenly as it'd started, it was all quiet like aga'n 'til tha sheriff says, 'round 'em up, boys.'

There was always a pause at this point in the retelling of the story, as if the narrator was as exhausted from recounting the shootout as the participants themselves, or perhaps more from the one last, mournful fact that Lon was the only townsman not to come out of it alive.

"Aft'r 'at, well, nothin' lef' ta do but bury 'em boys... an' poor ol' Lon." There was another pause. "If'n ya go on up ta tha cem'tary, you'll reco'nize Lon's headstone rat off. Always got tha mos' flowers... an' 'im without no kin."

*

"John," Lenore was the first to speak, "I'm so sorry for ya... 'bout your mother and family," and she reached over and held his hand in her's, the warmth he'd remembered still there.

"Thank you, but I have learned to live with it."

"That may be true, me boy," Rose added, "but this be the cruelest kind o' thing."

"I'm likin' da way ya handled dem gobdaws, John, but didn't ya say yer friend... Santin was it?... tol' ya killin' wasn't da way."

"He did say that, Tipper. But he also said the answer to a man like Strait lay with the townspeople. They were the ones who had to defeat him, in order to hold their heads high. I could not let them fight him alone. More good men would have died."

"So ya took to da killin'," Cam ended the thought.

"I did," he stated quietly, lost in his own thoughts for some moments, "but I am learning. I am learning."

"What about the last coupla years?..." Danny asked.

"These past years I have been on a journey to find something of my father's past... his family, relations, maybe only the place he once lived, anything that might tell me more about the man."

"Have ye had any luck, son?..." Rose wanted to know.

"No, not yet. I have only come across the name Connor once. It was in Pennsylvania, an Amish minister. He'd had no brothers. But there is this village in the state called Ohio that keeps speaking to me..."

"Speakin' to ye, John," Lenore mimicked, "how do ya mean?"

"I can only say I feel a calling whenever I pass through the town. It is a warmth, like the warmth I felt from the cooking fire in Two Bears' lodge when I was a boy. It is a comfort that is complete."

"Why don't ye settle in there, lad?..." it was Emilie now.

"I feel I will one day, Emilie. Now, however, I would see more of this land... my father's land."

"I don' think yer pa ev'r made up his scratcher in da Kitchen, John, else he couldn't a left such a fine life." And the men chuckled at Cam's remark.

"I'm sure you're right, Cam."

"Den what brings ya back, John?"

"I would see you, Tipper... all of you, once more."

The party and chatter would continue well into the wee hours with John telling tales of his recent life on the road, seeing much of the country's midwest... small towns, cities, taking the train when he'd stable Truth to fatten him up and allow him a few days rest. He'd had all manner of jobs — farm hand, blacksmith, saloon and shop apprentice, type setter, wrangler — enough to keep him off the hobo trail, although he explained his experience with that as well, saying he'd met some of the men he admired most around their campfires.

"So now what, John?"

He looked at Lenore. "I'll be leaving in the morning. Tipper is going to put me up for the... well, what's left of the night."

"Shall we den, John," and Tipper rose from his chair, as did Cam from his.

"We shall," John said. He extended his hand to Danny, "it was very good meeting you, thank you for your hospitality... and to you Lenore." Then turning to Rose and Emilie, "ladies..." and before the goodbyes might have become awkward, the three men were gone.

*

He got out of bed more slowly these days, but with no less interest for what might lay before him in the day ahead. He had come to appreciate that over the years... through two great wars, technological achievements, cultural and social shifts that, in the infancy of the twentieth century, were thought too preposterous to contemplate. The fact was, much of that early-on science fiction had become the reality of the mid-nineteen seventies. But during it all and in spite of it all, each day, whether it came with the look and sense of sameness as the one preceding it, was uniquely new, different, exciting to him. This never waned, once he'd learned how to look at the things around him, appreciating them for their differences more than anything else... much like his roses.

He reflected also as he had before that Santin had not come to him for many years until that fateful evening nearly two years ago now. But in his youth, just after he'd visited Lenore, Tipper and the rest of his Irish brethren on that balmy night in The Kitchen, breaking bread and telling tales, Santin had come often, showing him the way...

— "How do you know what to do, Santin?... when to act? Is there a sign?" Red Hand felt more than heard the reply of his spiritual advisor. 'Your pain will guide you to the purpose. The purpose will show you the way.'

The youth was slow but steady in applying this truth as he wandered the great land of his father in the early days. He recalled stepping into the middle of another battle for another town in Tennessee just after the new century had begun. He'd arrived in the tiny hamlet and had boarded Truth for what remained of the day until the next morning. As he crossed the street heading to the hotel, the sheriff and his deputy were speaking with two men who looked to be ranchers. Voices rose as he approached. Since they were directly in his path, he could hear part of the exchange.

"... So says you sheriff, but all's I know is I'm payin' Dixon fer the priv'lege o' waterin' ma cattle north o' town on free range, an' you know it. 'At ain't right."

"He claims it's his land... show'd me a bill 'o sale."

" 'At's horse droppin's... ain't no bill o' sale on free range."

"Well I cain't do nothin', Amos."

"Er won't."

Red Hand saw the others hidden in the shadows of a late afternoon behind the sheriff, and he understood the quarrel, and he felt the pain of the one called Amos, and his companion. As their pain rose up it entered his own mortal body, bursting within, savaging his belly until he drew from it strength, and purpose. He vowed these two men would not be slaughtered, as his family had been. He would not allow it.

"Sheriff, hold on."

The sheriff turned towards the boy. Not recognizing him, his look turned sour, "jus' who tha hell er you?"

He didn't answer the question. "The man is right. That is all free range. I have just come from there."

"Better take off, sonny, 'afore ya get hurt." The sheriff's hand was itching for his pistol, waiting for any excuse.

"Sheriff, you don't want anyone hurt over a simple misunderstanding, do you? You're the sheriff. You're job is to uphold the law."

"I know what ma job is."

"If you don't believe these men, ride out and see for yourself. There is no reason to pay. After all, free range is free."

Now Amos and the other rancher turned to see just who had come out of nowhere to their way of thinking, and they felt the power and the purpose Red Hand laid before them. A feeling of calm and readiness swept through them, and together they raised their rifles slightly, cocking them.

Red Hand said, "that won't be necessary. The sheriff will tell this Dixon you don't have to pay."

In a matter of moments, the sheriff's look of incredulousness at the intrusion of this... this boy turned to compliance, then to the point of cowering once the two had made eye contact. Red Hand's sky blue eyes glowed with an aura, boring a hole straight through the star on the sheriff's chest to his long dead soul, shaking the life back into it, demanding it reclaim the body that had strayed so far from the law.

"Is that not right, sheriff? You will tell Dixon."

"Yes," was all he said, quietly, the guilt he'd carried all these years leaving him barely able to stand.

"Hell, I ain't tellin nobody." It was the deputy. "An' I suspec' this here town's gonna need a new sheriff come election," and with that he went for his gun.

Amos was first to fire, catching the deputy in the right shoulder. As the man attempted to raise up his pistol with his left hand, the other rancher, Burkett, caught him full on the other side, shattering the other shoulder. The man never could put his own boots on again.

"Boys," the sheriff had command of his senses again and turned to the others, "git him outa here." Then to Red Hand, "son, I don't know who y'are er where yer from, but I feel, well... whole again," and he reached out his hand. "Much obliged."

*

Two years later he was riding from Huttonsville to Rock Cave in West Virginia on his way back to Ohio. As he approached the Buckhannon River he saw its banks eroding with the spring runoff, its white caps chasing one another in the surging waters. He'd have to wait until morning to chance crossing, that is if he could find a suitable spot. He looked north, then south, deciding on south as the likeliest direction to pursue since he could make out in the distance a slight bend in the river's path. Sure enough two miles down it did make a turn, and just after that, its color became an aqua blue. Shallow enough, he thought, but with the sun now setting behind the willow and the dogwood on the far side, throwing long shadows across the spot he'd picked out, better to wait until morning. If there were any sinkholes, he wanted every advantage to see them coming.

The next day the crisp air awakened him along with the cry of a cooper's hawk chasing its mate. After coffee and some of the hardtack, he rolled up his blanket and kicked dirt on the remaining embers of the fire before saddling up. That's when he heard him. At first just a slight yip, then louder. Then he saw him... a dog that'd been caught in the current, bobbing up and down along the far bank, unable to catch hold of anything, branch or boulder, to slow his progress or wrench himself from the rushing waters. Red Hand had no time to ease his way into the river aboard Truth and impede the dog's path, the animal would be directly across from him in a minute, maybe less. As he got closer, the dog yelped, a cry for help as clear as any human's. He felt the animal's pain, his terror, and he searched, begged his mind to find a way to help the dog, to heal his pain. This is when Santin spoke to him once again. 'You cannot ride or swim to him, you must find another way. Fly, you must fly to him, quickly, or he will perish.' Red Hand struggled with the thought as he felt the pain of the animal growing within him, its intensity quickening so rapidly he was becoming frightened himself. But he must find a way. His mind raced to Santin again... fly, fly, but how?... yes, now I see, like the eagle, swift and sure, strong... to pull the dog from the death waters.

His heart pounded as the dog raced closer, disappearing, then reappearing again in the raging waters, losing his strength with each attempt to breathe. Red Hand prayed to the Great Spirit to grant his wish, to effect the change in his physical state, and guide his way, and the Great Spirit smiled upon him. At once, he felt a burning within him as if a stream of liquid fire poured through every vein, every capillary until he imploded with a great gasp of fright and pleasure and wonder. When he opened his mouth to cry out, it was not the cry of his human form, but the cry of the eagle that escaped his lungs, and instantly he knew what he must do. His eyes scanned the river's far side, seeing nothing but the rushing water and white caps that traveled so swiftly with it. He took two short steps and bounded upward, flapping his great wings, hoping this would take him airborne. It works, he thought, and he was relieved he'd taken flight after only his first attempt as he cruized the river's far shoreline, looking for any sign of the little dog. He saw what he thought was a small animal surface for a moment, then nothing. He flew lower, slower, attempting to pace the flow of the river from where he thought he'd last seen the animal. Yes, there he is again, about twenty yards ahead. Then he disappeared. Faster, he thought, I must be directly above him next time. Red Hand dipped his great wings, gaining speed, then settled into the pace of the river a second time just off the water. Come on, little one, come up for air. Come now! And with that the little dog appeared, front paws struggling, a quick gasp for breath, then... then... then with his huge talons Red Hand grabbed hold of him, gently raising him from the current. He carried the little dog back up river to a grassy nest directly across from where he and Truth would soon cross. The animal opened his eyes, barely, as the great eagle placed him down to rest, whimpering a thank you before weariness turned to slumber.

A half hour later, Red Hand was back, kneeling next to the little dog, stroking his head, coaxing him to awaken. When the little one opened his eyes, he saw the same spirit before him, the same gentle soul, only this time in its human form. It did not matter to the little dog, this was the spirit he would serve for the remainder of his years.

*

The drums of war were crossing the Atlantic now as news spread of the Hun's push into France and Belgium. The Yanks, as the Americans were called, could not stay out of it forever, even though they were buffered by three thousand miles of ocean. The French were getting pounded at every turn, and the Brits would do well to stave off invasion of their own homeland, an invasion that would likely come sooner than later.

"What shall we do, fellas?"... John asked his two companions out back in the stable, Truth, and the little mutt he'd pulled from the river some ten years earlier, Life. As always, whenever he'd asked their advice, they both looked directly at him, Truth shaking his head, snorting and Life wagging his tail, signalling whatever he decided was just fine by him. This time, however, his decision would take him away from them, and for how long he did not know.

"I think it is time I see what this Great War is all about. After all, I am half white, and surely all Yank, as they say." Truth and Life nodded, snuffling and yipping in apparent agreement. So John added, "I will see Pris tomorrow and ask if she will tend to you while I am away."

"Priscilla Lantry had been a neighbor of John's in Granville for the past two and a half years after he'd taken the position of foreman at the Curley place. Elmira Curley was up in years, and after Zeb, her only son, had succumbed to a fall from a horse, she hadn't been able to keep up with the eighty-odd acres of good bottom land she'd owned since she inherited it from her pa, Old Zeb Deekins, back in '83. John had heard of the opening in town on one of his trips through from the bartender at The Friendly Inn, and as the sirens often do, they whispered to him... we've been expecting you, stay a spell. So the next morning he rode out and started that very same day. It'd been six days on, one day off ever since. The best thing about it, besides the wide trail he was able to cut while tending to the job, was meeting Pris at one of the town socials some three months later. He caught her looking his way as Elmira was introducing him around, but no matter. He'd already seen her chatting with two of the other women across the yard, saw her long, golden hair pinned up at the sides framing a slightly rounded face with a freshness and vitality about it that drew him to her, and he realized he wouldn't have left the gathering without making the attempt on his own.

"Nice meeting you folks," John stated kindly, "but I think I see someone I know. Excuse me."

As Pris turned from the stand after refreshening her cider, John was waiting, which startled her. However, his look of anticipation accompanied by a broad smile set her at ease.

"How do you do, Miss Lantry? I'm John Connor, your new neighbor."

"So I have heard." Looking directly at him now, a coy smile exposed a slightly chipped front tooth. "Excuse me for askin', but isn't that Zeb's shirt you're wearin'?"

"Yes it is. Mrs. Curley allowed me."

"Sad thing, what happened to Zeb."

"Yes, it must have been."

"So... what brings ya to our little neck o' the woods, Mr. Connor?"

"Please, call me John."

"John, then."

"What brings me here?... many things, some I do not fully understand quite yet, however one of which I do."

"And that is?..."

"My restlessness. It seems, it needed some rest of its own. At least, that is what the voices told me, the voices on the wind."

She thought the remark somewhat odd. "Do you often listen to the wind, Mr. Co... John?"

"Everyday," and he smiled broadly again, captivating Pris from that moment until the day he would leave three years later.

As he studied her, her sparkling light brown eyes now began to flutter some and she caught her breath and changed the subject, "so, how are things comin' along at Elmira's? From what I've seen, corn's up again, and it looks like that old barn's got a fresh coat o' paint."

"It does. First, a few repairs were needed, but we have made some progress. You should come visit. I will show you what we have done."

229

Over the next two years or more Pris visited often, the two talking of their lives, hers as one might expect not the adventure John had lived to this point. Granville was a small town where people worked hard, lived simply, and established an order to their lives that comforted them in knowing what lay ahead. Excitement was found in the dancing and goings-on at a wedding or holiday event, a good harvest or a good horse race, even wagering on the gender of a soon-to-be new born, at least by the men. A girl like Pris... well, she could see her life laid out before her by the time she was ten or twelve. With only a handful of children of similar age at any one time, pairs were matched by doting parents who then applied enough subtle pressure to the youngsters to see their plans prevail, unless of course the young man and woman were in connubial agreement, and constant companions. In that case, the wedding was moved up to a day before the bride-to-be started to show, which presented another opportunity for the men to place a small wager.

Pris, in fact, had been matched to Elias Bonham since they were fourteen, however her reluctance to advance the situation any farther for near eighteen years finally had the desired effect on her parents, and the community at large. Poor Elias could still be seen by one and all attempting to court her at every turn. May as well try to court that beauty of the silent screen Theda Bara herself, it was whispered behind his back. Only after John's arrival did Elias see the light of day. But he took no offense. Like some of the others before, a batchelor or a spinster here or there was accepted.

"Come to supper tonight, John?"

He agreed immediately, as he'd done on several occasions. John liked Pris's father, Walter, and mother, Millicent. They were hard working Ohioans, three generations removed from Sussex, England as her mother was wont to drop into conversation.

In fact, Millicent felt no compunction to repeat to him at various times her origins, reaffirming, "the family had a thousand hectares in Sussex... that'd be about twenty-four hundred acres here, but grandfather..."

"Millie," Walter cut her off, "I ain't so sure John wants to hear all 'at again."

"No, please, Mrs. Lantry, go on. I would like to hear."

"See, Walt... anyways, John... Lord Gathers, my grandpa, he was a lord, ya

know, but he was also a rambler... well, one day he just picks up the entire family...
my mother, that's Priscilla's grandmother, Eunice, along with her six brothers and
two sisters, and sets sail for the Americas. After a short three weeks in New York...
a vile hellhole of a place as grandpa put it... they all head west, settling here in the
summer of '47. Two years later, four of the brothers take off for the gold in
California. We haven't seen hide ner hair of 'em since. Two of them, Thad and Will,
wrote once er twice, but it's been years since we heard anythin' more. The rest o' us
stayed put. Roots are down now, good and strong. We ain't goin' anywheres... are we
Pa?"

"No, Millie, we ain't," Walter replied.

"John's spent some time in New York, Ma," Priscilla said.

"Oh, I'm so sorry for ya, John."

"Thank you, ma'am, but I found it to be an interesting city, very diffferent
from Ohio as you might guess. I also met some very nice people... like yourselves."

"Would you ever return?... that is, after knowin' what life's like here in
Ohio?"

"I will return. I have seen it."

They all smiled gently at John's remark, not understanding his meaning. A
year later, as he and Priscilla were sitting under a tree with a picnic lunch overlooking the valley, she finally did understand what he'd meant.

"John, hold me." She had not wanted to hear about his plans to go off to
war, but the news of the fighting had been growing worse these past months, and
John knew in his heart, saw in his mind, the souls of his white brothers dying by the
thousands in the land across the great water. On one of his long rides into the hills
above the town, praying silently by his campfire amongst the wild hackberry and
juniper and listening to the thrushes late into the evening, he saw himself fighting
alongside his white brothers, and returning home after. This is how he reasoned
with Pris, promising to return, knowing he would.

"I have seen it, Pris. You must trust me. It is as I have told you... the same as
Santin once told to me... some have the power. It is why Life has been with me all
these years, why I was able to save him from the river. It is a gift."

She only clutched him tighter, her heart beating faster, her breath shortening as she looked into his eyes. "I want to be with you, John... completely, before you go. I know it may not be wise, but I would be more the fool if I did not want it so." And they stayed on the hill that day until the setting sun brought with it the coolness of evening, all the while touching, caressing, ever gently, sharing a closeness they would hold sacred for the remainder of their days.

*

"What's yer name, boyo?"

After his last night with Pris, John had taken the 7:10 early the next morning to Pittsburg, then Scranton before changing trains to New York, finally pulling into the newly constructed Grand Central Station the following afternoon. He'd figured if he was going to sail back to the old country, might as well say a final farewell, for a time anyway, to the same commanding statue others from the ravaged towns and villages across Europe could only hope to see one day. So he had wired Tipper who'd wired back telling him men were joining the National Guard by the droves, heading off to fight in France with the 106th. The very next morning, after spending one night of gentle carousing with Tipper and Cam, catching up on recent years and asking them to bid his adieus to Danny and Lenore, Rose and Emilie, John went down and signed up as well. Six weeks later he was aboard ship heading to Southhampton where his regiment would take a train to their encampment at Gravesend just east of London overlooking the Thames. It was his third day there.

"I asked, what's yer name?"

"John," he replied from the bunk across the center aisle of Barrack 9. He studied the other soldier for a moment. The man looked a bit old for this kind of work, not being an officer, but John saw toughness there. "What's yours?"

"Monk."

So began an association begotten from the streets and alleyways of lower Manhattan which they discovered they had in common after only a few minutes of conversation. Monk Eastman had been the leader of one of the most notorious gangs that operated from The Bowery to Monroe Street, and up to the East River. The Cherry Street Gang and the Yakey Yakes, who roosted under the Brooklyn

Bridge, were allies of the Eastmans, and together with a combined twelve-hundred members they vied for territory with the Five Pointers from the mid-1890's until 1904 when Monk was hauled off to Sing Sing for shooting at a Pinkerton detective during the infamous Battle of Rivington Street. When he was finally parolled and returned to his old turf, he found the gang broken up. He became a pickpocket and dope dealer for a time, banging heads when he had to, surviving the only way he knew. And even though he had no effective control of the lower Eastside anymore, and no real muscle behind him, he was considered a man to be avoided.

In the fall of 1917, the Yanks, courtesy of one George M. Cohan, were heading 'Over There' in earnest. With no one left to fight at home, Monk decided, what the hell... why not join in the biggest dust-up of all. That's when he walked into the recruiting station in mid-town Manhattan with more scars and bullet wounds covering his body than the doctors at the National Guard had ever seen on one individual. With their approval, due not in small part to also observing his stoutness, Monk signed up.

"So you be da kid wit Tipper an' Cam an' the Dazzler 'at night in da Black n' Tan what sent dem culchies home in da proper Kitchen style."

"That's right, I was. But they had it coming."

"So's I heared. By da by, how'd ya get ov'r here? You a few years past soldierin' looks like."

"You mean, like yourself."

Monk laughed, knowing he'd met a like-minded soul with his own reasons for marching off to the Great War. "Say, how's ol' Tipper an' Cam deez days?... still on da job?"

"Yes they are... just watching out for their own kind, like always."

"Dat's right, dat's right... as it should be. 'Cept now ov'r here, weez all our own kind... fightin' da Boche. Eh, Johnny?"

John thought about the astuteness of the remark... that all any diverse group needed was a common cause to unite them. In fact, it was why he was here... with all of his American brothers. He promised then he would ask the Great Spirit to watch over Monk.

*

It was late in September of 1918, the air hot and sticky clinging to a canopy of clouds overhead as the bullets flashed by, grazing the very top of the trenches in which John and Monk and the rest of the company had been cowering for more than an hour. They were just west of the river Somme somewhere near Amiens and the Germans were not letting up. John was able to catch a glimpse only once, but it was enough to locate the machine gun perched no more than seventy yards off to their left overlooking their position.

"What da hell O'Ryan git us in dis time, Johnny boy?"

"Nothing good," and he looked over at his companion who was sweating, shaking visibly from the constant fire, attempting to dig deeper into the muck and the stench. Monk had told John about many of his exploits in the Kitchen, but now the real test lay before them. Back home had been child's play, mostly intimidation, banging heads, breaking bones here and there. Only now and again was someone killed, murdered more like... a contract hit. But this was mayhem, bodies strewn in and out of craters made from raining mortor, limbs draping familiar and unfamiliar torsoes like parsley on roast beef. The sight and smell was overpowering, unimaginable. As they lay huddled beneath a blanket of exploding shells and screams of the dying, the fear came, a fear so complete John looked to the sky above, through the smoke and the shrapnel, feeling the nearness of the death spirit who courted them, waiting to pounce upon the feeble and the weak of mind. With all of his inner powers, all of the wisdom he had reaped from his silent mentor Santin, John confronted the presence, chastising the spirit to come another day.

"O'Ryan must know something," he finally yelled over to Monk. "We're not called his Roughnecks for nothing."

"Oh, dat's reassurin," the reply came back.

"Cover me," John finally said, ready to test the vision he had of his own safe return. "Pass the word. We've got to silence that machine gun."

The fear was slowly, silently choking Monk's will to live like an odorless gas overcomes its victims in the night when his life on the streets passed before him. He saw all those he had beaten senselessly, mercilessly, quaking before him, and he felt shame. He looked at John and gathered himself, wiping the dirt and muck from his face before taking a deep breath and stating, "no ya don't, hero. I didn't git da name Monk fer nuttin'. I c'n scramble ov'r der like a striped ass ape in no time. You cov'r me," and with a brashness John had come to know, off he went, slithering over the top of the trench, through a hail of bullets and into glory.

By the time Monk Eastman, one Edward Osterman, had returned from the battlefields of France after knocking out countless enemy machine gun nests and rescuing many a wounded comrade, he was no more the feared hoodlum of his earlier years; he was a tried-and-true, one hundred percent American hero, acclaimed by the cheering throngs as he along with the rest of O'Ryan's Roughnecks marched down Fifth Avenue on a hot, August afternoon in 1919.

Just one year and four months later, on the day after Christmas, Monk was back in business, drinking with a shady Prohibition officer named Jerry Bohan in the back of the Blue Bird Saloon, a dive on the lower Eastside. When they exited the place, a shot rang out... then four more. The street thug, gang leader, ex-con and war hero lay bloodied on the turf he'd ruled for so many years. Three days later, with four-thousand in attendance, he was laid to rest in Brooklyn's Cypress Hill Cemetary with full military honors. In spite of Bohan's claim of self-defense, he was arrested and imprisoned. Eight months later, he was parolled.

Over the fifty-odd years since, when the first snow melts and the birds take to the wing and the air is crisp and clean, an old man looks to the heavens and sings of his fallen comrade, and they talk again in the spirit world as they once did when the sky raged red across the great water.

*

It was 5:30 A.M. The old man liked getting up early, figuring his aching bones needed the extra time to catch up with what his mind had planned for the day. Long about evening was when mind and body were again on the same page, and he could relax with his newspaper and the one neat shot of Wild Turkey he allowed himself knowing both deserved such. This evening, however, after spending the day at the library researching the Blackfoot leader Bear Bull, then picking up more mulch for his garden, he grew weary of the front page news. He set down the Dispatch, leaned back into the welcome of his armchair, and let his mind drift to earlier days...

— "Do you want me to fill it up and put a head on it, or should I put it on your head," John asked, walking up behind the coach as he watched the Tiger scrubs running wind sprints.

The coach turned around, gaping. "Why... why, is that you, John?..." Net asked before exclaiming once again, "it is!... it is you! My God, John," he was bear hugging him now, "it's wonderful to see you. What are you doing here?... how are you?" Before John could answer, Net told him to wait just a minute and blew his whistle, "men, come on over," and he allowed them to gather round. "We have a former player with us today, men, someone you've never heard of, and never will. But for one half of football back before any of you were born... back in our heyday, I'm proud to say I lined up in the backfield with this gentleman, and I witnessed first hand the greatest display of running I have ever seen on this historic field, or any field. Cast your eyes, lads... this is what a football player looks like."

"Net, enough."

"Riley," Net yelled, blowing his whistle again, "take over."

The two were up in the top row of the stands now talking comfortably, marvelling at the years that'd slipped by since those glory days of '96 on the gridiron, and the revelry at The Blue Boar Tavern afterwards, their jobs, travels, and now discovering at one point during the Great World War they were no more than ten miles from one another along the Somme in that fall of 1918.

"You mean to tell me you knew Monk Eastman?"

"He was a good friend, Net."

"I read about all the medals when he came back... and again after he was shot and they stirred up his hoodlum days once more." He paused then added, "I guess you take the bad with the good, eh, John."

"I believe so... no matter how bad or how good it appears a man is, you get some of both. That's the way of it for us all, that's the struggle."

They rehashed their days at The Tiger Inn, the meal fiasco when they first met... which they had another good laugh over, old Chester McGinley...

"Say, remember the night those four country boys came in looking for you? I never saw Chester so charged up. I was impressed."

"I, as well."

"Did anything come of that, John? Did you ever see those boys again?"

"As a matter of fact, I did." And John related the story of his escape with Lenore, his meeting Tipper and Cam and their run in with Jimmy and the other guards at the Black n' Tan.

"With a potato up each of their arses?! My God, John, what kind of fellas are these you were running with?"

"The best, Net. Some of the best."

Neilson Poe sat for a minute contemplating all that he had heard, shaking his head as he digested some of the specifics of his friend's adventures over the years, then asked what he had really wanted to know. "And how's Lenore, John? I admit, I'm dying to know."

"She's just fine. In fact, I saw her only two days ago in New York and told her I was stopping by hoping to see you on my way back home. She said to say hello."

Net's eyes bulged again as they did when John had surprised him. "She did?! Well, go on, what is she doing these days?"

"She's happily married to a fine fellow named Daniel Coyle, Cam's brother. He practices law for one of the banks in the city." Net's brow furrowed some, but he was pleased to hear of her happiness. "And Net, do you see the lad out there with your scrubs," John continued, pointing to the scrimmage in progress, "the one who just tackled the first team's quarterback for a loss..."

"That's Terry Coyle," Net finished the sentence.

"That's right, her and Danny's boy."

"Lenore's boy?!"

John watched as the information sunk in, watched the puzzle on Net's face turn to satisfaction, then to delight when he told John, "you know, he's the only one of my omelettes who's going to make the first team, and soon."

"Omelettes?"

"Yes, that's how the scrubs are known. They're all good eggs for getting their brains beat in every day."

"And?..."

"And... as they say, beat an egg and you get..."

"An omelette," they intoned together, John shaking his head.

They were watching Terry now as the first team lined up again. It was a pitch to the halfback who faked an end run then pulled up to throw the ball. When he let it go, Terry broke on it, picked it cleanly and took off down the sideline until the whistle blew. Slowing up, he didn't see the fullback hit him, the cracking sound of bone audible to even John and Net who rushed to him along with Coach Roper and some of the others.

"I didn't hear it," Jack Cleaves, one of the team's stars was saying, near tears, "coach, I didn't hear the whistle."

"It's all right, Jack," Coach Roper said, "now give us some room."

"What is it?"

"His knee. Looks like the damn knot end of a shillelagh, Net." It was Riley.

"Let me see," John said kneeling beside Terry who was grimacing, clutching his knee.

"Let go, lad, we've got to straighten it out if we can... slowly now," and Terry winced as John got the leg extended.

"I don't know, John... looks bad. Maybe we should try to get him to the locker room and send for the doc."

"We shouldn't move him just yet. Let me check for swelling..." which is when John rested both hands on the knee, carefully cupping them to cover the entire area of the break. He closed his eyes and raised his head, holding that position, praying silently, drawing strength from above, channeling the power through every fiber of his body until it poured forth from his cupped hands. The rush of the power was excruciating, and he sweated visibly from the pain as its healing strength was reassembling the puzzle pieces of Terry's knee. His pain rose as Terry's diminished, ripping at him as it deepened to the very marrow of his bones, intense, constant, until in the next moment, it vanished like the spirits do... in a flash, final and complete.

John looked up at Net and simply said, "no swelling." Then, "Terry, let's see

238

if we can get you up."

"I could've sworn that knee was all torn up," Riley was saying, scratching his head.

"How does it feel, Terry?..." John asked.

"Just fine, doc," Terry answered.

"No, I'm not the doctor. My name is John Connor. I know your parents, and the last time I saw you, you were just about three years, I would say."

"Mr. Connor, yes," reaching out his hand, "my parents speak of you often. I'm very glad to meet you... again."

"And you, Terry." He paused for a time. "Good luck."

"Thank you, sir," he half yelled running back to line up.

"How'd you do that, John?"

"Do what, Net?"

"You know... Terry's knee."

"Yes. There was no swelling."

Later, when they said their good-byes, Net refrained from asking again about Terry's knee. They shook hands warmly and promised to stay in touch, unsure if life would comply. Then he stood watching as John walked from the field towards the bell tower, the sun silhouetting him against a purple sky, and Net scratched his head wondering just who it was his friend had become.

*

When he arrived in town and had disembarked his train a few of the men recognized him and tipped their hat, one or two offering a 'good to see ya' or 'welcome home' and John acknowledged their remarks, thanking them. One woman he had not known well rushed up and hugged him like a mother does her young after finding them safe when she'd expected the worst, then she stepped back smiling warmly and continued on with the business of her day.

He went first to the Curley place to see Elmira and check on his two faithful companions, both longer in the tooth he noticed as he snuggled them until they would have no more of it, which took a time. Elmira remarked more than once how glad she was he came back to them in one piece, but all the while suggesting it would be best to get up to the Lantry place, he could fill her in on the details of his travels later. He understood, wondering just what he was to discover as he saddled up Truth for the short ride. He trotted him along the familiar trail bordering a stand of dogwood and tall, white ash that rose all about, then two miles farther on to the top of the rise that overlooks the little valley where the farmhouse sat, still and wait-ing. Over the final quarter mile and entering the front yard and tying Truth to the rail, he saw no one. He dismounted and walked to the front door. Before he could knock, he heard the metal latch on the heavy oak slide open, then the door swung wide. It was Pris. She looked older, much older than the two years since she'd waved to him when he boarded the train to far off lands. And he was worried. And she saw it in his eyes. He reached for her, but she stepped away.

"Pris, how are you? How's everyone?"

What she related, slowly, painfully, was something he could not have dreamed. Their last night together had born them more than a lasting memory, it bore them a son whom Pris had lost during childbirth. She was despondent of course, but worse she shut herself off from friends, the goings-on of the town, life even. She took her meals in her room, only venturing out to help her mother some with the house chores. After six months, she seemed to be doing better. There was color in her cheeks and, at times, Walter and Millie caught her smiling slightly at some humorous remark. One Sunday morning, to their surprise, Pris was waiting downstairs to accompany them to nine o'clock service. When all three arrived, the congregation applauded, and the minister noted the occasion with a reference to the Lord's abiding love for each member of His flock. She continued to appear at various social gatherings until three months later when her father, Walter, did not arrive to breakfast one morning at precisely six-thirty, something he had not altered since Pris was new to this world. She and Millie had called up to him, but there was no answer and they'd looked at each other and rushed up the stairs. He was slumped over sitting in the rocker fully dressed, his hands still clasping the laces of his right shoe. Three days later, the whole town saw him to his grave as the minister blessed his life and his passing without pain. Afterwards, everyone came up to the house and they all ate and drank and reminisced as long as they had a mind to, the last, some of the women from the knitting circle, leaving early the next morning after putting Millie to bed. Since that time, no one had been up to the house.

"Mother's not ready to receive anyone just yet."

"What about you, Pris?"

It took her some time to respond. "I'm... I'm not so sure I'm ready either, John."

"Pris. I'm sorry. I didn't know."

"I know. And I didn't know how to write you. Even if I'd had, I don't know if..." and she didn't finish her thought.

"Pris, it was I who should have written. But the news from over there was never good... only men dying."

"It wouldn't have changed what happened, John. Writing would have only meant me telling you of one more sweet soul passing on."

John felt Pris's pain now, but he was powerless to assuage it. The pain one feels within the spirit cuts too deep. You cannot help those so afflicted, Santin once told him... only the Great Spirit can help cure this pain.

"What about the place? Who will work it? I could..."

She cut him off, "John, I have come to understand my feelings... and my circumstances. These past months have taught me that... how to live with it. Mother needs me, I must tend to her first. As for the place... you remember Elias Bonham? He's been helping out... whatever needs tending to." John nodded as she continued with more affection now, "we had a wonderful two years, John," and it was Pris now who reached out, taking his hand in both of her's, "I will never forget it, John... I will never forget you." She kissed him on the cheek, resting her head on his shoulder until looking up once again. "I've got to go see about mother now," and before she turned away and the tears came, she added softly, "you take care of yourself, John... please take care of yourself."

He could only mutter, "and you, Pris," as she slowly closed the door. The sound of the latch sliding back into place ushered in a final silence, and he felt the coolness of the evening breeze wash across him and he heard Truth snuffling to go.

*

Over the next nine years, most of it referred to later as The Roaring Twenties, John allowed the spirit within to guide him on a more intensified search for his Connor kin in and around the townships of Ohio, eventually into parts of Kentucky and Indiana. Although the automobile had begun to take near total control of the roads and byways, Truth tolerated the noisy beasts without so much as shying once when one might roar past belching smoke and fire, and like always, Life was content to trot along beside them. During the second of those years they passed through a sleepy hamlet called Bethel and John thought he'd stumbled upon something... something in the land office that showed a forty acre parcel back in 1872 just south of town belonging to a family named Connor. After further investigation he discovered the name listed on the original document to be O'Connor, and it remainded such to this day... finding the third generation of one J.T. O'Connor still working the place.

He meandered farther south into Kentucky, but as he distanced himself from Ohio, the familiarity of home and hearth waned and he turned west arriving in another small town later that day just north of Lexington called Georgetown. After putting up Truth at the livery he went looking for a hotel room for the night, Life following along. I'm going to have to find some work soon, he reminded himself... going to be out of money within the week. Old Life yipped as if in agreement, and John smiled.

"Jus' you'n the animal?..." the woman asked.

"That's right."

"He ain't a piddler is he?"

"No, he'll do fine."

"All righty then. Dollar an' fifty cents fer the night. Here's the key. It's aroun' back."

"Thank you," John said paying the woman.

"Beddin's in the closet," she yelled after them.

Opening the door he surveyed the room to be tidy enough with one twin bed off to the right beside which was a nightstand and lamp, then on the far wall a larger table and wash basin. At the foot of the bed lay a throw rug that'd suit Life just fine John knew from experiencing much the same over the course of their travels. He visited the outhouse taking the dog with him to decorate a nearby tree, then back in the room after washing up and stripping to his longjohns, he began to doze, pleasant sleep only seconds away when he heard the first of the snores coming from the foot of the bed. The smile he wore for the next several hours dreaming of what he considered was a life to be envied — he traveling this expanse of land with his two faithful companions — would serve to refresh his body well. The next morning, while the sun peered through the paned-glass announcing the new day, his contentment would turn to despair.

"Oh, no... no," he said quietly, stroking Life's head, "I didn't even hear you go, little one. You shouldn't have been so considerate ... letting me sleep like that. I wanted to be with you... I wanted to hold you."

The hurt that followed, twisting his belly, tearing at him, doubled him over, and he lay beside Life for the next hour or more, he wasn't sure. When he was able he rose and dressed and got Truth and brought him back and tied him off to a tree in front of the room, then went to the office. The woman had just risen, an old pink and lavender robe with floral designs all over wrapped loosely around her, and she began right off stating, "no breakfas' here. Go on down to tha cafe if'n ya want breakfas'."

"No thank you. But I do want to buy that small rug in the room from you. Is five dollars sufficient?" And John handed her the gold coin.

She was taken aback, the words tumbling from her mouth unevenly, "why I s'pose... I mean... o'course... that'd be plenty."

"Thank you," and he turned to leave.

"Say, what ya want with 'at ol' thang?"

"My dog. He's grown fond of it."

*

It was the spring before the Crash of '29 when fortune smiled upon him as it sometimes does for no other reason than it's just a man's time. He'd been meandering through four states in seven years like a peripatetic seeking wisdom, lingering for a few days here, a few weeks there in towns like Carrollton, Seymour

243

and Oolitic taking jobs wherever they could be found — waiter, wrangler, shop apprentice — then farther north to Rosston and Middlefork where he earned his keep in the town laundry, finally east when he again felt the sirens calling, leading him through Rockford, Wapokoneta, Roundhead and Huntsville until they whispered to him again as they once had when he entered the tiny hamlet of Worthington one bright, crisp afternoon... 'remember, John... stay with us... settle in... it's time.'

"Well, old boy, here we are. Don't mind the looks of the place either. Now let's find you some bed and board," and he angled Truth onto High Street finding a livery about half a block down across from the village green.

"Can you put up my old partner here?"... John asked what turned out to be the owner, Milt Short.

"Sure can," he said right off, a pleasant quality attached to his manner. "How long ya gonna be with us?"

What John didn't know then was that his stay would span the next forty-seven years. "A few days. Maybe a week or two. That all right?"

" 'At'll be jus' fine," adding, "your companion here looks like he c'n use tha rest."

"That he can."

"What's 'is name?"

"Truth."

"Truth! Well, I'll be... 'at's one helluva moniker."

"It fits."

"I'm sure it does... I'm sure it does. Mine's Milton," he said, extending a hand, "Milt fer short, an' las' name's Short so 'at's how you c'n remem... anyways, I've 'ad this here livery goin' on twenty-two years. I'll take damn good care o 'im."

"I'd appreciate it, Milt. My name's John Connor," and he shook Milt's hand with a firmness that measured the man, and it was returned in kind.

"Say, did I hear ya correct?... John Connor?"

"That's right."

"Yer pa's name John Connor too?"

"Yes."

Milt stood for a moment with a 'Lord be praised' look on him before stating with all urgency, "you bes' get ov'r to tha Griswold," pointing across the street to the large, two-story inn located on the corner of High and Granville streets. "Ask fer ol' Lyle an' tell 'im who ya be. I'll take care o' Truth. Now go on with ya."

Lyle Gillam had arrived in Worthington in 1848 with his father, mother and three sisters when he was just a lad of four years. The family had emigrated to the Americas from Wales and, after spending a year and a month in New Hampshire, they'd come west to this hamlet from which Lyle hasn't strayed since. Being the town's eldest and longest tenured citizen for over twenty years now, he's become the local geneologist, having sat in lengthy conversation with every land owner, shopkeeper, doctor, dentist, businessman, minister and spinster, wife and schoolmarm regarding their bearers and forebearers. The fact is, and every one around these parts knows it, if you desire a brief or for that matter in depth history of any individual who's ever lived within fifty miles of town center for going on six generations, you ask Lyle Gillam. He's a regular living, breathing who's-who of Worhtington society, which is exactly what John discovered after a few minutes of conversation with the man he found reading quietly by lamp light next to the claystone fireplace in the lobby of the Griswold.

"...an' ye say yer name is John Connor, eh?... an' ye be 'bout fifty years give er take I'd make ye... 'at right?"

"Yes, I'll be fifty-three in June."

"Well, John, I knew yer pa, an' yer granpa, Ol' Joe Connor. He passed on some sev'n, eight years now. Nev'r did quite git ov'r losin' Martha to the consumption when yer pa was jus' a boy 'bout ten years. Then when John took off as young men do and nev'r come back, well ol' Joe was quieter after 'at. Not rude er orn'ry mind ya... jus' quiet."

"Was that the entire family?"

"Yes 'twas, son. Yer gramma, ya see, 'ad been sickly fer some time... 'at's why she passed so young. Mos' thought it near a miracle she's able to 'ave yer pa." Lyle hesitated, thinking back so long ago, so many years past. "Han'some woman Martha was... mighty han'some."

"Where did they live?"

"Yer granpa stayed on tha ranch 'til he passed. Bank bought the place but they 'aven't done nothin' with it... jus' boarded it up."

"Where is the old place?"

" 'Bout ten miles outa town due north. You'll see it on the east side o' the road."

"Thank you, Lyle. I appreciate everything you've told me."

As John was leaving, the old man added, "I believe there's some money in trust fer any kin, son... the bank expectin' yer pa might turn up."

The next morning with the sun rising over the gentle, rolling hills beyond casting rays that promised warmer days to follow, he trotted Truth along easily, seeing the speck in the distance off to his right swell to life with each passing mile. He had no expectations, no desire other than to walk the ground his father had walked and played upon... to feel anything from the land or the rooms or the walls this old house may yet have to offer. As he neared, its massiveness loomed before him, timeless, not yet ready to give up the land... and the closer he approached the clearer he could hear it beckoning. He pulled up Truth at the front gate. It was closed but not locked. He reached over, unlatching it and in the next move swung it wide. Another forty yards and horse and rider were stopped in front of a long rail hanging from a single support like a broken appendige. John dismounted and checked it and saw that it was firm enough so he could tie off Truth, so he did as much, throwing the reins twice over. Then looking up to the front porch he took in a long breath and walked into the ghosts of his past.

Finding the front door and windows boarded tight, he made his way around the far side and climbed through a window with a rotted out pane. He noticed cobwebs had overrun the interior but paid them no mind, brushing them aside as he stepped farther into the darkness within. He'd brought some matches for just such an eventuality and as luck would have it discovered an old coal oil lamp not ten feet to his right resting atop a desk. Over the next three hours it would illuminate a past rich with tales of the long since dead. He found letters from his grandparents relations in Ireland, one near eighty years old describing the country's constant fear of famine and the bitter consequences that would likely follow. There were photographs, torn and yellowed from the years, one unmistakeably of his father at about age eight, one of his grandparents, another with only the two men... his father now about eighteen, his grandfather with a noticeably dour expression. Upstairs there were three bedrooms and, in between, what looked like a sitting room. In one of the bedrooms he found an old trunk by the foot of a double bed containing the carefully folded clothes of a teenage boy, as well as riding boots and a heavy, brown leather belt with a silver buckle. In the largest bedroom, the clothes of an old man hung from a wrought iron tree in one corner. There was a stepstool by the side of the bed and next to that a chamber pot. The nightstand held some sheets of writing paper tucked under one foot of an electric lamp, with a quill and bottle of ink to one side. Just under the blank paper, barely visible save for a corner exposing the scratchings of two or three words, was a treasure John would hold close to his heart from that day until his last.

The letter was dated July, 1875, mailed from an outpost in Wyoming called Powell. It began, 'Dearest Father, I pray this letter will find you in good health. I am near the Shoshone with Ethan on a hunt for horses which, when we find a quality herd and sufficient number, will become a wedding gift for the father of my betrothed. My wife to be is a Indian maiden...'

The letter continued for four pages describing he and Ethan's discovery of the Sioux village, their meeting Two Bears and his family, his love for Willow and now the hunt that lay ahead. It concluded with hoping one day he would travel east with Willow and their own family to visit... one day he hoped would come soon.

John could not recall the last time he'd shed tears. But as he sat on the stepstool by the bed clutching the letter, hearing his father's words from so long ago, he held his head in his hands and wept for the loss of a man he never knew, for the years his father and mother were not able to share, for all their hopes and dreams... and for an old man who John realized had loved his father more than he.

*

Her name was Rae Tally and as far as anyone could recall she'd arrived in Worthington in the fall of '27, just before the snow flies. Two evenings after checking into the Hotel Central she'd taken her supper at the Griswold at the suggestion of the doorman as she was strolling High Street. After a quite delicious meal and respectable claret, she'd toured the premises. The very next day, along with her entire repertoire of belongings which consisted of two large trunks and several valises she arrived back in the lobby and promptly took a corner suite for an extended stay. After several weeks the hotel staff remarked on her pleasant manner, and how she kept to herself. Her routine included taking breakfast in her room at precisely nine-thirty, having her laundry picked up by eleven, and no later than one, weather permitting, gliding through the lobby and out the front door to wander the town discovering its small shops and eateries before reappearing back at the inn in the late afternoon.

This day, as usual, she was sitting at the table in the far corner of the dining room from where she had a clear view of the room as well as the long, mahogany bar which spanned the far wall. This was handy, she found, for gesturing to the bartender, Alfred, when she felt a taste for sherry, or for flagging one of the waiters, at this hour generally Pete or Francis, for a bite to eat or perhaps have her tea refreshed.

When the clock above the bar struck five she'd as yet not noticed the stranger, but raising her eyes from her book to call Francis over for more of the herbal tea and toast, there he was sitting at the far end of the bar, shoulders slumped, staring into his whisky. She asked Francis how long the man had been sitting there, and he replied "oh, 'bout thirty minutes, Ms. Tally." She continued reading the latest book of a young writer named Ernest Hemingway called A Farewell To Arms which she'd discovered in a shop the day before, all the while keeping an eye on the stranger whose mere presence somehow fascinated her. As the room began to fill, an additional complement of waiters hurried about with menus and pitchers of water. She motioned to Francis to please bring her a menu along with a notepad and quill.

"It's from the lady sitting at the table in the corner," Francis stated handing the note to John. He'd just finished his third whisky and was debating the intelligence of emptying the bottle of hearty sour mash sitting before him, knowing that its magical transformation from a musky tartness to liquid silk was only a disguise, and tomorrow, not only would the memories of his father and his father's father return in full, his head would be imploding. So he pushed the glass away and

attempted to focus on the piece of note paper. After blinking twice, he read...
'Would you care to join me for supper?' He turned on his stool and could make out
only the shape of a lady at the corner table, however he could see she held herself
with confidence, was pleasant of feature, but more, she had an overwhelmingly
charming way about her that was at once beguiling, and welcoming. In that instant,
despite the still active effects of the sour mash, John's spirit felt her touch, and he
thanked Francis and walked towards her, and into a new life with much to live for.

*

Their conversation over the leek soup started slowly, sharing the events of
their lives in generalities as two might before feeling a greater degree of comfort.
When the fried chicken with gravy and fresh greens arrived, Rae decided to dig for
more, not knowing if the result would be offputting to the man she was already
quite sure she wanted for her own.

"So, Mr. Connor, do you make it a practice of going through a bottle of
whisky of an evening, or is there a particular reason for the occasion?"

John thought about the question, only about how he might relate to her
the unexpected emotions of at long last discovering the roots of his white family. He
felt no imposition on her part, only curiosity... a desire to know. However, he also
saw her slight discomfort in not knowing if she had indeed overstepped unseen
bounds. So he reassured her.

"May I call you Rae?"

"Please do."

"Rae, there is nothing you can't ask me. I have nothing to hide. And I
would hope we can share our stories and hopes and dreams for many years to
come..." and the floodgates opened between them, spoken and unspoken, the
way her eyes softened and smiled at his words, her mouth parting, wanting him,
wanting his closeness, reaching for his hand across the white linen, fingers touching,
trembling with the thought of the days and nights to come.

Among the stories John shared late into that first evening over a glass of
rich port wine was his time spent in The Stockyard and later his escape riding the

rails north through the hobo camps of the eastern seaboard. She told him she was fascinated with those faceless, nameless men she saw walking the crossties across a lonely trestle in the afternoon sun, slowing time to a crawl. She said she often wondered if that might not be the road to travel in this life... to slow it down, breathing in every second. When he told her of his days in Princeton and The Kitchen, she immediately perked to the events as they unfolded and was as startled as Net had been with his tales of Tipper and Cam and the guards Irish escort out of town, potato and all. As the evening wore on, John stopped at one point, realizing he had commandeered the great majority of their exchange, and saying as much, he began asking the questions... her childhood, family, life, work. She looked at the clock on the far wall which read eleven, then to Francis who was waiting patiently for them to retire so he could clear their dishes, so rather than broaching a certain subject tonight, which she knew she soon must, she invited John along on one of her sojourns about town. In fact, why not the very next day.

"Tomorrow, John? At noon?"

"Tomorrow at noon."

"Goodnight, Francis," they said, walking from the dining room. Before going to their rooms, she reached for his arm, pulling him closer. "I would kiss you goodnight, but I fear I could not stop."

He hesitated, her strawberry hair falling to her shoulders framing sparkling brown eyes and fine features, her caramel skin pure save a small mole on the side of her neck, the scent of her intoxicating, yet he waited. "I'll see you at noon," he said softly, kissing her cheek, lingering, wanting more. "Sleep well."

*

It was when they were sitting on a bench in the park under a large poplar that she told him. They'd already haunted some of her favorite shops... she eyeing a parasol for the coming summer's heat before they stopped for a bite of lunch at The River Inn on the Paint, the sound of its gently flowing waters accompanying talk of their youth, her's in a little mill town called Lolo just south of Missoula, Montana.

With the rays of the afternoon sun splashing their faces through the trees, she took John's hand, then looked into his eyes. "Last night you asked me about my life... what my work has been. I'll tell you."

She reminded him of their conversation earlier about her life in the small farm house in Lolo, how her natural father had been killed in an accident at the mill... crushed by a log that'd broken free of its straps traveling down the sluice, how her stepfather had courted her mother six months after and how she'd relented and married the man without any love, only because she needed a man in the house... to help pay their keep and see to the kids which amounted to Rae, twelve at the time, and her brother Gent, ten. What Rae hadn't yet mentioned was the man, Frank, began keeping much too close of an eye on her, first when she was thirteen, spying on her through a knothole when she'd bathe, and later finding the boldness in a half bottle of whisky to climb into bed with her after she'd stayed home from school one day with the croup.

Rae's mother had been in town shopping and Gent was at school when Frank showed up home early from the mill to find Rae in bed rolled over on one side sleeping, covers off, it being one of those stifling Septembers where the heat lays overhead, still and thick, not the whisper of a breeze to offer solace to a body trying to breathe. He looks in the doorway finding her shift hiked halfway up her back from turning and tossing exposing her youthful backside, plump and pink. He could hardly contain himself, his member rising to a stoutness pronouncing itself ready to take control of a positive situation once presented, but he had not the wherewithall on his own to heed the call. What was required he determined was enough whisky to make him man enough, and give him the excuse he needed if necessary.

She remembered fighting him, scratching at his face, the stench of the whiskey on his breath and odor that comes off a man after a week's toil in the mill overcoming her as he pressed down on her, holding both her arms down above her head with a meaty hand, ripping at the shift with the other, her firm, young breasts before him witnessing the intrusion as he pressed on, plunging into her, grunting with each thrust until he was overcome with the explosion that raced through every limb and loin, his body collapsing on her, barely fourteen, ruined forever.

She told John of the dozen or more times over the next year Frank corraled her when her mother and brother were away, slapping her good when she resisted, threatening to kill her, kill them all if she spoke a word of it. It was a week after her fifteenth birthday, a week after Frank along with her mother, Sil, and Gent and a few neighbors sang happy birthday to her around the picnic table in the yard, that she left. She knew it was that or kill herself. She slid out of bed one night, packed whatever she could in one valise, made herself two cheese sandwiches then tiptoed into her mother's and Frank's room and emptied his pockets of the twenty-two dollars they contained. She walked into town arriving at daybreak and caught the first train to Butte which cost a dollar and twenty cents. She never looked back.

John was listening, still holding Rae's hand, feeling her pain as she recounted a time in her life he knew had been long stored somewhere deep within.

"You don't have to do this for me."

"I know. I think I'm doing it more for me," and she continued telling her story, saying it was only a month later when her money'd run out that she met a man she felt was heaven sent. She was in the train station again when he sat down next to her and asked her where she was headed. She didn't know.... didn't really care. When he discovered she was penniless he laughed saying he could fix that up and the next thing she knew she was going home with him... real nice place, big, two stories, where she could stay for a few days with he and his wife while he found her work. As he'd told her, he had many investments, knew just about everyone in town, it'd be no time before she was on her feet. As it turned out, the woman he was living with was his wife of the moment, meaning a girl he took a shining to from a passle he represented down on The Line in Butte's red light district. After a couple of sessions like old Frank had administered to her, Grim, that was his name, short for E.J. Grimsby... well, she said she just gave up and decided if she was going to have a roof over her head and eat regular like, she'd just have to learn to close her mind and soul to the job like Bessie, Grim's "wife," had told her.

"Ya learn to forget yerself, sugar, where ya are... almos' what yer doin'. I only got one er two reg'lars that I give two shits about... nice enough fellers, jus' married wrong. I try ta please them. But tha res'... shit, honey, ma mind's on some ol' African safari er flyin' through space like a dang bird with wings when I roll ov'r fer them boys. I'm gone."

252

For the next three or so years that's what I did, she said, just to survive. Grim got me a "crib" on The Line, or Venus Alley as it was called, which is a small cubicle with enough privacy where men could come and go, she said, smiling wryly at the pun. The cribs were lined up along the alley, each with a white light in front, lit when opened for business. If a man wanted to linger, there were callboxes for ordering drinks or something to eat from the restaurants and bars nearby. On the north side of the alley, some of the cribs were double deckers. The rowdier girls holed up there, taking on the groups of out-of-towners or frat boys who'd already had a belly full of booze, knocking off four or five at a time, filling their purses. Rae never did that. After the first couple of years, she'd made a reputation as the young beauty, quiet, refined, ladylike... and to be treated as such. That's when the idea struck. She went to Grim and said take me off the Line, set me up at the hotel as a regular, only for the richest... for those who wanted the best... and all night. She didn't want to age twenty years in five like she'd seen some do. Five or six men a week, that's all, at top dollar. She became known as the Queen, and if one of the town's politicians, or prominent businessmen, or rotary members was lucky enough to be one of the Queen's regulars, they stayed. And if the price went up as it did from time to time, they stayed and paid. Most of these men became personal friends, which after another year, prompted Rae to expand upon her original plan. She picked their brains, learning about real estate, financial planning, stocks and bonds, deal-making. She squirreled away almost three-quarters of her earnings every month which wasn't hard to do since her bed and board were shared by Grim and were no higher than the other girls' at The Dumas Hotel, her new digs. After six and a half years of screwing and saving, educating herself whenever possible which was almost every night, she was ready to move on. All she needed was the right opportunity to come along.

Rae stopped for a moment, then smiled, remembering the day one of Butte's sitting judges was talking with her about a consortium of investors he was putting together for a land deal just outside Hamilton in the southern Bitterroots. She was washing him up in the gilded iron tub in the corner of her room as he leaned back puffing on his cigar, sipping cognac.

"Sweetes' piece o' land ya ev'r seen. We goin' to buy it an' turn it aroun' within the year. Share's are five thousand a piece. Ah jus' need two more," he'd said, "an' we're off an' runnin'."

She wrote him a check for ten thousand dollars that very evening. Nine months later at twenty-five years of age and with mind and body none too the worse for wear, she was out of the whoring business, out of Butte and on to Denver with forty-five thousand dollars, all but a thousand of it waiting for her in the Bank of the Rockies where she'd had it wired the week before.

Over the twelve years since, she's invested in more real estate in three states, mostly turning those over in a year or two for a handsome profit. However, now that the stock market has been going through the roof, she's gotten out of her land dealings and is near one hundred percent in the market.

"Scares me a little, but what a ride. I can't tell you how much I've got now... it changes everyday." Then she grew serious once more, "John, I had to tell you about my past... all of it. I wouldn't have felt good about myself you not knowing. I'll understand if you..."

He squeezed her hand, cutting her off. "I told you, Rae, there's nothing you can't say to me. That life you lived is behind you, only because you were determined to change it. That's what I'll remember."

*

They married two months later at St. Luke's Cathedral on June 22nd, just three days before his birthday. Francis, who'd taken it upon himself to become their personal waiter at the Griswold, stood up for John, and Ellie McKensie, an ambitious twenty year-old who worked the front desk and volunteered to take care of Rae's personal errands, was the bridesmaid. The remainder of the attendees were hotel staff and acquaintances they'd made about town... one being Angelo Barri, the owner of the town's finest Italian bistro and who wouldn't hear of their continued opposition to his providing the food and beverage for everyone... "onna Angelo," as he insisted.

After their nuptials all were back at the Griswold feasting on various asiagos, crescenzas and fontinas with fresh apples and pears, clams and oysters covered in garlic over vermicelli and ziti, chicken and veal parmigiana, osso bucco, and the wine flowed... chianti, sangiovese, soave, bardolino. After dinner and through the revelry came the clinking of flatware on crystal, causing heads to turn towards Francis whose eloquence and sensitivity was well appreciated, particularly by John who rose to thank one and all for attending. Immediately following the comments a fine Grand Cuvee was served as bride and groom cut into an immense Torta Claudia, its rich, creamy five-layers composed of powdered cocoa, whipped cream, sugar and blanched almonds, then laced with brandy and grand marnier.

Later after Rae and John had said their farewells and all had departed, she turned to him in bed, smiling, "do you think anyone knows we've been sharing my bed for the past six weeks?"

"Of course not, my dear. All those winks Francis and Pete have been giving me were pure coincidence, I'm sure."

"You're not serious?!..." she exclaimed sitting up quickly, exposing perfect breasts to which John had come to pay particular attention. She grabbed for the quilt to cover herself, but he reached over, holding her hands as he began to carress first one, then the other, then back to the first, kissing tenderly, wetting her nipples until they were firm, erect, Rae moaning with pleasure, wanting more, pulling him closer until they melted into what remained of the night.

*

By early September of '29 the weather had already turned uncommonly cool as the two lovers lunched at the River Inn, a favorite of theirs. Two weeks earlier they'd returned from an extended tour of New England for their honeymoon, and now over a glass of claret and cake the question of John's family farm came up again.

"You're right, Rae, I have been putting it off and I will inquire about it tomorrow."

As it turned out, there was just over ten thousand dollars in trust for any next of kin, which John was able to prove by showing the judge the letter he'd discovered on his grandfather's nightstand. When asked if he was, in fact, that

Indian child, he offered to have half the Sioux nation travel to Worthington and vouch for him. That won't be necessary, Judge Purdy said, he'd known old Joe Connor personally for many years, and he could see the resemblance. So he authorized the proper documents, John signed them and was issued a check for ten thousand, four-hundred and forty-two dollars three days hence.

"By the way," the judge asked, "did'ya know the place is fer sale, son? Bank wants to cash out o' their land investments an' put it all in the market."

—"Is that right?!" Rae was excited as John told her the news later over supper. "Let's buy it! Think of it... our own place... your family's place!"

"I don't have enough money, even with the ten thousand..."

"I do." She could see him hesitating. "Honey," she went on, "we're married, we're one now... what's mine is yours. I don't know anything about running a farm, that's your part, you have the experience there... but I do know land. And what I do know is for the past few years investors have been getting out of land, deflating the market, and getting into the market. I'm guilty of that myself. But this is an opportunity we can't afford to pass up. Your family's place will never be this cheap again." He was weakening. "Honey," she took his hands, "let's do it." When he smiled she quickly added, "how much?"

"Thirty thousand."

"We'll offer twenty."

He smiled again, "you're tough."

"You didn't know that by now?..." she winked, kissing him.

Three days later the deal was done... for twenty-two thousand. "Sixty-day escrow," Russell Howell, the bank manager, had told them, but Rae said, "thirty... we need to restore the place. Looks like nothing has been done for years," glaring at the man.

"All right, I guess I c'n rush it through... end o' October then."

Rae countered, "as far as I can see by the calendar on your wall, one month would be the 26th."

"That's a Saturday," Russell Howell replied.

"Fine, we'll see you on the Friday before, the 25th then." He scowled as he drew up the documents, Rae and John staying late into the afternoon as she read them page by page.

When October 24th arrived, Russell Howell was paid a visit by Rae to make sure the final escrow documents would be ready the next day, which he assured her they would. The following morning she and John arrived precisely at eleven.

"Did you see what happened to the market yesterday," Russell Howell mentioned somewhat nervously as he gathered up the documents in front of them to sign.

"Yes, I did," Rae answered, pausing for effect. "That's why we're getting out of the market and into land." She paused again, "nothing like owning land, is there Mr. Howell?"

As they were leaving, John said to her, "that was almost cruel, what you said to the man."

"No it wasn't, honey, that was fun."

The following Tuesday, October 29, 1929, the New York stock index fell over thirteen percent in one day. Over the next two and a half years, it fell a full eighty-three percent from where it stood on that infamous Black Tuesday. And the world changed.

"You were right, Rae," John was telling her in bed that night. "I've got my ten thousand invested in the farm and you've got another twelve." John sounded pleased, then thought, "what about your other investments... what's going to happen to..."

"Don't worry, dear, let's sleep on it," and she began to chuckle at her own joke and couldn't stop until he asked what was so funny, and she said, "honey, I just thought... we are sleeping on the other investments." She caught her breath finally.

"Remember last week when I called my broker in Denver to sell off enough stocks to purchase the farm?... well, I got a strange feeling about the market, so I got out... totally. I had him wire the money to First Ohio Bank in Columbus and a driver took me down there last Wednesday when you were out at the place going through more of Grandpa's things. I planned on taking out just enough for the purchase price, but as I was packing it up, I got to worrying about the banks... about just how many Russell Howells might be out there... so," chuckling again, "I took it all... in cash. After what we paid Mr. Howell, the rest is in a satchel under the bed," laughing in earnest now, "all three hundred and sixty thousand dollars," she cried, barely able to speak, howling at the mere thought of it.

John jumped up. With the idea of that much money under the bed, his eyes bulged like a bullfrog's and he too broke up, howling with her, their pure joy turning once again into another long night of love-making... then into the next several months restoring the family farm to its former state, after which they threw the biggest, rowdiest 'howdy-do' these parts had ever seen... and finally, blissfully, it turned into a source of great happiness and tenderness between them. If for only the next five years.

*

They were holding hands, gently, like the doctor had told him.

"Our time together, even though quite short it seems, has been wonderful, hasn't it, dear?"

"Yes, my love." It was all he could muster.

"I remember so many things," she was rambling again, thoughts scattered, smiling, searching. "Remember... remember when that fella recognized me in the Palace lobby in St. Louis from my former days? He walked right on up, took out some money and said he wanted a date with the Queen. Remember, dear?... I tried to turn away but he wouldn't let me."

"Yes, I remember."

"I can see the faces on everyone as clear as day... mouths dropping when you picked him up and threw him like so much riffraff crashing into that table, dishes flying everywhere... you were my hero, John."

"You're my hero. You always have been...." particularly when the doctors told them of her condition... how she'd accepted it, never questioning why, only complaining it would shorten their time together. He thought of the times he tried to heal her pain, but to no avail. He called upon Santin, but he did not show himself. He made entreaties to the Great Spirit, but he was not up to the task. This sickness was too strong for them. It was her destiny, her life... her life ending. But then he would try, and try again. And on those nights when she saw him struggling with the effort, searching for a way to ease her suffering, she was the one comforting him... stroking his brow, whispering words of love. How ironic, he would ponder later... how utterly, eminently ironic.

—Those last few weeks they spent every minute together touching on bits and pieces over the years, she asking John to fill in the blanks like a teacher who calls upon one of her pupils to finish a sentence with the proper word.

"It was your idea for the 'home' as I recall, and I believe it was our best idea."

"It was something we were in a position to do... what with five bedrooms and nearly a hundred acres and the Depression having orphaned them all... at least for a spell. We couldn't just leave them on the street."

"What a menagerie it was... five boys and four girls... and the twins... remember our two little Cheyenne babies, a boy and a girl?... we gave them a good home 'til their folks could take them back, didn't we, dear."

"Yes we did."

"But those three years we had with them were special... not having kids of our own."

"Yes they were."

He pushed the button for the nurse as she began to cough, her eyes still smiling, only half open as she struggled to keep the man of all her hopes and dreams in clear view until she could no longer. He smiled back, stroking her hand. Her eyes began to wander as her coughing grew more pronounced. He pushed the nurses button again. And again. When her coughing stopped abruptly she squeezed his hand with all the strength that remained... and whispered, "John," for the last time. All he could do was watch.

It was five thirty in the evening when she slipped away, and for a long while after, John would not forgive himself for failing to heal the cancer. What offered him solace some time later was knowing Rae could, and would, find a place of peace and comfort in the great beyond... a place where she would await his arrival, however long that may be, before once again they continued their journey into the life to come.

*

It wasn't pretty to watch... John coming into the Griswald three, four times a week sitting on the same barstool where Rae had first seen him, only now ordering one whisky after another until he asked Alfred, at times demanding from him the bottle which he would caress as a valued possession and drain quietly, somberly before stumbling out to the green Phaeton he and Rae had purchased only six months earlier and somehow crank it over and weave the ten miles back to the farm. On each occasion, no matter how they tried, Alfred, Francis, Pete, none of them could reach him, engage him in convivial or otherwise more personal conversation before he was well into his cups. Then it was too late. He was lost in his thoughts and dreams of Rae, her face floating through his memories of their time together... perfect and pure.

It was on just such an evening Ellie got the notion to take a risk... one Pete and Francis advised against, but one she felt was now necessary... to attempt to reach out to John in a manner so unexpected he would have to react, good or bad, and face the reality of Rae's death as well as the life that remained.

He was well into a bottle when she slipped in a side door and took a seat in the same corner table across from the bar Rae preferred. On cue Alfred offered, "yes, ma'am, what can I get you?..." and John looked across his shoulder in her direction. She was wearing the dress Rae wore the night she invited John to join her for dinner, one of several dresses Rae had bequeathed to Ellie over the years. Her hair was done up like Rae used to wear it, and she held a book in her hand. After blinking twice to clear his eyes, John pushed the drink in front of him to the side and slid from the barstool, nearly falling as he made his way towards Ellie.

"What... who are...?"

"John, it's me, Ellie."

"What?... WHAT?..." his voice all anger and anguish, rage and regret, and more, a cry for forgiveness... forgiveness for not being able to save Rae.

"John," she took hold of his hands across the table, "it's Ellie, not Rae. Rae's gone. You know that." He looked up, barely, the pain in his eyes as plain as his need for finding some way to bear it. "She's with God... in heaven... waiting for you. John, look at me."

He tried to focus. "I... I..."

"You know that, John. You remember."

"I do... I do remember. But I... I don't want to..." And he broke down, shedding tears long due for all the days he had blamed himself for not finding the power to save the one person he would have given everything for... everything. And Ellie came around the table and held him, stroking his hair, gently whispering, "it will be all right, John... everything will be all right." And Pete and Francis and Alfred stood watching, and silently wept.

*

The alarm rang at six o'clock in the morning as the bite of an early fall spilled through a half-opened window opposite his bedside. John didn't mind, for it announced the few remaining days of summer's heat, and the coming of the fall harvest. He would require some help again this year... the corn was high and the soybeans plentiful, and after deciding to run some beef three years back, his dairy business was picking up, particularly the cheese the farm was producing. The problem was finding migrants to help. Tad Wellworth, the foreman he'd hired for the harvest every year since he and Rae bought the place, he could count on. But while fair, the old cob was particular. He wanted only seasoned workers as he told John when he started back in '30, and as John had noticed over the years, he wanted only white. This year, however, would be different. The annual corn and soybean yield had risen steadily, faster than the migrants available to harvest the crop. John knew they'd need to go out and find some additional help, seasoned or not, and fast. Which is when the idea struck him... with some assistance, he thought later, from two men he'd never met... one white and one black. Lutz Lang and Jesse Owens.

During the years when the drums of war were resurfacing in Germany, the leader of the Nazi Party, Adolph Hitler, had a message to send at the Olympic

Games of 1936... the predominance of the Arian race, which he meant to showcase on the world stage.

When the Games had ended John remembered reading about the long jump competition... about Jesse Owens, the best track athlete in the world, fouling jump after jump, unable to record a single good effort, that is, until he got some special help from Lutz Lang, a German. Lutz, Jesse's fiercest competitor, suggested he place a marker a few inches in front of the take-off board as his target point, so he wouldn't foul again. On his final jump. Jesse took the suggestion. Moments later, flying down the runway and hitting his mark perfectly in stride, he took off and, as he stated later, felt himself flying like a bird, never wanting to come down. And Lutz Lang?... well, he was the first to run up and congratulate him.

So John considered, why not? Why not here?...

—"Tad, how many hands do we have?"

"Eight. When the Ridley boys git here, ten."

"We're going to need twice that this year, wouldn't you say?"

"I suspec' near that, but they ain't available nowheres. I've inquired."

"Well I have an idea, Tad. I'm going to get word to my uncle and see if any of the young men at his place are interested."

"Sounds fine. But we need to geta goin' nex' week hell er high water."

"I know, I know. You take care of that."

Ten days later five young Yankton Sioux and three Hunkpapa from the Rosebud jumped off the back of a flatbed heading for Cleveland and walked the remaining half mile to the ranchhouse where John and Tad Wellworth were just finishing lunch. John saw them coming and pointed them out to his foreman, "here are your new hands," then sat back to watch the fun. Although to Tad's way of thinking, there was no fun attached to it whatsoever.

*

As John expected he would, Tad rode the Sioux hard that first week, as hard as he could without being downright malicious. He gave no account to the fact none of them had farmed before much less knew the meaning of the term. At each day's end, he inspected their bushel baskets closely, checking where each ear of corn had been snapped from the stalk, if the husk had been removed properly and that it was dry.

"Gawl dang it, Big Shoulders, yer half agin the size o' the rest o' these fellers an' ya got what... forty... fifty bushels. An' lookie here," grabbing a shucked ear, "this here ain't dry yet. How we gonna store that? It's got ta be dry afore we c'n shell it an' sell it. Un'erstand?"

As always, Big Shoulders nodded that he did understand although he never quite did catch on. Tad figured this a week later and so, for the remainder of the harvest, had Big Shoulders in the barn loading and unloading pallets, which to Tad's surprise he did as well as any two men.

"What's this?..." he asked looking at the baskets in front of another of the Sioux, a boy named Three Hands. " 'At's a shit load o' corn boy. You pick all 'at?"

The boy nodded yes.

"Lemme see here..." and Tad inspected a few ears and found them all snapped off and shucked right and dry. " 'At's damn good work. What's yer name?"

"Three Hands."

"I c'n see why."

It was later that John told Tad about Three Hands. His given name had been Black Moon because he was born on the afternoon of an eclipse, when a hazy sun obscured all but an outline of the moon just as the people heard the first cries of new life in camp. But as he grew and learned to break horses and build fires and hunt, there was none better or faster at braiding a lead rope, or gathering wood, or fashioning a good bow and quiver of arrows. So his name was changed to Three Hands by a proud father who bragged of his son's prowess as much as the others would allow.

"He had ov'r a hun'erd bushels in front o' him. Hell, I'd call 'im the Human Combine er the Injun Engine er..."

John gazed at his foreman with more disappointment than disapproval when he said, "don't forget I'm half Sioux myself."

Tad wanted to take the words back as soon as they left his mouth. "I know,

Mr. Connor, I know. But 'at's diff'rent. Yer the boss... always have been."

"And I've always been half Sioux."

Tad shuffled his feet some looking down at the rich soil beneath his boots which had given rise to the bumper crop of corn they were harvesting, and a thought that'd been swimming around his mind for some time finally took hold, and he looked back up at John. "Ya know, boss, I nev'r thought I'd see the day some-one'd out-pick Brice Ridley. But Three Hands... he's somethin'." He paused then added, "guess color don't matter. Jus' a man willin' ta do a job... do it proper."

And John allowed his foreman the time to consider his thought wholly... watching as he did the dissolution of the man's life long prejudices fall from his body like so much soil and sweat cleansed at day's end by the simple thought of equality.

—As it turned out, over the next six years Tad was back for the harvest every fall as well as the regular crew of migrants and a handful of Sioux from the Rosebud. Most often these were new faces who, like the original eight who jumped off the flatbed in '36, didn't know an ear of corn from a wedge of Gruyére, a rich, creamy swiss cheese the farm also produced from its dairy. However, there were two regulars from the reservation as well whom Tad was pleased to see... Three Hands and Big Shoulders. By 1938, he had Big Shoulders overseeing the warehouse making sure the corn was stored high and dry for top dollar. As for Three Hands, he had him instructing the pickers on how to increase production by a simple repositioning of the left thumb to allow for a better grip of the shucks. This way the shucks could be cleaned quicker to ready the ear for a final jerk off the shank which, despite no increase in production, saved John a week's labor in bread and board for nine of his migrants. Showing good business sense, John passed a portion of that savings on to his foreman who in turn passed some along to Three Hands and Big Shoulders.

"You boys made me look good," Tad was saying to his top picker and warehouseman. "How'd you like to string along with me an' work some o' these farms hereabouts in the off season. Plenty ta do... plantin', runnin' irrigation ditches, killin' grubs, shooin' critters. I'll pay ya top dollar."

*

They were a threesome after that working the Ohio Valley from Marion to Chillicothe in the spring and summer months, traveling in Tad's old Dodge half-ton with an open bed, most of the time sleeping under the stars and not wanting more. And every fall, when the first sign of summer's swelter began to wane, they would wind their way back to Worthington for the corn harvest at John Connor's.

It was the fall of '41 the last time John, or any of them, would see Three Hands. A month after the harvest-ending picnic John would throw every year for the men, the Sioux Indian lad read the Monday morning headlines on December 8 when he and Tad and Big Shoulders stopped for breakfast in Plain City. "Pearl Harbor Attacked by the Japanese," it read. To Three Hands way of thinking, there wasn't much to discuss. While working with Tad he'd developed a love for the land, a land he now considered his own, his country... once again. He would not allow an invasion of it. Having no knowledge of the Japanese or the whereabouts of Pearl Harbor or Hawaii even or how this "act that would live in infamy" might affect him was of no consequence. After breakfast he gathered up his belongings, waved good-bye to his two companions and caught the next bus to Columbus where he joined the Marine Corps. The very next day he was shipped to Quantico for boot camp. Nine months later on a hot September morning he was dug in with two buddies from his squad in a foxhole on the island of Guadalcanal. At the beginning of what would be called The Battle of Bloody Bridge, a quick burst from a Japanese sniper caught the three by surprise, raking their cover. Three Hands and a fellow named Terry Bailey were killed instantly. PFC Al Sims, crouched shoulder-to-shoulder between them, didn't receive a scratch.

*

It was mid-October. The cooling of fall had begun and the leaves were in full turn, their yellows and crimsons sparkling as the sun's rays shone through casting patchwork shadows on the country road. It would not be harvest time for John and Tad quite yet as the two drove north alongside the Keya Paha, back to the

Rosebud to attend Three Hands burial. John looked with affection at the rolling hills and valleys he roamed in his youth, and the trail he once traveled taking him to the small town of Mission for supplies... smiling when he thought of Two Bears' tobacco, and as his mind wandered, he wondered if he might have been able to do something for Three Hands... see him in his danger, even from so far distant, and somehow reach out to save him from the enemy's bullet. But then a voice, distant and faint, came to him. And as he strained to listen, to hear the words, he could only make out, 'you... could... not...' And he felt Santin's presence. And his heart was no longer heavy.

Later that day, witnessing Three Hands laying on his pyre in his Marine dress blues draped with buffalo robes, the boy's father, Elk Run, rose to speak of his son... of the infant Black Moon who had later become Three Hands because of his skill with the rope and the bow and the quiver... of the youth who had mastered the farming of the white man and who had made his own way in their world... of the first man of his tribe to sign up with the great war party that would travel so far from their homeland to fight an enemy they knew not of... of the soldier who had given everything for his people, who had died a good death. And as he spoke his tears began to flow over the jagged map of an ancient face, streaming onto his deerskins like the rushing of so many rivers. And the others of the tribe stood before the great fire with him. And they listened quietly, reverently, as he spoke of his son while the wind off the prairie rushing overhead carried Three Hand's spirit home.

*

John had come to realize in the years since Rae's death that he must immerse himself in something he held important, held dear, that would challenge his mental abilities certainly, as well as provide some tangible result, something to step back and observe and admire, or to critique and make better, or he would slowly, surely drown in his own self-pity.

So it happened, in the front yard of the little brown and yellow bungalow on Quincy Road where he had moved after the farm became too much, he took to growing roses — lush red Blazes and Dortmunds, Golden Beauties, and white

Icebergs and Prairie Stars — that is, only after he'd taken a trip out west. All who passed by of an evening or, later, making a point of doing so, remarked on their beauty, exclaiming them to be like no other. When John was tending them, the more curious would ask this or that about how he developed the interest, if these were own-roots or bare-roots, if he used cow or horse manure, mulch or peat and so forth, then pick his brain further in an attempt to discover some small clue or hidden trick or secret as to how to improve their own. John was only too happy to oblige every request, but no matter how diligently his neighbors and acquaintences, and their acquaintences, put his recommendations into practice in their own gardens, old John's roses remained the marvel of the town.

His second avocation, one which the crisp, cool air of fall had this morning reminded him was just around the corner, was football. This renewed passion had developed late one evening while reconciling the years and events of his life... and the words of Walks Over Them when he escaped The Stockyard, "you are the one."

He had been praying to the Great Spirit for comfort and guidance, as was his habit, when after some hours he looked up, the beads of sweat and tears mingling, dripping from his chin. As his eyes slowly focused, he was startled for a moment, then filled with a peacefulness that washed over him. It was the image of Santin sitting crossed-legged on the black bearskin rug in front of the fire, the embers still warm, casting a glow all around. John rubbed his eyes, blinking away the wetness, focusing again. Yes, it was his old friend. It had been so many years, but yes, Santin was there before him, beckoning him to sit, and talk.

"You have come to me again, old friend."

"Because you worry me, my son. How are you?"

"Saddened, as you know, by the death of my wife. Troubled, by what I have, or have not, become."

"To grieve for a loved one is good. But it has been many moons since your wife has gone. Time enough."

"I still miss her."

"You will see her again."

"When, Santin?"

"It is not for me to say. Now, tell me about what you have, or have not, become... how are you troubled?

"I was told long ago by an old friend that I was the one."

"The one? The one to do what?"

"I do not know. But I fear the events in my life have not fulfilled the prophecy, if you can call it that."

"Of which events are you speaking? Bringing purpose and meaning back into the lives of the men of Mission... saving the little dog... giving the sheriff of the small, white village his manhood back... inspiring a killer to become a war hero... the homeless to regain their homes... healing the young man's leg? Those events?"

"I'm, I'm not..."

"Maybe it is of your marriage you speak... taking a wife who had been with others, whom others would not have married had they known."

"No. I loved... love my wife."

"Then perhaps it was bringing Three Hands and Big Shoulders and the rest to the farm to learn the white ways, so those who might escape the reservation could, and survive. No, Red Hand, you were the one to do all of these things. Walks Over Them knew that. He knew that because he knew you would not rest until you found your white family. And he knew that because, like I, he knew you had the power."

"That is all true, Santin. But when I found my white family, they were all dead."

"Sometimes in the earthly world, my son, things are not as they seem. There is always much to learn... much to do."

"Much to do?"

"Yes, because you are still part of the earthly world, you must play a part... participate... share your knowledge." Red Hand's thoughts of his own inadequacies were somehow softened as he listened to the simple message of Santin. "What have you enjoyed the most in your time in the earthly world..." Santin could see clearly Red Hand's inner mind and soul, "other than your time with your wife?"

He thought for some minutes, "much, Santin. Travels, old friends," and he paused, "although all have gone now to the life beyond." Then with a twinkle in his eye and a look that stretched over decades past, Red Hand whispered the word, "football. To me, old one, football is not just a game. It is a life lesson, something to know, and if one is lucky enough, as I was, something surely to do."

"There is your answer. Do it, my son. Not the playing of it, that has passed. Participate by sharing the knowledge."

Red Hand relaxed completely, something he'd not done for months, and he smiled, "you are right, Santin, I will."

As his old mentor smiled, beginning slowly to recede from Red Hand's sight and thoughts and mind, he offered one more thought, "you need not call me old one. It is you who are old. I am young and strong, gliding on the wind in a world without time." And he was gone.

*

"John, how are you?" It was Joe stopping by practice to watch the boys, Joey and Eddie in particular, as Dave put them through their final paces before the season opener on Saturday. He'd seen the old man sitting high up in the makeshift stands set in the middle of the field as he had so often before. When he stopped to chat, Joe recalled it was only a couple of weeks ago that he'd started a dialogue with John and discovered, somewhat to his surprise, the old guy knew his stuff. During subsequent conversations, which had come to be daily, John related his experiences at Princeton with Net Poe and his one dash to glory which impressed the heck out of Joe because now, after ascending to the position of sports editor three years earlier, he'd researched college football's early years more for his love of the game than anything else and he knew all about the Poe Brothers.

"How does Ohio State look this year, Joe?"

"Solid on defense with Brudzinski anchoring the line and this new kid Cousineau backing him up."

"Yes, I saw Brudzinski in the Rose Bowl two years ago. Very strong player. In fact, the trip out there inspired me to begin growing my own... roses, that is."

"You know, John, I believe I've heard something of your roses. Word spreads."

"Well, I had to find something to do with my time."

"The Rose Bowl, huh... must have been some trip, John. Did you go with anyone?... a group?"

"No, no, I just decided I would like to go. It was two days after Christmas and all the news was about the coming bowl games and I had never been, so I just..." he was looking for the words, "took off."

"That's hard to do on short notice... what with hotels all booked up and the game sold out every year, and... how'd you get out there?"

"Oh, I flew."

"Flew! You must have been lucky to get a flight. How about the game? Were you able to get a decent seat?"

"Oh, yes. Excellent... view."

"It must have costed you."

"No... no more than I expected."

Joe was somewhat suspect of John's story, but he liked the old guy and knew he had no reason to make it up and after John went on to describe all the key plays of the game as well as the parade route along Colorado Boulevard and the looming backdrop of the San Gabriel mountains which Joe knew to be a fact, he was convinced old John was telling him the truth.

John could feel the wheels turning in Joe's head, so he asked, "and the offense?"

"Sorry?"

"The Buckeye offense, Joe? What shape is it going to be in with Archie gone?"

"Yes, the offense. I've got a feeling they'll be all right. This kid Logan has just been waiting for his chance. He could be a good one."

"Like little Joe out there," John said, pointing to the field.

"Or little Eddie."

It was then that Joe related the story of he and Eddie McCabe after John had asked about his own football exploits... if he had played, at what level, why he gave it up. John listened intently, and was struck not with Joe's prowess on the field back in the day, but more, he was taken with he and Eddie's broader story... their friendship and comaraderie, the closeness they developed, Eddie's untimely death,

Santin's prophecy. Could it be?... could it be true, at last?

Joe noticed the old man was off somewhere, in his own thoughts. It was time to go. "John... John!... will we see you at the boys' game Saturday?"

"Oh, sorry. Yes, yes, of course. I wouldn't miss the season opener.

"Good. I'll see you there then. Take care, John."

"You too, son."

How ironic, John thought later that night, smiling some, after one final conversation with Santin... how very ironic calling Joe son.

*

Saturday morning couldn't arrive soon enough for Coach Delmon and his team, and Evie and her folks, and Joe and Wendy. Most of all, old John made sure to catch the early bus on High Street to get a proper seat, although he enjoyed watching the pre-game warm-ups as well... the crowd gathering, bantering back and forth as they filled the stands, both sides mingling, anticipating the contest to come. As he leaned back against a metal pole in the top row settling in for the kickoff, the sun just now warming his bones, he heard a familiar voice from below.

"John..." it was Joe. "Come down and sit with us."

After making his way to the field, he asked, "is it all right?"

"Of course," and Joe made the introductions to Wendy and Evie who told him how much they'd looked forward to meeting him after hearing so much about his interest in the team. He thanked them, complimenting both on raising sons who, as he put it, had a gift for the game. The women smiled and said they would see them at half time.

Halftime, he thought?... before he heard Joe say to him, "come on, we're sitting on the bench."

—It was the middle of the fourth quarter, Bulldogs 12, Mustangs, 13. Dave and Joe hadn't expected this close of a game, particularly the Mustangs toughness on defense holding Joey and Eddie to about four yards a carry. The boys had each scored a touchdown, but only after two long drives without a play longer than twelve yards.

"Damn, we could've used at least one extra point," Dave said to Joe as he paced the sidelines, looking for a weakness in the Mustang's defense.

"We'll get 'em, Dave." Joe encouraged.

"Well, it better be damn soon," and he stalked off scratching his head thinking of some way to spring one of the boys as the clock ticked away... less than three minutes to go.

"Joe," John said to him, "have you noticed how their defense is only playing for a run... with eight, sometimes nine right up at the line of scrimmage?"

"Yes, but we only have so many blockers... and, well, Toby isn't that good of a passer to loosen them up."

"I know. But what if we lined up to loosen them up... you know, to give the boys more running room."

"How do you mean?"

"Spread the line. Double the space between center and the guards and tackles. Create holes."

Joe had never seen this before, but he thought... that could be brilliant.

"Hey, Dave... Dave!..." he yelled, "call time out."

He introduced John to Dave quickly and told him about the idea. Dave stood there, hands on hips hearing him out, then looked at John and rolled his eyes. He was turning to walk away when Joe said, "Dave, it's third and eight and there are two minutes left. You got a better idea?"

"Okay, okay. How do we block them?"

Joe never got the chance to respond.

"Block down, everything to the middle, and tell Joey to fake up the middle, then take it wide. I've been watching the boys in practice. They have good instincts. They can make one or two miss, and then be off."

Dave was silenced. He thought like Joe now... yes, that could work.

The referee walked over. "Dave, twenty seconds."

"All right boys," he turned to the team, "huddle up." After his instructions, Dave, his coaches and his starting eleven yelled, "Bulldogs!"... and the boys broke toward the field racing like hounds on the hunt until Toby lined them up, gaps double wide, and barking signals across from a confused Mustang defense.

It was a thing of beauty. When the clock started… one fifty-nine, one fifty-eight, with Toby yelling, "hut one, hut two, hut HUT…" the ball was snapped and the two Bulldog tackles and guards blocked down, taking two Mustangs each, jamming the middle as Joey took a straight handoff, dipped inside, then out, sprinting to the right, juking the cornerback before heading up the sideline. The safety barely got there, knocking him out of bounds after a twenty-three yard gain. First down on their own forty-four yardline with one thirty-seven to go. Now it was Eddie's turn, this time to the left side, linemen blocking down, Eddie juking and veering off tackle, then cutting back up field for eighteen yards before being tripped up. The clock kept ticking as Joey rushed in for him, the team scrambling to line up, forty-one, forty, thirty-nine, Toby screaming, "hut hut, HUT…" Toby looking left then wheeling, pitching the ball to Joey who was heading right again going full speed. He turned the corner just as the leftside linebacker planted himself for the tackle. This time, Joey didn't juke. He ducked low giving the boy a forearm, knocking him on his back as John, standing on the bench, smiled widely, every fiber of his body pumping with adrenaline, carrying him back all those years as he watched Joey, like himself, dash to glory, cutting upfield, leaving the Mustang defenders grasping for air as he sprinted to the end zone. When the gun sounded, barely audible above the roar of the crowd, the old scoreboard on the northside of the field read, Bulldogs, 18, Mustangs, 13.

Parents and grandparents, neighbors and friends along with the rest of the team were rushing the playing field as Dave turned and yelled to Joe, "one helluva way to start the season!"

"Sure is, Davey boy. But if John wasn't here," he winked, "who knows what might have happened."

"You're right. I should shake the old guy's hand." And he looked for him before asking, "hey, where'd he go?"

Sometime during the final two minutes of the game was the last time anyone had actually seen John. Joe remembered sitting next to him just before Joey had taken off on his run up the sideline; then he'd jumped up and sprinted alongside his son, cheering him on. Evie had glanced over to the bench and had seen him with about a minute to go, she thought. Even Wendy had caught him hollering, waving a program just before the game ended. But now?...

With the crowd melting into what remained of the day, the three Delmons and the three Cramers, the boys hand in hand with their parents, walked from the playing field leaving it to reclaim a peaceful serenity. It was then they heard the cry of the great bird behind them, perched on the railing at the top of the stands, and they marvelled at him. How close for an eagle. As they stared they saw it leap into the sky, flapping its great wings. It circled once high above, then dove down soaring on the wind, speeding towards them. When it angled past it threw off a great smoky contrail, and the sound they all heard was as loud as any jet fighter. Then just as swiftly the great bird turned skyward again, flapping his wings faster, ever faster, in a straight line towards the sun until it disappeared into the burning light, lost to eternity.

"Did you hear that!"... the boys exclaimed. They had all heard it they agreed... heard the great bird roar past them. But years later, lying in the comfort of their bed, Joe would tell Wendy what he heard that day had not been the sound of a jet fighter at all. What he heard was a great, mournful, yet peaceful whisper of the word, "father." And it has haunted him. And he fears it always will.

***

www.ingramcontent.com/pod-product-compliance
Lightning Source LLC
Chambersburg PA
CBHW052019020726
47501CB00004B/1141